Keri Arthur won the *Romantic Times* Career Achievement Award for Urban Fantasy and has been nominated in the Best Contemporary Paranormal category of the *Romantic Times* Reviewers' Choice Awards. She's a dessert and function cook by trade, and lives in Melbourne, Australia.

Visit Keri Arthur online:
www.keriarthur.com
www.facebook.com/AuthorKeriArthur
www.twitter.com/kezarthur

Praise for Keri Arthur:

'Keri Arthur's imagination and energy infuse
everything she writes with zest'
Charlaine Harris, bestselling author of
the Southern Vampire Mysteries

'Keri Arthur is one of the best supernatural
romance writers in the world'
Harriet Klausner

'This series is phenomenal! It keeps you spellbound
and mesmerized on every page. Absolutely perfect!'
FreshFiction.com

Keri Arthur
WICKED EMBERS

A Souls of Fire novel

piatkus

PIATKUS

First published in the US in 2015 by Signet Select
an imprint of New American Library
a division of Penguin Group (USA) Inc.
First published in Great Britain in 2015 by Piatkus

1 3 5 7 9 10 8 6 4 2

A CIP catalogue record for this book
is available from the British Library.

ISBN 978-0-349-40417-2

Printed and bound by CPI Group (UK) Ltd, Croydon, CR0 4YY

Papers used by Piatkus are from well-managed forests
and other responsible sources.

MIX
Paper from
responsible sources
FSC® C104740

Piatkus
An imprint of
Little, Brown Book Group
Carmelite House
50 Victoria Embankment
London EC4Y 0DZ

An Hachette UK Company
www.hachette.co.uk

www.piatkus.co.uk

WICKED
EMBERS

I'd like to thank all the usual suspects: my lovely editor, Danielle Perez; copy editor Jane Steele; publicist Nita Basu for getting the word out; and the totally amazing Tony Mauro for the cover art.

A special thanks to Miriam Kriss, agent extraordinaire; my crit buddies and best mates, Robyn, Mel, Chris, Carolyn, and Freya; and finally, but by no means lastly, my gorgeous daughter, Kasey.

CHAPTER 1

In the still darkness of this dream, Death was hunting.

Her scent filled the air, as heavy as the fog was thick.

I had no sense of where I was. There were no identifiable buildings here, no street signs, nothing that could provide a clue. Not even people.

Just me, the foggy darkness, and the huntress who stalked this place somewhere up ahead.

The night eddied around me but brought with it no sounds. Unease swept through me. In the hundreds of years I'd been dreaming of death, there'd never been one like this—one in which there was absolutely nothing that would enable me to pin down a time or location. And while I may have very recently sworn to stop interfering with fate and just let death take its natural path, I'd made that same vow dozens of times over the centuries, and it had never resulted in a dream like this.

The night continued to slide past me, gelatinous and uneasy. The sensation of Death was growing stronger, but I could neither see nor sense what form she was wearing.

And I had no idea why.

Usually when my prophetic dreams hit, I was not only given a clear image of the time and location, but I was also shown how that death would occur. But here, there was no such clarity. Some sorcerers and witches had the ability to hide their presence from either dreamers or astral travelers, but I was a spirit rather than a being born of flesh—even if I wore human form most of the time—and I could generally sense such magic being employed. But there was nothing here beyond the thick night and that steadily growing certainty of wrongness. It was almost as though my inner dreamer was having trouble pinning down the source of this death—and that in itself suggested whatever lay behind it was something I had never come across before.

It was a scary thought, given the many years and many lives I'd had.

Gradually, a sound that reminded me somewhat of the click of nails against stone began to echo through the fog. Loud at first, it grew ever softer, as if the source was moving away. And yet Death was nearer, not more distant. I frowned, confused, but I had little choice other than to keep moving. I knew from past episodes that the dream would not release me from its grip until the very end. It was an end I could stop if I chose to, but only if I was shown enough details.

The soft sound of nails continued to grow fainter, until it was barely audible again. But every intake of breath was filled with the foul presence of evil, and if I could have stopped, I would have. But the dream drew me on. Ever on.

Something flickered through the darkness ahead. It

was little more than a deeper patch of night, but I had no doubt *it* was the giver of death.

I drew closer. The shape of the creature was fluid and oddly disconnected; it seemed to be made of embers rather than mere shadows, and it flowed from one form to another with ease. Sometimes it looked like a cat, at other times like a large bat that made the night eddy and flow around it with every sweep of its wings. Gradually, though, it settled into the form of a monstrous black dog.

A black dog whose paws were on backward.

And even though I was close enough to see it now, the noise of its stained yellow nails hitting the surface under its paws was still oddly distant. It was as if there was a weird disconnect between reality and sound in this place; it made me wonder whether there was some form of magic at work even though I had no sense of it.

I followed in its wake, and gradually the darkness gave way to forms and shapes. A dark street stretched ahead of us, silent and empty. The road surface was slick with rain, though I was immune to its touch. The creature ahead was not, and the scent of wet fur soon filled my nostrils.

There were no cars parked in this street and no footpath. Butting up against the two old bluestone drains that lined either side of the road were varied fences— some were brick, some were wood, and some were little more than metal roller doors. Many were almost hidden by the old roses that scrambled over them, and tall trees—their tops lost to the darkness and the rain— towered above us.

The creature stopped and looked around. Its eyes

were large, bloodred, and filled with hunger. It raised its long snout and sniffed the air, as if searching for a scent. Finally, it snarled, revealing canines that were needle fine and razor sharp. Then it leapt over the nearest fence and disappeared.

The dream quickly followed, giving me little chance to do anything more than glimpse the graffiti that littered the old redbrick fence.

The yard beyond was small and strewn with rubbish. A clothesline that was little more than several strands of wire strung between two wooden T-pieces dominated the right-hand side of the yard, and to the left was a large lemon tree laden with fruit. As the creature moved up the concrete steps to the tiny house's back door, its shape became fluid again. With little effort, it slid underneath the gap between the door and the floor.

The dream forced me to do the same. The air inside the house was thick with the scent of garlic and meat, and it was so hot, the fires within my soul burned to life, as if eager to draw in the richness of it.

The creature slunk through the house; its movements were cautious, wary, but its hunger was now so strong it filled the heated air and made my stomach turn. This death would not be a good one . . .

Not that any of them ever were.

As I drifted in its wake, I studied our surroundings, trying to find something—anything—that would clue me in as to where we were. The kitchen was small and neat, although a pot on the stove was beginning to smoke. If it wasn't turned off soon, a fire was likely. But I doubted *that* was the reason I was here. I might be a phoenix, with fire mine to control, but this dream was about the strange creature and its intentions rather than about a house blaze.

A newspaper lay on the edge of the kitchen counter, and the date leapt out at me. August 25—today's date. But was the dream showing me a real-time event— something no other dream had ever done—or was it once again showing me the future, even if only a few hours from now? I had no idea, because I could see no clocks in this place. Even the one on the oven was out of focus.

We moved into a small hall. A stand holding several coats lay sideways on the floor—an indication, perhaps, that someone had left in a hurry. On the small table nearby were several unopened letters. *Mr. James Hamberly*, one of them read. *Forty-two Highett Street, Richmond.*

I finally had a location.

Now I just had to see the death and decide whether I should interfere. Most of the time, it was better not to—I'd learned *that* the hard way—but even so, there were some deaths I just couldn't walk away from, no matter the risk to my personal safety. Which was the reason why in *this* lifetime my back had become a mass of scars after I'd saved a child from a burning car, and why my heart had gotten all bruised and hurting again after I'd saved my ex's grumpy ass.

The creature paused and lifted its nose, then looked over its shoulder, its eyes bloody fire in the darkness. I wondered if it had some sense of my presence, but it made no move to flee and, after a few more seconds, it turned and went through the door on the left.

Inside was a dead man.

Shock hit me, its force so fierce and cold it briefly calmed the heat in the air and the fires in my soul. Why was the dream showing someone who was already dead? It wasn't even a particularly fresh death, because Death herself was nowhere to be seen.

So why was I here?

No answers came, but then, they rarely did. I watched as the creature slunk to the bed, its backward paws making no sound on the wooden floorboards. As it neared its prey, it seemed to grow, until it was almost the height of a tall human. It sniffed the covered form, then raised a paw and pulled the blankets back, revealing the man's flaccid form to the night and the heat. The creature sniffed him from head to toe, and the scent of anticipation filled the air. My stomach roiled and the heat grew, but I had no flames in this dream state and no way to stop what was about to happen.

The creature's tongue flicked out and, almost lovingly, it licked the man's rotund belly. I shivered again, despite the growing heat, guessing what was coming and not wanting to see it. But it wasn't as if I had a choice.

Again the creature's tongue flickered out, this time centering on the area above the liver. It was almost as if it was marking its spot for penetration.

It was.

With very little fanfare, the creature bared its teeth and pierced the exact spot it had marked. The cuts were small and precise, and it made no move to enlarge the wound. It didn't need to.

It was syphoning the man's liver through its teeth . . .

The dream finally dissolved, but the heat did not. I

thrust up into a sitting position, suddenly aware that the flames in my soul not only danced across my skin but also across the sheets and blankets. It was a sensation that was thick and warm and luscious, but it was also very dangerous, considering my bedroom had no special protection against the heat that was mine by nature.

But even as I started to draw it back into my body, the door opened and Rory burst in, his red hair burning in the light of my fire. He was a phoenix like me, but he was also my life mate—the spirit to which I was bound forever, and the being who meant everything to me, because neither of us could be reborn without the other's help. And yet, while I loved him, I wasn't *in* love with him. It was an unfortunate fact that paired phoenixes had been cursed with the inability to find emotional completion with each other, even though we could have children only with our decreed partner.

Of course, the other half of the damn curse was that love, for us, never ended happily—and it was something we'd *both* cursed more than once during our many lifetimes.

He didn't say anything, just sat down beside me, pulled me into his embrace, and drew the remaining heat and flames into his body. And though desire stirred between us, he did nothing more than simply hold me.

"It must have been a bad one this time," he said, his warm breath tickling my ear. "It's rare for your prophetic dreams to end in flames like this."

"It wasn't bad. It was just *weird*." I pulled free from his arms and swept the hair out of my eyes. Like Rory's, mine was red, though it strayed toward the copper

end of the spectrum more than was usual for phoenixes. "This time the victim was already dead."

He frowned. "Why on earth would you see *that*?"

I snorted softly. "Why on earth do I even *get* them?
It's not like it's an ability found in any other phoenix
we've ever come across."

He half smiled. "True. But then, you always were a
little different. It's what attracted me to you."

"Like you even had a choice in *that*."

My tone was dry, and he acknowledged the point
with a wider smile. When a phoenix hit sixteen years
old, a ritual was performed to reveal his or her partner
and, from that moment on, the two were bonded—
whether they liked said partner or not. Thankfully, I'd
never heard of a bonding in which the partners hated
each other, but it would certainly be a horrible situation
to be in, considering that each phoenix in the pairing
relied on the other for rebirth.

I swung my legs past him and rose. The carpet was
thick and warm under my toes as I padded across to
the chair, grabbed my jeans, and pulled them on.

"I take it you're going to investigate this death, despite being able to do nothing to prevent it?" His tone
held an edge that was both amused and resigned.

"Yes." I grabbed a sweater, gave it a sniff, and tugged
it over my head. "I don't think the death was the reason
I was there. I think it was the creature."

Surprise flickered through his amber eyes. "What
creature?"

I sat down and tugged on socks. "It was some sort of
shape-shifter, but nothing I've ever seen before."

"Given the number of shifters we've come across over the centuries, that's saying something."

"Yeah." I grabbed my boots. "This thing had multiple shapes, but the form it seemed to settle on was a big black dog with backward-facing feet."

"*Backward* feet? How did the damn thing even walk?"

"Without any problem, from what I saw." I stood up. "I have to see what is going on, Rory. I need to know why I was shown that thing."

He sighed and pushed to his feet. "I know. But please promise me you'll be careful. I would really love to get through one lifetime without either of us being killed before our hundred years are up."

I smiled as I walked over to him. While every phoenix could be reborn with the help of his partner, his life span each time totaled one hundred years precisely. I had no idea why or how that number of years had been allotted to us, but neither of us had ever gotten to that magical figure. The closest I'd ever come was ninety-eight.

I draped my arms around his neck and kissed him. It was a gentle thing, but the promise of fire ran beneath it. We both had other partners sexually, but it never erased our need for each other. In fact, phoenix partners *had* to combine energies every couple of days or we risked fading and could die—which was just another nail in the coffin when it came to finding happiness with whomever we fell in love with each lifetime.

"I'll promise to be careful if you promise to get your butt out of bed and actually make it to work on time this morning."

"Hey, my butt has made it to work with five minutes to spare on three occasions this week."

I grinned. "Then go for four—hell, even five. The fire chief will think all his Christmases have come at once."

"I just might, even if only to show you both it's entirely possible." He ran a finger lightly down my cheek before his touch settled on my lips. "I mean it. Be careful. I really don't like the sound of this dream, and I like the thought of your investigating it alone even less."

I kissed his fingertip, then said, "I know, but Jackson doesn't get back from the job in Sydney until tomorrow afternoon." I'd met Jackson only five weeks ago, after I became involved in the investigation into my boss's murder. We'd gotten on so well that he was now not only my lover but also my business partner, as he'd offered me a fifty percent share in Hellfire Investigations, his PI agency. But he didn't know about my dreams, and I really preferred to keep it that way. It was bad enough that I endangered my own life investigating them; there was no way I was going to risk someone else's.

And it wasn't as if we didn't have plenty of other problems at the moment without my adding to them.

Rory's concern deepened. "You haven't told him about the dreams, have you?"

Jackson knew I was a phoenix because my fire had helped saved his life, but I hadn't mentioned the dreams because there'd been no reason to. "No, but—"

"Em," he cut in softly, "don't make the same mistake with Jackson that you made with Sam."

"It's hardly the same thing," I snapped back. "Damn it, you know very well why I didn't tell Sam I was a phoenix, and he certainly didn't give me a chance to explain why I need you in my life."

"I know." He grimaced, caught my hands, and squeezed them lightly. It only made the anger flame higher. "Believe me, I *know*. But I was just thinking the other day—what if it's about honesty?"

"What?"

"The curse. What if it's all about honesty?"

"No one is sure if the curse theory is even true." I pulled free from his grip. "And it's not as if we *haven't* been honest. For fuck's sake, Rory, how many times has one of us been killed or burned because of honesty?"

"Too many." His voice was grim. "But we've never been honest with our partners from the very *beginning*, and maybe that's the point of the curse. Until we are, maybe we'll *never* find happiness."

"It's hardly practical to be honest when humans fear the unknown." I walked back to the chair to grab my leather jacket.

"I know, but baby steps and all that. Tell Jackson about the dreams, Em. Besides, if one hits when you're with him, he needs to be prepared."

"Maybe," I muttered, not convinced. "I'll think about it while I go investigate this creature."

He snorted softly. "In other words, no."

I didn't say anything—there was little point. We'd been together for a very long time, and he knew me very well. "I'd better go. The dream didn't pinpoint a time, so there just might be a chance of stopping this thing before it starts anything major."

"Maybe I should come—"

"No," I cut in instantly. "Remember our rule, Rory."

That rule—only one of us could ever step into a dangerous situation at a time—had been made for a *damn* good reason after a particularly nasty event had almost taken us both out several lifetimes ago. I might be getting a little weary of endless centuries of heartbreak, but I certainly *wasn't* tired of life itself.

He scrubbed a hand through his hair, leaving several bits sticking up at odd angles. "Okay, but take my bike. It's not like you're going to get public transport at this hour, and it probably wouldn't be wise to catch a cab in case you have to leave in a hurry."

I nodded and followed him into the kitchen. After grabbing the keys from where he'd dumped them on the counter, he tossed them over to me and added, "Just don't scratch her."

I grinned. "I think you worry about that bike even more than you worry about me."

"Well, it *is* a classic, and a brand-new purchase besides." Amusement teased his lips. "Give me a call once you figure out what is going on."

"I will."

I blew him a kiss, then grabbed my handbag and headed out of our apartment. Lights came on as I strode toward the elevator even as the shadows reclaimed the area behind me. They'd begun replacing all standard lighting in the building's public areas—except for the lobby, which was manned with security twenty-four/seven—with movement-activated ones nearly a year ago, but it was only in the past few days that they'd finally gotten up to our floor. I rather liked the idea of them, if only because they gave advance warning that someone was approaching. A handy thing, considering that we were now on the outs with the sindicati, the vampire equivalent of the mafia, and definitely *not* an organization anyone with any brains would want to be on the wrong side of.

But it wasn't like we'd had much choice. They'd not only kidnapped both me and Jackson, but they'd held *him* ransom in exchange for the missing notebook that held my boss's research on the cure for the deadly red plague virus. It was a virus that had the potential to turn the human race—and some supernaturals—into insane pseudo vamps, and even with Jackson's life at stake, there'd been no way I was about to let the sindicati get their grubby mitts on something like *that*. While I had no doubt that the sindicati, who had their fingers in just about every level of criminal activity imaginable, were a major headache to law enforcement, they'd be nigh on unstoppable if they got hold of a drug capable of changing the human race—and some nonhuman ones. Because they *would* use it to threaten and control.

So I'd arranged a little subterfuge of my own, and the exchange had gone off without a hitch. Almost. But at least the sindicati would find no joy in the notes, as the virus that had been placed into the computer that held them would activate the next time the device was booted up, and everything on the hard drive would be rendered unreadable *and* unrecoverable.

We were expecting reprisals, and the fact that they hadn't responded, several weeks later, was scary. But then, vampires did have all the time in the world to plot revenge.

A soft chime announced the elevator's arrival. I stepped inside its warm interior and pressed the basement button. The door closed, and, in no time at all, I was astride Rory's fierce black Norton Commando and thoroughly enjoying being able to stretch her out in the near-empty Melbourne streets.

Highett Street looked nothing like what I'd seen in the dream. For a start, the street was wider, with two lanes of traffic as well as room for cars to park along either side. And there were not only footpaths but big old plane trees that cast deeper shadows across much of the street and the nearby houses.

James Hamberly's house was hidden behind a six-foot green metal fence, and if the number of weeds and bushes scrambling over it was any indication, the front yard was as wild as the back. I parked the bike, took off my helmet, and immediately heard it—the electronic shrieking of a fire alarm. I swore and ran for the house.

"Is Jamie all right, then?"

I jumped and half swung around. The voice had come out of the darkness that enclosed the house to my right and, after a second, a woman appeared. With her white hair, pale skin, and the overly large dressing gown that flapped loosely in the slight breeze, she almost resembled a ghost.

I took a deep breath and walked on. "I don't know, because I'm not in there yet."

My somewhat offhand reply obviously didn't please her, because her voice was sharper as she said, "You know him, then?"

"Old friends." I paused to unlatch the rickety metal gate. "Could you go inside and call the fire brigade? That's the fire alarm going off."

I didn't wait for her answer, just ran up the old

wooden steps and headed for the front door . . . and discovered it was open. Just a crack, but since the creature hadn't entered the house this way, James Hamberly was either lax about security or, as I'd suspected earlier, someone had left in a hurry.

I pulled a sleeve over my fingers and carefully pushed the door open. Even without entering the house, I could feel the dance of fire; the heat of it washed across my senses, stirring the embers within my soul to life and making me hungry to taste its sweetness.

I stepped warily into the house. Air brushed heat past my face, and I glanced up, seeing a vent several feet away. The heating was not only on but turned up. Hamberly had probably cranked it up when he'd gotten home, just to take the chill off the air, but *why* would he then go to bed and leave a pot to burn on the stove?

Again the heat of the flames washed across my senses, but I ignored its siren call and headed into the bedroom I'd seen in my dream.

The creature was gone. Only the dead man it had dined on remained.

I swore yet again, then spun and headed for the kitchen; I needed to take care of the fire before I did anything else. The pot on the stove *had* caught alight, and flames raced up the walls and across the ceiling, fierce and bright against the darkness. I stepped closer, flung my arms wide, and called them to me. The fire reacted instantly; thick fingers of flame leapt from both the ceiling and the walls and flung themselves at me. It spun around me, the intensity of the fire increasing until it was a maelstrom that roared with heat and power. For several seconds I simply enjoyed the close dance of the storm that didn't touch, didn't burn, but only fed.

Gradually, though, I became aware of approaching sirens. With a regretful sigh, I drew the maelstrom into my body, and, god, it was *glorious*. And it made me wish Rory were here to share the heat and the passion that such a moment always created.

But *that* was not what I was here for, and time was running out.

With darkness once again in control of the kitchen, I rummaged through the kitchen drawers until I found a lid that fit the pot. After calling a sliver of fire to one fingertip, I seared the inside of it to replicate what would have happened had I actually capped the pot with it and dropped it into place. Then I grabbed the pullout mixer tap and quickly sprayed water across the walls and ceiling. With everything drenched and the real reason the flames had been so quickly doused covered up, I grabbed my phone and called the cops to report the death as I spun on my heels and ran back to the bedroom. The fire brigade would be here within minutes, so I needed to discover whatever clues the creature had left before then.

As in the dream, James Hamberly lay on the bed with the blankets pulled back and his body exposed. But what I hadn't noticed earlier was that—if the dents in the pillows beside his were anything to go by— someone had recently shared his bed.

So who was that person, and why had that person left in such a hurry as to have knocked over the coat stand and left the front door ajar?

I had no idea—but I had a feeling it would be very worthwhile to find the answers to both those questions.

Hamberly was a short, overweight man with steely gray hair and features that were not unpleasant. Death might have caught him unaware, but at least he'd died with a smile on his face.

My gaze dropped back to the area the creature had pierced with its teeth—only it hadn't done it once, but twice. There was another cut in his chest, right above his heart. There didn't seem to be any other marks on his body, however, and I wondered if the creature had simply come here to dine on those two organs, or whether its actions had been interrupted by the fire alarm. It certainly *seemed* like a whole lot of effort to go to for such a small gain, but until I knew for sure what this creature was, there was no way to know what it had really intended to do here tonight.

I stepped back and studied the rest of the room, looking for anything else that might provide some clue as to what I was dealing with. There were droplets of water on the wooden floor, but they could have dripped off my coat as easily as off the creature.

I closed my eyes, envisaging where it had stood, then looked for that spot on the floor. Other than the droplets, there didn't seem to be any other giveaway clues. Not even hair.

So why did the damn dream bring me here if not to uncover some way to track this creature down? I spun around. If the nearness of the sirens was anything to go by, I had maybe three minutes—if that—before the fire crew arrived. I tugged a sleeve over my hand, walked across to the beautiful old mahogany wardrobe, and carefully opened the door. One set of clothing, not two. Hamberly's partner either didn't live here, or she kept her clothes in another room.

I closed the door, then turned and scanned the bedroom again, just in case I'd missed something. Nothing appeared to be out of place; the creature really *had* come here to dine on a dead man. I shivered and wondered how it had even sensed the death when it obviously hadn't come from around here; then I thrust the question aside. The hows and whys were not important right now. But as I turned to walk out, an odd scent caught in the back of my throat. I frowned and took a deeper breath. Again that scent tickled my throat—foul and almost chemical in its taste. After several more breaths, I realized it was coming from Hamberly's direction. Confused, I walked back over and leaned closer to the wound above his heart. It was definitely some sort of chemical smell, and it was coming from the wounds themselves. Maybe the creature had injected some kind of liquid through its teeth to dissolve both the liver and the heart *before* it had sucked them out. It would certainly explain how it had managed to do so through teeth that, while sharp, were also needle fine.

I shuddered and walked out. The creature might have become little more than shadow and ash to get into this place, but it had regained dog form once it had. Maybe there was a clue somewhere else.

I investigated the other rooms as I passed them, but found nothing to suggest anyone else lived here. I walked through the kitchen, then into the little laundry. There was water here, too, and several puddles that vaguely resembled paw prints. I got out my phone and took a photo and, in the brief flash of light, caught sight of something floating in one of them. I flicked on the flashlight app and squatted next to the puddle. It was a hair—a short dark one. There was no certainty it belonged to the creature; for all I knew, Hamberly owned a cat or maybe even a dog. Hell, it might even belong to whoever had recently shared the bed with him. But there'd been no sign of animals in the dream, and there wasn't a litter box anywhere inside the house. It might prove to be nothing more than a random hair from a previous visitor, but it was better than nothing. And while I had no way of investigating whether the hair *did* belong to the creature, Jackson just might. I knew he had a secret source and, given the type of information he'd gotten from her recently, I very much suspected it was a cop.

I thrust upright, ran back to the kitchen, and grabbed a spoon and a sealable plastic bag. Once I'd claimed my prize, I shoved the bag deep into my purse and walked out of the house to wait for the fire crew and the police.

Several hours of questioning followed—not only from the fire chief and the police but also from the overly nosy neighbor—so it was almost dawn by the time I was allowed to leave. Rory had already gone to work when I got home, so I dumped his keys back on the kitchen counter and went to have a shower.

One of the many good things about becoming Jackson's partner was that I could now walk to work. Hellfire's offices were situated in West Melbourne, only a fifteen-minute walk from where Rory and I lived at Waterfront City. Once dressed, I grabbed my coat and bag and headed out. Though cold, the wind coming off the nearby sea brought with it the aroma of freshly baked bread. My stomach rumbled a reminder that while the spirit might have dined out on fire, the flesh had yet to feed, so I grabbed a couple of croissants and munched on those as I walked through streets that were surprisingly empty. Usually by eight in the morning, the place was packed—though admittedly, at this end of the city there was more car than foot traffic.

Hellfire Investigations was located on Stanley Street, and that was not only currently filled with early-blooming blossoms and wattles but also contained an eclectic mix of light industrial and old Victorian buildings. It was close to both the Queen Victoria Market and the Flagstaff Gardens, and the rent, I'd discovered, was horrific. But it had one major advantage that many other—cheaper—locations didn't: It was situated right next to a blacksmith's. Jackson was a fire Fae and, like most of the Fae, he had to be near his element regularly; otherwise he risked fading and, eventually, death.

Our building was a rather pretty, blue-painted double-story Victorian that was little more than two windows wide. I grabbed the mail out of the letter box, then opened the old wrought-iron gate and bounded up the two steps to the door.

Only to realize it was slightly open.

And it *hadn't* been that way when I'd locked up and left the night before.

Someone had broken into our office.

CHAPTER 2

I warily pushed the door open. Sparks danced across my fingertips, a weapon that was ready to ignite at the slightest hint of danger. The long, thin room that was our office appeared empty, but there was plenty of evidence that someone *had* been here, because the place was a mess. They'd ransacked our desks and filing cabinets and scattered paper everywhere. It almost looked as if the place had been hit by a snowstorm. The three computers were missing, although the screens and keyboards were still present and looked somewhat forlorn among the mess.

My gaze went to the spiral staircase that sat to one side of the lounge area at the far end of the room, and the tension running through me increased again. Just because I couldn't immediately see or sense anyone on this level didn't mean they hadn't hightailed it to the next. I pressed the door all the way open to ensure no one hid behind it, then quickly stepped to the other side.

Still no sense or sign of anyone.

I placed my bag on the floor, then clenched my fist to contain the sparks. The last thing I needed right now was to inadvertently set fire to anything. I cautiously moved forward. Paper crunched under my feet or whispered away in the breeze of my passing, but nothing else stirred. Nor was anyone hiding under the desks, although the drawers, like everything else, had been ransacked. Several had even been smashed, as if to ensure there were no secret compartments. Whoever had done this was either a little paranoid or just very thorough.

I continued on until I reached the staircase. Thankfully, the paper storm hadn't quite reached this end of the room, although there were a number of plastic cups in a nearby bin that hadn't been there yesterday evening. The bastards had obviously made use of Jackson's industrial-sized coffee machine while they'd ransacked the place— and *that* suggested a well-timed, well-planned raid rather than a spur-of-the-moment event. Just as the fact that they'd left the cups *behind* suggested they had no fear of being traced through their fingerprints.

I looked up to the next floor. Nothing registered on the sensory radar, but that didn't mean someone couldn't be up there. The senses of a phoenix, while far better than a human's, were nowhere near as sharp as those of a werewolf or vampire.

There was only one way I was going to find out whether the fear twisting through me was justified or simply the product of an overactive imagination, but I just couldn't force my feet onto the first metal step. Not in *this* form, anyway.

I glanced at the front door to ensure there were no passersby, then called to the fires within. They surged through me, flinging me from flesh to fire spirit in an instant. No longer constrained by physical limitations, I swept up the staircase and into Jackson's living area. The light of my flames danced across the room, lending warmth to the shadows and leaving nowhere to hide. Like the floor below, the area up here was one big expanse. The kitchen was centrally located, with the bedroom to the left and the living area on the right. There was no one or nothing up here; nothing beyond the usual dust and unwashed dishes, anyway.

I moved across to check the bathroom—which was the only separate room in this entire area—but again, there was nothing. I reclaimed my flesh form and finally relaxed.

While this area had escaped the paper storm, it had nevertheless been searched. They'd stripped the bed, pulled the mattress away from the base, emptied out cupboards, and upended the couches. It had been a very thorough search and, for that reason alone, I suspected the persons behind it were connected to the sindicati. They had to be, because who else had any reason to snatch the computers? None of Jackson's other cases—or at least, none of those he'd updated me on—warranted such action. The sindicati, however, didn't have access to the research notes they'd been promised, and no doubt suspected we *had* to have backups hidden somewhere.

Only we didn't—I'd given the only other copy of the notes to Sam Turner, who was not only my ex but also a cop working for the Paranormal Investigations Team, a specialist squad of humans and supernaturals who worked outside the regular police force to solve crimes that involved paranormals.

We'd neither seen nor heard from anyone at PIT since we'd handed over the notes. They even appeared to have pulled the tail they'd had on me. While I'd never been happy about being followed around, it had nevertheless been somewhat reassuring to know there was someone close who could come to my aid if things got ugly. Which they had, of course, and, in the end, the tail hadn't really been of much use. Maybe *that* was why it had been pulled.

I studied the room for a moment longer, then headed back downstairs. After calling the cops, I made a pot of green tea, then sat down to watch the security tapes while I waited for them. What the tapes revealed were raiders in dark clothing wearing black masks. Which wasn't exactly helpful, as the raiders had no doubt intended.

The cops weren't exactly helpful, either, when they finally arrived. They basically took notes, collected the security tapes, and disappeared. But then, other than write up a report, take a few photos, and dust for prints, what else could they do? If the sindicati *were* behind the break-in, the nearby neighbors wouldn't have spotted them. Not when vampires could wrap the night around their bodies and all but disappear to human eyes.

With the police gone, I closed—and locked—the door, then got down to the business of cleaning up. I was only halfway through the mess when the alarm on my phone went off, reminding me it was time to go meet Jackson at the airport.

I headed back upstairs to grab the keys of the car Jackson had rented until PIT released his truck—though why they even had it, I had no idea. The sindicati might have rammed it to snatch me, but I doubted there was a whole lot PIT could glean from the wrecked vehicle beyond the fact that the van that hit me was black—and they knew *that* from witness reports. And the longer they had it, the more likely it was that they would discover the three USBs I'd hidden under the seats. Given the trouble I went through to get the damn things, I'd be *seriously* pissed if they were taken before I'd even had a chance to look at them.

I found the car keys under an upended kitchen drawer and went back downstairs to reset the security cameras. Then I grabbed my handbag and headed out.

There was very little traffic on the Tullamarine Freeway, so it didn't take long to get to the airport. I parked in the short-term area, then walked across the bridge to the terminal. After checking the boards to see where his plane was coming in, I headed through security and walked down to the lounge. It was packed, so I found a pillar to lean against while I waited.

Thankfully, the plane arrived on time and, as people began to disembark, I straightened, my gaze, scanning the crowd of people exiting the air bridge. Not that Jackson was in any way hard to spot. He was a big, lean man who radiated sexuality and heat, and he towered over those nearest him by a couple of inches. If there was one thing literature and movies had gotten wrong when it came to the Fae, it was their stature. They were neither small nor winged, and the only ones who were ethereal in *any* way were the air Fae.

His grin, when his gaze met mine, was easy and delighted, creasing the corners of his emerald green eyes.

I moved forward to meet him. He dropped his carryall, then caught one hand and pulled me close. His body was not only delightfully muscular but deliciously warm. Fire Fae had core temperatures that ran a lot hotter than most humanoids, which, in many ways, made them almost perfect partners for beings made of fire. But Jackson was also perfect in one other respect: Fire Fae didn't do commitment, and Jackson was never going to want anything more than a good time from me—which was just as well, given Sam was this lifetime's heartbreaker.

"You," Jackson said, his voice gravelly and sounding as if it were coming from the general direction of his boots, "are a sight for sore eyes."

A smile teased my lips. "Don't try to tell me there were no seduction opportunities up in Sydney, because I won't believe you."

"It's true, whether you choose to believe it or not." His expression was woebegone, although the effect was somewhat muted by the amusement creasing the corners of his bright eyes. "The stakeout was in the middle of goddamn nowhere; the nearest I got to any sort of female was watching my target get picked up in the local pub."

"A chance encounter, or a deliberate one?"

"Oh, the latter most definitely. It was artfully done, but once they were back in her hotel room, it was all business rather than sex." He shook his head sadly. "Which was a total waste of a good bed and woman, if you ask me."

I grinned. "I'm gathering you ran a trace on the man she met?"

"Woman," he corrected. "And she's a courier for the

sindicati. But, for the moment, *that* is unimportant, because I seriously need to kiss you."

And with that, he did.

It was a long, slow, and extremely sensual kiss, one that was filled with desire and heat. I wrapped my arms around his neck and pressed my body even closer, enjoying all his luscious heat even as I fought the desire to draw it into my own body.

"Oh, for god's sake, get a room," a woman muttered as she brushed past.

Jackson chuckled, the sound vibrating lightly against my lips. "*That* is a damn good idea," he murmured. "Shall we race over to the hotel and grab one?"

"You have a perfectly good bed at home." Or, at least, he would when it was put back into place. "Besides, you might not feel so amorous when you discover what happened last night."

"It'd have to be a pretty dire event to stop a fire Fae from feeling amorous." His tone was dry. "But what happened?"

"We got raided."

His amusement faded. "By whom? PIT or the vamps?"

"I suspect the latter, if only because of the thoroughness of the search and that it happened at night. Besides, if PIT wanted something from us, they'd openly come and take it."

"And woe betide us if we, in any way, objected." He thrust a hand through his dark gold hair. "What was taken?"

"Besides the three computers, I'm not entirely sure. I'm only halfway through the cleanup."

He picked up his carryall, then tucked a hand under

my elbow and guided me forward. "Did the security cams reveal anything?"

"Yeah, men in dark clothes wearing ski masks."

He grunted. "If it was the sindicati, I'm guessing they were looking for the notes."

"And once they realize they're not on any of the computers, they'll be back."

"We knew something like this was going to happen."

"Yeah, but I was hoping we'd have more time." Even if more time would have only caused more anxiety. But at least now that they'd made their first move, we had a clearer path forward.

His expression was grim. "Well, I can tell you one thing—those bastards are *not* getting their hands on me again. Not without a major battle."

An understandable sentiment, considering the last time he'd been taken had resulted in a broken arm and leg. That he was walking now was only due to my having become spirit, allowing him to not only siphon my flames but use them to heal his body. It was something I'd never done before, and I had no idea whether there would be consequences for either of us. So far, it appeared not, but then, it hadn't been all that long since it had happened.

"We could install a better security system—"

"It wouldn't be of much use," he cut in. "We're talking about a crime syndicate, remember. I doubt there's a system out there they couldn't get around if they really wanted to."

His point was well proven. Not only had they gotten into both the Chase Medical Research Institute, where I'd worked before my boss had been murdered, and

Rosen Pharmaceuticals, the company that had hired Jackson, but they had also hacked into their computer systems and erased everything related to the research into the red plague virus.

"Besides," he added, "I doubt the next attack will involve our building. It'll be against us directly, and it'll be someplace dark and secluded." His gaze met mine, green eyes concerned. "Since dark and secluded are part and parcel of an investigator's job, we'd better start carrying."

I grimaced as we stepped onto the escalator and headed down to the bag collection and exit area. "My investigator's license hasn't come through yet, so that option is out for me. And my fire is a better weapon than any gun you could give me." Besides, it wasn't like a gun was going to stop a vampire attack—not when the bastards could move as fast as the wind.

Jackson must have been thinking along the same lines, because he said, "A gun might be useless against the speed of a vampire, but if you manage to get the drop on them, you can certainly blow their fucking brains out. But I wasn't actually thinking about *that* sort of gun."

I raised my eyebrows as we headed across to the parking lot. "What other sort of gun is there?"

Amusement touched his lips. "A water gun."

"A *water* gun?" I stared at him for a second. "You're serious, aren't you?"

"Totally." The amusement so evident on his lips warmed his bright eyes and had my pulse rate skyrocketing again. Not that *that* was a surprise, given both the desire he was still radiating and the fact my hormones were still physically unsatisfied after the delight of ingesting Hamberly's fire. "A small plastic gun loaded with holy water can make as big a mess of any vampire as any regular gun—and you have the advantage of being able to hold down the trigger and spray it in a wide arc."

I dug the parking ticket out of my pocket, paid the fee, and led the way across the lot to the car. "Why hasn't anyone ever developed this idea commercially? At the very least, the police would find a weapon like that extremely handy."

Hell, *anyone* would. Vampires might be more civilized these days—and attacks on humans few and far between—but that didn't mean they *never* happened.

"Oh, both the police *and* the military have developed such a weapon. They just don't use it during day-to-day operations." He dumped his bag into the trunk of the car, then climbed into the passenger seat. "Could you imagine what would happen if it became common knowledge it existed? There's enough trouble on the streets now with the antisupernatural squads without feeding them the knowledge that holy water really *is* an effective weapon against vamps."

That was true enough. While humanity had reacted far better than anyone had really expected when vampires and werewolves had revealed their existence during the height of Hollywood's love affair with all things supernatural, there were still pockets who believed nonhumans were a threat that needed to be eradicated—and who were willing to back this belief with action. Nightly "hunting" parties were becoming a real problem, and while they might be illegal, it didn't seem to stop anyone. Of course, it didn't help that some police and politicians who sympathized with the hunters were more than willing to turn a blind eye to their actions.

Which was the main reason why the rest of us hadn't come out. Heaven only knew how the paranoid would react if they ever actually discovered just how many other nonhuman races were living among them.

"It's hard to believe no one's ever realized it, though." I started up the car and headed out of the parking lot. "I mean, holy water is such a literary stable. Vamps might have spent years debunking the myth, but I would have thought someone, somewhere, would have tested it out anyway."

"They undoubtedly have, but remember, holy water burns rather than kills outright. If you hit a body part other than the face, you're basically dead meat. The vamp will be on top of you before you can scream."

"True." I paused to shove the ticket into the exit gate. "But that's also a problem that applies to both of us."

"Well, yes, except that we're both faster than humans, and we have other weapons at our disposal."

I glanced at him. "I have, but you need a source of fire before you can shape it."

"I have you." He shifted in his seat and gave me a wide grin. "Not only are you the best source of flame I've ever encountered, but you come wrapped in a very luscious package."

I snorted softly. "I'm being serious here—"

"Oh, so am I." He reached over and placed a big hand on my thigh. "You really *are* a luscious woman."

"Concentrate on the sindicati and what we're going

to do to avoid them," I said, ignoring not only his compliment but the warmth of his touch and the desire it stirred. "Because any plans you have for seduction might just depend on whether we can remain out of their grasp."

"I know." He sighed and removed his hand, though the heat of his touch lingered. "But the truth of the matter is, if they want us, they'll get us. We both know that. We can't run either the business or our lives around what they might or might not do—not indefinitely, anyway. All we can really do is watch each other's backs as much as is practical."

I mulled over his words as we merged into the traffic heading toward the city. While the reason Jackson had offered me the partnership in the first place was simply so that we could protect each other, he was right; it wasn't going to be enough. The sindicati had to have been watching us to know when to make their raid, and yet we'd had no sense of them. No sense of being watched at *all*. And as much as I'd promised Rory I would be careful, I'd lived long enough to know that, sometimes, the best defense was offense.

"What if we take the fight up to them?" I said eventually.

"It's certainly an interesting premise, although I daresay a dangerous one."

I glanced at him. "And this worries you?"

He grinned. "I'm a fire Fae. We live for danger."

"And here I was thinking you lived for sex."

His grin grew. "And you don't think sex can be dangerous? Darlin', you obviously haven't lived long enough."

"I'm a *phoenix*. I've had more rebirths than you've had years." My tone was dry. "And when it comes to sex, I've seen more and probably done more than you could *ever* imagine."

"Oh, I don't know about *that*." His expression was decidedly wicked. "I can imagine a whole lot."

"Well, just stop doing so right now, and concentrate on the matter at hand."

"A hard thing to do when my hand is itching to re-acquaint itself with all your lovely curves."

Which was certainly something I wouldn't have objected to . . . I mentally swatted away the images that rose with the thought, deciding I'd better take my own advice and concentrate. "We can attack them from two angles; we can go after Henry Morretti—"

"We were warned *off* the sindicati—and Morretti specifically—by your ex," Jackson said. "I don't think he'd take it all that well if we ignored that warning."

"But they've pulled my tail—"

"You only *think* they've pulled the tail," he cut in again. "Just because you can't sense them doesn't mean they're not there."

I raised an eyebrow. "Meaning you don't want to go after Morretti?"

"No, I'm just pointing out the probable consequences. The next time your ex catches us interfering, he might do a whole lot more than merely give us a drug-enforced warning." He hesitated. "And, just for reference, no air or fire Fae can survive jail time."

I couldn't, either, and for similar reasons. I might not need to be immersed in my element regularly, but I certainly needed time with Rory. But jail time was the threat we were currently under if we didn't give up investigating the death of Mark Baltimore—my former boss at Chase. Somewhat oddly, though, Sam had *not* offered the same warning when it came to investigating the disappearance of Professor Wilson, the other scientist involved in the research into the red plague virus. His notes, like those of my boss, were missing, and no one had any idea where they'd gone. Except, maybe, Amanda Wilson, who was both the professor's wife and a telepath for hire. She was also the woman who'd given me the USBs stashed in Jackson's truck. And if Sam *had* found them, she might be our only hope of uncovering what had happened to either Wilson or his notes. And Sam wouldn't stop us going after her—he'd told me she was of little interest to PIT. The trouble was *finding* her, as she was currently in the hands of one of the warring sindacati factions—but which one, we had no idea.

That there were two factions was something I hadn't even known when Mark Baltimore had been murdered and all hell had broken loose in my life. I still had no idea which faction we'd been snatched by, because we had only one name—Morretti. Whether he was the current power or the would-be power, I didn't know, and I certainly had no clue as to who his opposition was. Though I very much suspected the cool-voiced, ultrapolite vampire who'd been in charge when I'd exchanged Jackson for the laptop containing the research notes might have been it. And if that *was* true, it also meant I'd managed to annoy both factions. Because not only did I plant a virus on the laptop that would have destroyed the notes the minute he tried to access them, but we'd also foiled his plans to kill us. Although whether the kill plot had been his idea or that of the man in charge of the red cloaks—the nickname given to those infected by the red plague virus—was anyone's guess.

After merging into some more traffic, I said, "What if we don't go after him directly?"

I might fear Sam's threat, and had no desire to anger him any more than he already was, but there was a part of me—the very same part that had gotten me into more trouble than I could remember over the centuries—that couldn't walk away completely. Not only had my boss been murdered, but I'd been kidnapped, threatened, and drugged—and not *just* by the bad guys. I was pissed off, and I wanted answers.

Jackson half smiled. "I suspect your ex still *wouldn't* be pleased by a sideways approach, but I do so love your thinking. Who do we hit first—Amanda Wilson, Denny Rosen, or Lee Rawlings?"

Rosen was the man behind Rosen Pharmaceuticals, and Lee Rawlings was the vamp Morretti had hired to pick me up the first time I'd been snatched. Unfortunately for Morretti, things had not gone according to plan—I'd not only escaped and interrogated Sherman Jones, the initial bagman, but we'd intercepted and paid out Rawlings in exchange for information.

"Given the sindicati have Amanda, and it might take a bit of time to find Rawlings, why don't we tackle Rosen? You're due to report to him anyway, aren't you?"

Jackson grimaced. "I very much doubt he'll be able to tell us much about the sindicati."

"It's still worth a shot."

"Maybe. And he did call when I was in Sydney, enraged that I haven't handed in an update for several days." A smile flirted briefly with his kissable lips. "His bluster died somewhat when I told him PIT had become involved in the investigation."

I frowned. "Surely he had to be aware of that? I mean, they would have spoken to him when Wilson and his research went missing."

"They may not have identified themselves as PIT." His gaze met mine. "Or they may have simply read his mind from a distance. PIT aren't afraid of bending the rules or stepping on civil liberties, remember."

"But not everyone can be mind read—you said that yourself."

Certainly neither Jackson nor I could be, but then, neither of us was human. And while that rule didn't apply to all supernaturals, it had certainly saved our butts whenever we'd landed in PIT's grasp.

"And yet," he said, "according to Amanda Wilson, Rosen is something of an open book."

"Remember who made that statement," I said drily. "It's possible she was lying through her teeth."

"It's also possible she wasn't."

I acknowledged the point with a shrug. "But if she *wasn't*, then it might also mean anything he could tell us will have been investigated and/or dismissed by Sam and his people."

"True, but if she *was*, then PIT would have had to read him with specific parameters in mind. Few telepaths have open access to anyone's mind, remember."

And thank god for *that*. "It's highly unlikely that PIT would ask the same questions we would."

"This is PIT we're talking about. They were probably aware that Rosen was selling company secrets to pay off his gambling debts well before we ever knew."

I frowned. "But if they know *that*, surely they would have taken steps to have him removed from his position?"

"Why would they, when he's perfect bait to catch everyone else in the chain?"

"One of which is Radcliffe." Or, more precisely, Marcus Radcliffe III. He not only owned a string of second-hand stores that were little more than a front for a roaring trade in black market goods and information, but he also happened to be the man who owned Rosen's gambling debts.

"Precisely," Jackson said. "But who is *he* selling them to? He's not the end user—he's not that clever."

"He's clever enough to avoid the damn police." Or, at least, he *was* until I'd lured him into a hotel bedroom, and Sam had promptly stormed in and snatched away our prize. "I don't suppose you know if PIT ever released him?"

"No, and it's not a question I can ask my source, either." He shrugged again. "I guess the only way we'll find out is by asking at the casino if he's been back."

"It's worth a shot." If Radcliffe was the high roller we'd been led to believe, then he either had to risk illegal games or venture back to Crown, as it was Melbourne's only casino. And it wasn't like I could ask Sam what Radcliffe was doing. Aside from the fact he wouldn't tell me, the only number I had for him was a central number that collected the message and passed it on. "Speaking of your police source—"

"I never said she was police," he interrupted, his tone mild.

"You never denied it."

"No, and I won't ever confirm or deny it. It's too risky, especially now with your ex and PIT on the scene."

"I wouldn't—"

"I know," he cut in again. "I trust you, or I wouldn't even have mentioned her, but this is her decision, not mine, and I have to respect that."

"Which is fair enough." Especially if she *was* a cop. She was risking her career by feeding Jackson *any* sort of information. "Do you think either she or someone she knows might be able to get a DNA analysis done on a black hair I found?"

"Possibly." He studied me for a minute. "Did you find it at the office? Because, honestly, it could belong to any of at least a half-dozen recent clients."

"It's not from the office." I paused, still reluctant to tell him about my dreams, even if I knew deep down that Rory was right. Jackson needed to be prepared in case it happened when he was with me. "I found it in the house of a dead man last night."

"Which begs the question, what the hell were you doing in the house of a dead man? It wasn't one of our clients, was it?"

I half smiled. "No, fortunately. A dream sent me there." I gave him a brief explanation of the dreams, the problems they'd caused over the centuries, and what this particular dream had led me to find.

"So this hair may or may not belong to the creature," he said, "and it might be the only way of tracing it?"

"Unless I have another dream, yes."

"It's a hell of a long shot," he said. "You may get DNA from the hair, but you're not going to get a name or location."

"I know, but DNA will at least give me some idea of what I'm dealing with, and that, in turn, might give me some idea of a location."

Because just as different human nationalities tended to gather in certain areas, so too did supernaturals.

"There is no *me* in this equation," he commented. "And I'll pass the request on to my source. It really is a long shot, though."

"I know." I shrugged. "So, back to the office, or shall we go visit Rosen?"

"As much as I'd love to drag you up to my bedroom and prove just how dangerous sex can be, I've got a feeling we'd better go interrogate Rosen." Though amusement touched the corners of his lips, little of it reached his emerald eyes. "The sooner we can uncover who has Wilson's research, the more chance we have of getting everyone off our backs."

"Somehow, I don't think it's going to be that simple."

He shrugged. "It's a start."

And it wasn't like we had many other options right now, anyway. "So which is the easiest way to get to Rosen Pharmaceuticals from here?"

"Continue down CityLink and get off at Barkley Street."

I did so. Rosen Pharmaceuticals, it turned out, was situated in busy Power Street in a rather plain-looking four-story building with a café dominating one side of the ground floor and a lawyer's office on the other. It was very different from the dedicated building inhabited by their opposition—the Chase Medical Research Institute, which just happened to be owned and run by the ex whom Rosen hated.

"You might want to turn right onto Lynch Street," he said, "because there's no parking in front of the building."

"Oh yeah?" I slowed down and flicked on the blinker. "Obviously no one told the dipstick in front of us."

He grinned. "Maybe I should have said there's no legal—" He paused and leaned forward suddenly. "That's Rosen."

I glanced toward the building's entrance. A tall, somewhat weedy-looking but impeccably dressed man was exiting the building, accompanied by two other men. All three were heading toward the illegally parked sedan.

"Well, I guess he figures it's okay because he owns the joint."

"Yeah, but I don't think he owns the car," Jackson growled. "And I certainly don't think he's going willingly."

"What?" Instead of pulling out, I moved closer to the curb and stopped—and then saw what Jackson had already seen.

One of the two men accompanying Rosen was a

werewolf we'd met once before—when we'd rescued Amanda Wilson from his not-so-tender ministrations. His companion was even bigger, with thick hairy arms and thighs so large, he walked like an ape. We knew the first wolf worked as a thug for hire, and I was betting the second man did, too.

I had no idea where they were taking him or what they intended, but one thing was very obvious—Denny Rosen was in *serious* trouble.

CHAPTER 3

"What are we going to do?" I asked.

"Rescue him, of course," Jackson said. "But if we try it around here, someone's bound to call the cops. We don't exactly need that right now."

"Calling the cops might be the *only* way we're going to beat those bastards." Hell, I'd barely survived tackling the werewolf the last time we'd met, and I had no desire for a rematch. I might now be at full strength and more able to defend myself, but the bastard was *big*. And his friend was even bigger.

"You forget whom you're traveling with." Jackson twisted around and pulled a slender wooden box from underneath the car's backseat.

Amusement ran through me. "Don't you go *anywhere* without an armory as backup?"

"Well, I can't always rely on having a pretty lady made of fire at my disposal now, can I?" He pressed his thumb into the little scanner, and the case opened. "What would you like? The sawn-off shotgun or Glock semi?"

"I thought semiautomatics were illegal."

"It's a common misconception; they aren't, though there *are* strict ownership criteria to contend with." He got out the double-barrel shotgun and studied it for a minute. "I think even a werewolf built like a brick shit-house will respect this baby."

I wasn't so sure about that, given there were two of them. "I'll keep to my fire. I think it'll impress them more than a gun."

"It'll impress Rosen, too, so unless you want to out yourself as something more than human, you'd better take the Glock."

"Good point." He loaded both weapons, ensured the safeties were on, and shoved the wooden box back under the seat. Up ahead, Rosen was pushed none too gently into the rear seat of the car. Man-Mountain One squeezed in beside him while the other ambled around to the driver's seat. The car started up, but instead of pulling out into the traffic, the driver waited until there was a gap in the flow and did a quick U-turn. I did the same but kept several cars between us.

"Do you think this snatching means the sindicati believe Rosen might know more than Amanda uncovered?" I said.

"That depends on which sindicati faction employed Amanda and who has her now. It could be either the incumbent faction or the opposition, depending on who has what."

"Which suggests the people behind this are the ones who *haven't* got Wilson or his notes," I commented.

"Or maybe they *have*, and they're just being ultra-cautious and getting rid of evidence."

"Which again points to the possibility that Rosen knows something."

"Or that they realize he's a loose cannon and don't want to risk him talking to the cops or PIT." He shrugged.

"As you said earlier, if PIT thought he knew something, he'd be under watch. I can't see anyone else following that car right now."

"Doesn't mean they're not there. There *are* winged shifters, remember."

"Yeah, but if Sam and PIT still believed Rosen could be of any use to them, he would have warned us away from him, along with Morretti."

"Possibly." He glanced at me. "But PIT does like playing its little games."

I raised an eyebrow. "Meaning you've crossed swords with PIT before?"

"Once or twice." He shrugged again, his expression somewhat grim. "As I've said, the police in this town and I do not see eye to eye."

"You just get more and more interesting."

He grinned, though it failed to lift the shadows in his eyes. "There *is* more to me than my sexual prowess."

"I wouldn't be here if there wasn't."

"I'm so glad to hear that."

Up ahead, the big black vehicle put on its blinker and swung into the right-hand turn lane. Not wanting to pull up right behind him and risk Man-Mountain One looking back and recognizing us, I instead stopped on the left side of the road and waited. Only once the lights changed and the right-turn lane got the green arrow did I begin following him again.

We drove down Swan Street, then over the Yarra River, around past the Art Centre, and through several backstreets until we reached an area I recognized—Port Melbourne.

"Well, well," Jackson murmured. "Another industrial area. Imagine that."

An industrial area was where Morretti had wanted me delivered—and was probably where I'd been when the ultrapolite vamp had given me the option of exchanging Jackson's life for the research notes. If they were taking Rosen somewhere similar, I felt a little sorry for him. He was a gambler and a seller of secrets, and I very much suspected whoever was behind this action wouldn't be as considerate or as polite to him as they had been to me.

"We can't let them get to the location; not if we want any hope of rescuing Rosen."

"There're still too many possible witnesses around at the moment to take any sort of action. We really have no choice but to wait."

"I *hate* waiting."

"Says the woman who's lived for more centuries than I've had years."

"Patience doesn't come with time, let me tell you." And *impatience* had gotten me into trouble more than once over the years.

One of the two cars between our quarry and us turned left, leaving us with very little cover. Our rental car might have been a plain white sedan, but even the densest of drivers would surely have thought it suspicious that he kept seeing the same one practically right up his rear end.

Jackson obviously reached the same conclusion, because he got out his phone and Googled our location. "Okay, pull over to the side of the road. We'll see where they go at that roundabout."

I did so. The black car cruised on through the roundabout and kept going. I glanced at Jackson. "And?"

"Keep following, and hope they turn down Lorimer Street."

"Why?"

"Because at the very end of that street is one Sardine Street, which leads into an old transport depot."

"Abandoned?"

"Abandoned. If they go there, then it's to kill him, not question him." He flashed me a grin filled with both excitement and anticipation. "At least the odds are even; two against two."

"That's presuming there's no one else at the depot waiting for them."

"There won't be. I'm certain of it."

I wished I shared his confidence. Wished we could leave Rosen to his fate. But we couldn't, if only because he might know something useful.

The car ahead turned onto Lorimer Street, just as Jackson had hoped. We followed suit a few seconds later but remained well back. There were plenty of warehouses along this stretch of road, and plenty of cars and people about, too. But as we drew closer to the CityLink overpass, the warehouses became rattier-looking, or were in the midst of being demolished. There wasn't anyone about down this end of the street; even the demolition site was empty of life. The black car finally turned again—onto Sardine Street, as Jackson had hoped.

"Stop here," he said.

I did a U-turn and parked under the trees that lined the small parkland between the road and the Yarra River, then climbed out. Although there wasn't a cloud in the sky, the breeze coming off the water was cold, and I shivered. I could have very easily ignited my inner fires to warm myself, but if things went wrong in the next few minutes, I was going to need every ounce of heat and flame I could muster.

Jackson handed me the Glock, then led the way onto Sardine Street. We kept to the left, walking in the shadows between the old gum trees that lined the rubbish-filled parking bays. On the right-hand side, the wide concrete supports of the overpass dominated, and the roar of traffic was constant and unending. It would, I thought grimly, go a long way to covering the sound of any gunshots if we were forced to use our weapons. Down the far end of the street was a high metal fence, but the old gates lay on the ground and had been there for some time, if the weeds growing through the links were any indication.

The black car had stopped close to a couple of old shipping containers. Even as we approached the gates, Man-Mountain One climbed out of the backseat, then dragged Rosen out. Rosen wasn't screaming, wasn't fighting, wasn't doing much of anything. When the werewolf released him, he simply fell to his knees and bowed his head.

Accepting what was to come, I thought. It said a lot

about the state of his life if death was a better option than fighting.

With very little fanfare, Man-Mountain One pulled a gun out from behind his back and pointed it at Rosen's bowed head.

We'd officially run out of time.

I stopped, flicked the safety off the Glock, and fired off four quick shots. The first smashed into the car's rear window, the second pinged off the bumper, the third hit the tarmac near Man-Mountain One's boots and sent bits of asphalt spinning into the air, and the fourth smashed into his hand and sent his gun flying.

He roared, the sound one of fury more than pain, and lunged for the fallen weapon.

"Don't," Jackson warned, his shotgun aimed and ready even as he walked closer to the werewolf and Rosen—who, interestingly enough, hadn't reacted to the gunshots. Maybe he was drugged rather than simply resigned to his fate.

The werewolf froze, but the man still in the car took off so fast, the tires smoked. He didn't go far; he simply spun the car around and accelerated straight at us.

Jackson swore and fired the shotgun, the sound so close and loud that my ears rang. The car's windshield shattered, but the second went wide as the driver wrenched the car sideways. I raised my gun and fired, aiming for the tires, and getting one of the rears on my third try. It blew out, and the car spun widely.

Another bellow cut through the air; I looked around and discovered Man-Mountain One barreling at me.

I swore and fired, but I missed as he threw himself

sideways. He was up and running at me again with incredible speed, a wide grin of anticipation stretching his lips. I stepped back and squeezed the trigger again, only to discover I was out of rounds.

The werewolf laughed and lunged at me. I spun away from him and raised a hand. Fire leapt from my fingertips, forming a wall so fierce and hot that no sane person would risk traversing it. The werewolf might be furious with me, but he *was* sane. He propped and turned left, obviously intending to run around the fire-wall. I flicked my hand, twisting the fire into thick rope, and flung it at him. Again he threw himself sideways, hitting the asphalt hard before rolling onto his feet and running again, this time away. I hooked my flaming rope after him and lassoed his legs, causing him to stumble and fall. He cursed and fought, trying to free himself from the fiery strands that held him tight without burning. But as I twined my rope up the rest of his body and pinned his arms, he froze. His gaze, when it met mine, promised death. It wasn't the first time I'd seen *that* particular expression on his ugly mug, but it nevertheless sent a shiver of fear running down my spine. I'd just turned hate into obsession, and it was going to get *nasty*.

I thrust the thought away and spun around to see how Jackson was doing. And realized that shooting the car's rear tire out hadn't stopped the thing; it was now barreling straight at Jackson. He seemed totally unfazed by this turn of events; he simply raised the shotgun and rather calmly sighted.

And waited.

The car continued to speed toward him; even from where I stood I could see the wide grin of anticipation stretching across the driver's face as he fought to keep the car in a straight line. Jackson didn't move, and he didn't fire. At the very last moment, when it seemed totally impossible for the car to miss him even if he *had* fired, he simply leapt *up* and *over* the vehicle, landing elegantly and in complete control behind it.

And only then did the driver—and I—realize he'd been standing in front of another old shipping container. The driver slammed on the brakes and spun the wheel, but he was going far too fast for a car that was already unstable thanks to the shredded rear tire. It flipped, rolling once before landing on its roof and sliding driver's side first into the container.

Jackson ran toward it, the shotgun held at the ready. Metal groaned and the engine roared, but there was no sign of movement from inside the car. The airbag *had* gone off, however, and I had no doubt Man-Mountain Two was alive and well. It'd take more than a high-speed rollover to take out someone *his* size. My gaze went to Rosen. He still hadn't moved; in fact, he showed absolutely no awareness that anything untoward had gone on around him.

Frowning, I glanced back at the werewolf and wondered what in the hell the pair of them had given Rosen. The wolf returned my gaze balefully but remained mute. Of course, he didn't actually need to say anything, because his eyes promised plenty—and none of it was good. Thankfully, my flames were still holding him tight, so I followed Jackson across to the car. The farther away I moved from my fire, the more it tugged at my strength, but that was better than Jackson facing the bigger man when armed with only a shotgun.

"What, you don't trust my ability to cope with someone his size?" he said, clearly amused.

"In situations like this, it's sometimes better to play it safe than be sorry." I stopped beside him and squatted to have a look inside the car. Man-Mountain Two glared back at me. He had blood in his hair and dust and abrasions over his face, but otherwise he seemed intact. "He's awake, aware, and not happy."

"Can he get out?"

As Jackson asked the question, the big man growled and flicked the seat belt catch. It didn't retract. He growled again, then reached down into his boot and withdrew a knife. I narrowed my gaze and, a heartbeat later, fire erupted around the shiny blade and melted the metal before he could use it. Man-Mountain Two was *not* impressed by this; he roared again and threw himself against the seat belt in an effort to get free. He got nowhere fast.

"If you don't want to meet the same fate as your knife," I said conversationally, "throw out any other weapons you might have, as well as your wallet and cell phone."

"Go fuck yourself," he snarled. "I'd rather—"

I didn't let him get any further; I simply sent more fire his way, this time letting the front of his shirt smolder for several seconds before snuffing it out. His gun, wallet, and cell phone appeared in pretty quick succession. Big, but not dumb.

"Okay, he's pinned tight and safe for the moment." I rose and kicked the three items farther away from the car. "Shall we go question Man-Mountain One?"

Jackson snorted as he secured the shotgun. "Maybe this time we should ask the bastard his name."

"He'll probably just lie." I walked back over to the wolf and stopped in front of him. "You can't trust thugs who hire themselves out to the highest bidder."

Said thug hawked and spat. The globule landed inches from my toe.

"Hasn't anyone told you it's not polite to spit at a lady?" Jackson squatted next to the wolf, grabbed a fistful of shirt, and dragged him closer. "Do it again, and I'll relieve you of whatever teeth you have left after our last encounter."

The wolf snarled, revealing canines that were decidedly sharper than they should have been. The bastard was beginning to shift shape. Thankfully, despite what humans might believe, it wasn't an instantaneous process.

Jackson shook him—hard. "Go any further into your change, and the flames that bind you *will* burn you."

As he spoke, one of my flames crawled up the front of the wolf's shirt and danced across his chin. The smell of burned flesh and seared hair caressed the air. Jackson's doing, not mine.

The wolf gritted his teeth and hissed as sweat popped along his forehead. But after a moment, he said, "All right, all right; what do you fucking want this time?"

"Your name would be a good start. And don't attempt to lie." Jackson withdrew the fiery sliver, but it still danced across his fingertips.

The wolf glared at it, me, then Jackson in quick succession, and said, "What the fuck are you two?"

"Firestarters," Jackson replied. "And you have one second more . . ."

"My name is Theodore Hunt."

Theodore seemed entirely *too* posh a name for someone his size and shape.

"And your employer?"

He hissed again, though it was a sound more of frustration than anger. "Radcliffe."

Jackson glanced at me. "You believe that?"

I crossed my arms and half shrugged. The werewolf had nothing to gain by lying, but I suspected lies fell off his tongue a whole lot easier than the truth.

"I agree." He let the thread of fire tease Hunt's chin again. "Try again, wolf."

"Okay, okay, it was Morretti. He wanted Rosen put away, and we were employed to do it."

"Why?"

"How the fuck do I know? The sindicati aren't in the habit of explaining the why of jobs. They just expect them done."

"Meaning you've just landed on their shitlist again," I commented. "Somehow, I can't be sad about that."

Hunt's gaze narrowed, but after a quick glance at the fire that still danced across Jackson's fingers, he wisely refrained from saying anything.

"How were you supposed to be paid?"

"Via an exchange this evening."

"When, where, what, and who?" Jackson said.

"Seven p.m., the Grey Street fountain, and the bastard's left hand."

His left *hand*? That seemed an oddly specific choice. Why not his right? Or even his head? I shivered and rubbed my arms, though it wasn't entirely in horror. The fire was beginning to tug at my strength, and while I was a long way from being anywhere *near* depleted, I still didn't want this situation to go on for much longer. We had no idea when the sindicati would strike next, and there was no way I was going to get myself into the same situation as I had last time—out of fire, unable to shift into spirit or bird form, and left with only those skills that came with my flesh form to depend on.

Jackson glanced at me, eyes narrowed, then said softly, "Stop feeding the flames. I can keep them active."

Shock ran through me. He was reading my thoughts—or at least, reading *some* of them. He *had* to be . . . but how? Neither Jackson nor I was telepathic, and it was certainly something that had never happened before now. Only it wasn't *just* now—when I actually thought about it, he'd been answering unspoken thoughts ever since I'd picked him up at the airport.

He blinked, as if suddenly realizing what he'd done, and half smiled. "Interesting," he said, then returned his attention to Hunt. "You forgot the who."

"Because I don't fucking *know*. It'll be just another courier. The sindicati never put themselves in *any* situation that might bring down interest from the cops."

Which made their kidnapping of us all the more unusual—although it was blindingly obvious from their actions at the exchange that they hadn't *actually* intended to release us.

"And the payment?"

His breath hissed out. "Ten grand."

For murdering someone? Either these two worked cheap, or Morretti figured Rosen wasn't worth much anymore.

"You're not going make that meeting, I'm—"

"Fuck the meeting," Hunt growled, his gaze cutting to mine. "The third time's the charm, sweetheart. And the next time, the shoe will most definitely be on the other foot."

"If there *is* a next time," I retorted, "I'll burn your ass to hell and back."

And if I'd done precisely *that* when we'd stopped the bastard murdering Amanda Wilson, not only would I have saved myself future problems, but, considering how close he'd come to killing me, I probably could have claimed self-defense and gotten away with it.

I'd barely finished speaking when Jackson swung his fist; the blow snapped the wolf's head back and rattled his teeth. He was out of it before his bloody spittle hit the asphalt.

The flames binding him were immediately doused, leaving Hunt's clothes smoking slightly but his skin untouched.

With the bastard finally unconscious, I relaxed. "We'd better lock these two up if we want to make that meeting tonight."

Jackson pushed upright. "Wonder if Morretti intended to get rid of two birds with one stone and use Rosen's death to draw us into their net?"

"And do what? Kill us? I doubt they'd go to such lengths when we haven't exactly been hiding out. Besides, he's more likely to want Hunt dead than us."

"That's probable since Morretti doesn't take failure lightly, but I doubt he actually wants to kill us. Even vampires can't get answers out of the dead."

No, but the leader of the red cloaks could—*if* the victim had been infected with the virus before the death had occurred, that is. "As I said, if he wanted to question us, there were easier ways to go about it."

"Which is where the two-stones theory comes in. Why else would Morretti use someone we'd instantly recognize? Had anyone else escorted Rosen to that car, it's doubtful we'd have reacted." He toed the unconscious werewolf lightly. "Besides, the only reason *this* bastard isn't in jail right now has to be because someone with enough pull kept him out."

"Given the legal system's soft-sentencing tendencies on criminals, he probably just walked from court with a slap on the wrist." I frowned. "But Morretti couldn't have known we'd decide to visit Rosen—"

"Couldn't he?" he cut in. "They're obviously aware of our movements. In fact, given who they are, I wouldn't put it past them to be tracking the car."

"Great," I said, my tone heavy. "So from now on, no major discussions inside the car until we check it."

"That's *if* the car is bugged. As I said, it's probably just a tracker." He shrugged. "I'll check it. But it might still be wise to use a different mode of transport if we go to this meeting tonight."

"And to go fully armed." Especially if this whole thing *was* all part of a grander scheme.

Jackson nodded. "I'll dump Hunt in one of the shipping containers. Then we'll grab Rosen and take him somewhere safe."

I glanced toward the upturned car. Man-Mountain Two appeared no closer to getting free, but he had, at least, turned off the engine. "What about the other one?"

Jackson half smiled. "He can sit there and rot for all I care, though I daresay Hunt will free him eventually.

The containers will hold a wolf of his size and strength for only so long." He bent and, with a grunt of effort, hauled the unconscious wolf at his feet upright. "Why don't you go prepare a cage for our hairy friend?"

I jogged over to the two containers near Rosen. The rods on the first one had been bent at right angles and didn't have any sort of lock. The second one looked no less rusty than the first, but the rods were in place, as were the lock handles that opened them. I unlatched the right door, then moved across to the left and repeated the process. The doors swung open easily enough. Inside was a pile of putrid rubbish and what looked to be human remains. At least Hunt would have some company while he was locked in here.

Jackson dumped him inside, and then went through his pockets until he'd found Hunt's phone. He crushed it under the heel of his boot and left the remains for Hunt to find.

"Right," he said, closing the right-hand door after he'd exited. "Let's grab Rosen and get out of here."

I locked the left door, checked both were secure, then followed Jackson across to Rosen. He still wasn't responding to external stimuli, and his blue eyes had a glazed, no-one-is-home sort of look.

"Definitely drugged," I said.

"Yeah." Jackson seized Rosen's arm and hauled him upright. "Come on, let's get you somewhere safe."

"Okay," Rosen said.

Meaning he *could* see and hear; maybe whatever he'd been given simply made him pliable. It would certainly explain why he'd walked so willing into the arms of certain death.

We made it back to the car without incident. Jackson shoved Rosen in the rear seat and told him to sit still and be quiet—to which he got another soft "Okay."

After Jackson had done a quick search for bugs and discovered nothing, I started up the car and reversed out. "Where to?"

He leaned forward, turned on the radio, and said, his voice barely audible over the music, "We can't risk taking him back to either his house or the office. Once Morretti realizes things haven't gone as planned, they'll be the first places he looks."

"And for the very same reason, we can't take him back to our office."

"No." Jackson studied the road ahead for a second. "What about we all stay at that hotel we used after I rescued you from the sewer?"

"Good plan, except for the minor fact that we can't register in our own names because that'll also make finding us easier."

His sudden grin was wide and cheeky. "Did I register in either of our names the first time?"

"Well, no." I glanced at him. "That's one hell of a good friend you've got if you're still running around with his credit card."

"It may be his card, but I'm paying the bills, never fear." He shrugged. "Besides, as I explained, I saved his wife. He's come out and said, more than once, anything I want, I can have."

"And this is the first time you've asked for anything?"

He nodded. "I don't believe in abusing my client's gratitude. It's not a great way to get return business or recommendations."

"With that I agree, but many wouldn't."

"Which is why Hellfire survives whereas many other agencies don't." He twisted around in the seat and added, "Rosen, why did those men grab you?"

"They said Radcliffe wanted to talk to me." His reply was monotone, without life.

Jackson glanced at me, eyebrow raised. "Indeed? What about?"

"Gambling debts."

"Just how much do you owe Radcliffe?"

Rosen shrugged. "Eight, ten million, something like that."

"You don't *know*?" I couldn't help the surprise in my voice. While I'd never been much of a gambler, there had been times over the centuries where I punted more than I should have and paid the price for it. But I'd been fully aware of how much I owed, even if I kept digging the hole deeper in an effort to get out of it.

"What do a few million matter?" Rosen replied absently. "The company is worth billions."

Jackson snorted. "It's not going to be worth anything if you get caught selling company secrets."

"It's my company, and I pay my scientists good money to uncover those secrets. Why should I not be allowed to use them as I please?"

I shook my head, unable to believe what I was hearing. "They're not your secrets when it's the *government* paying you to do the research."

And I have to admit, I'd been surprised when I'd first discovered that. But—according to Jackson—it was part of a deep-level government initiative to outsource certain projects. Apparently, there were too many management types and too much red tape that came with government labs. Over the years, they'd discovered it was far easier to have a black slush fund and get certain projects done under the radar.

Rosen didn't say anything. Maybe he just wasn't willing to admit what he was doing was wrong.

"Has Radcliffe ever sent those two men to collect you before?"

"No."

"And you didn't think to check with him, just to ensure they *were* from him?"

"No, because he rarely sends the same people. It's safer that way."

"Undoubtedly." Jackson glanced at me. "So, was our massive friend telling the truth or spinning a yarn?"

I shrugged. "I think lying is a natural state for Hunt, but I really couldn't guess whether he was or not with us."

Jackson grunted, then glanced back to Rosen. "What do you know about the disappearance of Wilson's research?"

"Nothing more than the police have told me. The bastard got himself murdered, and persons unknown took his notes and erased the information off our hard drives."

"And you didn't have backup?" Somehow, I found that very unlikely. After all, Lady Harriett (who owned and ran the Chase Medical Research Institute, and whom Rosen had no doubt hoped to piss off when he'd started up his own company after their divorce) not only had a backup system, but her chief researcher (my now-dead boss) also had his *own* backup system. Maybe Wilson had as well.

"Of course I had backup." Rosen managed to sound indignant despite the compliancy in his tone. "The bastards found it."

"But did they find Wilson's backup?"

"No," Rosen said at the same time as Jackson said, "What?"

I stopped at a pedestrian crossing and, as several schoolkids scooted across, said, "Baltimore once told me the reason he backed up all his notes was because he'd once had his research stolen, and he wanted to be able to prove, beyond doubt, it was his. It's possible Wilson was similarly paranoid."

"If he *was*, wouldn't Amanda have known? And surely she would have mentioned it to Morretti."

"And yet, Rosen said no." The lights changed again, and I drove on.

"So he did." Jackson glanced back at the man. "Do you know where he hid his backup?"

"If I had any clue, would I have hired you to find them?"

Amusement briefly touched Jackson's lips. "You hired me to uncover who stole his notes, not find the backup ones."

"I was hoping the latter would be part of the process."

"Unlikely, given that up until now I didn't even know the things existed."

"Well, what sort of investigator are you?"

"A pissed-off one at the moment," Jackson said

rather mildly. "And that's *not* something you want, considering that, right now, we're all that stands between you and death. Did Wilson have any clubs, special friends, or places he went to regularly?"

Rosen shrugged. "I'm his employer, not his keeper. Ask that flirtatious wife of his."

"That flirtatious wife," I commented, "was a telepath working for the sindicati."

"Bitch." It was so mildly said, it was almost comical. And yet, anger practically vibrated off him. Maybe the drug was starting to lose a little of its influence—which was logical, since they'd really only need to give him enough to keep him pliant until they reached the kill zone.

"So, if you have no idea where Wilson kept his notes, why are you so certain they haven't been found?"

"Because people keep asking about them."

"People?" Jackson's gaze sharpened. "What people?"

"Radcliffe, PIT investigators, some damn investigative reporter." He shrugged. "I showed him the door quick smart, I tell you. Never did take a shine to vamps of his sort."

Something twisted in my gut. Whether it was instinct or a premonition, I couldn't say, but it nevertheless had me saying, "Describe him."

"He was tall, with close-cut gray hair and old-fashioned rimmed glasses that were perched rather absurdly on the end of his nose. He had an air about him—one that reminded me of a rabid dog."

Aside from the rabid-dog description, it was almost an exact match for Professor Heaton, whom Lady Harriet had supposedly employed to replace Professor Baltimore. Only trouble was, he'd been a vampire who'd had Lady Harriet under telepathic control, and my orders—to show him down to the labs and provide him with any help he required—had undoubtedly come as a direct result of his control over her. I'd chosen the safer option—running.

The lights ahead changed from green to red. I used the moment to grab my phone from my purse and bring up the picture I'd taken of Heaton. "Is this him?"

"Yes," Rosen said.

I threw my phone back into my purse and glanced at Jackson. "I'm guessing Heaton read Rosen's mind and discovered he didn't know anything new about the notes."

"Which is why it makes no sense for either Morretti or Radcliffe to have ordered him killed. Why waste a good future resource?"

I had no idea. But then, I wasn't a crime boss or a black marketer, and never had been, so it wasn't like I was coming from any level of understanding their thought processes. I turned onto Dorcas Street and swung into some underground parking near the hotel. If we did have a tracker attached to the car somewhere, parking here would at least make the sindicati's time finding us a bit tougher. Jackson ordered Rosen out of the car, then handed him over to me while he opened the trunk and retrieved not one but two largish carryalls.

"You've taken to carrying spare clothes with you?" I said, amused.

"After all the shit with the sindicati and whatnot, I thought it wise." He slammed the trunk closed. "I've got toiletries in here for you, but nothing in the way of clothes, I'm afraid."

I caught Rosen's arm and guided him toward the elevator. "Hoping, no doubt, that I'd run around naked."

"I always hope that, and I am constantly disappointed."

I snorted. "No fun and games during working hours. Your rules, not mine."

"Rules *can* occasionally be broken."

"Well, *that* isn't going to be one of them." Even if I *had* kissed him rather ardently at the airport. "For this partnership to truly work, there do need to be boundaries between our working and social lives."

He glanced at his watch, then flashed me a dangerous and downright sexy grin. "So at precisely one minute past five, I'm free to seduce you?"

"If we worked regular office hours, sure. We don't. Besides, we have a passenger in tow, remember? We can't protect him if we're doing the horizontal tango."

"You're a hard taskmaster, Emberly Pearson."

I just grinned and led Rosen into the street. Five minutes later, we were walking into the hotel's lobby. The vibrancy of the red feature wall behind the desk made me blink, just as it had the first time we'd been here, but at least *this* time I had more of a chance to look around—not that there was much to see. Other than the feature wall, the rest of the lobby was rather bland, even if it was clean and comfortable. Jackson strode over to the desk to organize accommodation and, in no time at all, we were once again in the elevator and heading for the tenth floor. As before, we didn't have a room but rather a suite, this time with two bedrooms as well as a generous living area, separate bathroom, and a small kitchen.

"Right," I said, leading Rosen into the smaller bedroom. "Lie on the bed and rest until the drug wears off. We're in the living room if you need us."

Rosen did as he was bid. I spun around and found Jackson peering out the living room window. "Problem?"

He shook his head. "Just scoping the street out of habit." He pulled the curtains closed. "If we're going to make this our base of operations, we need, at the very least, a computer."

"Since I also need clothes, I'll head back home and grab Rory's laptop." I still hadn't replaced mine after handing it over to the sindicati.

"Just be careful coming back. We know the sindicati have replaced at least one of your building's security guards with their own man; they might also have someone ready to follow you now that their office raid didn't net them the desired result."

"I'll be careful." I wrapped my arms around his neck and kissed him. It was long, slow, and totally wonderful.

Jackson groaned when I pulled away. "Damn it, woman, you don't play fair."

"Consider it a teaser for a later point when we have some alone time."

"With the way my luck has been running, Rosen will be with us for days on end."

I raised my eyebrows. "And why is that a problem?"

"Aside from the fact I'll be as frustrated as hell, I don't think the bastard can be trusted to behave himself for that long."

I frowned. "Surely if we explain the situation to him, he won't do anything stupid. I mean, he doesn't seem the type to have a death wish."

"He's a gambler," Jackson said heavily. "One who is so hopelessly locked into his addiction, he's stealing from his own company. You can never trust someone like that to do the right thing—even if it's something as simple as staying put to save his life."

"Well, we can't guard him twenty-four/seven—not if we want to find answers."

"True." He dropped a quick kiss on my lips, then stepped back. "You'd better go, before my hormones override my control."

"A fire Fae with so little control." I shook my head sadly. "What is this world coming to?"

"Neither it nor I are coming," he growled, but with amusement crinkling the corners of his eyes. "And *that* is the whole problem."

I grinned but grabbed my purse and keys and headed out. Jackson's caution was catchy, however, because I checked the street carefully, looking for anyone who seemed out of place before I headed back to the parking lot. And I double-checked the car—more thoroughly than Jackson had—but got exactly the same result. No bugs. So maybe they were following us. I hadn't spotted a tail, but then, if the sindicati worked with werewolf thugs, why would they not also employ shifters? As Jackson had noted, it would be easy enough for a winged shifter to follow us, and it certainly wasn't something we'd notice. Nor was it something we could do anything about.

Except, maybe, constantly change cars. Or steal them.

I glanced around and noted the security cameras. Stealing wasn't a possibility here, but it might be at another, less watched, location. I jumped into the car and headed out into the traffic. It was nearing rush hour, which meant it probably would have been quicker to walk home than to actually drive there. I found a parking spot a block away from our apartment and walked the rest of the way.

And discovered, as I walked into the lobby, Sam waiting for me.

CHAPTER 4

I stopped abruptly, my gaze locked on his and my stupid heart dancing about like a crazy thing. Just for an instant, the beautiful blue depths of his eyes warmed, and it would have been very easy to believe he was truly happy to see me. But the warmth disappeared all too quickly, cloaked by the shadows that seemed so much a part of him these days.

He uncrossed his legs and rose languidly from the chair, a big, lean man who exuded a dark sensuality—one that had somehow gained depth and power in even the brief time since I'd last seen him.

"What the hell are you doing here?" It came out a little huskier than I might have wished, but then, how could it not when every intake of breath was filled with his warm, woodsy scent? I was a being of fire, not stone.

Yet that same delicious scent now held an even deeper, more dangerous edge than before, and it was one that allured and repelled in equal amounts.

"I need to question you about last night's events." He stopped several feet away and shoved his hands into the pockets of his coat. I had an odd feeling they were clenched and that he was fighting the desire to reach for me. Wishful thinking, surely. He and I were over, thanks to his refusal to believe that Rory was a necessity in my life; while my heart couldn't move on, his obviously had. He'd made that more than clear during our recent meetings; hell, he'd drugged me, for god's sake and, as a result, had restricted my ability to use my fire and had almost gotten me killed. Why would he do that if even the slightest bit of caring remained?

"Why?" I said. "I told the cops everything I saw last night. I can't add anything else."

"You might have told them everything you saw at the scene, but I doubt you told them everything you know." His voice was as flat as ever, but much of the coldness that had been so evident in our recent meetings was absent. "I know you, Red. It wasn't by chance that you were in that neighborhood."

Was his use of my nickname just a slip of the tongue? Or was it, perhaps, an indication that maybe—just maybe—he wasn't as filled with hate for me as I'd presumed? I couldn't help hoping it was the latter even if I suspected it was the former. We might not ever be what we once were, but I'd like to think we could at least be friends. "And why would you think that?"

"Intuition." He waved a hand toward the doorway. "Shall we take this discussion to Portside?"

Portside was the small café not far away from my apartment building, and a place we'd retreated to several times in the past few weeks. I stepped to one side and motioned him forward. Something flashed in his eyes—amusement or annoyance, I wasn't sure which.

Then he strode past me and out into the crisp afternoon air. Once again he chose a table overlooking the marina but as far away from the other customers as possible. Not that there were many about at this hour; it was too late for the lunch diners and far too early for the dinner crowd.

I pulled out a chair and sat opposite him. Not only because it put as much distance between him and me as was possible on a round table but because the wind was behind my back rather than his, taking his scent away from me.

He picked up a menu and studied it for several seconds. Frustration swirled through me, but I knew from past experience that he wouldn't be hurried. He would say what he'd come here to say in his own good time.

That he was even here was odd, given his vow to stay well away from me. It wasn't as if he were just an ordinary, everyday PIT investigator; everything he'd said and done since we'd come into contact again led me to believe he was fairly high up in the organization. Surely if he'd wanted to avoid me, he could have.

Unless, of course, everyone else was out chasing mad humans infested with the red plague virus.

The waitress came over. After she'd taken our orders and retreated, he put the menu away and interlaced his fingers on the table. His gaze, when it met mine, was steady and determined. The dangerous darkness had, for the moment, retreated, even if it hadn't gone too far. I could still sense it, deep within him; it was a thick knot of shadows that stained his soul but hadn't consumed him. Not yet, anyway.

Whether those shadows were the aftermath of his

having had to kill his own brother after Luke had been infected with the red plague virus and it had made him mad, a result of his job at PIT, or something else entirely, I couldn't say. All I knew was that the darkness was to be feared.

And I hoped like hell that whatever it was, he didn't let it win.

I leaned back in my chair and returned his gaze steadily. If he wanted answers, then he'd better ask his damn questions. Rory's theory was all well and good, but Sam was holding just as many secrets these days as I was. I wasn't about to volunteer information unless *he* returned the favor.

But what if it's not just about truth? that annoying inner voice said. *What if it's our actions as much as our words in this lifetime that affect what happens in the next?*

It was a somewhat depressing thought, if only because I doubted anyone could ever be totally honest in thought *and* deed his entire life. Everyone made mistakes. Everyone lied—sometimes for good reasons, sometimes for bad. It was the *one* truth that *hadn't* changed, not in all the centuries of my life. If our happiness *did* depend on achieving such a high goal, then we truly were cursed.

"Why were you really in that neighborhood last night?" he said eventually. "I've done a background check on Hamberly, and he's certainly not someone you'd normally associate with."

"Maybe these days he is," I replied evenly. "Maybe I've suddenly gained a hankering for paunchy, middle-aged men since you and I split."

He raised an eyebrow. "Really?"

Amusement briefly touched my lips. "What is this about, Sam? Why has PIT stepped into what should be a regular homicide investigation?"

"Because it's not a regular homicide, and it's not the first time this murderer has struck."

I sat upright abruptly. "What?"

"Your reaction," he all but drawled, "is something of a giveaway."

It certainly was. But, damn it, if this wasn't the first time the creature had struck, why hadn't I dreamed about it before now? Generally, when the prophetic dreams hit, it was because a life hung in the balance—a life I could save if I so chose. That *wasn't* an option here. And if it was the creature I was supposed to stop, why didn't I see it when it first struck?

"How many others has this thing feasted on? And did it just take the liver and heart of those victims, or were other internal organs missing?"

"And just how," Sam said, the shadows in his soul becoming a little more evident, "did you know this thing had a penchant for inner organs? There was very little evidence of such an invasion on Hamberly's body."

I hesitated, but it wasn't really practical to hold back the truth in *this* particular case. Sam worked with PIT. They not only had vamps, weres, and shifters on their payroll, but all sorts of psi-gifted humans. If anyone could accept the reality of my dreams, it was he and PIT.

Even if, that inner voice whispered, *he hadn't been able to accept the reality of phoenixes.*

Or rather, I amended silently, the reality that, as a

phoenix, I could never be entirely faithful to the man I loved. Not if I wanted to spend an entire lifetime with him.

Of course, he hadn't actually given me the chance to explain I had no choice but to be with Rory. And as much as I understood his anger, it still hurt that he'd chosen to wipe me from his heart rather than simply listen to my explanation.

"I want the truth, Red," he said softly. "Not lies."

You can't handle the truth. The immortal movie line jumped onto my tongue and begged to be spoken, but I somehow kept it inside. Because the real truth was, anyone discovering the person they loved was apparently having an affair would have reacted the same way. Like it or not, our breakup was as much my fault as his, even if I'd spent a long time denying it.

"I saw the creature in a dream," I said. "I saw it enter Hamberly's house and watched as it began to dine on his body. I went there simply because I thought there was a chance I could stop it before it attacked anyone else."

Sam studied me for a minute, his expression closed and his body still. He reminded me somewhat of a predator about to pounce; there was the same sense of coiled readiness about him.

And yet it wasn't, in any way, aimed at me. Which was odd, considering that nearly every other time we'd met, he'd seemed too close to the edge; that at any second, the darkness within him could have reached out and killed me as easily as it would any villain.

Something had changed in the weeks since I'd last

seen him. The darkness was still there; it was still very dangerous and very much to be feared, but it was—for the moment at least—controlled.

"And these prophetic dreams—this is how you knew I was in danger?"

I nodded. "I generally see events before they happen. Sometimes I interfere, but I've learned over the years it's often better not to."

"So why rescue my butt? We both would have been far better off if you hadn't."

There was an edge to his voice, a bitter anger so deep and desperate, it brought tears to my eyes. And again, it wasn't aimed at me. Hell, if the blankness in his eyes was any indication, he wasn't even *seeing* me right at this particular moment, but rather, something deep within.

Something that had changed him forever.

His brother, that internal voice whispered. *But not the shooting.*

Which made about as much sense as vampires suddenly gaining wings and flying.

"No matter how much I might have hated you at the time of our breakup," I said softly, "I never wished you dead. I still don't, even if you've been the world's biggest bastard."

He blinked and life returned to his eyes; life and darkness. "You can hardly expect tender treatment when so many lives have been put at risk thanks to this virus—especially when your behavior and dogged refusal to be sensible were hampering investigations."

"You almost got both Jackson and me killed when you gave us the drug that restricted my abilities and made us obey your order not to pursue Morretti. Nothing we did justified that, Sam."

"Almost getting you killed *wasn't* our intention," he bit back. "We simply meant to get you out of the way."

"It might not have been your intention, but it certainly was the result."

"As I said, unintended." He paused. "Although we can hardly take *all* the blame—if you and Jackson had done as ordered and stepped away, you might not have fallen afoul of the sindicati."

I snorted. "Nothing I did would have stopped them coming after me, and we both know it."

Because they'd wanted the last of my boss's notes—notes that I'd inadvertently lost when I'd run into the coffee table in the middle of the night, sending the pile of them scattering to all corners of the room.

But if I hadn't, then the last of those notes would be in sindicati hands right now rather than in PIT's, because the bastards had broken into my home and stolen the rest of them before any of us really realized what was going on.

"Perhaps." Sam waved a hand, as if the matter were of no consequence. And I guess it wasn't to him. "What was so different about Hamberly's death that you decided to interfere?"

I shrugged. "In all honesty, I think it was simply that Hamberly was already dead. I've never had a dream in which I couldn't change the outcome, not in all the centuries I've been alive. It *had* to mean I was there for the creature, not the victim."

He leaned forward. Just for a moment, his scent spun around me, warm and enticing. But that still darkness was stronger with his closeness, and it instantly chilled the sparks of desire.

"Creature? Can you describe it?"

I hesitated. "It's a shifter of some sort. It's little more than shadow and ash, but it seems able to alternate between a cat, a bat, and a monstrous black dog with backward-facing feet."

He blinked. "Seriously?"

I nodded. "The closer it got to its victim, the farther away the sound of its footsteps, so I suspect some sort of magic is involved. But I've never come across its like before, and I have no idea what it is or what it might be capable of."

Sam scrubbed a hand across his jaw, his expression thoughtful. In the late-afternoon sunlight, his black hair gleamed with rich blue highlights, but his face was far leaner than it ever had been. It was almost as if every ounce of fat had been burned from his body, leaving only muscle and perfection.

"It certainly doesn't sound like anything I've ever read about," he said eventually. "Do you know if it has a human form?"

"It never took a human form when my dreams followed it, but that doesn't mean it can't."

He grimaced. "And you can't tell us anything else about it?"

The waitress came back with his coffee and my tea and carrot cake. I dumped the bag of green tea into the little pot, then picked up the spoon and scooped up some cake.

"Not really," I said in between mouthfuls. "I did notice a really weird chemical smell when I examined

Hamberly's body, and I think the creature might have injected something into the wounds to dissolve Hamberly's organs before it sucked them up."

"Your sense of smell is damn good if you picked that up."

I shrugged. "I'm not human, Sam. I don't suffer the same sort of restrictions."

"When you're wearing flesh, you're as human as anyone else. That much I *do* know."

Our gazes locked and memories rose. Everything that we'd been, everything that we'd shared; all the love and the laughter, all the heat and desire. It was right there, hovering between us, a ghost that flaunted the magnitude of what we'd lost.

Fate, I decided, was a bitch. It didn't need to bring this man back into my life. Didn't need to remind me how far I'd fallen from love everlasting in this lifetime, because I was more than aware of it.

I pushed the remainder of my cake away, poured myself a cup of tea, and then leaned back. It gave me time to recover, to think.

"That's true in some respects, not so much in others." I shrugged and directed the conversation back to slightly safer waters. "So how many times has this thing struck?"

He contemplated me over his coffee cup for a moment, then took a sip and said, "Hamberly was his third victim. The first attack occurred in a morgue, and the second was a junkie who'd overdosed."

I frowned. "So he's restricting his actions to dead people? That really *is* weird."

"The problem is, there's no guarantee he'll remain content with dead people."

"He's taken three now. With any other killer, that would be considered a pattern, wouldn't it?"

"Yes, but in this case, each victim has been progressively closer to life. The first had been dead a day, the second twelve hours, and Hamberly barely one hour. His actions are escalating, and we fear that the next time, he'll actually kill his victim."

It was certainly possible, given the fast-dropping timeline. "How often is it feasting?"

"They started nine days ago. There were five days between victim one and two, and four days between two and Hamberly."

So he had, at most, three days to find this thing before it killed again. No wonder he'd come to me; if the other crime scenes had been as clean as the most recent, they were obviously desperate for clues.

Except that Hamberly's house *hadn't* been absent of clues. And I still had that hair sitting in my purse.

"Did it take only the heart and liver of the other two?" I asked. "Because it seems a lot of effort to go through just to get those."

"Yes," he said. "And there are plenty of creatures out there who would rather feast on offal than flesh."

There were plenty of humans who preferred it, too, but I very much doubted we were dealing with anything human. "You've obviously found nothing at any of the crime scenes that would help."

"No." He contemplated me for a second. "Have you?"

I hesitated, but in truth I wanted this thing caught as much as he did, and it made sense to hand the hair over. Jackson's source might be able to help us out, but Sam and PIT were far better placed to go after this thing. We had trouble enough coping with Rosen, the sindicati, and keeping our clients happy. We didn't need anything else lumped onto our plate.

Though *that* wouldn't stop me from going after this thing if I dreamed of it again.

I reached into my purse and pulled out the plastic bag that contained the hair. "I found this in a paw-print puddle."

He plucked the bag from my fingertips and held it up to the sun. "It's a black hair."

"Whether it's the creature's or not, I can't say. But Hamberly didn't appear to have any pets, and while he obviously had a partner, she wasn't there at the time."

"No." He tucked the plastic bag into his pocket. "Anything else?"

I shook my head. "The dream wasn't really that helpful."

"Are they ever?"

"Sometimes." They'd certainly given plenty of details when I'd saved his life, just as they'd done when I'd plucked the little girl from the flames that had left my back scarred. But this creature—and this situation—was different from anything else I'd ever dreamed about.

"If you dream again, I want you to contact us," he said.

It was an order rather than a request, and the inner bitch sparked to life. But I bit back the instinctive retort and took a sip of tea. He'd been extraordinarily talk-ative this afternoon—at least compared to other recent meetings—so maybe it was time to try to grab some much-needed information. The worst that could hap-pen was he could tell me to go to hell, and I'd been told that more times than I cared to remember—and by men more bitter than him.

"I will," I said eventually. "On the condition you an-swer some questions."

A smile twisted his lips, but it held no warmth. Though I fully expected a rebuke, all he said was, "That would depend on the questions."

"The first one is easy—has PIT released Radcliffe?"

"Yes. And before you ask, I have no intention of tell-ing you what information we did or didn't get out of him."

I snorted. "Trust me, I'm well aware of *that*."

"Then what is your second question?"

"Why is PIT still holding Jackson's truck?"

"We're not. It was taken to the impound yard yester-day and a letter sent." He paused, then reached into his pocket and pulled out a USB. My heart sank. It was one of the USBs I'd hidden under the driver's seat when the sindicati van had smashed Jackson's truck into a tree in a well-planned, well-timed, and very successful at-tempt to kidnap me. I guess it had been naive to think that PIT *wouldn't* search the truck. If one thing had be-come obvious since this whole mess had begun, it was that PIT was ruthlessly efficient. And sometimes, sim-ply ruthless.

But, as he'd said, they were dealing with a virus ca-pable of wiping out a good portion of both the human and nonhuman populations, so they could hardly be blamed if they occasionally resorted to heavy-handed methods.

I just wished they wouldn't use them against *me*.

I opened my hand, and he dropped the USB into it. "Why am I getting this one back?"

"Because there's nothing relating to Wilson's research on it."

"Meaning the others *did* have information?"

He simply gave me another of those cool smiles. "Anything else?"

I hesitated. There *was* one question I was burning to ask, even if it would be stupid to do so. I had to move on from this man and what might have been, I knew that, but Rory's words had stirred something within me, and I just couldn't let go. Seeking answers certainly couldn't alter what had already happened in *this* lifetime, but it might well be the difference between heartbreak and happiness in all our future ones.

I opened my mouth to speak, but my throat suddenly felt drier than the Sahara, and the words refused to come out. I picked up my cup and took another sip. It didn't really help the dryness, but I nevertheless managed to croak, "If I'd been honest from the very beginning about what I was and what that entailed, would it have made any difference?"

He leaned back in his chair, his expression closed and his eyes shuttered. The darkness within him was still, but it was *not* unthreatening. It rose around him like a cloak, making him suddenly appear more shadow than a man of flesh and blood.

I blinked and the shadows fled, making me wonder

if it had been my imagination or some sort of prophetic glimmer. Was my subconscious self—the being that was spirit and fire—seeing more than the physical senses of my flesh counterpart? I had no idea, and that was frustrating.

Sam remained still and silent. Tension wound through me, but as much as I tried to relax, I couldn't. I needed an answer; needed to know if disclosing the truth would have made any difference to us, or whether it would simply have killed all hope of *any* sort of relationship, leaving me without even memories to survive on.

Eventually he sighed and leaned forward. There was something in his eyes—a spark that spoke of sadness— that had my stomach plummeting.

"That is a question I've asked myself a hundred times since you came back into my life." His voice, like his expression, was closed. Only that fading spark gave any hint there might be more happening behind the shutters than the stillness suggested.

I swallowed heavily and said, "And did you ever come up with an answer?"

In the deeper shadows that haunted his blue eyes, hunger flared. It spoke of need—not just the need for emotional closeness but for something much deeper, much darker. It was a caress of flame that promised so much and yet threatened even more. It was almost as if he were a man of two very different souls, one born of light and the other of darkness. The former was the man I'd fallen in love with; the latter the man he'd become. Right at this precise moment, the two seemed to be on equal ground, but whether the status quo would or even could remain was anyone's guess. But his darker half had certainly come out to play during some of our previous meetings, and I had no desire to come into close contact with *that* part of him any more than necessary—even if some tiny, somewhat insane part of me desperately wanted to understand what was going on with him.

"Why does it matter now?" he said eventually. "Neither of us can change the past or what happened."

"No," I agreed even as I wondered if he would want to, given the chance. "But it might just affect my future. Or rather, how I approach relationships in the future."

"I would hope that you'd approached them honestly." His flat voice oddly hinted at anger. "We both know the damage anything else can cause."

"And yet, such honesty can result in just as much harm," I replied evenly. "They may not burn witches at the stake anymore, Sam, but that sort of mentality is still very much in existence."

"But only in a very small portion of the human population. For the most part, people are accepting of non-human existence."

I wasn't sure about that, but it wasn't something I was about to debate. "And would you have been accepting?"

"Of your being a phoenix? Totally." But even as those words left his mouth, his gaze became fierce. It was anger and hurt and confusion all mixed in with that deeper darkness, and it made my heart race as much as it sent chills across my skin. "But of a phoenix's need to be with another man? I don't know. I'm not the man I was back then, but I'm also even less inclined to share. And that, basically, is what loving you will always mean. I'm not sure I'm capable of that, Red. I'm not sure I'll ever be capable of it."

He rose so abruptly, his chair flipped backward, the noise drawing the gazes of the few diners who were here. Sam stepped to one side, righted the chair, and tossed some cash on the table. His gaze, when it finally met mine again, was calm. The turmoil I'd glimpsed had been erased, replaced by the still, cold darkness. "Make sure you call us if you dream of the creature again."

Us, not him. A bitter smile twisted my lips as I watched him walk away. I'd gotten my answers, but it really hadn't helped my situation. Not in this lifetime, and not for any other lifetime. And if truth *was* fate's ultimate lesson for us, then it certainly wasn't making the discovery—or even the desire to chase it—any easier.

I sighed and gathered the bills Sam had dumped on the table. He'd left enough not only to pay for his coffee but for my tea and cake, so once I'd given the money to the waitress, I headed home.

The smell of meat cooking hit my nostrils the minute I opened the door. I took a deep breath, needing to erase Sam's scent from my nostrils and memory.

"Smell's lovely." I dropped my purse on the nearest chair and walked into the kitchen. Rory stood by the stove, stirring what looked to be a meat sauce. "Lasagna?"

He nodded. "I wasn't sure whether you'd be home tonight or not, so I thought I'd make something I could easily freeze."

"Good idea." I kissed him, then grabbed a spoon and scooped up some of the sauce. It was delicious— but then, he'd always been a better cook than me. I was okay at the basics, but he was more adventurous. More imaginative—in the kitchen and out.

"What happened with your creature chase?" he asked.

I leaned against the nearby counter and crossed my arms. "The best thing about it was the night ride through the street. That bike of yours can move."

A grin split his lips. "Why do you think I bought it? It's the next best thing to flying." He paused. "So if the creature chase was a bust, what has you so uptight? Is Jackson okay?"

"Totally." I gave him a quick update on everything that had happened, then added, "Jackson is with Rosen now, and I'm going back there."

"So what's stressing you out?" He paused again, his gaze narrowing. "Sam."

I sighed. "Apparently, the attack I witnessed last night wasn't the creature's first. He wanted to know why I'd been there."

"And did you tell him?"

I half smiled. "That whole truth theory of yours got me thinking. So yes, I did. Besides, it's not like I've got the time *or* the desire to go after this thing."

"Unless, of course, you dream of it again."

"Exactly." I shrugged. "Sam was surprisingly reserved today. I don't know what was different, but something was."

Rory gave me a long look. "Don't go falling for him again, Em. It won't end happily."

I snorted. "I can't fall for him again simply because I never fell *out* of love for him—"

"You know what I mean," Rory cut in. "Just guard

your heart and your hopes. I don't want to be picking up the pieces twice in one lifetime."

"You won't. His behavior is really puzzling, that's all. Today there were glimmers of the old Sam, and they just made me all the more curious as to what happened to him."

"It's probably better not to know."

It probably was, but that wasn't something that had often stopped me.

Rory switched the stove off, then tugged me close and wrapped his arms around my waist. "I know *that* look. You're going to chase this, aren't you?"

I hesitated. "It's not like I actually can. Sam won't tell me anything—hell, he only comes to question me because he has to—and I doubt if any of his old friends will talk to me, even if he *has* confided in them."

"Which doesn't mean you won't go ask them."

"If this was another time, another situation, then probably." I sighed and rested my cheek against his chest. The steady beat of his heart was oddly reassuring. "But I've got an odd feeling Sam's on the edge right now, and I really don't want to do anything to tip him into complete imbalance."

"Says the woman who declares she has no intention of getting hurt a second time."

I pulled back a little. "He *is* this lifetime's love, Rory. I can't help caring."

"I know." He brushed a stray hair out of my eyes, his touch light. "Will you be back home later tonight?"

I shook my head. "As I said, Rosen needs guarding, and we need to keep out of sindicati sight until we figure out what we're going to do about them."

He frowned. "Wisdom suggests you do nothing but avoid them."

"Or that we figure out a way to stop them from coming after us."

"I really don't think—"

I placed a finger on his lips, halting the rest of his words. "We may have no other choice. But we're not about to do anything stupid, and we certainly won't do anything without letting you know first."

"Good. But if you get dead, expect a right tongue lashing when I resurrect you."

I grinned, rose on my tippy toes, and kissed him. "I won't get dead. I want to be alive long enough in this lifetime to complain about the wrinkles and gray hairs."

He snorted. "Are you staying for dinner?"

I hesitated, then shook my head. "I might, however, be tempted by a quick recharge, because who knows when I'll get back here."

"Well," he drawled, "how can I possibly resist such a sultry invitation?"

I pulled back and said, a mock note of haughtiness in my voice, "If you're going to be like *that*—"

He laughed, pulled me close again, and swept me up into his arms. Sparks ignited where our bodies touched, tiny fireflies of anticipation that spun through the shadows as he headed for our special room. It was, technically, the third bedroom of our large apartment, but as soon as we'd bought the place, we'd completely stripped it of all fittings and installed the very best fireproofing money could buy.

He nudged the thick door open with his foot, then

kicked it closed again once we were through. The room was completely empty, and pitch-black aside from the sparks that danced between us. He stopped in the middle, deposited me back onto my feet, and said, "Clothes on or off?"

I raised an eyebrow. It wasn't as if our clothes would actually be harmed if we flamed. The magic that allowed us to shift from one form to another also took anything that was touching our skin—clothes, watches, etcetera—with it. "And isn't *that* the ultimate in seduction talk."

He laughed again, then flamed; his flesh and his clothes gone in an instant, and all that was left was the heat of his soul. I threw back my head, my nostrils flaring as I sucked in its fierceness. It surged through me, primal and hot, and ignited the fires deep within. It was a firestorm that ripped through every muscle, every cell, breaking them down and tearing them apart, until my flesh no longer existed and I was nothing but fire.

"Oh lord," he murmured, "that feels *so* good."

I didn't answer. I couldn't. I was too wrapped up in sensation. He was heat and energy, life and love, need and necessity, and I was lost to the glory of him. As our fires grew fiercer and fingers of flames reached for the ceiling and crawled across the walls, his essence began to flow across every corner of my soul, reaffirming the connection between us and assuring life went on.

He drew me close again, and we began to dance, entwine, the fiery threads of our beings wrapping around one another, tighter and tighter, intensifying the pleasure, heightening the need. Soon there was no separation—no him, no me, nothing more than a growing storm of ecstasy. And still the dance went on, burning ever brighter, until the threads of our beings were drawn so tightly together that they would surely snap. Then everything *did*, and I fell into a fiery pit of bliss.

Several minutes later, I took a deep, shuddering breath and came back into flesh form. I was still embraced in Rory's fiery grip, but his flames quickly rolled back and he regained human form. He pressed his forehead lightly against mine. "Are you sure you won't stay for dinner?"

"I can't. The sindicati are probably watching my movements, and I really don't want to do anything that would make them believe you're anything more than a boarder."

He frowned and pulled back. "Why would they think otherwise? It's not like anyone saw me up at Hanging Rock."

"No, but the fact you took out their sharpshooter is a good indication someone else was up there, and it's easy enough to put two and two together."

"Only if they know a whole lot more about phoenixes than what the myths would have everyone believe. And let's face it—very few of *those* are actually based in truth."

"I know, but—"

"Em," he said gently, "I'll be okay. As far as anyone is aware, I have nothing to do with either the search for the missing research and disks, or the ongoing investigation into the deaths of Baltimore and Wilson."

"Maybe, but I have this really bad feeling that someone out there knows more about us than we think." I touched a hand to his cheek, ignoring the heat that burned into my fingertips as my gaze searched his. "I really want you to be careful, Rory. No risky behavior."

"I'm a fireman—risk comes with the job."

"That's not what I—"

"Em, relax." He caught my hand, then dropped a kiss on my palm. "I'll be careful. I won't do anything untoward until all this is over. I won't even risk dusk flights, if that'll ease your fears."

I smiled, but it felt tight. Uneasy. "It will. Thanks."

He nodded. "Then you'd best go shower and leave. If you *are* being watched, the less time spent here, the better."

I squeezed his hand, then pulled free and headed for the shower. Twenty minutes later, dressed in jeans and a thick sweater, I was out the door, Rory's laptop in one hand, a hastily made roast beef sandwich in the other, and a carryall containing enough clothes and other essentials for the next few days slung over my shoulder.

I couldn't see anyone following me and there didn't seem to be any birds acting suspiciously above me, but I still headed back to the hotel via a very circular route and parked in a different lot. As the saying went, better safe than sorry.

Jackson glanced up as I walked into the room. "Ha! Just the person I wanted to see—look what I've bought for you."

He held up a mousy brown wig and what looked suspiciously like a nurse's outfit. I raised an eyebrow. "And why did you buy me these things? Or did you have a sudden desire for sexual dress-ups? Because if you *did*, your idea of a fantasy needs a little more work."

He grinned. "Hey, anyone with *any* sense knows there's nothing better than a sexy woman in a short, tight nurse's uniform." He tossed me the outfit. "Your hair means you're too easily recognized, Em, and you can't risk using either of your other forms at night."

"Yes, but a nurse's uniform? A wig and a coat would have done just fine."

He grinned. "Maybe, but where's the fun in that? Besides, with two major hospitals on either side of Grey Street, no one is going to glance suspiciously at a nurse."

"What about Rosen?"

"He'll be out of it for a couple of more hours. I dropped a little something in his coffee."

My eyebrows rose again. "Was that wise, seeing as we have no idea what Hunt gave him?"

"Considering how belligerent he was being before I doped him, yes it was." He glanced at his watch. "We'd better get moving if we want to make it to Grey Street on time."

I quickly stripped and put on the uniform, all too aware of the hunger radiating from Jackson. He sighed wistfully when I finished. "That show was over far too quickly."

I grinned as I slipped my shoes back on. Thankfully, I'd been wearing sneakers, which didn't look too out of place with the uniform. "I do have to strip off again, remember."

"And I fully intend to do more than merely watch, let me warn you." He rose. "I've arranged another rental car for the evening."

I grabbed my bag, slung it over my shoulder, and followed him out. Although it was the tail end of rush hour, it didn't take us all that long to either pick up the new car or to get across to Grey Street. Finding parking was another matter entirely and, in the end, Jackson stopped just down from St Vincent's Hospital and let me out.

"I'll cruise around the block and meet you back here," he said. "If the sindicati are at the fountain, don't approach them without me."

I raised my eyebrows. "You don't think I can handle them?"

"No, I just don't trust them." His eyes glittered in the light coming from the car's dash. "Remember, they might also have intended to use this meeting to get rid of Hunt and his partner, and they'd know it'd take more than one vamp to achieve that particular goal. If you *do* spot anyone suspicious, call me. I'll dump the car and come a-running."

"The whole point of my wearing a disguise was *not* to be recognized. Your running in kinda spoils that."

"Yes, but—"

"Jackson," I cut in, "I'll be fine."

"Oh, I know *that*."

"Good, then quit worrying, and let me do my job."

I slammed the door shut. As he took off, I grabbed my phone and headed over to the park, pretending to text as I crossed Clarendon Street and walked toward the beautiful old fountain. There were only three people near it—a young couple cuddling on one of the park seats opposite and an old man clutching a bottle sheathed in a brown paper bag as if his life depended on it. None of them immediately screamed sindicati, but maybe that was the whole point. I skirted the fountain, passing within a couple of feet of the old man as I walked over to the seat opposite the couple. He smelled of urine and stale, unwashed flesh; if it was a disguise, then it was a damn good one, because his odor swamped my senses and made me want to gag. Neither he nor the couple paid any attention to me, and there was no one else in the immediate area. I sat down, crossed my legs, and waited. Time ticked over slowly. People walked by, in groups or alone, most of them barely doing more than glancing absently at me as they strode past. If the sindicati or their representatives were here, then they were well hidden.

My phone beeped. I glanced down and saw it was a message from Jackson asking what was going on. My reply was simple. *Nothing.*

No one there? he responded.

A couple and a drunk.

A few seconds passed; then he sent back, *Vampires?*

Hard to tell. The old guy's reek is killing my senses, and I've no reason to get closer to the couple to check.

Meaning it could be a bust. Do you want to come back to the car? I can't find parking, but I'll be back near the drop-off point in five minutes.

I was just about to reply when a shadow peeled away from a group of nearby trees and strolled toward the fountain. I kept my eyes down and watched him surreptitiously. He was big and muscular and walked with a slightly bow-legged strut. A man who exuded confidence, power, and danger. Even from this distance, it was obvious he was something more than human.

A werewolf just turned up, I sent. *One who could almost be Hunt's brother.*

Once again, Jackson's reply wasn't immediate—no surprise, given he was driving—so I raised my phone and took several shots of the wolf as he was looking the other way. I also took some of the old man and the couple, just in case.

The werewolf drew closer. There was a tension in him, an odd tightness to the set of his shoulders and arms that spoke of a man ready for action—an impression backed up by the fact his gaze was never still. It swept over me briefly, settled on the couple for several seconds, and moved on to the old man. Judging us, I thought. Or rather, judging the threat we represented.

He was here for a reason, and while that reason might *not* be me, it still had tension rolling through me. I could definitely look after myself, but I'd really had my fill of fighting man-mountains today. Besides, since I hadn't actually spotted *him* until he'd peeled away from the tree, it was very possible that he wasn't here alone.

The phone beeped again. *It could be someone from a rival pack,* Jackson wrote back. *Wolves have little compunction about getting rid of the opposition, especially if it gives them some sort of advantage.*

The wolf skirted the fountain and came toward me. I kept my gaze down and typed a reply to Jackson, though every other sense was tingling with awareness. The wolf's gaze was a weight I could feel—a heaviness that seemed to press down upon me. It was almost as if he were willing me to look up and spill all my secrets. But he was a werewolf, not a vampire, and wolves in general were not telepathic.

What sort of advantage would getting rid of Hunt give them, though? I sent back. *He was little more than a thug for hire.*

The wolf stalked past me. Surprisingly, the heat radiating off him was filled with anger—fierce, furious, and very dangerous anger. The hairs along the back of my neck rose.

I understand werewolf politics even less than I do vampire, Jackson wrote back. *Just found parking in Clarendon Street, so I'm nearby if you need help.*

Good, I replied. *Don't like the feel of this right now.*

The werewolf had moved past me, and the sudden release from his regard made me feel lighter than air, even though the tension in me was increasing. I studied the wolf's back as he moved toward the couple again. They paid him little attention, yet the closer he got to them, the angrier he seemed to become, until his whole body vibrated under the force of it.

Then, with little fanfare, he pulled a gun out of his pocket and shot them.

CHAPTER 5

I jumped to my feet without really thinking about it, a gasp leaving my lips and fire briefly skittering across my fingertips.

The wolf turned and aimed the gun at me. Fire shot through me, and just for an instant my skin glowed a dangerous orange. But I sucked the heat down, waiting to see what the wolf intended. The mere fact he *hadn't* shot me, either when he'd approached me or right now, surely meant he wouldn't unless provoked.

"You see nothing," he growled. "You hear nothing. Don't call the cops and don't tell them anything afterward, or I *will* hunt you down. I have your scent in my nostrils, lady."

I nodded and sat down again. He stared at me for a few seconds more, then turned his back to me and studied his two victims—who weren't dead, I realized. Nor was there any sign of blood; instead, there were faint wisps of smoke rising from the wounds where the—obviously silver—bullets had ripped through their shoulders. And that—along with their lack of screaming in agony—meant they were vampires rather than humans.

"You," the wolf growled, snapping my attention back to him. He reached forward, grabbed a fistful of the young man's shirt, and hauled him upright, until his feet were dangling several feet off the ground. "You were here to kill Theodore Hunt, were you not?"

The young man merely snarled, an action that revealed two very pointed canines. He was, I suspected, only young in vampire years. An older one wouldn't let a werewolf push him around so easily, even with silver embedded in his shoulder.

"Answer me," the wolf said as he shoved his gun into the face of the woman, "or she gets a bullet to the brain. And we all know even you lot can't recover from *that*."

"Yes," the young man all but hissed. "We were."

Did that mean Jackson had been wrong, and Morretti hadn't set this all up as an elaborate trap? Or simply that the vampire wasn't admitting to anything else?

But despite his anger, there was something in his expression that set off all sorts of alarms. I looked around and noticed the drunk had moved. He now stood slightly to the left of the fountain, a position that gave him a full view of the proceedings. No one else seemed to be in the immediate area or taking any undue interest in events, though. And yet, I couldn't escape the notion something was definitely off.

My phone beeped, indicating another text from Jackson had arrived. The noise was as sharp as a gunshot, and the werewolf's gaze snapped around. I held my hands up and half shrugged. He studied me a second longer, then returned his attention to the young man. It did nothing to release the tension still building within me.

Wolf just shot the couple, who are vampires, I surreptitiously sent back to Jackson. *He's from Hunt's pack. Think the vamps have backup here, too.*

Even as I hit the SEND button, the drunk moved. He reached into his pocket, drew out something big and silver, and aimed it at the wolf's back. Without really thinking about it, I called up flames and sent a hot lance arrowing across the darkness. It hit the drunk's gun and wrapped around the barrel, the heat so fierce, the metal instantly began to melt. As the drunk swore and dropped the weapon, the werewolf reacted. He simultaneously threw the vamp he was holding into the female and brought his gun up and fired—not at me but rather at the drunk. But *he* was already on the move, and with such speed that he was almost a blur.

Jackson appeared out of nowhere and launched at the drunk. They went down in a tumble of arms and legs, hitting the ground hard and rolling several times before they stopped. Thankfully, Jackson was on top, and he had a rather large gun shoved hard in the vamp's face.

"Twitch," he warned softly, "and I'll blow your fucking brains out the back of your head."

The vampire immediately stopped, but even from where I sat, I could feel the heat of his anger. We'd just made ourselves another enemy. Joy.

"Well," the werewolf said, his gaze and his gun back on the two other vampires. "This has turned into a very interesting situation, indeed. I take it you're the two firestarters Hunt was complaining about."

"Yes." I rose from the seat and walked over to Jackson. The vampire glared at me and his hand twitched—a hand that still held part of a gun, I noted, but only because he had little other choice. The heat of my flames had melted the barrel onto his palm. "Who might you be?"

"Scott Baker, alpha of the city pack."

My eyebrows rose. While I'd known wolves ran in packs, I hadn't been aware that only one pack controlled Melbourne. It was a large city and a lot of ground to hold against the other packs; either the city pack was huge, or its wolves were badasses. Looking at the wolf in front of me, I suspected the latter, even though Baker seemed a whole lot more civilized than Hunt.

"And why would the alpha of the city pack come out here alone to deal with three vampires?" Jackson asked. "Especially since it's well-known that the city pack runs many operations in conjunction with the sindicati?"

"*Those* operations are the reason I'm here," Baker growled. "This city is *our* territory. If the vamps wish to operate both within it *and* with us, then they do so under *our* rules."

"And I'm betting the sindicati bosses would give us much the same reply," Jackson said.

"Given at least one of the sindicati factions currently sees itself as superior to us, that is undoubtedly true." He reached down, grabbed the young male vampire, and hauled him upright. "It is *not*, of course."

The vamp bared his teeth but otherwise remained quiet.

"Except perhaps, when it comes to one Theodore

Hunt," Jackson drawled. "He's not exactly the sharpest knife in the drawer, is he?"

Baker's gaze flashed to Jackson, a quick half snarl that I think was more instinct than anything else rumbling up his throat. Then he laughed, a short, sharp sound. "Yeah, but he *is* good at what he does, and what he does is kill. You two, I'm afraid, have reached his hit list."

"And the city alpha approves this action?" I asked.

Baker's gaze met mine. His expression gave little away as his sharp brown gaze briefly swept over me. "I neither approve nor disapprove. You have now intervened in two operations, and have subsequently placed Hunt's life in danger. And yet you saved my life, a debt I must now repay."

"Meaning you'll call Hunt off?"

His smile was one of cold amusement. "No. But I won't condone his actions, either. If you kill him in self-defense, the pack will not seek retribution."

That was probably better than nothing. We already had the sindicati after us. We didn't need the local wolf pack joining in on the fun and games.

"Thank you," I said, meaning it.

He nodded. "And, as I said, I now owe you. If you need assistance in the future, contact me."

"Again, thanks."

He bowed his head slightly, the gesture oddly regal. "I will now ask you both to leave. I need to send a little message to our sindicati partners via these two pond scum, and I really prefer not to have witnesses."

Said pond scum didn't look at all worried by this news; either they hadn't had much to do with werewolves before now, or they weren't very smart. Looking at the both of them, I was betting on the latter.

"And this one?" Jackson asked.

Baker's gaze briefly rested on the vampire held down by Jackson. I had a sudden suspicion he would not be seeing another night rise. "Knock him out. I'll deal with him afterward."

Jackson did so, then rose and glanced at me. I motioned him to lead the way and, without another word, we left. It was only once we were back on Clarendon Street and well out of the hearing range of the wolf that he said, "Well, that was an interesting turn of events."

"Yeah, but it didn't exactly help us out with the Hunt situation."

"Maybe not, but we are now owed a favor by one of the biggest packs in Victoria, and that can't be a bad thing with the sindicati on our tails."

I grunted, not entirely convinced. The werewolves were known associates of the sindicati—would they betray a partner to help us? Somehow, I doubted it. Not unless there was something in it for them, anyway.

"Are we heading back to the hotel now?"

Jackson nodded. "I'll grab some takeout on the way, though, because I'm starving. You feel like anything in particular?"

"How about Chinese? I've a hankering for black bean steak and fried rice."

"Done deal."

Half an hour later, we were back in the hotel room. I changed back into jeans and my sweater—much to Jackson's horror—while he dished out not only the steak and rice but sweet and sour pork and honey chicken. As we ate, Jackson booted up Rory's computer and Googled myths and legends, looking for creatures that could change form and who fed off the dead.

"Anything?" I asked, leaning a shoulder against his as I looked at the screen.

"Hundreds, apparently." He hit the first search result. It turned out to be a list of mythical creatures that could change form.

"That one," I said, pointing to the third-to-last one on the list—something called an Aswang. "Sounds rather like our creature, even if it doesn't mention its form being ashlike at night."

"No, but it does say it has a human day form."

I frowned. "Does it mention if there's any obvious difference between it and a regular human? Anything that could help us find it?"

He half shrugged. "Other than bloodshot eyes, no."

"Given a good percentage of the human population has bloodshot eyes at any particular moment," I commented, "that's not really a practical way to hunt the creature."

"No, it's not." Amusement crinkled the corners of his eyes. He clicked on a couple of other links, but there wasn't much more to be found—nothing that really matched what we were looking for, anyway.

He Googled Aswangs next. This search revealed a heap more information about the creatures, including the useful tidbit that they could be killed via decapitation or—rather weirdly—by using a whip made entirely of a stingray's tail. But there was nothing solid on how to find such a creature, other than one article stating that a special oil extract—made from boiled and decanted coconut meat, mixed with plant stems—could be used to determine whether an Aswang was nearby.

Jackson closed the computer with a sigh. "Well, that didn't help much."

"No." I ate some chicken, then added, "Maybe we need to find someone who can tell us a little more about Aswangs."

"We're not even sure if *that's* what we're really hunting."

"We're not hunting it," I pointed out. "PIT is."

"Which is why we just wasted time looking for information."

I grinned. "Only because it doesn't hurt to be prepared if I have another prophetic dream about the thing."

His expression was one of disbelief, and I flicked a bit of chicken at him. He caught it with a laugh and shoved it in his mouth. "So until that happens, we concentrate on finding the research notes and getting the sindicati off our backs."

"The latter being the more important for our long-term health," I said. "I think we should try to find Radcliffe. If anyone might know something, it'll be him."

"He's been in PIT's hands. Anything he did know has either been erased or checked out by now."

"Maybe." I grabbed the sweet and sour pork and scooped some of it over the rice on my plate. "Sam wasn't exactly effusive when he came to information about what Radcliffe did or didn't tell them."

"Gee," Jackson cut in, "that's surprising."

I made a face at him. "The point is, we know something PIT and Sam don't—Radcliffe has a wife."

"Actually, we *don't* know that. It's just something you believe."

"True, but I'm right. I just know it."

He snorted. "Even if you *are*, I can't see how it helps."

I grinned again. "And there speaks a man who's never been married or even formed a deep connection beyond sex."

"That's because we Fae rather sensibly gave up all that muck eons ago. Life is much more peaceful without the drama of intimacy and emotion."

"It can also be lonely."

He studied me for a moment, his gaze contemplative. "And are you?"

"I have Rory, so I'm never lonely."

"But he's your must-have, not your deepest desire."

"True." I shrugged. "But there's not a whole lot I can do about the situation. It is what it is."

"And yet you still hope. I have to wonder why."

"Because if I give up hope, I might as well die." I shoved away my plate and rose. "I don't want to live like you, Jackson. I have to believe that, sooner or later, I will get my happy ending. You want a coffee?"

"Yes, thanks," He leaned back in the chair and pulled his phone out of his pocket. "I'll contact my source and see if she can find a marriage certificate for Radcliffe."

"It might not have happened here in Victoria, or even in Australia." I dumped some instant coffee into a mug and a tea bag into another, then flicked on the kettle. "He might have been married interstate or overseas."

"I'll get her to check that, too. And I'll send a text to

my friend at the casino and see if Radcliffe's been back there."

"If he hasn't, we've hit another dead end. I doubt he'll be contactable via any of his businesses."

I made coffee for Jackson and tea for myself and headed back to the table with the two mugs. Jackson finished sending the two texts, then put his phone back into his pocket and accepted his coffee with a nod of thanks.

He took a sip, then said, "No, he'll probably be lying low for a while, especially after experiencing the delights of PIT's interviewing techniques."

"They wouldn't have drugged him like they did us. They'd have no need."

"We don't know that. Radcliffe might well be resistant to telepathic intrusion, like us."

I frowned. "I thought rats were *more* susceptible than most, not less."

"In some respects, yes, in that they're more easily influenced on a surface level. But they're also intuitive when it comes to sensing psi abilities in others."

"Which would explain how Radcliffe managed to avoid PIT for so long."

"Undoubtedly. Doesn't help us find him, though."

"No." I took a sip of tea and grimaced slightly. Black tea was not a favorite, but it was better than using the little packets of long-life milk the hotel supplied. "I wonder how that creature knew James Hamberly was dead. I mean, it obviously wasn't from the area, and it's not like the newly dead have any obvious odor."

Jackson raised an eyebrow, his expression somewhat

ironic. "And here I was thinking you weren't interested in tracking the creature down."

"I'm not. I'm just curious."

"Believing that. And you know what curiosity did to the cat."

"I have one advantage over the cat—I'll be reborn. Besides, it's not like we have a lot of other avenues to explore right now. Not until either of your sources comes back with some information."

"Beyond the fact he's dead, we haven't exactly got a lot of information on James Hamberly, either."

"And why would you be interested in James Hamberly?" Rosen said behind us, his tone abrupt and decidedly displeased. "What has *he* got to do with anything?"

I glanced around. Rosen leaned against the door frame, his arms crossed and his expression annoyed. With his rumbled clothing and his short hair sticking out at odd angles all over his head, he looked more like a hobo than a man who owned and ran a billion-dollar company.

I raised an eyebrow. "You know him?"

"Don't answer a question with another question, young woman," Rosen snapped.

Annoyance rose, but before I could reply, Jackson said, "I wouldn't be using that tone on someone who just helped save your life." His voice was mild, but the anger that gleamed in his green eyes was even fiercer than mine. "Not unless you want me to toss you back to the sharks that had you."

"Sharks?" He glanced at the two of us. "What the *fuck* are you on about?"

"You don't remember?" I asked, surprised.

"Remember what?" His gaze moved to the apartment's main door, as if he were judging whether he could get it open and get out before we stopped him.

"Being escorted from your office by sindicati goons and then taken to a deserted location to be shot," Jackson said. "We're the only reason you're not rat meat now."

"Why the hell would the sindicati want me dead?" Rosen pushed away from the wall and cast another look at the door. "I've never had anything to do with them. Only Radcliffe."

"Meaning Radcliffe is connected to the sindicati?" I said.

"I don't know. *And* I don't care," he added, bristling again. "Neither Radcliffe nor the sindicati have any reason to get rid of me. In fact, I'm more useful alive given the amount I—"

He cut off abruptly and looked even more belligerent—as if it were our fault he'd almost admitted one of his sins.

"It's okay," Jackson said. "We know all about your gambling addiction and how much you owe Radcliffe. You, I'm afraid, sang like a bird to both the sindicati goons and to us."

"I wouldn't—"

"You were drugged," I cut in. "It made you both pliable and *very* verbal. And given what you said in the car, it's probably not the first time they've done it."

Rosen's face lost some of its color, but he didn't run for the door, as I half expected. Instead, he moved—

rather unsteadily—toward the table. "I don't believe you."

"And it's your god-given right not to," Jackson said, "but it doesn't alter the facts. Now, how about you answer the question—do you know Hamberly?"

"How is Hamberly involved with Wilson's missing research?"

"He's not," I replied.

"Then why are you discussing him?" Rosen plopped down on a spare chair and helped himself to a plate and some food.

"Because he was murdered last night," I said.

Rosen harrumphed. "Can't say I'm sad to hear that."

"Then you do know him?"

His gaze met mine briefly. Judging how much we needed to know, I thought. Or rather, how much he could trust us with the information. "Since Hamberly has no relation to the reason I'm employing you, I can't see why you're even interested in him."

"Because," Jackson said, his tone holding very little of the annoyance that practically vibrated from his body, "we were the ones who found the body, and we're curious as to what, exactly, killed him."

Rosen glanced up sharply at that, a spoon of steak and rice hovering halfway to his lips. "What, not who?"

I met Jackson's gaze with a raised eyebrow. Rosen definitely knew Hamberly; or, at least, someone he was close to did.

"Yes," I said. "He was killed by what we think might be an Aswang."

"Never heard of it." He got back to eating. But tension still rode him—it was evident in the set of his thin shoulders. "And I'm paying you good money to chase those research notes, not some mythical creature that did the world a favor by killing a leech like Hamberly."

"And what if the two events are connected?" Jackson mused.

That raised my eyebrows again. He flashed me a brief smile but added quite sincerely, "It's always possible that, given your obvious connection to Hamberly—however tenuous—that either you or someone close to you might be next in line."

"That is highly unlikely. If there was any such possibility at all, the police would have already contacted—"

"Except that it's PIT investigating these murders," I cut in, "and they are not only notorious for holding back information, but they have no love for you."

Which wasn't exactly the truth, at least as far as he was concerned, but hey, if we were going to be shady with the truth, we might as well go the whole hog.

He frowned. "I've had very little to do with PIT, so I cannot see why they would form such an opinion. I am, after all, the CEO *and* owner of a large—"

"Who is in debt up to his eyeballs to a wererat with possible links to the sindicati, and who has probably sung his heart out on all sorts of secrets during the many meetings he's had with said rat." My voice was surprisingly even, considering my growing dislike of the man. "I suspect the only reason you're not in jail at the moment is because those with PIT are more interested in uncovering information about Radcliffe and his connections than you."

He looked rather ill at the thought of that, and I couldn't help a sliver of satisfaction. It might or might not be the truth, but Rosen's actions were still unforgivable. He really *did* deserve to be in jail right now, rather than free to wreak more harm on his company.

"None of this is relevant—"

"We cannot say what is and isn't relevant," I snapped, my patience suddenly slipping, "until we know all the facts. So how do you know Hamberly?"

His glance moved from me to Jackson and back again. His expression was still displeased, but there was also fear in his eyes. He was only just realizing what his actions could cost him. "I don't. My son does."

"And your son's name?"

Jackson's tone was a hell of a lot more polite than mine, but hey, someone had to play the good cop in this outfit. And while he obviously already knew the answer to the question on the table—he'd mentioned the son's name when he first told me about Rosen Pharmaceuticals—it was always better to be safe than sorry. For all we knew, Rosen might have a veritable stable of illegitimate sons he wasn't acknowledging.

Rosen hesitated, then said somewhat reluctantly, "Denny. Denny Joseph Rosen Junior."

"And his connection to Hamberly?"

His hesitation this time was deeper, and a hint of color crept into his cheeks. "I cannot see how knowing that can possibly be relevant in this situation."

"It was a sexual relationship, wasn't it?" I said matter-of-factly. "And I'm gathering you disapproved?"

Anger flashed in Rosen's eyes. "Of course I disapproved! Hamberly was a leech, always trying to get more and more from Denny, be it time or money or whatever else he fancied."

I had a feeling Rosen's disapproval stemmed just as much from disappointment that his son was homosexual as from hatred for his son's choice of partner. But he wouldn't be the first parent to face that, and he probably wouldn't be the last—though, thankfully, attitudes like Rosen's were harder to find these days.

"We'd like to speak to your son, if possible," Jackson said. "If only because we need to warn him—"

"*I* can do that," Rosen cut in crossly. "There is no need for you to get involved with him."

"Perhaps, perhaps not," Jackson agreed. "But given your obvious rancor about his choice of partner, it's possible he will completely ignore anything you say. And *that* could be a fatal mistake if this creature *is* after him."

"But hey," I added, "if you'd rather have PIT speak to him than us . . ."

Rosen slammed his hands on the table so hard that the plates rattled and tea jumped out of my mug, splashing across my fingers.

"If you *dare* mention his name to them, you're off this damn case!"

I shook the hot droplets from my hand, but the rather angry reply that jumped to my lips died at Jackson's warning glance.

"You can choose to fire us anytime you please," he said, "but it would be wise to remember that no other private investigator will get as far as we have. Not with PIT involved. Nor will I share any current information with competitors. If you *really* want to uncover Wilson's notes, we are still your best option."

Rosen said nothing for a second or two, his gaze darting between us. Then he made a low sound deep in his throat and sat back down. "He lives in Elwood." He gave us the address, then added brusquely, "But I don't want you chasing this Aswang thing on *my* dime."

"Speaking of which," I said, "where do Radcliffe's men take you whenever you have a meet and greet?"

Rosen blinked, then frown. "A coffee shop, I think."

"Can you remember the name of it, or the location?"

"Not really." His frown deepened. "That's odd, isn't it?"

"Not if you were being drugged," Jackson said. "You can't remember much of today's events, after all."

Rosen scrubbed a hand across his jaw. "I really can't believe he'd want me dead. He has too much to lose . . ."

"Radcliffe may not have had a choice," I said. "It depends on who's pulling his strings."

"Even so—" He paused, his gaze narrowing. "However, if what you're saying *is* true, then there is one place you might find him."

"Where?" Jackson and I said together.

"Some place called Wirraway." He grimaced. "I remember one of his buffoons mentioning it—he said the boss wanted them back at Wirraway ASAP."

Which wasn't a whole lot to go on, but better than the nothing we had. I glanced at Jackson. "Then we need to find that place, and stat."

And *before* Radcliffe—or whoever else might be after Rosen—made another attempt on his useless life. The comment was on the very tip of my tongue, itching to be released, but I somehow managed to stop it.

"Right." Jackson downed the rest of his coffee in one large gulp, then gave Rosen a hard glare and added, "If you value your life, Mr. Rosen, I highly recommend you stay here—and don't contact anyone."

Rosen didn't comment, but he looked decidedly unhappy. If he was still here when we got back, I'd swear off sex for a year. Which, given how much I liked sex, said a lot about my confidence.

"Let's hope that confidence is well placed," Jackson murmured as he leaned past me to grab his coat. "I don't think my swimmers could endure such frustration."

I smiled and elbowed him in the ribs. His soft laugh whispered past my ear, rich with promises and heat. I ignored the rush of desire, grabbed my purse, and rose.

"Lock the door after us, Mr. Rosen," I said. "Don't let anyone in, not even hotel staff."

"If you insist."

I stared at him for a moment longer, then turned and followed Jackson out the door. Rosen was an adult; if he wanted to risk his life, he was free to do so.

Evening rush hour was well and truly past, so it didn't take us long to drive across to the address Rosen had given us in Elwood. I climbed out of the car and stared up at the apartment building; it looked like a series of cantilevered glass boxes stacked on top of one another, and seemed rather out of place against all the older, more-regular-looking brick buildings that surrounded it. But given its closeness to both the beach and the nearby shops and nightclubs, it was undoubtedly expensive. Daddy obviously looked after his son, despite being uncomfortable with said son's sexual orientation.

Jackson led the way over to the gate and up the

steps, and pressed the doorbell. A few seconds passed; then a plummy voice said, "Yes?"

"Denny Rosen Junior?" Jackson said.

"Yes, it is. Who are you?"

"My name is Jackson Miller. We need to talk to you about James Hamberly."

"Why?"

"Mr. Rosen," Jackson said, "we can do this out in the street, where anyone can hear, or we can take it inside. Your choice."

He hesitated. "Are you police?"

"No. But we can take our information to them, if you'd prefer."

"No." A buzzer sounded, and the door clicked open. "Come on up."

Jackson ushered me through. Despite the late hour, the lobby was bright, white, and almost entirely filled with an assortment of expensive-looking bicycles and helmets. The stairs, like the apartment itself, were nearly all glass, no doubt a means to help create the illusion of space where there really was none. The sound of footsteps echoed; then a man appeared at the top of the stairs. He was wearing bicycle skins under a loose black sweatshirt, and his short brown hair was dark with sweat. He shared the same build as his father—tall and thin—but he was very well toned.

"Who are you, if not the police?" he asked.

Jackson flashed his badge. "I would suggest that *that* is a question you should have asked before you let us in."

Denny raised a hand. In it was what looked to be a small square unit. "Panic button," he said. "Building security could be here in ten seconds."

Ten seconds was plenty of time to kill someone. Hell, I could burn the unit from his grasp before he even twitched.

"We're not here to harm you, Mr. Rosen." Jackson climbed the stairs but paused several steps below Denny, forcing me to do the same. "As I said, we just need to talk to you about James Hamberly."

"Then perhaps you'd better come in. Coffee?" He turned and walked away.

"No, thanks," I said as I followed Jackson into the main room.

The apartment was an open plan and, like the downstairs foyer, all white, from the walls and ceilings to the kitchen units and furnishings. The only splashes of color came from the large photographic canvases that dotted the walls. It would have been a rather sterile environment if not for those and the large expanse of windows, which seemed to bring the nightlife right into the room.

"Why would James Hamberly be of interest to two PIs who are supposedly investigating the theft of research notes for my father?" He stopped at a coffee machine even more industrial-looking than Jackson's, and proceeded to make coffee.

"Rosen Pharmaceuticals is not the only case on our list," Jackson said. "As much as your father would have otherwise."

"Yes, he can be rather demanding." Denny motioned us toward the pristine leather sofas, then made his way to a nearby chair. Despite what he was wearing, there was a very elegant air about him. "So why is James of interest to you?"

Jackson glanced at me, one eyebrow raised; he was asking me to do the dirty work.

"Because," I said softly, "he died last night."

Despite his gasp and shocked expression, I very much suspected Denny Rosen Jr. *wasn't* surprised. Not only was his grip on the mug far too steady for someone who had just been given shocking news, but there was an odd sort of watchfulness behind his reaction.

"How did it happen?" He leaned forward and placed the coffee mug on the dust-free glass coffee table, then crossed his arms, shoving his hands out of sight. The cynical part of me wondered if it was an attempt to cover up the fact that they *weren't* shaking.

"Heart attack, we presume," Jackson replied.

"I did warn him that his lifestyle would kill him in the end. I'd rather hoped I'd be wrong, though." He paused and frowned. "But if it was a heart attack, why are you two investigating his death?"

"Because of what happened *after* his death," I said.

The odd tension riding Denny increased, although there was still little evidence of it in his expression. His father might have little in the way of self-control, but Denny had a ton of it. "I don't understand what you mean."

And *that* was a lie. He knew, all right. He might not have been there when the creature had feasted on Hamberly's cooling organs, but he certainly knew *something* had happened to him after his death.

But how, if he wasn't actually there?

"I'm afraid that James Hamberly was—" Jackson paused, then made a brief motion with his hand. "There's no way to put this nicely. He had his internal organs sucked out of his body by a shifter of some kind."

Denny's face lost color—the first honest reaction we'd seen since our arrival. "How can you possibly know that? The coroner wouldn't have even examined the body yet."

"We know it because I saw it happen," I said. "I'm a psychic, of sorts. I actually went to your partner's home to stop it from happening, but the creature had already left by the time I got there."

"He wasn't my partner. We were just good friends." The reply was absently said, and it made me wonder how many times he'd repeated the same line to his disbelieving father.

"And lovers," Jackson added.

Denny's gaze shot to his. "Sexual partners, not lovers. There is a difference."

I raised my eyebrows. "Here I was thinking they were one and the same."

"No. We were friends, as I said. I didn't love him, but I could talk to him, and I trusted him." His mouth twisted. "Believe me, when you have a father who is not afraid of buying people off, trust is something you cling to when you find it."

"Your father was of the opinion that Hamberly was a leech."

Denny snorted, the sound bitter. "Yeah, he would. But he can't buy me, and he couldn't buy James."

"So all this?" I waved a hand around the pristine apartment. "It does not belong to your dad?"

"No." Anger edged his tone. "Everything here is

thanks to an inheritance from my mother—his third wife—and my skill as a semiprofessional bicycle rider."

Jackson held up a hand. "We didn't mean to offend you."

Denny took a deep breath, then released it slowly. "I know. But do you know how often I have to hear that particular accusation?"

"I'm guessing your father isn't a particularly easy man to deal with." We might have been here to discuss Hamberly, but there was little point in missing the opportunity to uncover a little more about Denny Rosen Sr. Presuming, of course, his son would actually tell us anything about his father. Family loyalty was sometimes stronger than hate.

Denny snorted. "No. And he's getting worse now that the cards aren't falling his way. The fool's going to lose everything at this rate—and I can't say I'm sad about that."

But there again, sometimes hate overrode loyalty.

"Anyway," he continued, "this has nothing to do with what happened to James. Are the police chasing this thing?"

"They are," I said, "and will undoubtedly come calling, given your relationship with him."

"I can't tell them anything. I left before he died." He thrust up from the chair and moved across to the window, staring out at the darkness almost blindly. But even from where I sat, it was easy to see the tension; his body practically vibrated with it.

"So you left without turning off the stove?" I asked. "And in such a hurry that you knocked over the coat stand and left the front door open?" It was a guess, but a pretty sure one.

"No. I mean, yes." He shrugged. "We'd argued. I was angry."

"James Hamberly died with a smile on his face. That does *not* imply an argument."

He didn't say anything. He just shrugged again.

"Mr. Rosen," I said, trying again, "this thing has killed before. We need to find it—stop it—before it kills again."

"But it didn't kill James. A heart attack did."

The reply was soft but edged with slivers of remorse—and perhaps just the slightest hint of guilt.

"You *were* there, weren't you?"

Again he said nothing.

"Why didn't you ring for an ambulance?" I continued. "There was still a chance he could have been saved."

"There was no chance, because it was already too late," he finally said. "It must have happened when I went into the kitchen to prepare dinner. By the time I went back into the bedroom . . ."

His voice trailed off and he half shrugged, as if it didn't matter, though the raw edge in his voice said otherwise.

"Even so," Jackson said, "you should have notified someone. Why didn't you, Mr. Rosen?"

His gaze swept past Jackson and rested on me. In it, I saw not only the stirrings of grief but also fear.

"Because," he said eventually, "I felt the creature coming."

CHAPTER 6

Of all the answers I'd expected, *that* certainly wasn't one of them. "You *felt* it?" I said. "You're psychic?"

He shrugged. "I've never been tested, but sometimes I see things. Feel things."

"And you felt this creature?" I couldn't help the slight edge of excitement in my voice; Denny Rosen had just handed us a means of finding this thing . . . if we were to go after it.

"And we're not, remember?" Jackson murmured.

I made a face at him but didn't comment as Rosen said, "Yes, I did." He paused and rubbed his arms. "It felt old. Evil. James was already dead, and it would have killed me had I stayed. I had to get out. I just *had* to."

And no one could blame him for *that*. "Is there anything you can tell us about the creature? Something that might help us locate it?"

"No." He hesitated, frowning. "Well, maybe. When I sense things, I sometimes get hit with multiple images. It's like there's a movie projector set on high speed inside my head, and I get flashes of images or information about whatever person or event I'm seeing. This time it showed me the creature changing from a cat to a bat to this massive doglike thing with needle-fine canines, but the first image was human."

I glanced sharply at Jackson. He simply rolled his eyes, his expression somewhat resigned. "Can you describe him?"

"Her, not him," Denny corrected. His gaze returned to the world outside his windows again. "She was tall, thin to the point of being gangly, with dark hair and strange red eyes."

"Bloodshot or actually red?" I asked.

He hesitated again. "Hard to say. That particular image was weirdly upside-down."

"And there were no other distinguishing marks?" Jackson said.

"No, but she held a cleaver in one hand. You know, the sort butchers use to cut up meat." A ghost of a smile touched his lips as he glanced at us. "I used to go out with one, so I recognized it."

"Was her human form old or young?" I asked. "I know you said she *felt* old, but did she look it?"

He hesitated. "She looked preserved, if that makes any sense. It was almost as if her skin were stretched too tight over her bones, with very little room for wrinkles. But old? Not really."

So we were looking for a middle-aged, plastic-looking woman with weird red eyes and a cleaver in her hand? *That* should be simple.

"Mr. Rosen," Jackson said, "you need to tell the police—"

"No," he cut in. "Definitely not."

"But surely you want to catch this thing, before it dines on anyone else?" Jackson said.

"*That* is not my concern. Trust me, I know how police treat psychics. I'm not going there again."

"PIT is different." Jackson gave me a somewhat wry glance even as he said it, undoubtedly because of the way they'd treated us when we'd been in their hands.

"I don't care. Besides, I have a race to get ready for and no desire to be hampered by endless rounds of questions."

I guess he couldn't be blamed for his stance; the police *could* be somewhat skeptical when it came to psi talents, even in this day and age. But it was also frustrating when the information he held might just help PIT track down this thing.

Of course, I could always pass it on. But Sam was the only contact I had, and while part of me was more than a little happy at the prospect of talking to him again, the other, somewhat saner, part was remembering Rory's warning and taking heed.

"Are you sure there's nothing else you can tell us about this woman?"

He hesitated again. "She will take another victim soon, and this time that person will be living rather than dead."

Alarm ran through me. "Why are you so certain of this?"

He shrugged. "If you're psychic yourself, then you know there's no accounting or controlling the information that comes through your visions. I just saw that this is something of a pattern for it—it starts off with the older dead, then works up to younger, sweeter flesh."

The alarm got stronger. "Meaning it's likely to go after *children*?"

"Eventually, yes."

And he didn't want to help us—or rather, the police—stop it? It took every ounce of strength I had *not* to punch him for such an uncaring attitude—even if this sort of reluctance was something I'd seen time and again in my lifetimes as a cop.

But maybe this escalation was the reason why I'd been shown the creature on its third kill rather than the first. If I wanted to—if I could find the thing—I could stop it before it started dining on the living.

Rosen glanced at his watch, then said, "Is that all? Because I have a meeting to get to, and I need to shower and change first."

"It is for now." I rose, then hesitated. "You said before that your father was in danger of losing the whole kit and caboodle—just how much do you know about your father's gambling problem?"

"Enough." His gaze narrowed slightly. "Why? What has this got to do with anything?"

I hesitated again, glancing at Jackson. He shook his head slightly, an indication that we shouldn't mention the attempt on Denny Rosen Sr.'s life.

"Because," I said, thinking fast, "we suspect his gambling problem might be related to the missing notes."

"I doubt he's the reason the notes are missing," Denny said. "The stuff he's selling is only minor— information on new pain meds and other drugs that can be easily sold on the black market. I doubt he'd risk anything major. He's not that much of a fool."

I wasn't so sure about that—especially if either Radcliffe or the sindicati were regularly taking him for drugged-up "discussions."

"Is Marcus Radcliffe the only person he owes money to?"

"I don't know. It's not like he actually confides in me or anything." He paused. "But he did mention a warehouse in Laverton North once. I got the impression it scared him."

Laverton was a big suburb, but a warehouse in Laverton North just happened to be the place I was supposed to be taken the first time I'd been kidnapped. Coincidences happened, but I doubted this was one of them.

"He didn't say why?" Jackson asked.

Denny shook his head. "No. But he has a morbid fear of vampires, and I suspect that's who was involved in the game."

Jackson rose and got out his wallet. "Well, thanks for your help, Mr. Rosen. And if you remember anything else—or sense this creature again—please contact us."

"If I sense that creature again, I'll be running." But he nevertheless accepted the business card Jackson handed him.

With that, we left.

"Well, that was all very interesting," I said once we were back in the car. "And he doesn't seem like much of a gadabout to me."

"The definition of a gadabout is a habitual pleasure

seeker. Junior is a playboy millionaire who doesn't work and who flits from one lover to another."

"He seems pretty serious about his cycling."

"Yeah, but not on a professional level. He keeps with the amateur ranks. He has the potential to go further, but not the dedication, according to the gossip rags."

I raised an eyebrow. "You've really checked into him."

"I always make it a habit to check the backgrounds of my clients. It often reveals all sorts of pertinent information."

"I'm guessing they don't know about these checks."

"Not unless I need them to. Unfortunately, Denny Rosen Junior didn't actually give us any useful information to track the creature with."

I grinned. "I wasn't intending—"

"Perhaps not," he cut in, "but you were certainly *thinking* about it."

"And *that* is something else that needs answering," I said. "Why the hell are you suddenly catching my thoughts?"

"I'm not catching your thoughts. At least, not all of them." He frowned as he checked the rearview mirror, then pulled out. "And certainly not on a conscious level. I just seem to occasionally know what you're thinking. And you're obviously catching bits and pieces of my thoughts, too."

I wrinkled my nose. "As you said, not directly. It's not telepathy or anything like that. But it *is* weird."

"Yeah, especially since neither of us are telepathic."

I shifted in my seat to look at him. "Could it have something to do with my allowing you to siphon my heat to heal yourself?"

"I've never heard of anyone ever doing that before, so I can't say." His gaze met mine. "You're the one with all the various life experiences—have you ever done anything like that before?"

"No. But as I said, I figured it was the only chance we had of burning the red plague virus from your body. Which it obviously did, because you haven't turned into a psycho pseudo vampire."

"No, but I just might go psycho if I don't get some loving soon."

I grinned and patted his leg. "There, there, you'll survive."

"I wouldn't be so sure of that." His expression was woebegone, but amusement gleamed in his bright eyes. "A Fae can live only *so* long without sex."

"Lack of sex won't make you fade. It's lack of fire that does that, remember?"

"It's all one and the same—fire, sex, it's all about the heat."

"As the saying goes, all good things come to those who wait." I contemplated the road ahead for a second. "I guess it's entirely possible that, given just how deep that connection went—"

"Deep is underdescribing it," he cut in, amused. "I was *flame*, for fuck's sake. There was no separation between either of our beings—just fire and heat."

And it had felt incredible—without, in any way, being sexual in nature. "Which means it's entirely possible we've somehow hotwired an informal connection between us. But I have no idea how, or if it'll get stronger or weaker with time."

"It could be very handy if it got stronger—especially

if we keep getting ourselves into tight situations." He braked lightly as the traffic signal ahead went red. "I don't suppose there's anyone you could ask? An older, wiser phoenix or mentor?"

A smile twisted my lips. "Not really. Not given how old *I* am."

He gave me a somewhat speculative look. "Just how old are you?"

"A lady never tells."

It was primly said, and he grinned. "So, no parents or anything?"

"I have them. I just haven't seen them for centuries."

"So phoenixes, like Fae, don't go into that whole warm fuzzy family-unit thing, then?"

"Oh, we do. But it becomes harder once children reach maturity and find their soul partners. It's very difficult for two pairings to share the one territory—even if one of those pairings includes a child of your own."

"Why?"

I shrugged. "Safety, mostly. Our coloring makes us more conspicuous, especially back when the world was not so populated."

"I would have thought there'd be safety in numbers. Or at least, that was what wolves discovered over the centuries."

"Werewolves naturally pack, and territories are generally handed down through the generations. We can't do that, because we're reborn into adulthood every one hundred years. People tend to notice things like that."

He glanced in the rearview mirror and accelerated again as the light went green. "Meaning either you or your children have to move on?"

"Yes. Hanging around past one lifetime is safer these days than it used to be, but even so, Rory and I will probably have to establish ourselves elsewhere in a re-birth or so." Maybe once the world became aware that vamps and werewolves weren't the only nonhumans out there—and actually accepted us—that might change. But right now, when some parts of society were still forming nighttime hunting parties, it was simply easier to move.

"That must be hard—building a life, then being forced to abandon it."

I shrugged again. "It's safer than getting dead before your time. I've done that a few times, and it's rather unpleasant."

"I'm guessing it would be." A smile touched his lips. He flicked on the blinker and glanced in the rearview mirror as he turned right. "So how many children have you and Rory actually had?"

"Five. We are not an overly fertile race. Generally a pairing only breeds when another dies."

"Really?" He shook his head. "Given all the other curses you lot have, that almost seems the worst."

"Trust me, it's not. Besides, it's something of a neces-sity that our numbers remain small. As I've said, it's hard to conceal what we are." I glanced at him. "Are there any little Jackson Millers running around out there?"

"Sadly, no, but I'm hoping to find me a delicious Fae lady and remedy that soon. I'd hate to think the Fae gene pool would miss out on the fabulousness that lies in my DNA."

I snorted softly and punched him lightly in the arm. He chuckled, but his gaze went to the rearview mirror again, and my curiosity stirred. "Have we got a problem?"

"We might. Black car, three back."

I flicked down the vanity mirror and checked it out. "The BMW?"

"That's the one. It's been following us since we left Denny Rosen's."

"And you don't think it's a coincidence?"

"No, I don't." He contemplated the mirror for a moment, then added, "But I believe we need to find out whether it's sindicati or Radcliffe's goons in that car before we go anywhere near the hotel."

"I believe you could be right. What's the plan?"

"That we have a cozy little chat somewhere we're not likely to be seen or overheard."

A smile touched my lips. "I'm gathering you know such a place?"

"I do indeed." He swung left, then accelerated hard, gaining some distance between the BMW and us without totally losing him. "There's a cul-de-sac at the rear of some factories two turns ahead. I'll brake, jump out, and you can slide across and take over driving duties."

"They're just going to reverse out the minute they realize what we're up to."

"Oh, they'll certainly try." His wide grin flashed, filled with anticipation. "When I give you the word, call up some of the mother's lovely flame."

He meant the earth mother; she was the heat that could be found deep in the earth, the energy that gave life to the world around us. I raised an eyebrow but didn't comment. Jackson kept to the speed limit, making no attempt to lose the car behind us. We turned left into a street that was all trees, concrete buildings, and thick shadows.

"Okay," he said, unclipping his seat belt, "get ready."

I undid my own belt and gripped the dash hard to steady myself as he swung sharply right. Once in the much smaller lane, he braked, threw the shift into park, and was out the door in one smooth motion. I scrambled over the center console with a whole lot less elegance and got the car moving again—but much slower, because the headlights were now shining on the tall, graffiti-littered wall dead ahead.

The night behind me lit up as the BMW swung into the lane. I continued on as far as I could, then braked. I couldn't see Jackson in the rearview thanks to the brightness of the headlights behind me and had no idea what he intended. It was, I thought, slightly irritating that the connection between us seemed to flare at times of its own choosing rather than when it would be truly useful.

I pulled on the hand brake and got out of the car. The thick walls of the buildings that towered on either side of us filled the lane with thick shadows. The night air was cool and filled with the aroma of rotting rubbish, undoubtedly thanks to the huge Dumpsters that lined the right side of the lane.

The BMW stopped, but the people didn't turn off the lights, didn't get out, and kept the motor running. I crossed my arms and waited. There was no sign of Jackson or any hint as to what he was up to.

But he was here. I could feel him—a sharp, familiar warmth hovering near the end of the lane.

The semi-standoff remained. My tension increased

as the minutes ticked by, and it was all I could do to remain still. For all intents and purposes, I was a sitting duck, and it was only the knowledge that the sindicati— if that was who was in the car—still needed me that had me staying put.

"Where is Jackson Miller?"

The question came out of nowhere, and I jumped, my heart racing a mile a minute and sparks glittering across my fingertips. Then I realized the voice had a tinny tone; they were using a speaker of some kind.

"He's not here," I said. "Who are you, and what do you want?"

"He was in the car when you left Elwood. What happened to him?"

"I dropped him off a street or so ago, so who knows." I shrugged. "Why were you following us?"

They didn't answer. Instead, the doors opened and four men got out. As they did, Jackson yelled, "Now!"

A bin slid into the lane, blocking the BMW's exit. A second quickly followed. I raised a hand and flung fire; not at the men or the car but rather in a ring around them, creating a wall of flame that prevented them from attacking and threw them into deeper shadows. Or perhaps they *were* shadowing, indicating they were vampires, as Jackson had guessed.

But those flames were not enough. I reached to the force of the world, to the mother herself, and felt the trembling in the ground underneath me as she responded. Her energy surged through me, powerful and wild and difficult to contain. I held on to her fiercely, weaving her flames into a net that surrounded the car and forced shadows to flee. These *weren't* ordinary flames; these were the flames of the mother herself, and she burned with a fire that danced with the colors of all creation.

And her light was the only way I could force vampires out of shadow.

But I couldn't hold on to her indefinitely, because there was always a cost in calling to such power. We needed to question these vamps and get the hell out of here, before my strength was drained too far.

The vamps, however, had other ideas.

The two at the front stepped away from the doors, raised several weapons, and simply fired. So much for their not wanting me dead.

I flung myself down, even as I flung more energy into the flames between us. Incandescent fingers broke away from the main body of fire, capturing the bullets and melting long before they got anywhere near me.

I rolled to my feet and walked closer to the flames. Their energy pulled at me even as the heat washed over me, enticing and delicious. "Gentlemen, please put down your weapons. As you've just witnessed, it's useless trying to shoot us."

They didn't even glance at one another, but as one, they lowered their weapons. They were all tall and slender with very little in the way of fat—a common trait among vampires. It was almost as if the effort of turning from human to vampire burned every ounce of fat from their body, leaving them with little more than bone, muscle, and flesh. And a diet consisting of only blood certainly wouldn't put much of that lost weight back on.

The heat radiating off the mother's wall had to be uncomfortable, but none of them were showing any emotion, not even anger. But then, if they were indeed sindicati—and I suspected they were—then they would be familiar with these flames, as I'd used them against the organization before.

"Who are you?" I repeated. "And why are you following us?"

"I suspect you are well aware of who we are." The driver's reply was polite and without inflection. If he was at all annoyed by the turn of events, he wasn't showing it. "Just as you are undoubtedly aware of what we seek."

"The trouble is, we haven't actually *got* what you want." A glimpse of movement had me glancing past the flames. It was Jackson, walking between the remaining bins and the ring of fire, his face aglow with heat as he made his way back to my side.

"That would indeed be a shame," the driver replied, "because the possibility of possession is all that is currently keeping you alive."

A grim smile touched my lips. "How about you send a little message back to those who control you. Attempt to kill me, and your asses are ash. And I don't care if I have to burn half the damn city down to do it."

He stared at me for several seconds, judging whether I meant it, his dark gaze contemplative. Then he glanced at the fires that burned all around us, and a small smile touched his lips.

"You are obviously capable of such a feat, but the reply is not one that will please our people."

"Right now, I'm not particularly caring. Stop following us, and don't consider hurting or kidnapping anyone I know. Otherwise, I *will* follow through with the threat."

He nodded once, the movement small and oddly regal. "I will deliver the message, as you wish. You do, however, need to release us."

I glanced at Jackson. He nodded, looking relaxed despite the flickers of fire that danced across his fingertips.

I drew in a deep, somewhat shuddery breath, then released the energy—but not all of it. I kept hold of the flames that burned between the vampires and us, not trusting that they wouldn't attack if given the slightest chance.

"The Dumpsters you can move yourself," I said.

Again a slight smile touched his lips. He glanced at the two men behind him, and instantly they moved. In very little time—and with very little effort—they rolled the large metal bins back out of the way.

The driver's gaze met mine a final time. "We may yet meet again."

"I would suggest we don't," I said. "Not if you value your life."

His slight smile grew. I had an odd feeling that he rather respected my actions, which was weird, considering my actions had stopped him from completing his task and—if everything I'd heard about the sindicati was true—would result in his being penalized.

He got into the car and they reversed out of the lane, disappearing into the night. When I was sure it was safe, I released my hold on the remaining flames; they shimmered brighter for several seconds, then dissipated, returning to the air and the earth itself.

Weakness washed through me, and I grabbed at the nearest bin to steady myself. I got Jackson instead.

"Whoa," he said. "Are you okay?"

I nodded. "It's the price I pay for using the mother's flames. It'll pass as soon as I eat."

"Are we talking food or fire?" Jackson asked. "Because there's a lovely little furnace that runs night and day next to our office."

I took a deep breath and released it slowly. My limbs felt steadier, but the weakness remained, making my head spin a little. "Definitely the latter."

"Then that's where we'll go next."

"That might not be safe—"

Jackson waved my concerns aside. "The sindicati and whoever else will be watching the front of our building, because there is no rear entrance or windows. They will not, however, be watching the blacksmith's, and I just happen to have a key to both their front and rear doors."

"And just how did you get that?" I swung around and walked to the car. Jackson hovered close, obviously ready to catch me if I stumbled or fell.

"I pay them a weekly retainer. It comes from my personal accounts, not the business's, never fear."

"I wasn't." I nodded my thanks as he opened the door and ushered me into the seat. "But I *am* worried about leaving Rosen alone for that long. I don't think he can be trusted."

"The man might be a gambler, but he isn't a fool." Jackson slammed the door shut, then ran around to the driver's side and got in. "So, what do you want— furnace or hotel?"

What I *wanted* was sex and sleep, though not necessarily in that order. But the former was dangerous when my reserves were low; though I'd never yet lost control and drained anyone of all their heat during sex—thereby killing them—I certainly didn't want Jackson to be the first.

"Furnace. We don't have to be there long."

"Done deal." He threw the car into reverse and headed out of the lane. The BMW was nowhere in sight, and neither of us spotted it during the trip across to West Melbourne.

We parked in the shadows of several old elms one street over from ours and made our way back to the blacksmith's. Jackson paused near the fence, his gaze scanning the night, then nodded and unlatched the gate. It opened without a squeak. The double-story brick building loomed above us, a big sturdy structure that had an odd, almost Victorian elegance about it. A double roller door dominated the left side of the building, while there were several bricked-up arched windows on the right.

"How often do you have to use this place?" I hunkered down in the shadows as Jackson moved across to the lock.

He shrugged. "At least once a week."

I was silent while he sorted through his keys, then opened the lock. The door went up as quietly as the gate. Heat washed over me, an enticing dance of energy that called like a siren to me.

Jackson caught my hand and led me forward. Ahead, the heat of the coals glowed, casting orange shadows across the vast space. Aside from the old-fashioned brick furnace, there were several tables, cabinets holding all sorts of tools, and metal projects in various states of completion.

"Do you just draw the energy in," I asked as we wove our way through the room toward the fire, "or do you have to meld with it?"

"We don't meld with flames; not in the same way a phoenix does, anyway." He glanced at me. In the orange light of this place, his eyes burned with both fire and desire.

He wanted me. Here. Now.

Excitement surged, but all I said was, "Does that mean you simply draw in its power?"

"To give it a new-age term, we commune with it. It's an intense and very satisfying experience."

"Sexually satisfying?"

His grin flashed. "No. Which is why I generally need a willing partner afterward."

"Ha," I said. "That explains those nights you came back hornier than a six-peckered tomcat."

He raised an eyebrow, his expression bemused. "Is there even such a creature?"

"Well, if there was, he *would* be horny."

Jackson laughed, the sound warm and rich in the vast space. "Undoubtedly."

He made a motion with his hand and, in the furnace ahead, flames leapt to life. Their heat ran across my senses, and, deep inside, the part of me that was spirit and fire reached out, quickly drawing it in. The closer we got, the stronger the pull, the more I fed. It was a glorious feeling.

We stopped next to the furnace. I closed my eyes and opened my arms, drawing the heat and the power of the flames into my body. It felt like I was glowing. Felt like I was a part of them, even though I was still flesh and blood.

"Better?" Jackson's breath whispered past my ear. He was standing so close to my spine that I could feel the tension thrumming through him.

I nodded and eased my grip on the flames, still drawing them in but not so completely that I was unaware of anything else.

"You look so beautiful right now." His lips briefly brushed the nape of my neck, and a shiver of delight ran through me. "So alluring."

He kissed my neck again, the touch featherlight, teasing. I closed my eyes and clenched my fingers against the need to reach for him. If I did, this would be over far too quickly; his need was every bit as fierce as mine under the light of these flames.

He slid his hands down my waist, then caught the hem of my sweater and lifted it over my head. The T-shirt soon followed, and both were tossed onto the nearby table.

"Glorious," he murmured as he slid his hands up my belly and cupped my breasts through the silk of my bra. He kissed between my shoulder blades, then lightly bit my shoulder as his clever fingers began to caress and pinch my nipples. Tremors ran through me, thick with delight, and I leaned back against him. The heat of his body burned into my spine, as delightful as the force of the flames in front of us. Despite the layer of clothes still between us, I could feel his erection, thick and hard with desire as he pressed against my butt.

He continued to tease, kissing and nipping and

pinching, playing me as easily as any master did his instrument.

Then his caress moved down, his nails skimming my ribs and my hips before moving across to my belly. Slowly, surely, he undid my jeans, then slid one hand past the silk of my panties. He touched my clit and delight shot through me. I groaned, my body arching into his touch, wanting, needing, so much more.

He chuckled softly, then withdrew his touch and stepped back. I tried to turn, to take control, but he stopped me.

"Don't move," was all he said. His voice was husky, edged with desire and hunger.

I closed my eyes and waited. My bra soon joined my shirt and sweater on the table, and, a heartbeat later, his tongue touched up my spine, tasting, teasing. I shivered again, lost in sensation, as he slowly made his way up the ruined landscape of my back. Then his hands gripped the waist of my jeans and pushed them down my legs. As I kicked free of my clothes, he quickly stripped, denying me the pleasure of watching. Not that it mattered. This was his fire, his rules. My turn would come later.

His touch returned to my skin, sliding up my thighs, then around my waist as he pressed me close again. His cock slid between my legs, teasing me when all I wanted him to do was thrust so very deep inside of me.

Which was the one thing he *didn't* do, of course.

He continued to play me, teasing and arousing, bringing me close to the edge, then backing away. And he did it time and again, until my entire body was feverish and shaking, and all I wanted, all I could think about, was being taken—consumed—by him.

Then, finally, with a soft growl filled with desperation, he swung me around and kissed me hard. I wrapped my arms around his neck and pressed so close, it would have been hard for anyone watching to tell where his skin ended and mine began. Desire and heat burned around us, until the air itself seemed to be on fire. I drew it in, letting it feed my soul even as it ramped up my desire.

He slid his hands down my back and cupped my butt, lifting me with little effort. I wrapped my legs around his waist as he carried me across to the table and placed me on the hard surface. A heartbeat later, he was in me. It felt like heaven, and for several seconds, neither of us moved; we just enjoyed the sensations and the heat that came with this simple joining of flesh.

Then the fiery need that burned between us became too great to ignore, and he grabbed my hips, holding me tight as he thrust deeper and harder. He paused again, as if to control himself, then resumed at a slower pace, his movements belying the urgency that trembled through us both. Flames flickered across my skin and leapt to his, until it seemed as if we were two beings of fire rather than a Fae and a phoenix. He bent down and caught one nipple between his teeth. Pleasure shot through me, and I gasped and threw back my head. He repeated the process, again and again, until my nipples ached as fiercely as the rest of me, and it was all I could do to keep hold of the desire that threatened to burn out of control.

His grip on my hips suddenly tightened, and his movements became more urgent, until my whole body shook with the intensity of them and it felt as if I were about to shatter into a million different pieces.

Then my control crumbled, and everything *did* shatter as my orgasm swept through me, intense and violent. A heartbeat later, he groaned, the sound one of ecstasy as his body stiffened against mine and he came.

For several minutes neither of us moved. Then he took a deep, somewhat shuddering breath and shifted his hands, cupping my cheeks as he kissed me sweetly.

"I think we both needed that," he said eventually.

"That," I said, my own breathing still very shaky, "is an undeniable truth."

He laughed, dropped another kiss on my lips, then released me and stepped back. I jumped off the table, grabbed my clothes, and quickly dressed. He did the same, then snuffed out the flames in the furnace, leaving them little more than glowing coals once more. We retreated, locking the door behind us, then made our way back to the car. It was well after midnight, but despite the hour, a good number of cars were still on the roads. None of them appeared to be following us, however, and we made it back to the underground parking lot near the hotel in good time.

"I," Jackson announced casually, as we walked through the near-deserted streets to the hotel, "am still very hungry."

"You," I replied, in the same offhand tone, "are apparently insatiable."

He laughed. "That is *also* an undeniable truth. Unfortunately for me, I've a feeling Rosen's presence will hamper my intentions."

I glanced at him, eyebrows raised. "I thought Fae were exhibitionists?"

"Oh, we are, but I've a feeling you phoenixes are not. At least, not to the same extent."

"You'd be surprised. However," I added as a gleam of anticipation sparked in his emerald eyes, "I really don't think Rosen would appreciate our creating a little noise. And I actually don't think it would be wise to be so unguarded when someone apparently wants him dead."

"All too true." He grimaced. "You want first watch or second?"

"Second. I need a shower and sleep, in that order. I didn't exactly get much sleep last night thanks to that damn dream and creature, and it's been a long day."

The elevator opened as we neared it. Jackson punched the button for our floor. Then, as the doors closed, he said, "I'll do a search for the place Rosen mentioned—Wirraway, wasn't it?"

I nodded. "And if we can't find anything, then our next step has to be that warehouse in Laverton North."

Jackson pressed a hand against my back, lightly guiding me forward as the elevator stopped and the doors opened. "As I said before, I don't think your ex is going to be too happy if we do that. And I'm not even sure I'll be able to, given the drug-induced order he gave us to stop chasing Morretti and go nowhere near that warehouse."

"The drug's influence will be voided by now." I kept my voice low, not wanting to wake anyone in the nearby rooms. "And even if it *had* been capable of such long-term behavior restrictions, the fires of our merging would have burned it from your system."

"None of which negates the fact that things could get ugly if he discovers we've gone against his orders."

I stopped beside our door and gave him an amused look. "And this worries you?"

"Anyone with any sense would be worried by PIT's presence in their lives." He opened the door, then stepped back and waved an arm, ushering me in first. "But their ugly is more than likely to hit you first, given your connection with the man. I just want to make sure you're ready for it."

"I am." I glanced around the room but couldn't see Rosen anywhere. Maybe he'd gone back to bed. Or maybe, as I'd suspected earlier, he'd run.

"Are you?" Jackson said. "Because I'm not so sure of that."

I glanced over my shoulder as I made my way toward the second bedroom. "And why would you think that?"

"Because you still love him—"

"Yeah, I do," I cut in. "But my heart can't be broken twice in one lifetime. He's already done that, so I'm safe."

And if I said that often enough, maybe I'd believe it. The only trouble was, while it was true no one had ever heard of a phoenix getting her heart broken more than once in a lifetime, it didn't mean it *couldn't* happen. And Rory was certainly worried about the prospect.

Rosen wasn't in the room. I knew he wouldn't be found in any other room, either, but I nevertheless swung around and headed for the larger bedroom, checking it before moving toward the main bathroom.

"The heart is not a practical organ," Jackson commented. "It doesn't think. It only feels."

I snorted. "Such sage comments from a man whose race shuns deeper emotions."

"True." He frowned, watching me for a moment. "What's wrong?"

"It's Rosen." I swung around and faced him. "He's gone."

Chapter 7

Jackson swore and thrust a hand through his hair. "I thought the damn fool had more sense than that."

"Obviously not." My tone was grim. "You want to go out and look for him?"

Jackson hesitated, then shook his head. "He could be anywhere. We need to rest and recuperate, before anyone else flings shit our way."

I raised an eyebrow. "Rest, huh? That's not what you were talking about a few minutes ago."

He shucked off his jacket, then began undoing his shirt as he strode toward me. "No, it wasn't. And right now I'm thinking shower, sex in the shower, bed, some more sex, and then sleep. How does that sound?"

"How about we reverse the last two? I really *do* need to sleep."

He sighed. "The lady has no stamina."

"Not right now she hasn't."

He laughed and gathered me in his arms, kissing me soundly. "Shall we go get wet?"

"Let's."

We did. And when we finally slept, I did so with a smile on my lips.

"I've Googled Wirraway," Jackson said from the living room. "It appears it's a street in Port Melbourne."

I pulled my sweater over my still-wet hair, then tugged it down as I headed out of the bedroom. Jackson had obviously made use of the room service menu, because the smell of warm toast and bacon teased my nostrils, and my stomach rumbled a reminder it hadn't eaten any food in a while.

Jackson had already tucked into his bacon and eggs, and he was currently intent on demolishing a six-stack of toast in between studying the search results on the laptop.

"Big street or small?" I sat down, took the cover off my bacon and eggs, and began eating.

"It's on the smaller side, but it's an industrial area, so there're lots of warehouses." He contemplated the screen for a moment. "I guess we could do a drive-by and see what we can find. We might get lucky and spot someone we know."

"Hopefully that someone won't be Man-Mountain One or Two."

He grinned. "Oh, I don't know—I wouldn't mind the chance to knock out Hunt's remaining teeth."

"Be careful what you wish for," I said, waving a fork filled with bacon at him. "Next time it just might be third time unlucky."

"For *them*." He grabbed another piece of toast and slathered Vegemite on it. I shuddered. I didn't mind Vegemite, but it needed to be *thinly* spread rather than slapped on like butter. "I tried to call Rosen while you were in the shower. He's not picking up."

Which didn't sound good. "Work or home?"

"Work and cell. His secretary said he wasn't expected in this morning."

"Meaning he's been in contact with her, and that he could simply be in hiding."

"Possibly."

I studied him for a moment. "But you believe not."

"I think it unlikely." He grimaced. "If someone hasn't snatched him, then it's highly probable he's either back at the tables or found a card game to join."

"Neither of which is easy to check." I scooped up the last bit of bacon, then grabbed a piece of toast to mop up the remaining egg. "But we could at least head to his house. He might be there and just not be answering."

"You believe *that* even less than I do."

"Yeah, but I still think it's worth checking. Have you got his home address?"

"No, but I doubt it's hard to find. Hang on a sec." He used the laptop again and, after a few minutes, said, "There're only three Rosens listed. One of them is Junior, and one lives in Bendigo. I seriously doubt Senior is the country-town type."

"No." I paused. "If I had to guess, I'd say he's more the luxury apartment on Albert Road, South Bank, type."

"I'm thinking that's *not* such a guess." His tone was dry.

"No." I frowned. "This whole sharing-random-information-and-thoughts scenario is going to take a bit of getting used to—though it could undoubtedly be helpful if we find ourselves in the hands of the sindicati again."

"Undoubtedly." He grabbed the remaining bit of toast, repeated the Vegemite slathering, and rose. "What's say we go check out Wirraway Drive? If that proves to be useless, it frees up time to concentrate on either finding Rosen or chasing the damn notes."

"I still have one of the USBs Amanda Wilson gave me, remember?" I picked up my coat and purse, then followed him out the door. "Sam might have said there's nothing on it, but it could still be worth checking."

"I'd forgotten about that damn thing. We'll do it as soon as we get back."

"Why not now? It's not like we have a limited time to either check out Wirraway or find Rosen or Amanda."

He pressed the elevator call button, then shoved his hands into his pockets. "That's the thing—I have this really weird feeling we need to get over to Wirraway."

Surprise rippled through me. "So Fae really *do* have clairvoyant tendencies?"

"We commune with nature and our elements, not idiots intent on gambling their fortune and their businesses away." The elevator door opened, and he ushered me inside. "But *you* get visions. Maybe this is another side effect of sharing flame."

"Maybe." I shrugged. It wasn't like I'd ever done anything like it with anyone other than Rory, so anything was possible.

We headed out to the hotel, but rather than walk to

our car, he caught my elbow and led me in the opposite direction.

"The sindicati will have no doubt registered the make and plate number of the car we used yesterday. We're getting another."

"Three rentals is pushing it a little, isn't it?"

His grin flashed. "The business can afford it. And we'll return yesterday's tonight."

"If they continued to follow us after last night's con-frontation, they'll be aware we're staying at the hotel. Changing cars won't matter."

"No one followed us here, Em. I'm certain of that. Not in a car, anyway."

We just had to hope he was right. It took little more than half an hour to sign all the paperwork and get another new car—this time a nondescript Ford Focus—and by then the traffic had eased up, and we were able to drive across to Port Melbourne in relatively quick time.

"Right," Jackson said as he swung onto Wirraway Drive and slowed the car down. "Keep those pretty eyes of yours peeled for anything that screams rats or Radcliffe."

I snorted. "It's an industrial estate close to a major river. There're going to be rats everywhere."

His grin flashed. "True that."

I smiled but scanned the nearby buildings. The street was wide and lined with gum trees, most of them fairly young. A few cars were parked on the roadside, but most people made use of the parking lots the various warehouses or businesses had available either in front or to the side of their buildings. It was a little hard to tell what any of the businesses actually were, because the only signage on most was simply a name.

The road curved left. As Jackson followed it, I spotted a row of what looked to be empty shops, at the end of which was a series of outdoor umbrellas shading white tables and randomly colored chairs.

"Didn't Rosen mention being taken to a café?"

"He did." He glanced at the café. "And it's a very well-secured little café, too."

It certainly was. There were at least two security cameras that I could see, and they were the type that was constantly moving, scanning the immediate surrounds. "It might just be worth going in there to buy a coffee."

"I totally agree."

He drove on. Wirraway Drive curved right one more time, then came to a dead end. Jackson swung around, drove back, and pulled into the café's small parking lot.

"Shame we haven't got that nurse's uniform." He leaned his forearms on the wheel and studied the building. "You could have gone in and gotten the drinks without raising suspicions."

"He may know me by sight, but he doesn't know you." I watched several workers come out of the café, drinks and bags of food in hand. "And it may just be what it looks like—a café doing a roaring job catering to all the nearby warehouse workers."

"Possibly." He unclipped his belt. "What do you feel like?"

"A green tea if they have it, hot chocolate if they haven't. And a vanilla slice wouldn't go astray."

"Didn't anyone ever tell you that pastries makes you fat?"

I grinned. "Not a problem for us. We burn too hot."

"Fae, too. I shall grab three."

He climbed out of the car and strolled toward the café. His hands were in his pockets and his gait casual, but I had no doubt he didn't miss a thing. I continued to watch the flow of people in and out of the place for several minutes, then shifted and studied the other buildings—and caught sight of yet more security cameras. The one on the end, closest to the parking lot, had stopped sweeping. We'd been made.

I got out and walked across, just as Jackson was coming back out.

He immediately stopped. "Trouble?"

I nodded toward the still-watching camera. "Big Brother has been watching."

"Idiots, giving the game away like that." He placed the drinks and the vanilla slices down on the nearest table. "Shall we go introduce ourselves more formally?"

"*If* there's anyone left to introduce ourselves to, sure."

He spun around and headed back in. I followed. It was a cheery-looking place, filled with color, warmth, and great-smelling food. There were more tables lining the right wall and several customers being served by an equal number of staff. Jackson ignored them and headed for the swing door at the rear.

"I'm sorry, sir," one of the women said, dumping her tongs on the nearby counter and hurrying after us, "but you can't go in there."

"It's okay," he said over his shoulder. "Mr. Radcliffe is expecting us."

"But there's no one by that—"

She was talking to air. Jackson was already through the door. I followed, but a quick glance over my shoulder as the door swung shut behind us revealed she was now on the phone. Even if, by some miracle, Radcliffe *hadn't* been aware of our presence, he surely was now.

The next room was a small kitchen. I gave the chef a nod as we passed through, but he basically ignored us. A pointer, perhaps, to the fact that we weren't the first strangers to stroll through this place.

The next room was a storeroom. It, too, was small, and filled with shelves loaded with stock and kitchen paraphernalia. There were several personnel lockers in one corner and two more doors, one of them open. Jackson stopped in the middle of the storeroom and studied the various shelves intently. I continued on; the open door led out to the rear of the building, but there was nothing in the lane beyond the exit other than several half-filled Dumpsters. The second door led into a bathroom. It was tiny, especially with the six personnel lockers crammed into it.

"Well, this is a bust," I said as I returned and stopped beside him.

"No, it isn't. There's a breeze."

"Well, yeah, the back door is open."

"Yes, but it's coming from that wall, *not* the door." He waved a hand to the wall in front of us. "And it's colder than the breeze outside."

"There's no air-conditioning in either the café or the kitchen." I glanced up. "There're no vents in here, either."

"No." He paused. "It suddenly strikes me that the

café is a whole lot wider than both the kitchen and the storeroom."

I blinked. Even with the width of the storeroom and bathroom combined, he was right.

"Meaning," he continued, "there just might be another room hidden behind that wall."

"Rats do like their hiding places." I contemplated the shelving for a second. "If there *is* some sort of entrance here, I can't imagine they'd be wanting to move the shelving to get to it every time."

"No," he agreed. "But does it seem at all odd to you that there're personnel lockers in a store that holds kitchen equipment and supplies? Isn't that against all sorts of health regs?"

"I haven't worked in the food industry in any of my recent rebirths, but I was under the impression staff facilities had to be separated." I walked across to the lockers. They were all padlocked, but the locks weren't particularly robust. I melted the one on the first door and opened it—only to have it continue to fold open. The lockers had all been connected and hollowed out, so they were little more than an outer shell that protected the doorway Jackson had sensed. It was heavy-duty and sporting a rather industrial-looking, key-coded locking system. I burned it out, sending sparks flying, then raised a foot and booted it open. The room beyond was brightly lit and apparently empty. I doubted it actually *was*, even though I could neither see nor sense anyone else near.

"I do so love the way you work," Jackson murmured as he ducked into the lockers and stepped cautiously into the next room.

And almost immediately was sent flying by a fist to the jaw.

I grabbed the arm and slammed it back against the door frame before the man could deliver a second blow. A howl of pain followed; then the stranger's body filled the doorway as his other fist came flying toward me. I ducked the blow, then released him, swung around, and booted him hard in the gut. He grunted and staggered several feet backward, but he didn't fall, as I'd half hoped. Instead, he simply growled and launched straight at me.

I scrambled backward, flames flickering across my fingers and skin. The big man either didn't see them or didn't care, and he was on me before I could do anything else. We went down in a tumble of arms and legs and skidded across the storeroom's floor, hitting the wall opposite hard enough to force a grunt from both the big man and me. I tried to break free, but his weight had me pinned down even as he wrapped his fingers almost lovingly around my neck. It felt as if he were trying to snap me in two.

Maybe he was.

I swore—though it came out more a garbled rasp of noise than anything actually understandable—and punched him hard in the face. As my fist mashed his nose and sent snot and blood flying, my flames hit his skin, cindering his flesh. The foul stench seared the air, and he roared—a sound that was filled with pain and fury. But he didn't let go. He simply squeezed harder.

As lights began to dance in front of my eyes, I did the only thing I could do—become flame rather than flesh.

Energy roared through me, sweeping me from one form to another in an instant. But the flames of a phoenix burned far hotter than any regular fire, and the big man went up in an instant. He screamed again, truly screamed this time, the sound high and terrible. I wrapped a slither of flame around his neck and wrenched him off me, then simultaneously put him out and retained flesh form.

And just in time.

The door behind us crashed open, and the chef appeared. "What the *fuck*?" His voice trailed off as he stared at the still-smoking man near the bathroom door.

"Call an ambulance," I said, then added, when he didn't immediately answer, *"Now!"*

His gaze came to mine, eyes wide with shock and perhaps horror; then he nodded and retreated. I spun, ran back through the lockers, and dove into the other room.

One man lay on the floor to my right, groaning in pain, one leg lying at an odd angle to his body, a leg bone visible.

Jackson was still fighting two others. The smack of flesh on flesh was loud and deadly sounding, but even as I rolled to my feet and stepped toward them to help, fire flickered across Jackson's fists, then ignited; the flames hit one man, sending him flying backward, while Jackson's fist took care of the other.

Neither man got back up. I walked across to the flame-thrown thug, quickly dousing him, then checking his pulse. He was out cold but okay. So was the second.

I glanced at Jackson and nodded at his still flaming

hands. "I'm guessing that's another side effect of our joining."

His expression became somewhat confused. "I can't make flame—you know that. I can only redirect and reuse—and you set the other guy alight. I felt the sweep of ignition."

"Yeah, but I doused him almost straight away." I motioned down at the unconscious figure at my feet. "There was no flame active when you did this."

"Well, don't those side effects just get more and more interesting." He studied his flaming hands for several more seconds, then doused them. A second later, the flames reappeared; just not as bright or strong. His grin flashed as his gaze met mine. "As a fire Fae, I cannot be unhappy about the prospect of being able to create my own flame, even if it contains only a fraction of the potency of yours."

"For now," I commented. "Who knows what will happen as time moves along."

"Again, I'm not complaining."

"No." I swung around and studied the room. "Radcliffe's skipped out."

"Rats have a habit of doing that."

He walked across to the large table that dominated the end of the long but narrow room. Papers were scattered everywhere and the chair was upturned, evidence of a hasty departure. On the wall beside the door were several small screens, one showing constantly moving views of the road and parking bays outside the café, and the other locked on the front door. We'd definitely been watched as we'd entered.

"But how did he leave?" I shoved my hands on my

hips and glared at the walls around us, seeking answers they were very unhelpfully *not* providing. "There're no windows in this place, and the only door is the one we came in."

"It may be the only regular door, but I'm betting there's a trapdoor here somewhere." He walked around the desk and studied the floor. "He can't have moved the desk, though—it's bolted to the floor."

"I don't think I want to know *why* he'd do that." My gaze swept the room again and came to rest on the small sofa at the other end of the room. One side of it was sitting slightly out from the wall. I walked over, grabbed the end, and pulled it fully away. There, on the floor, was a trapdoor. "One rat hole found."

Jackson walked over. "I'll go down first."

"Just be careful this time. Your pretty face is bruised enough."

He snorted. "We men prefer to be called handsome, my dear, not pretty."

"But they can definitely be both."

He rolled his eyes at me, then grabbed the trapdoor's handle and heaved it open. The air that rushed up to greet us was thick and dank, filled with the aroma of rotting carcasses and rubbish.

"A bloody storm drain," I groaned, wrinkling my nose in distaste. "I should have guessed."

Sparks danced across Jackson's hands, but they were barely bright enough to lift more than an inch or two of the darkness that hovered below. He glanced at me. "I guess the honor is yours."

I called to my flames, formed them into a ball of fire, and tossed the ball down into the darkness. It hit the trickle of water that lay at the bottom of the drain, sizzling and spitting but not going out. The drain it revealed wasn't a big one; in fact, I doubted I, let alone Jackson, could stand up in it. But Radcliffe didn't need to; all he had to do was change form and run for it.

I dropped on my knees and bent to get a closer look, but Jackson stopped me. "Remember the fist that greeted me when I stuck my mug through a gap."

He flicked a finger, and my ball of flame began to grow, expand, until it formed a wall of fire slightly wider than the circumference of the trapdoor. "Now you may look."

I did, but there was nothing to see. The rat had well and truly fled the scene. I sighed and sat back on my haunches. "There's probably not much chance of finding him, even if we do go after him."

"No." Jackson rose, then offered me a hand, helping me up. "But I'm guessing the cops have also been called, so we might as well give this place a quick search, before the shit truly hits."

I frowned. "It might be better to leave."

"No. Leaving the scene of a crime will only make us the aggressors in the cops' eyes—"

"And we were."

"Yes, but I've got a swollen jaw and you've got bruising around your neck, so self-defense is not unreasonable." He shrugged. "And we're in the den of a known criminal. Trust me, I doubt they'll come down too harshly on us."

I hoped he was right. As he'd noted previously, neither of us would do too well in jail—even if there was actually a human jail that could hold me. Or, at least, hold my fire form.

I stepped over one of the still-unconscious men and moved to the desk. The sound of approaching sirens was now very clear, so we really didn't have much time left to uncover anything. I picked up a couple of bits of paper and noticed the odd indents on the desktop. They weren't big, but they *were* deep. It almost looked as if something had been nailed to the desk. Repeatedly. Suspecting I really *didn't* need to know the reasons for that, I glanced back at the papers in my hand. They seemed to be financial records of some kind, though I didn't recognize any of the names on them.

"Anything?" Jackson said, moving across to the filing cabinets.

"Nothing useful." I righted the chair, then sat and began opening desk drawers. "You?"

"The cabinets are locked, and it probably wouldn't be wise to force them."

"No." The first drawer was filled with basic office paraphernalia, as well as some not-so-basic items, such as long letter openers that had been filed down to really sharp points—points that would undoubtedly match the odd dents in the desktop.

Bloody images rose of body parts being nailed to the desk by an angry Radcliffe; I shivered and shoved my imagination back in its box. I'd come across far worse than Radcliffe in my time, but the lengths some people—both men *and* women—were willing to go to for the sake of the almighty dollar never ceased to surprise me. I slammed the drawer shut and moved on to the next one. It turned out to be a random junk drawer. I searched it anyway but didn't find anything useful. I also didn't find any more sharpened office implements, for which I was extremely grateful.

"You know, it's interesting that no one from either the café or the kitchen has actually come to investigate what we're doing or to stop us from leaving."

I glanced up. Jackson stood in the doorway, his back to me. Studying the man who'd attacked us, I thought, as a sliver of remorse ran through me. He was going to have a long, difficult road to recovery—*if* he could, in fact, recover. Very few people survived such close contact with my spirit form. Jackson had, but only because he was fire Fae and really *couldn't* be burned by his own element. The sheer force and power of my natural being might have killed him—probably *should* have killed him—but it wouldn't have actually burned him.

"I suspect Radcliffe's employees learned long ago that curiosity is *not* a good thing." I opened the bottom drawer—and discovered not only car keys but a wallet and phone. "Guess what I just found?"

"The keys to the kingdom?" He turned to face me, a smile teasing the corners of his mouth. I held up the wallet and phone, and his smile grew. "I wasn't *that* far off."

"That depends on whether there's anything interesting to be found on either item." I tossed him the wallet and flicked on the phone. "It's key coded."

"The only thing surprising about *that*," Jackson commented, "is that it's not thumbprint coded. It's easy enough to break numerical codes these days, and Radcliffe surely has to know that."

"He probably does, but why do you? And does that statement imply that you've done it?"

"Well, not me personally. I haven't the time nor the inclination to sit there and physically type out numbers until I crack the right one."

"Then how?" The sound of sirens was now so close, the noise echoed through the small room. They had to be right outside the café, meaning we had a minute, if that, left. I grabbed the car keys, shoved them and the phone in my pocket, and rose.

"With the help of a forensic program capable of copying the encrypted data off a cell phone and then attacking it. Once it hits the right combination, all the data is unencrypted and can be read."

"Without the phone being affected?"

"Exactly. The user never knows his device has been compromised. Very handy." He shoved the wallet into the back pocket of his jeans, then added, "The ambulance and cops just arrived."

"Yeah." I glanced around as one of the men stirred. He did little more than groan, so I let him be and walked across to stand beside Jackson to wait for the incoming police and ambulance officers.

What I didn't expect was to see Sam among them.

CHAPTER 8

"What the *fuck* has been going on here, Em?" Sam's voice was low but so thick with anger, it vibrated.

We were standing outside, well apart from both the paramedics rushing the man I'd cindered toward the waiting ambulance, and the woman who was interviewing Jackson. She was PIT, like Sam, but not someone I'd met before—not that I'd met that many of them. Just Rozelle, Sam's bed partner and a Fae like Jackson, and Adam, the vamp who worked with Sam during nighttime incursions.

I crossed my arms and met Sam's gaze evenly. The outward calm, however, was little more than bravado. The darkness within him had risen to the surface again. The force of it was so fierce, it swept away any warmth or comfort I might have gained from the morning sunshine, and left my insides trembling. Unfortunately, *that* part of my reaction wasn't just fear.

"You *know* what we were doing here, Sam, because you know who this place belongs to."

"Yes, but to attack—burn—Radcliffe's man like that—"

"The bastard attacked *me*!" I grabbed the collar of my shirt and pulled it away from my neck so that the bruises became more evident. "You saw the size of him—what else was I supposed to do? He had me at the point of unconsciousness. My only way out was to shift."

His gaze rested on my neck, a dangerous weight I could feel through to my very core. "You could have used a thread of fire to lasso him away or something like that. I know you're capable of it."

Knew because he'd seen me do it? I frowned, thinking back to the forest and the gray-cowled stranger who'd ordered the red cloaks to attack us. That figure hadn't been Sam; I was certain of that—even if he had the same vibrant blue eyes—but I couldn't escape the notion that there *was* some sort of connection between them, however tenuous. And then there was the whole "You will be mine" threat that oddly implied we'd met previously.

Of course, it was also possible that *that* stranger was a cloak Sam had attempted to kill and, in his attempt to seek vengeance, was concentrating on erasing all Sam cared about. Sam *had* admitted when I'd saved his ass in Brooklyn—the apparent hot spot for red-cloak activity here in Melbourne—that he'd made it something of a personal crusade to kill every one of the bastards. It would certainly explain the gray cloak's odd fascination with Sam—although if he knew anything at all about Sam, he'd know we were no longer an item, and that my death wasn't ever likely to affect him. Not in the way the stranger seemed to think it would, anyway.

"And how would you know that?"

"How do you think? PIT has a dossier filled with general information about the abilities of a phoenix."

The intensity of Sam's gaze seemed to be growing, and it both repelled and allured. I wasn't sure why that should be, but it oddly reminded me of the glamor vampires could sometimes place on their victims, making the unwilling willing.

I frowned and briefly looked away. Even so, the weight of his gaze had my knees threatening to buckle. Or maybe *that* was simply his closeness, and the wash of his scent across my senses, a rich mix of woodsy earthiness and musk.

"You're right," I said eventually. "I probably should have. But I was on the verge of unconsciousness, as I said, and instinct took over."

He made a low sound in the back of his throat, then lifted his gaze and looked past me. The abrupt release from the weight of it actually had me taking half a step to steady myself.

Which was strange—almost as strange as the man himself. But then, Sam had *never* been normal. His dedication to his job, the fierce way he cared about the people in his life, his sheer *love* of life combined with his adventurous nature, were part of what had attracted me in the first place. The addition of that dangerous darkness just gave him more of an edge.

As Jackson had noted, the heart really *wasn't* a sensible organ.

Sam took a deep breath and released it slowly. "Okay, just tell me why you came here. There wasn't much more than thoughts on that USB I gave you, and certainly nothing that provided a link between Wilson's missing research and Radcliffe."

"Maybe not, but Rosen certainly has links to him."

His gaze rested on mine again. I rubbed my arms against both the chill that ran across my skin and the desire that stirred in the deeper recesses.

"We're aware of that."

"And I'm guessing you released Rosen rather than charge the bastard because you want to uncover who Radcliffe is selling the secrets to."

He didn't deny the statement but simply said, "Rosen won't be selling any more government secrets to either the sindicati *or* the city pack—not unless they're ones of our making."

The werewolves were buying government secrets? I'm not sure why that surprised me, given what Jackson had said earlier about the werewolves working with the sindicati, but for some reason, I'd expected better of them. Which probably just came down to naïveté and a lack of interaction with them on my part.

"Good." I paused. "Maybe that's why the sindicati— or, at least, two wolves who claimed they'd been employed by the sindicati—tried to kill him yesterday."

"*What?* When?"

"In the afternoon, just after four. I daresay you're familiar with one of the two goons who took him— Theodore Hunt, the werewolf who almost killed Amanda Wilson."

"If the sindicati *are* Radcliffe's buyer, it makes no sense that they'd want him dead. Our enforced restrictions only apply to government projects, not privately funded ones. Believe me, his company is working on a couple of projects the vamps would love to get their hands on."

So why didn't PIT protect those? Was it simply a matter of the other projects' holding no threat to humanity in general? If that *was* the case, then what else was Rosen's company working on? Maybe that was a question we needed to ask Rosen—if we ever found him again, and if PIT's restrictions didn't also apply to us.

"Of course," Sam added, "it could also be someone wanting to *implicate* the sindicati. Did they give you a name?"

My smile held as little humor as his had earlier. "Morretti."

"This mess just gets more and more interesting," he murmured. But before I could ask why, he added, "Where's Rosen now?"

"We don't know."

He frowned. The shadowed darkness that haunted his soul seemed to have retreated a little, but that only increased my awareness of him.

"What do you mean, you don't know? You rescued him, didn't you?"

"Yes, and took him somewhere safe. Only trouble is, we left to talk to his son, and he was gone by the time we got back."

His frown grew. "What the hell has Rosen's son—" He paused, and I could almost could see the cogs turning. "He was Hamberly's lover, wasn't he? Did he see anything?"

"That depends on your definition of 'see.' He's something of a psychic."

"So he saw the creature coming and ran out on his

partner?" Sam's tone held a thick edge of dislike. "It would seem the son takes after the father."

"Except that he claims Hamberly was already dead, just as he would have been if he'd stayed."

"Was he able to give you much information?"

"Not much." I smiled, and Sam's pupils widened. While that was generally considered a sign of sexual interest, I wasn't sure it was one I could rely on here— if only because there was little other indication that he was, in any way, still attracted to me. Certainly not in his expression, which remained ungiving. "Most of it made no sense. He did say the creature had human form—that of a thin, middle-aged woman with dark hair and bloodshot eyes."

"We'll talk to him."

I raised an eyebrow. "I'm surprised you haven't already."

His sudden smile held very little humor. "Sometimes even PIT can be behind the eight ball—and we've only got indentations on the pillows and a hair removed from the scene to initially go on. Forensic results don't happen overnight, as much as we might wish otherwise."

And even forensics couldn't grab a name out of DNA. The paramedics finally slammed the ambulance doors closed; in a matter of seconds it was gone, racing my victim toward the hospital.

"So why," he added, "were you here? Don't make me bring you into PIT again, Em."

I sighed and pulled my gaze from his once more. And noticed that our drinks and vanilla slices were still sitting on the table where we'd left them. The folk around here were obviously honest.

"Rosen told us that Hunt and his muscular friend had been sent by Radcliffe, *not* by the sindicati. We were just coming here to clarify whether that was the truth or not."

"And you didn't think he'd scarper the minute he saw you on the security cams?"

"We didn't see them until it was too late." I shrugged. "We took a chance that the rat didn't have an escape route. We were wrong."

He grunted and glanced across to the woman interviewing Jackson. She gave him a slight nod, then said something to Jackson and rose. No handcuffs appeared, and surprise rippled through me. "You're letting us go? Just like that?"

"Until or unless it can be proven that you didn't act in self-defense, then yes." A ghost of a smile—a real smile—touched his lips, and my stupid heart did something of a happy dance. "And we both know how unlikely it is that any of Radcliffe's men will speak."

I was *counting* on it. Granted, we didn't technically attack first, but we sure as hell *did* break and enter. "And Morretti? You're not going to warn us off pursuing him in any way?"

His smile faded, and part of me mourned its loss. The stupid part, obviously. "I don't have to. Morretti was murdered last night."

By Scott Baker, perhaps? He'd certainly seemed intent on sending the sindicati a message, but I'd been under the impression he intended to do it via the vampires who'd been waiting for Hunt rather than by killing someone so high up in sindicati ranks. *That* sort of reaction could spark a war, and I doubted that was what Baker actually wanted. "Who by?"

"And why would you think I'd actually *answer* that question?"

I squinted up at him. "Because you're a kind, generous, and very giving soul?"

My attempt at humor was met by an even stonier expression. "That might have been true once, but not anymore."

I didn't say anything, because there was little point. What he said was an obvious truth no one could deny—not if they'd had any recent interaction with him.

But even as that thought crossed my mind, I remembered the warmth and caring that had been so obvious between him and Rozelle the one time I'd seen them together. He wasn't stony to everyone; it was just me, obviously.

I glanced away. "I don't expect an answer, Sam. I don't really expect anything. Is that it? Can we go?"

He studied me for several seconds, and it was very much a silent demand to turn and look at him. I didn't and, after a moment, he said, "Where are you staying, just in case we need to get hold of you?"

"If you need to get hold of me, just ring."

"Em, don't be difficult. We know you're not spending much time at your apartment, and you certainly haven't been staying at the office since it was raided, so where?"

I crossed my arms and met his gaze again. "So you're still having me followed?"

He hesitated. "No. But we *are* keeping tabs on your whereabouts. Given your refusal to stop investigating Baltimore's murder, it is a logical course of action."

"Except that we're working for Rosen, looking for

Wilson's missing research notes. We haven't even thought about Baltimore recently."

Which was the truth, as far as it went. But that didn't mean we wouldn't change investigation streams if we came across anything relating to Baltimore's research notes or his murder—although could it really be considered a murder now that he'd risen from the dead either as a vampire or one of the red cloaks?

And Sam obviously knew that. His thin smile held little humor as he said, "Maybe, but unless you want to go back to being followed twenty-four/seven, tell me where you're staying."

I blew out a frustrated breath and gave him the address of the hotel.

"Thanks. And remember, if you learn anything else about that creature, we need to know."

"No problem."

With that, I turned and walked away. The weight of his gaze pressed against my back, and once again desire stirred deep inside. But I resisted the urge to look back at him and just kept moving. Jackson grabbed the drinks and vanilla slices we'd left on the table, then met me at the car.

"Well, that turned out a whole lot better than I'd expected," he said. "Any clue as to why they've simply let us go, without even a caution?"

"No one died. Seriously," I added when he raised an eyebrow.

"Fair enough." He unlocked the car and we climbed in. "But it seems damn odd that we weren't even given a warning not to pursue Hunt, the sindicati, or even Morretti."

I took one of the slices he offered me. "That's because Morretti was murdered last night."

His gaze snapped to mine. "Who by?"

"Sam didn't say."

"Can't have been Baker. That sort of action would start a war."

"My thought exactly." I bit down on the slice and hurriedly shoved a hand under it to catch the thick, gooey custard that oozed out the sides of the puff pastry.

"Maybe it was the sindicati faction that's seeking to control the whole kit and caboodle."

"Or someone who was simply pissed off about Morretti's lack of recent results." I shrugged. "Either way, we should definitely check out that warehouse in Laverton North."

"I agree. But I'd wait a day or so, until the hubbub over Morretti's death dies down a little."

We finished the slices and the now-cold drinks. Then Jackson started the car, and we headed out.

"Where to next?" I tossed the rubbish into the empty middle console and brushed the pastry crumbs from my clothes.

He pulled Radcliffe's wallet out of his pocket and handed it to me. "Radcliffe's driver's license gives us a home address. I think we should go investigate it."

"He's unlikely to go there since he now knows we're after him."

"True, but we might just find the elusive Mrs. Radcliffe you're so certain exists there."

"Also unlikely." I retrieved Radcliffe's driver's license from the wallet and typed his home address into the GPS. "If he's denying her existence, she won't be living at an address so easily checked."

"Also true." He shrugged, and we continued on in silence.

Radcliffe lived—somewhat surprisingly—in the rather middle-class suburb of Keilor East. His home turned out to be just as surprising—a standard 1970s redbrick house, which was single story in the front and double at the rear. A large brick patio that looked to have been added on at a later date covered the entrance to the front door, and to the left of the house was a two-car garage. There was little in the way of a front garden, but the lawn had been recently mown. There were no cars in the driveway, and the blinds were all closed.

Jackson stopped in front of the neighboring house and twisted around to look back. "I can't see any security cameras."

"Which is decidedly odd if Radcliffe *does* live here," I commented, "especially given all the technology at the café."

"Yeah." He turned and studied the rest of the street. "What do you think?"

"I think if Radcliffe owns this place, then he's probably got an escape route ready to go."

"My thoughts exactly. You take the front; I'll take the back. Hopefully we'll catch the rat somewhere in the middle."

"One of these days, breaking into places is really going to get you into trouble." My tone was dry as I opened the car door and climbed out.

"Undoubtedly." His expression was amused and

uncaring. "But until it does, I shall continue on my merry way."

"Is this need to walk the edge of danger a Fae thing, or just an inherent desire of yours?"

"In my case, a bit of both." He shrugged. "But it does take a little craziness to attempt to restrain the power of the elements in *any* way, and I have seen more than one Fae consumed by it."

I nodded. It could happen to us, too, if we held on to the earth mother's power for too long. Using her always came at the cost of our own strength, but the ultimate payment was death itself, with all that we are, all that we'd experienced, being drawn into her vast bosom. I had no idea if it was possible to be called back to the mother—I'd never actually heard of any phoenix being caught like that. But it was a warning handed down from generation to generation, and there were very few such myths that weren't at least based on *some* truth, however tenuous.

Jackson jumped over the small brick fence and headed for the rear yard. I continued on to the driveway and walked across to the front door. It was plain and painted white, but there were cobwebs in the corners of the frame, and the locks were old and not particularly strong looking.

I glanced around to see if anyone appeared to be watching, then stepped back and gave the lock a good kick. It sprung open with little fuss. I darted forward to grab it before it could smash back into the plaster, and I was hit by the scent in the air—it was musty, as if no one had opened a window and let in fresh air for a very long time.

If *anyone* actually lived here, let alone Radcliffe, I'd give up sex.

I closed the door, then looked around. There were two more doors—one directly in front and the other to my right—while on my left was a long corridor that ran past a staircase and had several other rooms running off it. I went right and found myself in the living room. The carpet was pristine, but the geometric pattern and the brash red and black coloring looked to have leapt straight out of the 1970s. The furniture was similarly dated, with dark wood and heavily patterned fabrics. The room was L-shaped, with a dining area in the other corner. Off this was a kitchen. A couple of recently posted envelopes were on the counter, but both had been opened and were now empty. It did, however, suggest that someone came here fairly regularly, even if only to collect the mail. I continued on and found myself back in the hall.

Jackson appeared out of one of the rooms. "Anything?"

I shook my head. "No sign of either a rat or a rat hole."

He grimaced. "I'd guess, from the smell of the place, he's using it for license purposes only."

I waved a hand at the stairs. "I'll head up."

He nodded and walked into the first room past the stairs. I bounded upstairs, the sound of my footsteps muffled by the awful carpet. There were four bedrooms up here as well as a large bathroom, and all of the bedrooms were unfurnished. I checked the wardrobes, just to be sure, but there was nothing except dust and dead spiders to be found.

I walked back down and met Jackson in the hall again.

"Well," he said when I shook my head, "it was always a long shot."

"Yes, but he has to live somewhere, and it *isn't* underground. That suit he was wearing at Crown was damn expensive, and neither he nor it smelled even vaguely of sewers."

Jackson pressed a hand against my back, lightly guiding me out. "I'll contact my source and see what she can come up with."

"Given the trouble PIT has had pinning him down, it's unlikely she'll be able to come up with much."

He shrugged and slammed the door shut. "Even a few more addresses to check could be helpful."

And it wasn't like we had many other options right now, anyway.

"True," Jackson said, obviously catching my thought as we walked back to the car. "I'm thinking we go back to the hotel and check out not only what is on that USB you have but see what sort of information we can drag from Rosen's phone."

"When I was talking to Sam earlier, he said there wasn't much relating to Wilson or his research on the USB." I flashed Jackson a smile of thanks as he opened the passenger door for me. "And Rory's computer hasn't got any sort of program capable of cracking key codes on it."

"It soon will. They may have stolen our computers, but they won't have gained access to the information I store in the cloud." He slammed the door shut and ran around to the other side of the car, climbing in.

"If you've got a program capable of cracking key codes, then surely the sindicati will have something similar to crack passwords."

"Undoubtedly. But my cloud isn't any of the regular service providers. A friend of mine runs one of the larger ISP companies here in Australia and has given me space off-grid, so to speak."

I raised an eyebrow. "You seem to know some very well-placed people."

He shrugged and pulled out of the parking spot. "Fae tend to live a long time, remember, and that gives us the opportunity to build contacts."

I shifted in the seat and studied him. "Fae aren't exactly 'out' to the general population, so how do you get around the problem of living longer than humans without their noticing?"

"We move around, like you." He shrugged again. "And admittedly, most of my friends are Fae, just like me. It's easier than explaining."

"I thought Fae were loners by nature?"

"We are, in that we don't live in one another's pockets month by month. Hell, I don't see some of them for years. But if I ever need help, I can call on them and know they'd be there."

"So this secret police source of yours is another Fae?"

"You," he said, flashing me a smile, "are entirely too quick at connecting the dots."

"Which isn't actually a yes." My tone was dry. "So, you've backed up all the office files on this cloud service?"

"Just active cases and programs I don't want to lose. My friend is generous, but I haven't got an infinite amount of space on his system."

"And will I ever get to meet these friends of yours?"

"Considering you've become a fixture in my life, more than likely."

I smiled. "Being called a 'fixture' isn't exactly a term of endearment."

"No, but it's certainly a truth." His grin flashed. "After all, light fixtures shine brightness on otherwise dark and dreary days, and that's certainly what's happened since you cannoned into my life."

Which was a rather sweet thing to say, even *if* he'd initially started seeing me in the hope I might be able to help out his investigation into Wilson's disappearance.

It was close to six by the time we'd returned our rented vehicle and got back to the hotel. We ordered burgers and chips from the room service menu, then booted up Rory's laptop and shoved the USB into it.

Sam hadn't been lying—there wasn't a whole lot of information about either Wilson or his research on it, but there *were* a lot of observations, in the form of notes, that Amanda Rosen had made about the sindicati and anyone else she happened to meet.

The stuff on the sindicati was enlightening, providing a whole lot of information about them. Apparently, the sindicati, like the mafia, had originated in Sicily, but unlike its human counterpart, the organization was ruled by a council. Unfortunately, there was no information on who was on this council or how they were chosen. The only people who had access to the council were the four generals—one of whom had been Morretti—and it was through them that the council's wishes and rulings were relayed. It also suggested the reason for the recent split was all about control—

Morretti's faction was considered old-school and out of date in its methods and beliefs, and many younger vampires believed it was time to change. And the leader of *that* section was one Anthony De Luca.

"Have you heard of him?" I picked up my mug of tea and stared at the screen thoughtfully. Amanda must have been a very strong telepath if she'd picked up *this* sort of information about the sindicati. As Jackson had said, telepaths didn't have open access to human minds, but rather they had to have a specific target in mind, and both vampires and werewolves were usually harder to read than humans. That ability was undoubtedly the reason she was still alive: The sindicati—and whoever else had been in the darkened room I'd been taken to after the truck crash—really *did* have plans for her. But if she'd been working for Morretti, did that mean De Luca now had her? Or had it been someone in Morretti's own faction—perhaps even the person responsible for his death?

Jackson shook his head. "But that's no real surprise, considering how little inaction I've had with the sindicati. What *is* surprising is that PIT left all this information on the USB."

"They obviously checked it. Maybe they just didn't think we could or would use it."

Someone knocked on the door. I put my mug down and walked over, checking the peephole before opening the door. A smiling hotel waiter brought our food in, accepted his tip, and then headed out again. I closed and locked the door, my mouth watering as the delicious aroma of hamburgers and fries filled the air.

"And to be perfectly honest, we really *can't* use it."

Jackson took the covers off the meals and handed me one of the plates. "It's handy background information, but it's very fragmented. We haven't got either addresses or images to chase down."

I picked up my burger and bit into it. The meat was thick, juicy, and cooked just right, and I all but groaned in pleasure. Jackson chuckled but got down to the business of demolishing his two. It was only when we'd finished the meal and I had another mug of tea in my hand that I said, "The solution is, of course, to find someone who *can* connect the dots."

He leaned back in his chair and contemplated me for a moment. "Someone like Lee Rawlings?"

"Well, he works for hire, and he had no qualms about handing over Morretti as the person who'd wanted me kidnapped—"

"Only if we covered the fee he would otherwise have missed out on," he cut in.

"And *that* is the entire point." I shrugged. "Getting hold of him will be the main problem."

"Not really," Jackson said. "He said it was a commission rather than a job."

I frowned. "There's a difference?"

"A huge one. Accepting a commission means the job didn't come through the sindicati themselves, but rather through nonallianced representatives." He paused to drink some coffee. "It also means Rawlings is not sindicati himself—as evidenced by his being so willing to sell them out."

"But why would they hire an outside source? They're the *sindicati*, for fuck's sake—surely they have plenty of muscle in their own ranks?"

"Yes, but even the sindicati will have certain actions or situations that they do not want linked back to them. Kidnapping you might have been one such case."

"If that were true, then they wouldn't have told Rawlings the job came from them."

"They may not have. Rawlings could have picked up that information through other means. He's empathic, remember."

"Empathy is not telepathy," I said. "He can't read minds, just emotions."

"Yes, but he also appears to be a very old vampire who is working as a bagman and surviving *outside* the sindicati circle. I'd place bets on his not only being able to uncover a whole lot about a person from just his emotions, but knowing a hell of a lot more about the sindicati than the average thug. He'd have to."

"All of which is undoubtedly true, but if the sindicati didn't give him the commission themselves, then who did?"

"The coalition."

I raised an eyebrow. "You're telling me a political party put out a contract on me?"

Jackson threw a leftover fry at me. I caught it with a laugh and ate it.

"Not *that* coalition, idiot. Its official name is the Coalition of Nonhumans, and it's an independent resource center for vampires and werewolves, funded by member contributions."

"So, something like a union? And why would such a union come after me?"

"The CNH wouldn't in and of itself, because that's not its main brief. Its priority is both the protection of nonhuman rights in the workforce and the promotion of nonhuman-friendly legislation at all government levels. I'm surprised you haven't heard of it."

I shrugged. "I've no reason to be aware of an organization like that, and I certainly can't remember its being mentioned on the news recently."

"The CNH tends to keep itself low key, especially with the rise of the antiwerewolf and vampire squads."

I frowned. "Wouldn't the CNH provide those squads with the perfect hunting ground? If vamps and weres are constantly coming and going, it's virtually a smorgasbord of targets."

Jackson grimaced. "That actually *did* happen when the CNH was first set up. It now has twenty-four-hour security installed, and there's been a law passed that makes it illegal for anyone to loiter outside the building."

"Obviously the lawmakers weren't aware of the existence of long-range weapons when they passed *that* particular ruling," I said. "It wouldn't be exactly hard for someone to make a hit from a distance."

"Again, that *has* happened, but the assailants were quickly caught." Jackson's smile held an edge of grim humor. "PIT has werewolves in its ranks, and they can track scents as well as any hound, believe me. After two particularly well-publicized cases, the rate of more professional hits has dropped to practically zero."

"Which is just as well. If the hunting squads got too well organized, it'll result in a war that could only ever end badly for everyone." I sipped my tea. "So if the CNH's main brief is nonhuman rights, where does the whole contract angle come in? And why, if we want to get hold of Rawlings, would we go through them?"

"Because some twenty-five years ago, when the CNH was seriously cash strapped due to some poor investments, someone got the idea of establishing a small off-the-records department to handle nonhuman business activities that were not only a little less than legal but that required anonymity. That morphed into the current contracts department. It has no official phone number, so even if you try to contact them via the main switchboard, you won't get put through. You have to submit job requests via snail mail."

"That's a rather old-fashioned means of doing things, isn't it?"

"Yes, but it's also virtually untraceable once said mail is destroyed. The CNH *is* a legit business; the contracts division just happens to be a behind-the-scenes but very profitable sidearm."

"It can't be too behind the scenes if you know about it." I paused and yawned hugely. Although it was barely nine, my lack of sleep over the last couple of nights seemed to be catching up with me. "And if you know about it, PIT surely does."

"But, as is the case with the sindicati, they can't prosecute unless they have evidence of a crime, and getting *that* is difficult. The CNH itself is too handy an organization, and few are willing to rat it out, even if they don't agree with the activities of the contracts department."

I was betting PIT didn't actually need evidence of a crime. If Sam's actions with the red cloaks were anything to go by, if they suspected wrong doing, they'd go in and stop it, regardless of who or what was involved.

"So, in order to talk to Rawlings, we need to send them a letter, state what we need and what we're willing to pay, and wait for contact?"

Jackson nodded. "If Rawlings is willing to accept the commission, he'll contact us. If not, we'll have to think of something else."

I yawned again, then waved a hand in apology. "Sorry."

He grinned. "You've no stamina, that's the problem."

"No, the problem is that *you* have far too much of it. Or you did both last night *and* this morning."

"Hey, I didn't hear any complaints at the time." His gaze swept over me, and his smile faded a little. "You do look tired, though. Why don't you just head to bed?"

"You're suggesting I go *alone*?" I leaned forward and pressed the back of my hand against his forehead. "Are you ill?"

He laughed, caught my hand, and kissed it. "Probably. But I also need to download the key-code program onto the laptop, and it'll take time to set up. There's nothing you can do, so might as well catch some Zs."

"Thank you." I kissed his cheek and rose. "I'll feel you later."

"You will."

I left him to it. My head had barely hit the pillow when sleep hit, and it was deep and dreamless.

But it didn't stay that way.

Images began to stir through the shadows of slumber, pulling at my consciousness, waking me and yet not.

The creature was hunting its next victim.

Once again its form constantly changed, but this time the embers of its being didn't settle on the one shape but rather swirled through them all, as if it were unable to decide which shape was appropriate.

We were in a lane barely wide enough for a car to pass through. It was dark and deserted, and the brick walls of the buildings on either side were lined with street art that gave the immediate area a bright and cheerful feel. But that soon gave way to more regular graffiti and grime as we moved deeper into the lane. The creature's ever-changing form was ghost quiet, and the night was still. Even the water that trickled from the downpipes and ran down the lane's center drain made no sound. As before, the dream was hushed. Ungiving.

At the far end of the lane were several green Dumpsters sitting in front of a gray roller door, but the lane itself made a sharp right turn. Once again the creature paused, and its embers condensed enough to form the long snout of the dog I'd seen last time. It sniffed, and its hunger rolled over me, thick with anticipation.

It had found its next victim.

The embers shifted, condensed, until what stood in front of me was an abnormally large black cat. It moved forward, its backward paws making no sound on the wet asphalt. We swept around the corner; on the right-hand side of the lane were more green bins, interspersed between roller doors and building exits. On the left were the clean concrete walls and upper windows of an office building.

For a minute, the darkness failed to reveal what the

creature had scented. Then, as the creature paused and its form grew even larger, I saw, huddled in the corner of one of the exits, the bundle of stained rags clutching a bottle sheathed in a brown paper bag.

And, as Denny Rosen Jr. had predicted, he was *alive*.

I wanted to scream. Wanted to run forward, shake him, and wake him. Wanted to grab the creature and somehow stop the play of events.

Wanted to wake up and *not* see what was about to happen.

But the dream's grip was fierce, and it would not release me.

The creature stepped forward and carefully sniffed the stranger. He stirred and mumbled something incoherent, and randomly waved a hand. The creature ducked the feeble blow, then raised a gigantic paw and smacked the man hard across the head. The blow sent him sprawling; his head hit the nearby bin as he went down, and the scent of blood began to taint the air. He didn't move, but the contents of the bottle he'd clutched so fiercely emptied into the lane and joined the water running down the center drain. In the shadows of this dream, it looked like blood.

The creature raised a paw and slashed the man's tattered clothing. It peeled away with little resistance, exposing his emaciated body. The creature's tongue flickered out, lovingly tasting his flesh and marking the spots for its violation. I clenched fists that weren't real, fists that were aflame and yet held no heat and posed no threat to this thing, helplessly watching as the creature's needle-fine teeth pierced the stranger's body above his liver, then his heart, and consumed them both.

While the old guy was undoubtedly now dead, that wasn't the end—not of the dream or this creature's atrocities. Because this time, it gutted the stranger and ate his intestines.

And the dream forced me to watch.

Fire burned through me, around me. Dimly, I heard someone calling my name, but the dream went on relentlessly.

The creature finally rose, blood and flesh dripping from its teeth and mouth as it studied the street at the end of the lane. Its body began to shrink, until it was little more than the size of an ordinary house cat. Then, without a backward glance, it padded forward.

I followed and finally saw the clue I so desperately needed—the name of the lane.

The dream snapped and I woke. The fire that had burned through me in the dream burned around me in real time, but it was little more than an orb of fire and smoke that was restricted to my flesh and the bed immediately beneath me. Through the haze of its heat I saw Jackson; his expression was distant, distracted. He was controlling my flames, constraining them to the small bubble of heat that surrounded me.

I took a deep, shuddery breath, then sucked all the heat, all the fire, even the smoke, back inside. As it flushed through my limbs and lit my soul, my gaze met Jackson's.

"That," he said grimly, "was one hell of a dream you were having."

"It wasn't a dream." I scrambled out of bed and grabbed my clothes. "The creature's chosen its next victim. We need to get there and stop it."

"Finlay Lane runs between Little Lonsdale and Queen streets—it shouldn't take us that long to get there from here."

I glanced at him sharply as I shoved my boots on. "You shared the dream?"

"Only bits and pieces, and only once I started trying to control your flames." He rose and walked back into the living room, grabbing his coat and the car keys before heading for the door. "It seems the presence of fire strengthens our link."

Another interesting development—but not one I had the time to worry about right now. I picked up my coat and purse and followed him out. It was, according to the clock on the wall, three a.m. It seemed the creature had a liking for the extreme hours of the morning.

Once we'd left the hotel, we ran for the car. I didn't bother checking whether we were being watched or followed, because right now it didn't really matter. I had a bad feeling the dream's warning *hadn't* come with a lot of time to spare, so if we wanted to stop this thing, we had to get to that lane. *Fast.*

As Jackson started the car and blasted out of the parking lot, I pulled out my phone and dialed Sam's number, leaving him a message with the details and location of the possible murder. And hoped like hell he got there before us—even though I doubted that was even possible. It was the middle of the night, for fuck's sake, and he was most likely asleep.

Jackson roared through the empty streets, not even bothering to stop for red lights unless forced to by cars coming through the intersection. I bit my lip, hoping against hope that we'd get there in time to save the old guy, even as the deeper, more intuitive part of me said we probably wouldn't.

Jackson swung onto Queen Street and slammed on the brakes just outside the beautiful old building that housed the Registrar General's Office. But I didn't wait for the car to come to a complete halt; I didn't even wait for Jackson. I just scrambled out and ran across the road to the lane.

And there, feasting on the old man, was the creature.

It looked up as I appeared, and snarled, its bloodied teeth glowing white in the shadow-filled lane even as the rest of it began to disintegrate. I cursed and flung a lasso of fire, trying to ensnare the thing before it totally disappeared.

The stream of flames shot down the lane, turning night into day and momentarily halting the creature's transformation. It flung itself sideways and scrambled under the nearby Dumpster, embers trailing behind it. I raised a hand and made a sweeping motion. My flames swung around, but even as they did so, the creature's form became full embers and it bolted—not down the lane or back toward me but up the side of the building.

I swore, but there was no way on this earth I was going to let that thing escape me now. I became full flame and gave chase.

As ash and fire we raced up the side of the building, then over the parapet and onto the rooftop. The creature streaked through the cooling towers and antennas, its form barely visible. I flung another ball of fire and caught the tail end of its embers as it leapt onto the rooftop of the next building. Several cinders spun away from the bulk of the creature's body, flaring a vivid red before they flamed out and fell lifelessly downward. The creature squealed, the noise a weird mix of cat and dog, but it didn't stop.

And god, it was *fast*.

Even in spirit form I was having trouble keeping up with the thing. As we raced through the cooling towers of another rooftop and leapt across a small street, the creature was slowly drawing ahead, becoming more and more difficult to see. If I didn't do something soon, I'd lose it. I flung more fire, but this time the creature's embers parted, allowing the flames to pass right through the middle of it before reforming and racing on. I cursed but didn't recall the fiery orb; instead, I held it ahead of me, close to the creature's tail in an effort to keep the night at bay and to stop the creature from fully disappearing.

Two more rooftops flew by. Then, on the next one, the creature hit a flock of roosting pigeons. Feathers and birds flew everywhere, creating a cloud of gray and white impossible to see past. Several hit my flames and were instantly cindered, causing even greater panic among the rest of them. I slowed; I had no choice. By the time the birds swept upward, into the night sky, the creature was gone.

I swore again, long and loud, though anyone standing near me would have heard little more than a roar of flame. I became flesh and walked to the edge of the rooftop. Down below, lights twinkled, golden and bright in the night. Several cars passed by, but there was no sign of a cat or a dog or even a bat. And definitely no scent trail—not that any of my forms were all that proficient at following scents.

Maybe the damn thing had taken to the skies in the middle of the surging pigeons, though I couldn't imagine birds wanting to be anywhere near such a form. The bats here in Melbourne might be fruit bats and no threat to pigeons, but even they'd sense the differences in *this* particular one.

I blew out a frustrated breath and headed back across the rooftops, only switching to spirit form when necessary. Once I neared the lane that held the old man, I leaned over the parapet to check whether the coast was clear.

It wasn't. The police were there, blocking the entrance into the lane.

And Sam was also there.

So much for his being asleep.

Jackson was standing near the Queen Street end of the lane, talking to a thin, tall man with blondish hair. It took me a moment to realize it was Adam, the vampire who worked with Sam.

I pulled back. With so many people down in that lane, I couldn't risk shifting to spirit form; PIT and Sam might know what I was, but I wasn't about to advertise the fact to anyone else. I walked across to the other side of the building to check the lane's other exit and, unsurprisingly, discovered it blocked by a police car. The vehicle's blue and red lights cast an eerie glow across the colorful artwork, as well as on the two cops who stood beside the car, looking bored.

With little other choice, I turned and retraced my steps over the top of the other buildings, searching for somewhere I could get down to ground level without being seen. I was close to Elizabeth Street before I found another suitable lane. I became spirit and flowed down the side of the building, landing lightly and in human form. Only then did I make my way back to Finlay Lane.

Sam was squatting next to the victim, and Adam was farther down the lane, looking upward, but both glanced my way as I appeared. Adam nodded briefly and went back to studying the building—it was the one the creature had fled up—but Sam didn't even nod. He simply went back to inspecting the body.

I stopped beside Jackson—not only because I had no wish to foul the crime scene any more than I already had but because it was safer for my sanity and heart if I at least *tried* to keep some distance between me and Sam.

"When did they arrive?" I asked softly.

"About three minutes after you flamed up that building. Which, by the way, looked rather spectacular."

Sam and Adam had obviously been out on another job and nearby when my call came in. But the question was, why? Vampires might not need to sleep—it was more a habit left over from their time as humans than any real necessity—but Sam *was* human, and he'd worked the day shift. And while he'd always considered the job more important than his own health, surely even he couldn't run twenty-four/seven without a toll being taken. "And?"

"They've been okay. Polite even." A wry smile touched Jackson's lips. "Of course, that could all be because they obviously need our help on *this* particular case. I expect a return to regular hostility once this thing is caught."

"Emberly," Sam said, his voice every bit as soft as ours but carrying clearly across the night. "Come here. Miller, remain where you are."

I grimaced but obeyed. I stopped when I was still a few feet away from the old man and shoved my hands into my pockets. This close to him, the odd, almost chemical smell that had been on Hamberly was very evident here, as was the scent of blood. The old man hadn't yet been covered up, and the remains of his intestines spilled over his stomach and onto the road surface, a mix of grayish purple and red that gleamed wetly in the darkness.

I swallowed heavily and briefly looked away. "We were too late to save him. We tried."

"At least you got close enough to *give* chase, and that's more than we've been able to achieve." His gaze was on the dead man rather than me, and there was an odd mix of anger and sympathy in his expression. "The poor bastard was alive when the creature did this, wasn't he?"

I nodded, even though he was still staring at the old man. "But it knocked him out first. I'm not sure whether it was intentional or not, though, as he made a swipe at the creature when she was sniffing him."

Sam grunted and finally glanced at me. His face seemed thinner than it had earlier today, and there were deep shadows under his eyes. But that wasn't so surprising; there were probably shadows under *my* eyes, too, given the continual lack of sleep. But despite the shadows, the blue of his gaze was luminous in the darkness and oddly reminded me of the night we'd met. It had been in a nightclub rather than a seedy lane, but then, as now, it was this blue glow as much as the warmth and love of life so evident with it that had caught my attention.

Something flickered across his expression—memories, perhaps, of happier times. Then it faded, as did the warmth, and the night seemed somehow harsher.

"Did you uncover anything else about the creature?" His voice was cool and businesslike—not that *that* was surprising. "Anything that might help us catch it?"

I hesitated. "It's fast, and it can shape-shift on the run. And even in ember form, it can be hurt by flames—I cindered its tail two roofs over."

"How did it give you the slip? I would have thought you'd be pretty fast in flame form."

"I am, but I'm still a spirit, not Superwoman."

Amusement flared briefly in his eyes, warming them, warming me.

"How did you lose it?"

"The creature flew into a flock of pigeons and used them as cover to escape."

"Unfortunate."

"Frustrating, more likely. I was so damn *close*."

He grimaced and rose. "Welcome to my world."

No thanks; not when your world involves red cloaks and dangerous darkness. I crossed my arms and somehow kept the words inside. As Jackson had noted, Sam seemed to be in a rather good mood, and I didn't want to do or say anything to change that.

"So tell me exactly what you saw in the dream, and what happened when you and Jackson arrived here."

I did. Once I'd finished, he stepped over the victim

and walked over to the Dumpster. "So it went under about here?" He motioned to a point slightly off center.

I nodded. "My flames seemed to have prevented it from fully changing, so it was half cat and half ember. It was only once it hit the darkness under the bin that it fully shifted."

"Interesting." He squatted down and studied the ground intently. After a moment, he pulled a glove out of his pocket and carefully picked something up.

"If the creature's main form is embers, then this might just be a piece of it." He held up what looked like a large piece of sooty-colored skin.

"Do you think you can get DNA from it?"

"Possibly." He placed it into a plastic bag and sealed it. "We'll search the entire area, as well as that rooftop where you flamed it. If we can pin down what we're looking for, it might make the job of finding it easier."

"If it's an Aswang, it also has a human day form. It's not going to be easy to track."

His gaze came to mine again. "What makes you think it's an Aswang?"

"Google." I half smiled. "It seemed the best fit for what we know of the creature so far."

"It's certainly one of the possibilities." He glanced down at the old guy again, and the wave of anger that rose from him was so fierce, it momentarily snatched my breath. "We will find it, and we *will* stop it."

It was softly said, and very much a promise to the dead. I didn't say anything, just watched him. He might be completely different from the man I'd fallen in love with, but when the darkness within him was being held at bay, I could still see glimmers of who he'd been.

And they just made me wish . . . I chopped the thought off abruptly. *Move on,* I told myself fiercely. *Just get over it and move on.*

Easy to think. Harder to do.

"Do you need me to make a statement or anything?" I asked.

He shook his head. "Not in this particular case."

I frowned. "Why not?"

"Because the regular cops weren't called in to investigate."

"But they're here now, guarding the lane entrances."

"And that's *all* they're doing. As I've said before, PIT works under very different laws—and it's not as if the things we hunt were going to get their day in court, anyway."

Meaning they really *were* a kill squad. But what was even more chilling was that the government actually deemed them necessary. Were things really that bad, or was it more a case of prevention being better than a cure? Were PIT and its powers a warning to the nonhuman world that there were boundaries beyond which they should not step? That there *would* be serious consequences for those who did?

"So, we can go?"

He glanced past me for a moment, and then nodded. "We know where to find you if need be."

"Thanks." I hesitated, and added in a softer tone, "Good night."

"Night, Em."

It was absently said and held little in the way of

emotion. His attention had already returned to the body and clue seeking. A wry smile twisted my lips. Why on earth had I expected anything else?

I turned and walked away. This time, I didn't feel the weight of Sam's gaze between my shoulder blades. Didn't feel much at all, really, beyond sadness. Mine, not his.

Jackson fell in step beside me and hooked his arm through mine. It was only once we were on our way back to the hotel that he said, "I didn't get much information out of Adam. I'm supposing you didn't do much better with Sam?"

"No." I rubbed my eyes wearily. "And the trouble is, the creature now knows I'm after it."

"Just as it'll be aware that the police and PIT are after it. That hasn't stopped it from hunting. I doubt tonight will, either."

"It might be better if it *did*," I muttered. "At least it would give us more time to find it before it decides to kill someone else."

"You keep using this 'we' word," Jackson noted. "Even as you keep denying the desire to go after it."

"I can't help that desire—it's inbuilt. Believe me, I've tried so many times over the centuries to ignore the dreams and let fate take its course, but I just can't." I shrugged. "But I also can't chase what can't be found, so unless I get another dream showing me either this thing's day form or its den, then it's PIT's problem, not ours. Did you load the break program onto the laptop?"

He acknowledged the change of topic with a wry smile. "Yes. It's working as we speak."

"How long will it take?"

He shrugged. "Anything from a couple of hours to days or even weeks. It generally depends on the complexity of the numerical code."

"I can't imagine a four-digit phone code would be too complex."

"No. We'll probably be able to access the information being stored on the phone sometime in the next twenty-four hours."

I grunted. "In the meantime, maybe we'd better start looking for Rosen."

"Not tonight, we're not." The gaze he cast my way was etched with concern. "You're pale and drawn, Emberly. You need to sleep."

"What I need is fire and heat more than sleep." I was tired, there was no doubting that, but the chase across the rooftop had also depleted my energy stores, and while I was nowhere near exhaustion, I really didn't want to push myself into that state. Not with everything that was currently going on.

"Then we'll swing by the furnace and you can top up." He did an abrupt U-turn and headed back into the city. "I want to grab a couple of things from the office anyway."

I raised my eyebrows. "You're not coming in with me?"

"That will only lead to sex, and while I wouldn't mind, I really think now is not the time."

"Good god, a Fae backing away from the possibility of sex? You really *are* sick!"

He chuckled softly. "No, I'm just momentarily being sensible. Don't expect it to happen too often."

"I should hope not. I'm not sure I could cope with a sensible partner."

It didn't take us long to drive to the office. As before, Jackson parked around the back, out of sight, then stopped the car and handed me the key to the rear roller door.

I climbed out and headed in. The heat emanating from the fire's coal was a siren's call that guided me through the darkness. I stopped beside the furnace and reached for it, calling to the heat within the coals. Fire immediately answered, and fingers of flame leapt upward and enveloped my hand. It was a caress that had anticipation shivering through me. I brought the fire to full life and threw my hands and head back, calling it to me. But I didn't immediately feed, instead allowing the flames to play around me for several minutes, enjoying the fierceness of them, the rush of heat, energy, and pleasure that came with them. Then I sighed and somewhat regretfully drew them deep within.

With my skin still glowing with heat, I banked the fire and headed back to the car.

"Better?" Jackson asked, starting up the vehicle and heading off again once I was belted in.

"Much." I touched his leg and his muscles jumped, as if stung by fire. "Thank you."

His smile was wry. "You're welcome. But if you don't remove your hand, I'm going to stop the car, rip this seat belt off, and jump you."

I grinned but did as he bid. "Not only sick, but holding no self-control. Shameful, really."

"Woman, you have no idea just how *much* control I'm asserting right now." Despite his stern tone, amuse-

ment danced around his lips. "You're practically glowing with heat and desire, and that's something few Fae
can resist."

"Ah. Sorry."

"Don't be. Just be prepared for our next lovemaking
session to be short and sharp."

I laughed and glanced at the side window as we
swung onto Stanley Street. A few cars were parked in
the center strip, but there was little sign of activity. It
was too early for any of the other businesses to be open,
and the few houses scattered along the street were dark
and silent.

Jackson pulled up in front of his building and
climbed out. I did the same and headed for the stairs—
only to stop abruptly halfway up the steps.

The damn door was open again.

Jackson did a quick sideways step to avoid cannon-
ing into me. "What's wrong?"

I didn't answer, just motioned to the door. He swore
softly, then moved around me and cautiously pushed
the door open . . .

To reveal Rosen, his throat cut and splayed out like
a sacrifice, lying in the middle of the floor.

CHAPTER 9

"Oh fuck," Jackson said. "This is all we need."

"I'm guessing it's not exactly what *he* needed, either."

I ducked under Jackson's arm but didn't immediately enter the room. Except for Rosen, the place was exactly as I'd left it—half cleaned up, with piles of paper sitting on the desks and most of the ransacked cabinets still open and empty of files.

Rosen himself was wearing different clothes from those he'd worn yesterday, but they didn't look brand-new, so he'd probably gone home to change. What he'd intended to do after that—whether it was to go to work or back to the hotel—was something we'd now never know.

Just as we'd never know what additional information he might have told us.

There was a gaping wound across his neck, as well as cuts and bruising around his face and on his hands. He certainly *hadn't* gone meekly to his death this time.

"Call PIT," Jackson said. "I want to get a closer look at the body."

"Why?" I pulled my phone out and hit Sam's number again.

"Because he wasn't killed here, and I think he's clutching something in his left hand."

I frowned and looked. Though it was barely visible through his clenched fingers, Rosen definitely held something small and white in his hand.

Sam's message service came up, so I detailed what had happened, then followed Jackson. I stopped on the other side of Rosen's body and shoved my hands into my pockets. This close, the wound on his neck looked anything but neat.

A shiver went through me, chased by horror. I'd seen wounds like this before. And, in the past, experienced one.

Rosen's throat had been ripped open by a vampire rather than any sort of man-made weapon—and it *hadn't* happened here. There would have been a massive spurt of blood after this sort of attack, and not even a vampire could have sucked away all evidence of it.

Jackson pulled gloves out of a nearby drawer. Then, once they were on, he squatted beside Rosen's hand and carefully pried his fingers apart, revealing a small square of paper.

Jackson carefully unfolded it. His expression, as he read it, grew even grimmer.

"And the shit," he said softly, "just hit the fan."

I frowned. "Why? What does it say?"

He didn't answer; he just offered me the note. I hastily put on some gloves, then accepted it.

It was both a street address and a warning. The street was in Brooklyn—right in the very heart of red-cloak territory, and a place I was already familiar with—which in itself was scary enough. But it was the warning that made the hair on the back of my neck stand on end and my blood freeze.

This time, we play by my rules, not yours. You will meet me at the above address at midnight on the twenty-fourth. You will not contact PIT, and you will come here alone. If you do not, Rory will suffer as Rosen suffered, only the weapon of choice will not be the teeth of a vampire but the talons of a cloak. He will, with the help of magic to curtail his flames and his ability to burn the virus from his system, become one of us. We both know that is a fate you would not wish and might not even survive.

It wasn't signed. It didn't need to be. This letter hadn't come from the vampires. It had come from the figure I'd spotted in the forest—the gray-cowled man who controlled the red cloaks. The one who had said, "You will yet be mine."

He was obviously intent on keeping his word.

"Fuck," I whispered. "They know about Rory." But, scarier still, he'd obviously witnessed how I'd saved Jackson and now knew that to infect us, all he had to do was stop us from attaining flame form.

"Yes." Jackson's tone was as grim as mine was fearful.

"But *how*? The only person I've told about Rory's importance in my life is you—" I stopped, a sick feeling twisting my gut.

"PIT knows, don't they?" Jackson guessed.

"Through Rory. He told Sam that he was a necessity in my life and that there could be no me if there was no him."

"So either Sam is connected to the sindicati and the gray cloak, or PIT has a mole in its organization."

"Sam may have changed over the years since our breakup, but he's not sindicati. I'd bet my life on it."

"And you just might be."

"It's *not* him." I thrust to my feet. "I have to ring Rory."

Jackson shoved the note into his pocket. "I'll study the security tapes and see if there's anything there. I dare say PIT will take them once they arrive."

I nodded and walked back to the front door, studying the night as I dialed Rory's number. The phone rang and rang, and my fear ramped up, until I could barely even breathe.

"Hello?" he said eventually, his voice groggy with sleep. "Em, what's wrong?"

I released the breath I'd been holding in a huge whoosh. "Oh thank *god*, you're okay."

In the background, bedsheets rustled, and a soft voice murmured something I couldn't quite catch. He replied just as softly and, after a moment, I heard footsteps, then the click of a door closing.

"What's up?" His voice was tense, worried.

"Rosen's been murdered, and whoever did it left a note threatening to make you a red cloak." I paused, and swallowed. "It could only have come from the man I spotted in the forest. The man cloaked in gray."

He swore. "Sam is the only person who knows how necessary we are to each other and, as much as the bastard might hate me, I can't believe he'd betray you like that."

"He wouldn't, but PIT is a different matter. There's obviously a mole in the organization."

"It's certainly the most logical explanation, though I doubt even Sam would have reported something like that."

"Well, someone uncovered the information, so if not Sam or Jackson, then who?"

"I don't know. It's not information I've handed out, not even to Rosie."

Rosie was a widow who worked at the fire station alongside Rory, and the two of them had struck up a "friends with benefits" relationship a few years ago.

"Regardless of how they got the information, you need to disappear. Take leave from work as of now—you've got plenty of it up your sleeve."

He was silent for a moment, then sighed. "Fine. But I'm not leaving you and Jackson alone to handle this. If they want you, they're going to have to come through me to get you."

"Rory—"

"No," he cut in, his tone sharp. "They've dragged me into this, Em, so let them pay the price. We hunt them, and we end this; they've given us little other choice."

I scrubbed a hand across my eyes. He was basically echoing what I'd said to Jackson not so long ago, but his intentions were far bloodier than mine had been.

And I had a bad feeling the price we would pay might be higher than either of us would wish.

But, as he'd said, what other choice did we now have?

"Fine," I said. "We're going to be stuck at the office

until PIT gets here. Why don't you head to the hotel we're staying at and wait for us there?"

"Will do."

"And, Rory? Be careful. Don't go home."

"I won't. I have clothes here at Rosie's, and neither Sam nor PIT should be aware of her presence in my life. We've kept our relationship quiet at the station, as they tend to frown on that sort of thing."

I hoped he was right, but I feared he wasn't. But I didn't say anything, just hung up and walked over to the desk that held the security monitors. I leaned on Jackson's shoulder and studied the black-and-white images being fast-forwarded. They showed nothing more than an unchanging landscape of mess and a firmly closed front door.

"Anything?" There obviously wasn't, but there was always a chance I might have missed something when I was talking to Rory.

"Not yet."

The unchanging officescape rolled on for several more minutes, until, at twelve forty-eight, the screen finally revealed a shot of the front door opening. Jackson immediately hit PLAY, and the tape rolled on at normal speed. Two figures walked into the room, both clad in black and wearing masks. A weird sense of déjà vu hit me as I watched them carefully search the ground floor. One moved upstairs but reappeared quickly enough; then he and the other man moved back to the door, opening it wider before standing to either side.

Two more black-clad figures came in, Rosen held between them with his throat ripped open. Given we'd spotted no bloodstains between the door and where the two men placed him, he'd obviously already been drained of blood. They placed Rosen's body on the floor; then all four walked out.

"So the note was already in his hand when he was carried in," I said.

"They'd know that we'd have to call in PIT, so they wouldn't have wanted *that* caught on-screen." He sped up the tape again. "We'd better erase all evidence of our finding it."

"Which will only alert PIT that we've found something."

"Yes, but better that than their stopping us from going to that meeting—or worse, turning up themselves."

I bit my lip. "Actually, *that* may be the most logical course of action."

"Logical maybe, but practical? Not so much." He swung around to face me. "If PIT *does* have a leak in its organization, then whoever is behind that note—be it the gray cloak, a sindicati faction, or both—will be warned. And that'll only mean the next time they hit us, it'll be full force and without warning."

I scrubbed a hand across my eyes. "I know, but—"

"You said it yourself earlier," he cut in. "Our best option now is to bring the fight to them."

"But I didn't actually mean going to war with them!"

"I know, and maybe it won't come to that. Maybe we can talk some common sense into these people."

I snorted. "Yeah, talk sense into insane pseudo vamps and the man who controls them. Like *that's* going to happen."

"Whoever did *this*"—Jackson made a sharp motion

toward Rosen's body—"might *not* be the faction working with the crazies, in which case, we have a chance—"

"Stop the tape!" Even as I said it, I dove past him and hit the PAUSE button.

The tape froze on the image of a man walking into the room nine minutes after Rosen had been deposited in our office. Unlike those others, he wore neither black nor a mask, and he was also looking directly at the camera. He was tall, immaculately dressed, with gray hair and old-fashioned rimmed glasses perched precariously at the end of his long, somewhat regal nose.

And I knew him.

"Who is it?" Jackson asked.

"That," I said softly, "just happens to be the elusive Professor Heaton."

"The vamp who chased you at the Chase Foundation?"

"Yes." And he obviously still wanted me, though for what I had no idea. But it was damn scary that he still seemed fixated on me.

"He obviously has no fear of being recognized." Jackson hit the PLAY button. "He knew the camera was there, because the first thing he did when he walked in was look at it."

"Which also means he has no fear of being traced."

On the screen, Heaton walked across the room and squatted beside Rosen's body. Like us, he retrieved a pair of gloves, then carefully plucked the note from Rosen's hand, read it, and placed it back.

"So whoever he is, he knows about the meeting." Jackson briefly froze the image and hit the PRINT button. A second later, the printer booted up.

"Which could be good or bad, depending on who

he's working for." I walked across the room to collect the image printout.

"If you ask me, he doesn't actually look the type to be working for *anyone*."

No, he didn't. And in the brief time I'd been in his presence, he'd certainly given off the vibe of a leader rather than a follower. "I wonder if Rawlings would be able to tell us who he is."

"I'm sure he could, if the fee was right."

I folded the photo and shoved it into my pocket. "Well, considering grabbing me only cost a grand, I can't imagine selling info on the sindicati, or whoever Heaton is, would cost much more."

"And in that, you might be wrong. If he tells us who that man is, he might well be placing himself in the firing line."

"He seemed eager enough to sell out Morretti."

"Morretti might not have been as powerful as this fellow."

"According to Amanda's notes, he was one of the four generals who ran the sindicati's day-to-day operations. You can't get much higher than that."

"Unless, of course, we're talking about the mysterious council that apparently rules them all."

"I seriously doubt any of *them* would lower themselves to interview anyone, even if they *did* know the whereabouts of the missing research notes."

"You might be right." Jackson shrugged. "What's Rory going to do?"

"Get involved." I grimaced and rubbed the back of my neck. Instinct was screaming it was a bad idea, but there'd be no dissuading him now that his mind was made up. I'd learned very early on in our relationship that while he was slow to anger, once he *was* there, watch out. By sending us this note, the gray cloak had just pushed one button too many.

"That may not be a great idea. If the worst happens—"

"I'm well aware of the damn cost, Jackson," I snapped. "And so is Rory. He just doesn't fucking care in this particular case."

Which wasn't true and it wasn't fair—not to Rory, and not to Jackson. I took a deep breath and waved a hand. "Sorry."

He looked more amused than taken aback. "So the redhead *does* have a temper. Good to know."

I smiled reluctantly. "You'll be pleased to know she doesn't fire up often."

"Sad if true," he drawled. "I found the flash of anger rather attractive."

My smile grew. "Let's be honest here—you'd find the flash of *anything* rather attractive."

"Very true."

The sound of sirens began to invade the silence. I took a deep breath that did little to calm the nerves or the tension riding me, then placed a hand on Jackson's shoulder. "I'll go meet Sam. You erase."

"I'll need five minutes. Delay them if you can."

"Another thing I doubt will happen. Just hurry."

I stripped my gloves off and shoved them into my pockets as I walked across to the door. Dawn was beginning to break across the night sky, its pale pink fingers contrasting sharply against the star-sprinkled black. The air was crisp and rich with the promise of daylight and heat, and I hoped like hell that I'd live long enough to feel the wash of it through my lungs for many more years.

A black car appeared at the far end of the street, its tires squealing as the driver took the corner too fast. "PIT just turned up."

"Just a few minutes more," Jackson replied, "and we're safe."

The black car halted in front of our building; a second later, Sam and Adam climbed out.

"PIT *has* got other investigators," I commented, crossing my arms. "So why do they keep sending you two out?"

Adam walked around to the trunk, but Sam came toward me, stopping on the step two below mine. The shadows in his eyes were even more disconcerting when we were basically eyeballing each other.

"Because I'm lead investigator on the ongoing red cloak and missing research investigation."

"Are you also lead investigator on the Aswang problem? And do PIT expect their operatives to work twenty-four/seven?"

"No, I'm not, and yes, if necessary." He practically growled the answer. "Now, kindly stop blocking the doorway and let us in."

I raised an eyebrow, crossed mental fingers that Jackson had finished erasing files, and then stepped to one side, grandly waving him in. "Be my guest."

He brushed past me. His body was oddly cool— almost as cool as Adam, who went by a minute later, carrying several bags.

I followed them in. Jackson was at the back at the

room, making coffee, but his gaze immediately met mine and a slight smile touched his lips. Relief spun through me. As much as I wanted to involve PIT in tomorrow night's meeting, Jackson was right. We couldn't risk their being warned through whoever was leaking information.

"Would you gentlemen like a cup of coffee?" Jackson said, raising one of the two mugs he held.

"No, thanks." Sam stopped close to Rosen's body while Adam began setting up equipment. "Tell us what happened."

I did so. He grunted and pulled on a set of gloves. "You haven't touched or moved the body?"

"No." I gave Jackson a smile of thanks as he handed me a mug of tea. "I really don't understand why he was left here like this."

Sam glanced up. His expression gave little away, but I had an odd feeling he didn't believe *that* particular statement. "There was nothing left with the body? A warning of some kind?"

"Nothing." I shrugged. "Maybe it was some sort of payback for rescuing his ass yesterday."

"Highly doubtful," Adam commented. He was setting up some sort of electronic equipment, but the brief gaze he cast our way was every bit as skeptical as the looks I was getting from Sam.

"Have you checked the security tapes?" he asked.

"Yes," Jackson said. "They come in at twelve forty-eight. It reveals them bringing Rosen's body, but the system was shut down after that, so it's not of much use."

Sam continued to study the two of us. "Did you recognize any of them?"

"They were in black and wearing masks," I said. "So no."

Sam glanced at Adam. "Interesting."

"Why?" I said.

A brief smile touched Sam's lips, though it held little humor. "*That* is of no concern of yours."

"Actually, it *is*." Jackson motioned toward Rosen. "This was obviously meant to be a warning—and it's one we need to understand."

"If it's a warning, then I daresay it's to step away from your current investigations." Adam pressed a button on the recorder he'd set up, then put on some gloves and squatted beside Rosen's body. "Something you'd no doubt be forced into anyway now that the man who employed you is dead."

"Rosen Pharmaceuticals is more than one man," Jackson said. "And I have no doubt his heirs will want the research found just as much as Rosen himself did."

Sam's gaze sharpened. "Rosen believed there was still research missing?"

I hesitated. "He believed Wilson had backup, yes. But he had no idea where that might be."

"And before you get all dark and threatening," Jackson added, "we have no leads as to its location, if indeed it *does* exist. My initial brief was to uncover who stole his notes, not find the backup ones."

Sam's disbelief was clearly evident even if his expression continued to give little away. But at least in *this* particular instance, we were telling the truth. And maybe he sensed that, because, after a moment, he grunted and looked back down at Rosen.

"We'll need to see those tapes."

"Help yourself. The control panel is on the desk behind you, and there's no password needed."

"Meaning the security system in this place isn't actually so secure?" Adam shook his head. "Not wise, given the current situation."

"Up until the current situation, I didn't *need* the system to be secure. And it's not like private investigators find the body of their client splayed out in the middle of their office all too often."

No one could miss the sarcasm in Jackson's voice, but neither man reacted to it. There wasn't even a flash of the deeper darkness in Sam's eyes. Maybe the tiredness so evident in his face was forcing *that* into retreat as well.

"You might as well go," Sam said. "We know where to contact you if we have further questions."

Jackson gave me a sharp glance, and it didn't take a genius to realize why. If Sam knew where we were, whoever was leaking the information from PIT probably did, too.

And I'd just sent Rory there. *Fuck.*

"Am I able to go upstairs and collect some things first?" Jackson's hand slid over mine and squeezed lightly as he spoke.

It was meant to be reassuring, but it didn't do a whole lot to ease the tension and fear that had ramped up another couple of notches. I needed to get out of here and call Rory. While I doubted the gray cloak or his allies would make a move on him before the meeting tomorrow night, it was better if we didn't take chances from now on.

Sam's gaze flickered briefly downward. He hadn't missed Jackson's reassurance attempt; what he thought of it was anyone's guess. "Did the intruders go up there?"

"Yes, but only to double-check no one was home," I said. "They weren't up there long enough to do anything."

"Then you can go up."

Jackson squeezed my hand again, then put his coffee down and quickly headed upstairs. I finished my tea and waited. Sam and Adam continued their investigation, making comments as they went. If they suspected Rosen had been holding something, they made no mention of it.

But then, if they'd suspected *that*, I doubt they'd be letting us walk. Not without forcing us to hand it over.

Jackson reappeared, several large carryalls slung over his shoulder as he clattered down the metal steps and headed for the door. I pushed away from the desk and followed.

But just as we reached the door, Sam said, "If you two are withholding information, there will be hell to pay."

I glanced over my shoulder and met his gaze evenly. "Everything we know about Rosen's death, we've told you."

"I wasn't referring to Rosen's death."

"Then I can't help you, because I have no idea what

you think we might be withholding." I motioned to the door. "Make sure the place is locked up when you're finished."

And with that, I left. Jackson popped our rental's trunk open, threw the two carryalls in, then slammed it shut again. I climbed into the passenger side and pulled my phone out of my purse again.

"You'd better ring Rory," he said, climbing in without actually looking at me.

"One step ahead." I flashed the phone his way. "Only trouble is, I need a location to give him."

Jackson sucked in a breath. "I have plenty of people who'd willingly give us beds, but I don't want to drag them into this sort of situation. It's too much of a risk."

That it was. "We're going to have to presume PIT knows what alias you're using by now, and that means everyone else just might, too. It makes using hotels a somewhat precarious proposition."

He pulled out of the parking space, the rear tires squealing. "I'll stop at the nearest ATM and grab some cash. From now on in, that's probably our best option; it's far harder to trace."

"Agreed, but how many hotels take cash and ask no questions these days?"

"There are a few." The glance he gave me was one of distaste. "But some of them are far from great places to be."

"Trust me, they couldn't be any worse than some of the places I've stayed at over the centuries." I hesitated, frowning. "And wouldn't the sindicati expect us to go to a dive in a seedy part of town? It might be better to do the opposite."

A smile touched his lips and momentarily lifted the concern. "It might, except that most upmarket hotels want photo ID if the customer is paying by cash."

I swore softly. "Where, then?"

"Let's try the Journey Man in Collingwood. It's a backpackers' hostel, but it also has several longer-term, self-catering rentals out the back."

"We can pay cash, no questions asked?"

He nodded. "I used it once in an undercover op. As I said, it's pretty basic, but the bedding is clean even if the shower is not."

"One out of two isn't bad."

I dialed Rory's number. He answered almost immediately. "What's up?"

In the background, I could hear people talking as well as someone announcing the arrival of a train. I quickly told him what had happened, and then asked him to meet us at the Journey Man instead.

"I'm currently at Flinders Street, so I'll just change platforms and meet you there."

"I'll text the room number when we have it."

"No prob."

He hung up. I shoved my phone away, then said, "What did you have in those bags beside clothes? There was a decidedly large clunk as you put them down."

He grinned. "I had to go rescue a few of my toys, just in case PIT uncovered them."

I gave him a long look. "You have a stash of guns in your office *as well* as in your car?"

"Of course. You never know when you're going to find yourself in need of one."

"But haven't Fae got an aversion to too much metal?"

"Only cold-forged iron. Anything else doesn't count, including guns, which are generally made from a mix of alloys and steel." He flashed me another grin. "But in this case, some of them are plastic."

That raised my eyebrows. "Plastic?"

"The latest in weapon hardware. These, however, are more of the water variety."

I blinked. "I don't suppose they come loaded with holy water?"

"Well, no, because that would just leak out over time and be wasteful. Holy water is very expensive to source and buy, let me tell you."

"And here I was thinking holy water was simply fresh still water consecrated by a priest."

"It is, but they do tend to frown on its being used for anything other than religious purposes. Hence its becoming a black market item—especially since vampires and werewolves came out in the open." He swung to the left side of the road and halted in front of an ATM. "Won't be a moment."

He jumped out and raced over to the machine. Within minutes, he was back in the car, with a large amount of cash, and we were moving on.

It didn't take us that long to drive over to Collingwood. The Journey Man was actually a two-story pub on Johnston Street. Its exterior was basic—the concrete walls were an odd green-gray color, and the ground-floor windows had been painted black. Though they were large, each one was made up of at least twelve smaller panes, many of which had obviously been broken over the years and replaced by different-colored glass. The upper floor had smaller sash windows in serious need of repainting. Several were open, allowing the curtains to spill out; tattered red and green flags fluttered limply in the breeze. The place looked shabby and cheap—exactly what Jackson had said it was.

He swung onto Harmsworth Street and found a parking spot about halfway down. "I'll go organize a room. Stay here."

He didn't wait for an answer; he just jumped out and headed in. I scanned the area, seeing little in the way of life across the mix of light industrial buildings and newer housing developments that filled the street. But then, dawn was still busy coloring the night sky; only the very eager would be up this early on a weekend.

Jackson reappeared a few minutes later and opened my door. "We have a back apartment on a week-by-week basis, cash up front, no questions asked."

I climbed out and gave the building a dubious glance. "I'm hoping we're not going to be here for a week, let alone more than that."

"Well, so am I, but better safe than sorry." He handed me the two bags from the trunk and a set of keys. "It's 1B, first on the right just through that gateway."

The gate he motioned toward was as battered and in desperate need of painting as the rest of the place. "Where are you going?"

"To dump the car elsewhere."

"That's going to make getting around awfully difficult."

His grin flashed over the top of the vehicle. "I've arranged another."

"Don't tell me—the hostel's owner has one available on a cash basis and no questions asked."

"Well, he's the manager rather than the owner, but otherwise, yes. And at least we won't run the risk of it being recognized."

The vehicle might not be, but we undoubtedly would. But all I said was, "Be careful."

"You, too." He jumped in the car and headed off. I hefted the bags over my shoulder and went through the decrepit-looking gate. Our apartment—though *that* was altogether too grand a name for something that looked to be little bigger than a shoe box—was squeezed into a small rear courtyard that contained several other tiny buildings. It was two-story, with two windows on either side of the door and three on the top level. Fly screens that had definitely seen better days covered all the windows, and there was also a security door that looked to have been kicked in more than once, if the dents and bent metal in its middle section were anything to go by.

I unlocked the screen door, then the main door, and somewhat warily entered. It was little more than one room that contained a small kitchen and living area, but the furniture was functional and tidy, and the air smelled fresh and clean. I headed up the stairs at the back of the room. The next level had a bathroom and a bedroom containing two double bunk beds. But again, it was clean and functional, even if the walls were in desperate need of a fresh coat of paint.

I dumped the bags on one of the bunks, then got out my phone and sent Rory the room number. *Be there in ten,* he sent back.

I headed back downstairs, found the kettle and a surprisingly good supply of coffee and tea bags, and made myself a cup. Eight minutes later, there was a soft knock at the door. I put my mug down and walked across to check the peephole. Rory smiled back at me.

"You're looking decidedly chipper for someone who just received a death threat," I said as I opened the door.

"I found pizza." He held up several boxes. "And it's not like we've never received death threats before."

I locked the door and followed him across to the small table. "But this is decidedly different from those others, because he's not actually threatening to kill you. And I have no desire to uncover what becoming one of them would do to us both."

"Nor do I." He put the pizza on the table, then caught my hand and drew me into his embrace. "It'll be okay, Em. We'll figure something out."

I closed my eyes and rested my cheek against his chest, enjoying the momentary sanctuary of his arms. "It's just that I have this really bad feeling it's all going to go to hell."

"Which you've had before, and often nothing has come of it." He kissed the top of my head, then pulled back. "Where is the third member of our hunting party?"

"Out hiding the rental car."

"Ah. Good idea." He flipped open the pizza boxes, revealing Hawaiian and barbecued chicken—my two favorites. "But if he doesn't hurry, he's going to miss out."

I snorted softly and helped myself to a slice of the chicken. Though it was early in the morning, I was famished. The furnace may have fueled my soul, but the flesh needed sustenance as well.

Jackson returned fifteen minutes later. He sniffed the air as I unlocked the door and let him in, and he said, "Pizza. The breakfast of champions."

"My sentiments exactly," Rory stated. "And there's even some left."

"Excellent." He grabbed a slice of the Hawaiian and sat down. "The car's stashed over near Melbourne Uni. We'll retrieve it once all this is over."

If any of us are still alive when it's all over, I wanted to say. I headed over to the kitchen to make another round of coffee and tea instead.

Jackson's gaze followed me, making me wonder if he'd caught *that* particular thought. "And I bought this."

He retrieved something from his pocket and placed it on the table. It was a map of Greater Melbourne.

"Why not just use the phones?" I picked up the three mugs and headed back to the table. "Google's street view will be a whole lot more useful when it comes to showing us the layout and streetscape."

"Yes, but it's easier to plot our moves with something much larger." Rory shifted the pizza boxes and unfolded the map.

The part of Brooklyn that the red cloaks had apparently taken over was sandwiched between the West Gate Freeway and Geelong Road, with Millers Road and Grieve Parade being the other boundaries. Or, at least, they were the roads that signified the no-go section.

"Here's where I'm supposed to meet them." I

pointed to the area on the map. "It also happens to be the same area where I rescued Sam."

Both men glanced up sharply. "That can't be a coincidence."

"No, I don't think it is." I wrapped both hands around my mug in an effort to warm them, but it didn't do much to ease the chill running through me. "The gray-cloaked stranger seems to hold a whole lot of hatred for Sam."

Jackson leaned back in his chair. "But why go from attempting to kill him to attempting to kill you?"

"Maybe he's aware of Em's past relationship with Sam. Maybe he presumes killing her will affect Sam more than his own death."

"Dying is a pretty permanent result," Jackson noted drily. "It'd certainly affect anyone at the wrong end of it."

A smile twisted Rory's lips. "You know what I mean."

"I do. But why would this gray cloak think Sam still harbors feelings after five years?"

"He can't. He's probably just presuming." I took a sip of tea.

Rory didn't look convinced. "That doesn't explain the whole 'He will not get you' statement."

"No." Jackson's gaze met mine as he grabbed another slice of pizza. "Maybe that's something you need to ask this person tomorrow night."

"I'm not asking him anything. I'm going to cinder his ass to hell and back, and make the world a safer place."

"If he was in the forest, he's aware of your capabilities," Rory said. "I doubt he'll expose himself to such a risk."

"Which doesn't negate the fact that he will be ash if I'm given the slightest chance."

Rory grinned at me. "I do so love it when you get fired up."

I made a face at him. "So, what's the plan?"

Jackson glanced at Rory. "Do you know how to use a long-distance rifle?"

"It's been a while, and the technology has undoubtedly changed, but I should be able to get the hang of it quickly enough."

"Then the plan is, we head to a distant rooftop and shoot the fuckers Em doesn't burn."

"Sounds good to me."

"Emberly?" Jackson glanced at me, eyebrows raised.

"I'll be in the street confronting them. As long as you've got my back and you don't get hurt, I'm happy." I contemplated the map for a minute, trying to remember the street and the buildings around it and how many hiding spaces there were—for me as much as them. "Getting in is going to be the problem. Both of you are somewhat recognizable, even from a distance."

"Which is why we will be wearing disguises. The gray cloak may have his troops out on watch, but from what I've seen of them, they're not the sharpest tools in the shed."

They didn't have to be. Not if theories were true, and they were working on some sort of hive mentality. The gray cloak would know what they knew, see what they saw.

"Besides," Rory added, "it would probably be better

if we went in before dusk. The red cloaks may be active and on watch, but I doubt they'll be expecting anyone to enter that place before night settles in."

"I wouldn't bet on that."

"Neither would I," Jackson agreed. "But they haven't got infinite resources yet—not if what Sam has said about the number of infections is true. They can't watch every street in and out of that place; not without leaving the meeting point short."

It did make sense that they'd put most of their effort into ensuring I couldn't escape the meet zone. The gray cloak had witnessed what I was capable of in the forest, and he knew that when it came to close-up fighting, it was going to take numbers to outlast me.

But that also meant he'd know long-range options might need to be employed as well.

"Which is a possibility we'll need to be aware of once we're up there," Jackson said.

Rory glanced at the two of us, frowning slightly. "I get the feeling I just missed part of the conversation."

"You did." I briefly explained what had happened in the forest after Jackson had been wounded by the red cloaks, and the subsequent effects that were now beginning to appear.

"Wow," Rory said. "That was one hell of a risk you both took."

"Yes, but the worst thing that could have happened was me being consumed by Em's fire." Jackson shrugged. "I'd rather death than life as a red cloak."

"Who wouldn't?" Rory contemplated us for a second. "It'll be interesting to see how deep the connection goes, and what it means physiology-wise."

I blinked. "My physiology hasn't changed. You'd know it if it had."

"Yours hasn't, but Jackson's *has*. He became, however briefly, a being of fire. He wasn't full spirit, but he was no longer just flesh. There *will* be greater changes, even if they're not evident just yet."

Jackson scraped a hand across his jaw. It sounded like sandpaper being rubbed across a rough surface. "I'm already able to bring fire to life without a source being near. What else could there be?"

"*That* is the million-dollar question." Rory didn't look overly concerned, but then, it could take months—even years—for the full consequences to be known. "But if threads of our fire have been left in your being by the merging, then it is also possible you will have gained the drawbacks. Our fire comes from our being—our very soul—and we can be drained to the point of death if we are unwary."

"As can a fire Fae who is remiss in keeping close to his element." Jackson held up a hand, halting Rory before he could actually say anything. "I know, and I'll be careful. But until we know the full result of the merging, conjecture is pointless." He tapped the map gently. "For now, let's just worry about getting through tonight."

Which was a goal I could totally get behind. "It might be better if you reveal your presence tonight only if absolutely necessary. Let me take out whatever cloaks I can with fire—including the gray cloak if he's there—"

"Oh, he'll be there," Jackson said, his tone grim. "He hasn't missed any of the fun so far, and I doubt he'll miss this when it's on his home turf."

"Agreed, but for safety's sake, it's better if you're backup rather than a first assault. Besides, I doubt the bastard will make an appearance until the odds are stacked in his favor anyway."

"All of which makes sense," Rory commented. "But the minute I even *sense* you're in trouble, we start firing." He glanced at Jackson, who nodded in agreement.

"Which is perfectly fine by me." And I hoped that by that point the cloaks would be too busy trying to subdue me to send anyone looking for them.

Rory pulled out his phone and brought up Google street view. Jackson leaned forward, and the two of them began plotting and arguing about which building rooftops provided the perfect mix of cover and line of sight.

I leaned back and left them to it. I had no doubt that this meeting was nothing more than a trap, and that meant I really had only one task.

To stay alive.

CHAPTER 10

The last time I'd entered Brooklyn, it had been bitterly cold, and it wasn't much better now. The night sky had disappeared behind a curtain of clouds, and it was raining—not heavily, but still enough to soak the bits not covered by my jacket. The wind howled through the lonely streets, rattling the boards covering the windows and pirouetting plastic bags and other rubbish down the middle of the damp street.

I shoved my fists deeper into my jacket pockets and scanned the nearby buildings. Broken glass, shattered brickwork, and rot abounded. It was no better or worse than what I'd seen last time, except for one thing—this time, the icy air held a hint of desperation and fear.

And I wasn't entirely sure whether it was radiating from the area itself or from me.

I continued walking down the middle of the street. There was little point in keeping to the shadows, because the red cloaks were undoubtedly aware of my presence by now. Besides, there were no longer any working streetlights in this part of Brooklyn. In fact, the whole area had been reduced to darkness, and there was absolutely no sign of life. Even the rats seemed to have deserted the place.

But then, rats were smarter than most people gave them credit for.

The desire to look up, to scan the rooftops, and check whether I was being watched, was so fierce, it took every ounce of willpower to resist. But I didn't want the cloaks—who were undoubtedly watching, even if I couldn't see them—to think I might be looking for someone. Rory and Jackson had ventured into Brooklyn several hours earlier, but they weren't positioned in this street. They were at either end of the cross street where I was to meet the cloaks. It was the same cross street where Sam had been fated to die.

Was that to be my destiny?

As much as I feared that possibility, logic and instinct said no. If this *was* all about making Sam suffer, then the cloaks and their shadowy leader wouldn't even attempt to infect me. Why would they, when they'd witnessed what I'd done in the forest and more than likely had a source in PIT? They'd have to at least *suspect* I would not be infected or turned by a scratch, as others had been.

No, what I feared was capture. Feared that my flames, Jackson, and Rory would not be enough, and I'd end up as bait.

Though I had to wonder how much the cloaks *really* understood about PIT if they thought holding me would be enough to force their lead investigator to come here. Sam had warned me often enough that no one's safety was greater than the mission. Not even his.

And I doubted he'd risk his life for me, especially

now, when we were no longer an item and I'd done nothing except gotten in PIT's way.

Which made the gray cloak's obsession of getting to Sam via me even stranger.

My footsteps slowed as I drew close to the intersection. There was still no sign of movement, no indication they were even watching me. The rain continued to drizzle down, making the night more and more unpleasant. Aside from the creaking bones of the nearby buildings and the soft whistle of wind through cracks, the night was silent. Even the squelching of my wet boots seemed flat and lifeless.

I hit the middle of the intersection and stopped. Nothing happened. Fire burned through me, eager for release, but there was no target, no threat. Not yet, anyway. I clenched my hands so tight, my nails were digging into my palm. Pain slithered through me, but it didn't help ease the tension.

The minutes ticked by. Despite the cold and the rain, sweat began trickling down my spine. My muscles were wound up so tight that they'd surely shatter if something didn't happen soon . . .

A whisper of a footstep behind me . . . I spun. About halfway down the street I'd just traversed were six red cloaks. They weren't doing anything. They were just watching.

Another footstep, this time down the left arm of the intersection. More cloaks down that street, but again, they weren't moving. Fear ratcheted up several more notches and flames flickered down my entire length before I snapped it back under control.

I *really* didn't like the feel of this—and *that* was probably the whole point of their actions.

I pulled my hands out of my coat pockets and flexed them. The desire to become full flame and get the hell out of here was so fierce, my body ached with heat and repressed energy.

Another set of six cloaks appeared on the street directly opposite. Which left only the right arm of the intersection . . .

The minutes ticked by. No cloaks appeared down that street, and none of the ones who were present moved.

Because they were waiting for something.

Or someone.

I slowly turned and faced the street that was free of cloaks. The swirling wind caught the misting rain, making it seem like there were ghosts dancing in the night. Nothing else moved, however, and I had no sense that there was anything or anyone down there.

But why protect every street but that one?

Because they want me to head that way.

I took a deep breath and, for all of two seconds, thought about doing the exact opposite. But that wasn't going to solve our red-cloak problem. Meeting with the psycho in charge of them might not, either, but I had to at least give it a try—if only so I could do as I'd threatened and cinder the bastard to hell and beyond.

After another deep, somewhat shuddery breath, I forced my feet into action. But the minute I moved, something sharp hit my butt and buried deep into my skin. I half yelped and swept a hand around to see what it was.

It was a dart.

Oh fuck . . .

That thought had barely crossed my mind when dizziness swept over me; whatever was on the dart tip was fast acting.

I flamed. I had no other choice. I had to become spirit and burn whatever was on the tip of that dart from my system before it could take full effect.

As I swept from flesh to flame, the red cloaks found life and ran toward me. But other than the slap of their footsteps against the wet road surface, they made no sound. I twisted around and flung fire in their direction. Several were instantly cindered, but the others simply parted around the lance, then regained formation and ran on.

I turned and sped down the empty road. My flames burned away the shadows and threw a fierce orange glow across not only the grime and neglect but also the barricade of stone and metal that formed an almost sheer wall at the far end of the street.

Not that *that* would stop me. I might not be able to burn stone, but there wasn't a barrier yet built that I couldn't get over in fire form. Except *that* would give us no answers . . .

As I was contemplating my options, I spotted another street on the right just before the wall. It wasn't blocked, meaning that was where they wanted me.

If I went in, I'd do so without backup. Neither Rory nor Jackson would have any sort of line of sight into that road from their current positions. They could—and no doubt would—change position, but that would still leave my back decidedly unprotected for too many minutes.

I slowed and went in anyway.

And almost instantly felt the magic. It burned across my skin, an unclean fire that made my flames itch. There weren't many things that could restrain or even kill my spirit form, but magic was certainly one of them.

As I stopped, the red cloaks surged into the small street. I raised a thick barrier of fire between us, then reached for the earth mother, calling to her energy; I knew I'd need it if the cloaks were to be fully halted. My flames might burn them, but it wouldn't cinder them all instantly. With the magic so close, I couldn't risk anyone breaking through and coming at me.

In spirit form, my connection to the mother's energy was stronger, and she sang through me—fierce and warm and joyful—before she exploded from me and formed a secondary barrier. All the colors of creation spun across the night, lending the blackened, desolate road a luster it wouldn't normally have possessed.

And just in time. Several cloaks lunged through my barrier, their bodies aflame and their mouths open in a scream that was never heard. They hit the mother's barrier and were cindered in an instant. Her fire rippled and her colors momentarily darkened, as if even she were horrified by what those things were.

I turned around. Down the far end of the street, untouched by the mother's light and standing with his arms crossed and the wind teasing the edges of his gray cloak, was the blue-eyed stranger.

"This," he said, his voice little more than a guttural whisper but carrying easily despite the distance, "is *not* how I'd planned events to go."

I didn't answer. I just shot flame at him. It burned

down the street, faster than a blink . . . only to bounce off some sort of barrier about ten feet away from him and go spearing into the night.

The magic wasn't designed to harm or entrap me. It was protecting *him* from me.

Fuck.

Our only hope of killing the bastard right here and now was shooting him—if Rory, who was down at this end, could get into position in time.

Which meant I had to give him as much time as possible—and to do that, I had to shift back to human form. Rory and I could understand each other as spirits, but few others would.

But the minute I changed back to flesh, the mother's pull on my strength increased. This body wasn't as strong as my natural form.

"It hasn't exactly gone as *I* planned, either," I growled back. "Otherwise, your ass would be toast right now."

He laughed. He actually *laughed*. It was a cold, cruel sound, yet there was something about it that stirred distant memories.

"You cannot kill a foe that is one step ahead of you."

"And pride comes before a fall." I smiled, but it held as little warmth as his laugh. "Why did you want me here?"

"I suspect you already know."

"I suspect I do. But why do you think my capture would, in any way, affect Sam Turner?"

"Because you and he were once an item."

"The key word being 'once.' I'm nothing to him now, so you can stop with the whole 'He will not have you' thing. He doesn't *want* me. He hasn't, for a very long time."

"Except *that* is not entirely true."

"So you know him intimately?" I said, raising an eyebrow. "You can read his thoughts and know his emotions? Because, as you're no doubt aware, I saved the man's ass, and he was neither pleased to see me nor happy to be saved."

"Be that as it may, it does not negate what I feel and know. You will be mine, as he will be when the fighting stops. And when it does, I will destroy him, as he attempted to destroy me."

When the fighting stops? What the fuck was that supposed to mean? That he had plans in place to destroy PIT? "So what you're saying is that you can read his thoughts?"

"His thoughts? No, that I can't do."

Meaning he *could* read Sam's emotions? That would be possible if he were an empath, but even then, he'd have to be standing near Sam to be able to read his emotions. I seriously doubted empathy was a talent that could be shared through the hive mind—especially since few in the red-cloak army seemed to have much in the way of street smarts or intelligence, let alone psychic talents—so he couldn't be reading Sam via them.

Or did he mean he had access to someone with that talent? PIT undoubtedly had both telepaths and empaths on the payroll, so maybe one of them was working for the cloaks. Though *how* that could happen, given the precautions and security PIT obviously had in place, I had no idea.

"Yeah, well, whoever your source is in PIT, they're feeding you a few whoppers."

"Oh, but they're not. You can trust me on that."

Meaning he *did* have a source in PIT. Fuck, Sam needed to know, and fast. I scrubbed a hand through my hair; sparks spun away into the night, tiny fireflies that quickly died long before they traversed the distance that divided me from the gray cloak. Sweat was dribbling down my back again, and the background headache was starting to come to the fore—a sure sign that both my fire and the mother's demands were affecting my strength.

"Whatever," I said. "I'm here only to give you a warning—if you or any of your hive buddies come near me or Rory or Jackson again, we'll cinder this whole damn place around your ears—and then do the same to the lot of you."

"A big threat, but one not even you—"

The rest of the sentence was cut off as he jerked abruptly. For a second I wondered what had happened; then I saw the blood on his arm. He'd been shot. *Rory*.

Relief filled me, but it was short-lived because the shadows began to roll around him, swirling up his legs as it began snatching him from sight.

A vampire trick, but a very useful one in this instance, especially when the barrier prevented my flames from reaching him.

Something zinged past my ear and smacked hard in his chest. He staggered backward but didn't fall. Nor was there any sign of blood, though there should have been. That shot had hit him square in the chest, and cloaks *did* bleed. The wound on his arm was evidence enough of that.

Either the bastard had no heart . . . or he was wearing a bulletproof vest under his cloak.

The darkness completed its journey and swept him from immediate sight. And while he wasn't concealed from my senses, he would be from Rory's. The clip-on thermal scope he was using wasn't strong enough to pick up the much lower body temperature of a vampire— or even that of a pseudo vampire, as the cloaks happened to be.

I swore and flung fire at the barrier but directed it upward to test its boundaries and limits. The lance of flame skimmed the surface of the unseen barrier, revealing it to be a dome. As my fire dipped toward the road's surface, I flicked it sideways to get a feel for the circumference and discovered it was more U-shaped. The barrier began and ended directly against the building on the right—protecting the doorway that our quarry was now heading for.

"You will pay for this deception," he growled. "Pay in blood—"

"And attempting to dart me wasn't a deception on your part?" I snapped.

But he continued on as if I hadn't spoken. "I will dine on your blood, and my victory will be all that much sweeter after the years of rejection."

Years of rejection? What the hell was this fellow smoking? But even as the thought crossed my mind, another rose. One I really *didn't* want to believe. Because it wasn't just his blue eyes and his cold laugh that seemed familiar, but also his fierce anger at being rejected. And if *I* was right, I really *did* have to get hold of Sam—the sooner the better.

Because the man the stranger reminded me of was none other than Sam's brother, Luke.

"Sam *will* watch you die," he continued, "and then I will have—"

"Oh, just fuck off with the threats."

I hit the building with everything I had. It might be brick, but even brick, when hit with enough searing heat, would explode. Dizziness swept through me, but I ignored it, concentrating everything on that building. Behind me, my flames dipped and fizzled out, but the mother's fire still raged. She would not go out until either I willed it or she completely drained me. As the heat radiating off the bricks began to boil across the darkness and flames erupted across wooden sashes and the rooftop, I added, "Because you really are playing with fire. And I promise you, we are the last beings you *ever* want to make angry."

He didn't answer. He just flung open the door and left. Two minutes later the building exploded.

As bricks and metal and fire erupted into the sky, I flung myself into flame form. The force of the explosion buffeted me from pillar to post, but it also fueled me. I sucked in the heat and the energy, then spun around. The red cloaks were no longer throwing themselves at the mother's barrier; they were running. Not toward Rory's building but down into rat holes; down into the sewers.

I sent several lances of fire after them, but even with the building fire burning so close, my strength was slipping alarmingly fast. I released the mother, felt her caress as she slipped reluctantly away, and felt no stronger for it. I moved into the fire, fully immersing myself into it. It was a dance of energy and power that sang all around me, but one in which I could not stay long. The explosion would not have gone unnoticed by the cops who patrolled the perimeter of this place, and while it was unlikely the fire brigade would be called in, they'd be watching. And the last thing Rory and I needed was to be spotted by one of them.

I ramped up the fire and sent several lances of flaming material into the night, directing one of them in Jackson's direction and then following it. Rory was well able to protect himself, but Jackson, though a capable fighter, might need a hand if the cloaks went after him. Though he could now create flame on his own, he was still flesh and blood and—as Rory had pointed out—we had no idea what toll my flames would take on his body when he used them. It was better to be safe than sorry—and even Jackson had admitted that when we'd discussed the possibility of things going sour.

I flamed out as I neared the rooftop he was stationed at, hitting the concrete in a tumbling roll and jumping to my feet. I didn't immediately see or sense Jackson, but, half a minute later, I caught a slight flicker of flame several buildings away. I raced across the adjoining rooftops and quickly joined him.

"As the saying goes, let's get the hell outta Dodge." He grabbed my hand and led me toward the building's old fire-exit ladder.

"Could be a good idea. I suspect they're going to be furious once they get over the shock of that explosion."

He glanced at me, green eyes bright in the shadows. "Your doing?"

"Yeah. I was a little pissed." I climbed over the building's parapet and jumped down to the stairs. Though I landed lightly, the metal vibrated and groaned—a clarion call to action if there were any cloaks in the near vicinity.

The metallic groan deepened as Jackson joined me on the ladder and motioned me forward. "And the gray cloak? Did either of you get him?"

"Not with my flames. The bastard somehow knows magic that can stop a phoenix's fire." I headed down the stairs, trying to be both fast and quiet and really not succeeding. "And he was also wearing body armor."

Jackson swore. "I guess we should have allowed for that possibility. Or simply aimed for the fucker's head."

"A head shot from that distance when you're not a marksman isn't exactly easy. The body shot was the safer option, considering all we really needed was him down so my flames could finish the job."

I jumped off the few remaining ladder rungs, hit the ground in a half crouch, and looked around. The small lane was dark and silent; no surprise since the whole area—apart from the section now on fire—was dark. I could neither see nor sense any red cloaks, but I doubted they'd remain hidden for long. They'd give chase if they spotted us—unless, of course, their lord and master had ordered otherwise.

And if he was dead?

If that *were* the case—if he'd been caught by either the fire or the explosion and *actually* killed—then they'd still probably give chase. A hive without a leader was rudderless, and if no one else stepped up, they'd swarm. And I didn't want to be anywhere *near* the area if that happened. I rose and stepped to one side to give Jackson room to get down.

"What about the explosion?" he said. "Did that take him out?"

I hesitated. "I don't know. I'd like to think it did, but I suspect he went down a handy hole like the rest of the rats."

"I guess we'll know soon enough."

I guessed we would. I accepted the weapon Jackson handed me, then followed him out of the lane. Aside from the distant crackle of the fire, the streets remained deathly quiet. Tension wound through me as we made our way toward the perimeter, but the cloaks didn't come out to play. Getting past the police and PIT patrols was simply a matter of timing and patience.

Twenty minutes later, we reached our meeting point—the McDonald's on Millers Road—and, after securely locking the weapons in the trunk of the car, we headed in. Rory was already there, having claimed a table and ordered burgers, fries, and Cokes for us all. As the last vestiges of tension left me, my legs felt weak and all I wanted to do was sit.

I slid into the booth opposite him. Despite the flicker of relief that ran through his eyes, his expression was less than happy. "I missed."

"No, you didn't."

I grabbed a Quarter Pounder and a bag of fries. Jackson slid in beside me and did the same.

"The bastard disappeared into *shadow*," Rory growled. "That implies life rather than death to me."

"Yes, but that doesn't mute the point that you hit him—twice." I bit down on the burger and savored its taste for several seconds before I explained what had happened.

Rory swore and rubbed a hand across his eyes. It was an action filled with weariness and frustration. "So we're basically in the same shitty position that we were?"

"Maybe. Maybe not." Jackson shrugged as he began demolishing fries. "Our actions here tonight will at least inform our cloaked felon that we are not to be messed with lightly. And we can always hope the fire takes hold and rages through the rest of Brooklyn. They'll find it harder to move about without the protection of that place."

"There're always the sewers." Rory leaned back and idly picked at the fries that remained in his bucket.

"The police—or PIT, as the case may be—have placed a watch on the perimeter," Jackson said. "I'd imagine they'd be doing something similar in all the main sewer tunnels coming out of that place."

"It wouldn't be a watch *I'd* volunteer for," I muttered. "Especially since they still have no clear idea about just who this virus can affect."

"If they're smart, they'll be using movement-sensing weapons as first *and* second lines of defense," Rory commented. "PIT aren't stupid, and I doubt they'd allow humans, vamps, or weres down there without adequate protection."

"Agreed," Jackson said. "So where does that leave us now, beyond being in that well-known creek without a boat?"

Rory's gaze came to mine. "I think the first thing you should do is talk to Sam. He needs to know what was said tonight and what we suspect. And we need to know what the hell his connection to this gray cloak is."

"Like he's going to tell me *that*." I licked the meat juice from my fingertips, then reached for another burger.

"He probably won't, but we have to at least try. He might even surprise us and be reasonable."

"I agree," Jackson said. "And at the very least, he needs to be warned that the gray cloak is gunning for him."

"I know," I said. "But I'll do it in the morning."

"No," Rory said. "Do it now. We need to plot our next move, and that may very well depend on what Sam tells us."

"Or what he doesn't," I said. "Hell, he might just throw our butts in jail and toss away the key."

"Even *he* would not be that unreasonable under these circumstances." Jackson held up a hand, halting my protest before I could make it. "I know, but that whole drugging episode aside, he *has* been more reasonable of late."

"It depends on your definition of reasonable—especially when you're not the one who has to talk to the man."

"It's better to talk to him than allow him to walk unknowingly into some sort of trap." Rory's voice was soft, but it was etched with pain. "We may be fated for unhappy love lives, but knowing they are out there and *alive* is far better than being faced with their death."

My gaze met his and, just for an instant, the misery and endless heartache of discovering Jody—his fiancée at the time—had been murdered shone in his eyes and rippled across his energy. We had no idea why she'd been targeted, and neither, apparently, did the police. Rory was still in regular contact with the officer who'd been in charge of the investigation, but there'd been no new clues for several years.

I wrapped my hand around his and squeezed lightly. There was no point in saying anything. While it wasn't a situation we'd faced very often, it was still one we'd both endured over our many centuries. And there was no point in words, because in such a situation, words were always going to be useless.

"I'll talk to him. I'm just bitching."

"And you do it very well." Jackson's voice was almost contemplative. "And with such style and grace, too."

It broke the wash of sadness through Rory's eyes and forced a somewhat reluctant smile to his lips. "Try listening to it for a few centuries. You might change your opinion."

I flicked a fry at him, then got out my phone and called Sam. Unsurprisingly, I got his message service. I told him I had vital information and asked him to contact me ASAP, then hung up.

"You know," Jackson said, "if PIT *has* been infiltrated, it might be worth getting rid of our phones. We can be tracked through them all too easily."

I frowned. "Using his source in PIT to do that would

be a rather large risk for our gray cloak to take. Police computers are monitored twenty-four/seven to ensure both the system and security measures are working properly, and to prevent unauthorized use."

Jackson raised his eyebrows. "And how do you know this?"

"Aside from its being basic logic, I was a cop in a previous lifetime."

"Huh. That explains why you make such a natural PI."

"And why she's forever sticking her nose where it does not belong," Rory commented drily. "The creature hunt being one such example."

"I'm not hunting it—"

"No," he agreed, "but only because you have no leads on the thing. That will change the minute you do, and we both know it."

It was a truth I couldn't deny, so I simply made a face at him and finished eating my burger.

"But," he added, "I agree. The cloak may well take the risk and use his source to find us after tonight, so we need to go dark on the electronics front."

I nodded, but before I could say anything, my phone rang loudly, making me jump. I answered it somewhat cautiously.

"Do you have another lead on the creature?" Sam said without preamble.

"No. It's possibly worse than that."

I could almost see his frown. "Then what?"

I hesitated. "I can't tell you over the phone. We need to meet. Now."

"Emberly—"

"Sam," I cut in. "Just trust me."

He made an exasperated sound, then all but growled, "The usual place?"

"No." I hesitated again, thinking fast. "There's a McDonald's near the Melbourne Market. Meet me there in half an hour."

"This had better be worth it," he growled. I could almost hear the fierce darkness radiating through his tone.

"It is. And, Sam?"

"What?"

"Don't bring your phone and don't use PIT's car."

There was a long moment of silence. Then he said, "What the hell is going on?"

"I'll tell you when we meet. Please, just this once, trust me and do as I ask."

He grunted and hung up. I blew out a relieved breath and met Rory's sympathetic gaze. "Fingers crossed he actually does as I asked."

"He will. He has nothing to lose, after all," Jackson said.

Rory and I shared a glance. He looked about as hopeful as I felt. But he didn't say anything; he simply plucked the phone out of my hand. A few seconds later, the sim was out. It was a process he repeated for both his phone and Jackson's.

"Can the phones still be tracked without a sim?" I watched somewhat dubiously as he dunked the three of them into his half-finished Coke.

"If we keep them off and the battery flat, I wouldn't think so. They track through GPS and location apps, as far as I'm aware." He put the lid back on the Coke, then picked it up along with the empty trays. "Shall we go?"

I rose and followed the two men out. Once we were in the car and under way again, I said, "Are you two heading back home after you drop me off?"

"No." Rory twisted around to look at me. "We've no way to contact you if Sam doesn't show up, and I'm not about to leave you alone too long, given what just happened in Brooklyn."

"But I'm not sure how long I'll be, and it might be a better use of your time to return to the hotel room and grab Radcliffe's phone." Which, rather stupidly, we'd left at the hotel along with everything else. But then, how could we have known that things would get so bad so quickly, and that we wouldn't get the chance to go back until now? "If Sam gives us nothing, then at least we can still work on finding the missing notes."

"Agreed," Jackson said, "and if nothing else, finding those notes and handing them over to the appropriate people will get the sindicati off our back."

"Or piss them off more," Rory commented. "We'll swing by the hotel, as suggested, but then we'll come back here."

I wasn't sure they could be any more pissed off—especially if they happened to be working closely with the red cloaks. "Fine. Just don't come into the restaurant if Sam is still with me. Given what I have to tell him, he's going to be angry enough. Seeing you might just push him over the edge."

Rory nodded in agreement. We reached the McDonald's near the market with five minutes to spare. Jackson halted just up the road. I opened the door to climb out, then hesitated. "Be careful, you two. That hotel might be under surveillance."

"We will, as long as you are. Don't leave the restaurant until one of us comes in to collect you."

"And take one of the guns from the trunk," Jackson said, popping it open. "It's always handy to have a backup."

"I will," I said. "See you soon."

I grabbed one of the pistols from the trunk and checked the safety was on before shoving it in the waist of my jeans, under my coat. Then I slammed the trunk shut and slapped it twice. Jackson took off. I gathered the ends of my coat together, then spun and headed for McDonald's. Sam wasn't there, so I ordered the largest cup of tea possible as well as a couple of hot apple pies, then retreated to a corner that had a good view of all entrances. By the time Sam arrived, I'd finished both pies and was halfway through my tea. He paused in the doorway, his gaze meeting mine briefly before sweeping the rest of restaurant. The rain dripped off his leather jacket and plastered his black hair, and his face was pale. There wasn't any color even in his cheeks, which looked sharper than usual in the bright lighting. It oddly reminded me of the gauntness that happened to some vampires when—generally for reasons of distaste—they refused to take the blood their bodies needed.

Though why you'd become a vampire if you didn't like the idea of taking blood, I have no idea.

Sam headed over to the counter, grabbed a coffee, and walked across to my table.

"So," he said as he pulled out a chair and sat down opposite, "why the cloak and dagger? What's going on?"

I hesitated, but there was really no easy way to ease into it. "I think you've got a mole in PIT."

He leaned back in his chair, an almost condescending smile flirting with his lips. "A comment like that shows just how little you know about PIT. Trust me, it's not possible."

"And yet, the gray cloak states otherwise."

That wiped the smile from his lips. But it also raised the darkness in him; the force of it was so strong—so all-consuming—that I had to lean back in an effort to get some fresh air.

"When the *hell* were you talking to the gray cloak?" It was softly said but full of threat.

"Tonight." I took a quick gulp of tea, but it did nothing to ease the fluttering of my pulse—and I wasn't entirely sure whether the cause was fear or the rain-washed cleanness of his scent.

"Why the fuck would you do that?"

"Sam, if you'd just—"

He waved a hand, the movement sharp, angry. "Damn it, you know how dangerous those things are, Emberly. Why the fuck are you going anywhere near them?"

Annoyance surged. "Because I had *no* choice—"

"There's *always* a choice. You just have a history of making the wrong—"

"Oh, for god's sake," I cut in. "Can the threatening demeanor, shut the fuck up, and *listen*."

It seemed to be my night for telling people that—and once again it felt decidedly good.

Surprise flickered through his eyes, briefly extinguishing the shadows. He contemplated me for a second, then leaned back and made a sweeping gesture with one hand. "By all means, go right ahead."

His tone was as bland as his expression. I wrapped both hands around my cup of tea, drawing in the reassuring slithers of heat as I told him about the note we'd found on Rosen. His anger stung the air, and I held up my hand, stopping him from saying anything.

"Yes, I know, we're bad, we withheld evidence. But we were warned not to tell you and PIT—otherwise they'd make Rory one of them."

"Phoenixes aren't affected by the virus, so that's an impossible threat."

"Not if our ability to take flame form is curtailed, and both you and PIT know that's possible via drugs." And magic, but I wasn't about to mention that in case he wasn't aware of it.

"But how would the cloaks or their leader have fucking known if you'd told us?" The blandness had very definitely left his expression—and his voice. "PIT is totally secure—"

"No, it's *not*." I met him glare for glare. "He said in the note he would know if PIT was informed. Besides, if there *isn't* a leak in PIT, how the *hell* would he have known I can't live without Rory? The only people I've told are you and Jackson—and Jackson's basically been with me twenty-four/seven. So who did you tell, Sam?"

"No one. I wouldn't do that to you."

I snorted. "Not even to get rid of a rival?"

"What fucking good can *that* do?" he bit back. "Killing him would kill you, and I couldn't stand losing you—"

He cut the rest of the sentence off, but the words seemed to echo through me regardless. *Couldn't stand losing you a second time.*

The gray cloak was right. He *did* still harbor feelings for me. They might be nothing more than ghosts—a pale reflection of what had once burned between us—but he still felt.

"And that," I said softly, "is something the gray cloak is very aware of. He wants to capture me—use me—to get to you."

"He can't possibly know—"

"Unless someone told him." I met his gaze steadily. Despite the darkness that shone in his eyes and washed between us, my fear was dying. His anger wasn't aimed at me—at least, not at this minute. It was aimed at himself—at whatever the source of the change in him was.

"Who at PIT did you tell about our relationship, Sam?"

He didn't immediately answer. Then he swore and scrubbed a hand across his eyes. "It can't be her."

"Rochelle?" I guessed.

He nodded. There was an odd bleakness in his eyes. "She was curious about you after I called her in to get that composite of the man who killed the guard at Chase."

"And you told her what, exactly?"

"Only that we were once an item."

"Nothing more?"

"No, because there is nothing more to tell." His gaze was unflinching. Remorseless. "We are history, not here and now."

History. How I hated that word. I took a sip of tea, then said, "You told no one else?"

"No one else but Rochelle had a need to know."

Because he and Rochelle were lovers, not just work companions. And lovers talked. Shared.

Except that I didn't. Hadn't. Because I'd been afraid of losing him, as I'd lost everyone else I'd ever cared about. I took a deep breath and pushed the ache back down. "Did you also tell her that you'd warned me away from the Baltimore investigation?"

He frowned. "Probably. It was in the report, at the very least. Why?"

"When we rescued Amanda Wilson from the sindicati's goons, Hunt said, 'You should have done as the cop suggested, because now you have to die.' The only way he could have known what you said to me was either by you or someone else telling him." I grimaced. "Maybe I'm being naive, given you had no qualms about drugging me, but I'd really like to think it wasn't you."

He didn't answer. But the anger and the darkness in him were stronger. And with that strengthening came an odd sort of desolation.

"What the hell is going on, Sam?" I asked softly. "Why is the man in charge of the cloaks so determined to destroy you? And if the leak *is* Rochelle, how the hell is she linked to him?"

I half expected him to tell me it was none of my business: that I needed to walk away and just stick my nose *out* of PIT business. But I couldn't, because the gray cloak had made PIT and whoever was feeding him information my business.

And there was something in his expression that suggested he was very aware of that.

"The reason he's after me is undoubtedly because

it's become a mission of mine to kill as many of the bastards as I can."

It was more than that. I very much doubted the gray cloak cared two hoots about the safety of the red cloaks—or, at least, the semi-insane ones marked with the scythe on their cheek. I'd killed more than a few of them, and he certainly wasn't coming after me because of it. No, this was personal.

But all I said was, "Because they infected Luke, forcing you to kill him?"

"Yes." He scrubbed a hand across his eyes, and I got the feeling he was trying to do the same to the memories of that moment. His gaze, when it met mine again, was bleak. "You really should have let me die, Red."

"Would you have let me die, given the same information and circumstances?"

The smile that touched his lips was bitter. "Maybe. I'm not the man I once was."

No, he certainly wasn't. But whatever had happened to him, there were still remnants of the man I'd loved remaining, and I couldn't watch those die.

"I can't take back my actions any more than you can," I commented. "But one question does occur to me—are your incursions into Brooklyn PIT sanctified? Because how else did those cloaks know the precise moment you'd reach that intersection?"

"I wouldn't go into that place without informing PIT. I can't."

I frowned. "Why not? Surely they wouldn't object to the cloaks being culled? Not considering the threat they pose to the rest of us."

"Oh, they don't object to me—or anyone else—

killing them." His tone was wry, but the bleakness in his expression was stronger. "They just object to not knowing my movements twenty-four/seven."

My confusion increased. "Does that rule apply to every PIT operative? Because that's one hell of a demand—and not one I'd imagine the unions would approve of."

"No, they wouldn't. But then, Rochelle and I are somewhat . . . off-grid . . . when it comes to unions and legalities."

Fear was beginning to creep through the confusion. I very much suspected I knew what he was leading up to, and I really—*really*—didn't want to believe it. "And why would that be?"

He took a deep breath and released it slowly. It did nothing to ease the desolation in his eyes or the dark anger staining the air. And it only increased the fear in me—but it was fear *for* him, not *of* him.

"You remember I once told you that all red plague survivors who don't run off to join the rest of the hive have a remote-controlled suicide pill implanted?"

I nodded. My heart was beating so fast, I swore it was going to leap out of my chest, and fear was a fist implanted deep in my gut, making it hard to breathe.

"Well, both Rochelle and I are recipients of said pill."

Dear god, no . . .

But the words remained locked inside. I could only stare at him.

"Yeah," he said softly. "We're both infected with the red plague virus."

CHAPTER 11

"When?" I somehow croaked. "How?"

He grimaced. "Do you remember what I said about Luke?"

"About his being one of the first to be infected by the virus?"

He nodded. "Well, he wasn't alone that day. I wasn't working with PIT back then—I was still a detective with metro. We had some information about the sindicati's activities in Brooklyn—information that linked Luke to them."

"So because he's your brother, you went in to confront him about it." It was a statement rather than a question. It was very much the sort of thing he would have done for anyone he cared about. He and Luke might have been estranged for years, but blood was still thicker than water. He would have wanted to talk to him before he did anything official.

"Yes. I was bringing him in when we were both attacked." He shrugged, the movement oddly angry. "I can't tell you how we got out of that place, but I woke up in a very secure military hospital."

I wished I could offer some form of comfort. Wished I could reach across the table and hug him. But his forbidding expression suggested any such action would be *very* unwelcome.

"And Luke? Was he also there?"

"Yes. But he wasn't exactly pleased to be in a military hospital, and he went a little crazy." His voice was grim. "To this day, I have no idea whether that craziness was the virus or simply his hatred of both authority and being cooped up."

I leaned back and crossed my arms in an effort to stop the growing desire to reach out to him. "What happened?"

"You know what happened." It was tersely said. "I shot him. I *killed* my own brother."

"And how many people did he kill or injure before you took him down?"

"Too many," he said. "But I could have maimed him. I didn't."

"Because maiming him wouldn't have stopped him, and we both know it." Hell, if setting the bastards alight didn't immediately stop their onslaught, bullets in the extremities certainly wouldn't.

"But I didn't know that then. I was just angry. Furiously angry."

"At him?" I frowned. "Why?"

"I'm told it's a side effect of the drug. Even now, I sometimes struggle with it." He scrubbed a hand across his eyes again. "Anyway, none of that is relevant."

"Except that I think it is."

His gaze sharpened. "Why?"

"Because I don't think the past is buried. Not in this instance."

"Meaning you think this gray cloak is aware that I killed Luke?" He frowned. "Why would he care? I've killed plenty of his soldiers over the last year, and he's never particularly worried about *them*."

"Because he's not related to them. He's related to you."

He crossed his arms. It was a defensive action just as much as it was angry. "No, that's not possible."

"How do you know?" I replied evenly. "Have you checked his grave of late? Are you certain his body is still there?"

"I don't *need* to. He was held in containment for a week, which was long enough for him to regenerate if he was going to. He didn't."

"What if he's one of those people who regenerates at a slower rate? People who imbibe vampire blood to become one have different rates of change, and all vampires recuperate at different speeds after injury. Why wouldn't that apply to the cloaks?"

"Because it's a man-made virus—"

"That no one fully understands," I said. "But it only partially turns the infected, so it's more than possible that wound recovery is also only at partial speed."

"It's not Luke." It was stubbornly said. "It can't be."

"Then explain why he keeps saying, 'He will not have you.'"

"Because, as you said, he seems to believe I still have serious feelings for you, and it's a good tactical move to target the people your quarry cares about." He shrugged. "Besides, Luke basically ignored you all the time we were together. I was under the impression he hated you."

"He probably *did* after I rejected his seduction attempt." As the saying went, in for a penny, in for a pound. Besides, what was the point of holding anything back now? "If this *is* Luke, then that event could also be playing a part in this whole drama."

"And *that* is something *else* you should have told me at the time." His voice held none of the anger I'd expected. He merely sounded resigned. Sad. And that probably stung more than anger ever could have. "That you couldn't speaks volumes about our relationship, Emberly."

"I was trying to protect your relationship with your brother," I snapped back. "As I said, I dealt with the situation. It didn't happen again, so there was no point in mentioning it."

"So if the gray cloak is indeed Luke, why would he be so determined to get you now?"

"Because he's a sicko infected with the red plague virus, and determined to rule the world?"

"I'm a sicko infected with the virus, remember. It doesn't make me determined to get you back, let alone rule the world."

"Because, according to him, you're fighting it." I hesitated, but it was only fair he knew everything that had been said. "He also said the fighting would stop eventually and, when it did, he would destroy you, as you attempted to destroy him."

"I'll never stop fighting. I'll die before I stop fighting."

The odd mix of determination and bleakness in his voice had tears stinging my eyes. I blinked them away. "Does Rochelle feel the same?"

"Of course. Hence my belief the leak can't be her."

"But what if she's not doing it knowingly? I asked the gray cloak if he could read your thoughts, and he said no. But I got the impression he *can* catch at least some of your emotions. What if he's catching both from Rochelle?"

"If he could read her thoughts, more missions would have gone ass up. They haven't."

"Which still doesn't mean she couldn't be the leak." I studied him for a minute. "It has to be checked, Sam. Just as Luke's grave will need to be checked."

He didn't say anything, and his expression gave very little away. But I had no doubt he'd follow up on both things, if only because he wouldn't want to put anyone at PIT in danger if he and Rochelle *were* inadvertently feeding the gray cloak information.

And if it *was* true? What would that mean for both him and Rochelle? PIT surely wouldn't risk having them as part of the team—not until after the cloaks were all caught and killed, anyway.

I contemplated him for a moment longer, then said, "If you and Rochelle can't go off-grid without setting off alarms, does that mean you told them you were meeting me tonight?"

Because if he *had*, I was damn glad Rory and Jackson were coming back for me. If the illustrious leader of the cloaks *was* Luke, and he'd survived both the fire and the explosion, he'd be murderously angry—maybe enough to send his insane army swarming after me.

Because the *only* time Luke did *anything* without thinking it through first was when anger got the better of him.

The smile that touched Sam's lips once again held very little in the way of warmth or humor. "I may hate that I'm now the monster I accused you of being, but I'm not yet ready to give up either the fight or life. So, yes, I rang my boss and told her what I was doing."

"No one else?"

"No." He paused. "Though she would have informed the surveillance team. An alarm would have been raised when the tracker in my body told them I was on the move but both my car and my phone remained stationary."

"Has Rochelle got access to the surveillance team or system?"

"No one has but the team itself. All systems are monitored twenty-four/seven, and all personnel are tracked when they're on the clock. We're not a big team, and we can't afford to lose anyone."

"Ah. Good."

"From that perspective, yes." His fingers tapped lightly on the table. "Is there anything else you need to tell me?"

"The fire in Brooklyn was me. And I threatened to burn the entire place down if he went near either Jackson or Rory again."

This time, the smile that twisted his lips was so small, it was barely even noticeable, but it nevertheless made something inside me sing.

"But not you?" he said.

"If either he or his cronies come near *me*, I'll burn their asses to hell and back. I told him that, too."

"Good."

"Maybe not. I think I may have just made the situation worse."

The smile became stronger, and it lent his cool features a warmth that harked back to the Sam of old. "I seriously doubt the situation *could* get any worse."

"Maybe not." I smiled, but only briefly. "Do you think the scientists—or whoever else is now working on this thing—will eventually be able to help you and Rochelle?"

He hesitated, then shrugged. "We don't know, because right now they're working on a vaccine rather than a cure. That has to be the first priority, even if this thing doesn't get out of control. But they've also taken lots of blood from us, in an effort to understand why some people survive intelligence intact, while others do not."

"I thought what form of red cloak you became depended on who infected you?"

"It does, but that doesn't negate that some become crazed and some do not. Remember, this outbreak was the result of one man."

That man being the scientist who thought he'd hit pay dirt—that he'd discovered the enzyme that gave vampires immortality—and very unwisely had decided to use himself as a guinea pig. He'd eventually been tracked down and killed, but not before he'd infected dozens of others.

"But surely studying your blood and why the likes

of you and Rochelle don't become mad pseudo vampires will help them develop a cure?"

"That's something no one can or will commit to." He picked up his barely touched coffee and rose. "I had best go report in. Are you going to be okay here?"

I nodded. He half turned, then stopped. "And, Emberly? Thanks."

With that, he walked away. I watched him leave the restaurant and become one with the night, my relief so fierce, my whole body shook. *That* had gone a whole lot better than I thought it would.

At least I now knew what that darkness in him was. It was a darkness he might never be free of, even if those who were now undertaking the continuation of Baltimore's and Wilson's research found a vaccine. A vaccine wasn't a cure and, as Sam had noted, no one had any idea if a cure was even possible.

Which meant that maybe the best he and Rochelle could hope for was that by destroying Luke—if indeed he was the leader of the cloaks—they'd at least destroy the insidious call of darkness. I had no doubt that Luke's desire for full control was at least partially the reason the darkness within Sam seemed to be in a constant state of flux whenever he was with me. Because when he *was*, he was fighting emotions and memories more than the virus, and it gained a greater hold on him.

Of course, that could also be the reason why Luke was so certain Sam still cared for me. He was catching snatches of emotions during those same moments.

Which meant the best possible thing I could do for us all was stay away from him—and yet that was probably the one thing that was nearly impossible to achieve.

Certainly fate itself seemed determined to continually throw me back into his path.

I pushed up from my chair and walked across to the counter to get another cup of tea and a McFlurry. It was probably just as well my body burned energy at a far higher rate, because with the amount of crap I'd been eating of late, I'd be the size of a shed in no time.

I was about halfway through the icy treat when Rory walked in. He didn't bother checking the restaurant or going to the counter; he just walked straight over to me.

"You okay?"

I nodded but nevertheless rose and wrapped my arms around his neck. "Sam's infected. The virus is the darkness I sensed in him."

"Oh fuck. I'm sorry to hear that." He held me tight for several seconds. "I may hate how the bastard treated you, but no one deserves that fate."

"At least he's one of the saner ones. And while he's alive and fighting, there is at least hope."

Because without hope there was nothing. Not for him, not for me.

Rory dropped a kiss on the top of my head, then pulled back. "And the leak?"

"It may be Rochelle. She's also infected. He doesn't believe that she's willingly feeding anyone information, however."

"Maybe not consciously." He picked up my unfinished tea and waved me toward the door.

"I told him that," I said, heading for the main door. "I also told him my suspicions as to who the gray cloak is."

"And?"

"And, he didn't react favorably, as you'd expect."

Jackson pulled up as we stepped out of the restaurant.

"But he's going to exhume the body regardless?" Rory asked.

"He didn't say as much, but I suspect he will."

"A successful meeting, I take it?" Jackson said as Rory slammed the car's rear door shut, then got into the front.

"You could say that." I updated him on everything that had happened, including the information that Rochelle was one of the infected.

He swore vehemently. "There go any seduction ideas I may have held."

"Yeah, but it's also a confirmation that Fae *can* be infected. If we hadn't used my fire to burn the virus from your system, you might well be one of them now."

"Yeah." His expression was bleak when it met mine briefly in the rearview mirror. "And I hope that one of you will kill me cleanly if it turns out that the virus *isn't* burned but rather just dormant."

"I don't think this virus does dormant. From everything Sam has said about it, the change hits within the first week or so. You're past that now."

"Be that as it may, you will put an end to me if necessary, won't you?"

I didn't want to even think about the prospect of doing something like that. Not to someone who had so quickly become a friend. "Being infected isn't the end of everything. Sam and Rochelle are proof enough of that."

"Maybe so, but the concern of infecting others is not something I'd want to live with." His expression was bleak. "Promise me, Em."

I closed my eyes for a minute, then softly said, "If it comes to that, I will."

"Good."

Silence fell. There wasn't much traffic on the road at this hour of the morning, and we arrived back at our bolt-hole without any sign that anyone was even remotely interested in us. By that stage it was close to five in the morning, and all of us were bone tired. We simply trundled up the stairs and crashed into separate beds. I couldn't say how long it took the two men to get to sleep, but I was out almost as soon as my head hit the pillow.

Only to dream yet again.

This time, however, it had nothing to do with monsters and dire events, but rather desire.

Because I dreamed I was being cradled close by arms that were warm and strong and familiar. Arms that belonged to a man with vivid blue eyes and a wild, dark scent.

And while I knew it was nothing more than the inner prophet taunting me with possibilities that could never be, I nevertheless allowed myself to sink deeper into sensation and enjoy it. Being wrapped in the imaginary arms of the man I loved was better than nothing.

I woke about ten, grabbed a shower, and then clattered downstairs. Rory was in the kitchen, frying up bacon and eggs for breakfast, and Jackson was sitting at the table nursing a mug of coffee.

I made myself a cuppa, then sat opposite him. "You look like shit."

He scrubbed a hand across his unshaven chin. "That bed is far too soft for my liking. And my feet stuck out the end of it."

I smiled. "And here I was thinking you enjoyed soft things."

"When it come to the female form, yes." Amusement crinkled the corners of his bright eyes. "In fact, the more curvaceous they are, the sexier I find them."

"So if a sexy-looking waif made a pass at you," Rory asked as he walked over with three plates piled high, "you'd tell her to keep on walking?"

"Well, no, because I'm a fire Fae with a high sexual drive. I'm just stating preferences."

I snorted softly and tucked into my breakfast. When we were all finished and the dishes cleared, Jackson retrieved the laptop and Radcliffe's phone from the trunk of the car and placed both on the table.

"So, what's our next move?" I picked up the phone and inspected it. It didn't tell me any more than it had yesterday. "Is that program of yours any closer to busting this thing open?"

"It shouldn't be too much longer." Jackson shrugged. "In the meantime, it might be worthwhile doing a search of Wilson's place. If he *did* have backup of those files, it could be there. If he'd kept a backup system at either the office or on a cloud service, someone would have found it by now."

Someone had certainly found Baltimore's cache— but only after torturing him to get it. And Wilson was already dead . . . maybe. If the attack on him by the red cloaks *had* been nothing more than a ruse to get him into their ranks, then he might well be alive and blabbing right now.

"Surely Amanda would have known about the cache if he did have one at home?" Not to mention the fact PIT would have searched the place thoroughly after his murder. They wanted the research notes as badly as anyone else, after all.

"Amanda may have been a powerful telepath, but—from what you've said—she could only read him during sex," Jackson said. "That being the case, she was probably concentrating on recording his daily progression with the virus rather than whether he was making a private backup of the information."

I frowned. "So why would Rosen be so convinced that he *did* have a private backup?"

"Given Rosen was backstabbing his own company, maybe he figured his top man was doing the same thing." Rory's expression was contemplative. "A cheater, whether it's sexual or money based, often expects the worst in others. It helps offset his own guilt."

"Maybe." I wrinkled my nose and tried to imagine Rosen simply sitting back and letting Wilson gather top-secret information. I couldn't, because Rosen had—in the brief time I'd met him—come across as both arrogant and confident in both his place in this world and his own self-worth. If he thought Wilson was stashing research and maybe even toying with the idea of selling it—something Rosen himself was already doing—then he would have undoubtedly put a stop to it. He might have even fired Wilson.

If he *had* known about Wilson's backup, it could

only mean he'd given Wilson his approval. Maybe it was Rosen's way of ensuring he could still get his hands on all the research if his deal with Radcliffe went sour.

Which it certainly had.

I put the phone down and picked up my mug of tea instead. "Amanda was doing a pretty thorough job of plucking information from Wilson's brain, so why wouldn't she have picked up info on a secret stash?"

"She may have," Rory commented. "Perhaps that's why the sindicati kept her alive rather than simply letting her die when they snatched you both. Maybe they're waiting for her to recover enough from her injuries so they can grab the info from her."

"The sindicati are an organization of vampires," I said. "It's not like they can't mind-rape her or something to get the information if they really wanted to."

"Except that, as I've said, telepaths often can't be read—even forcibly—by each other." Jackson opened the laptop and hit the START button. "Either way, I still think searching Wilson's place is a good plan."

"And not just the house itself, either," Rory commented. "It could be somewhere obscure, like a shed or something."

Radcliffe's phone chose that moment to come to life, the ringtone's music harsh and unpleasant, and the words all but incomprehensible. In fact, the only word I *could* understand was the term "ball-breaker." Unfortunately, while caller ID popped up on the screen, it simply said MJ and a number. Jackson scribbled it down, then motioned me to answer it. I did so cautiously.

"And just who the fuck are you?" a woman said, her voice teeth-grindingly strident.

"Angie," I said, giving her the first name I could think of. "Who are you?"

"Who I am is none of your damn business. What are doing answering this phone?"

"Mr. Radcliffe is currently in a meeting and asked me to vet all calls."

The woman snorted. "And we both know 'meeting' is just a euphemism for a fuck session."

My eyebrows rose at the vehemence in her voice. Whoever she was, she really *didn't* like Radcliffe. "I'm afraid I have no knowledge of what his meeting involves. Can I take a message?"

"Yeah, tell the rat bastard RJ's concert is tonight and he'd better fucking appear."

And with that, she hung up.

"Well," Rory commented, "she's a charmer."

I grinned. "Totally. Wonder who she is."

"According to Google and a number search," Jackson said, turning the laptop around, "she's Mrs. Mary Johnson, and she lives in Coburg."

"Wonder what her relationship to Radcliffe is."

"She could be anything from your much-theorized hidden wife, to his sister, or just someone he's seriously pissed off." Jackson shrugged. "Whatever the case, I think we need to go have a little chat with her."

"You'd better pack some earplugs," Rory said, his expression amused. "I suspect you might be greeted with some rather colorful language the minute you mention Radcliffe."

I raised an eyebrow. "You're not coming?"

He shook his head. "I'm better off staying out of your regular investigations. If the cloaks do come after you, it leaves me free to come in and save the day."

"So you have a hero hankering?" Jackson said, his expression contemplative. "That's interesting."

Rory gave him "the look"—the one that said, "Grow up." I knew that, because he'd given it to me a few times over the years. Although, as I often said to him, he could hardly tell me to grow up when he was often just as bad.

"I'm not entirely sure it's a great idea to leave you here alone." Doubt edged my voice. "Especially after the threat the gray cloak made."

"Em, we're safe here, at least for the moment. I'll stay and do some research on the creature. Because," he added, his tone dry, "I have no doubt it will feature somewhere in our near future."

I didn't deny it. I just flashed another grin at him. He rolled his eyes and motioned toward the door. "You'd better go, just in case Mrs. Ball-breaker decides she needs to go out."

We went. Mary Johnson's house was a small and neat redbrick house in a street filled with similar-looking houses. Her front yard was filled with sweet-smelling roses, and the car parked in front of the garage was a small Toyota that looked more than a few years old.

"If she's Radcliffe's wife," I commented, "then he's pretty damn mean with his money."

"Rats aren't good at sharing." He reached past me and grabbed Radcliffe's wallet from the glove compartment. He must have caught my surprise, because he added, "Hey, if she *is* his wife—or even just a poorly kept bit on the side—she might be receptive to a little monetary inducement."

"And why offer ours when his wallet is filled with both cash *and* credit cards?" I commented, amused.

"Precisely."

We climbed out of the car and walked to the front door. I pressed the doorbell. After several seconds, footsteps approached; then the door opened.

The woman who answered was not what I'd been expecting. She was six feet tall and slender with sharp but pretty facial features. A garishly pink hairband loosely held her neat brown hair back from her face. It was only when you met her unflinching brown gaze that you saw any hint of the harridan we'd heard on the phone. Her gaze was definitely on the steely side.

"Mrs. Mary Johnson?" I asked.

"Yes. Who the hell are you?" But even as she asked the question, recognition flashed through her eyes. "You're the woman on the phone—and obviously *not* the bastard's secretary."

"Jackson Miller and Emberly Pearson, from Hellfire Investigations." Jackson showed her his ID. "We're looking for Marcus Radcliffe—"

"I really don't give two figs about who you're looking for or what you want," she cut in abrasively. "Bugger off and leave me alone."

"Fine," I said mildly. "Sorry to have bothered you. We need to go talk to Morretti anyway, so I guess we can ask him about Radcliffe, as well as you and RJ." Morretti might be dead, but I was banking on few outside the sindicati and PIT actually being aware of that.

Her skin lost its color, but her eyes blazed with fury. "You wouldn't *dare*."

"Don't count on it," I said, "because right now your fucking husband has information we need—"

"He's *not* my husband," she snapped, then glanced past us, her gaze briefly sweeping the street. "You'd better come in."

She stood to one side and opened the door wider. Jackson stepped in first, tension evident in the set of his shoulders. He, like me, was waiting for a nasty surprise—or, at least, someone or something to jump out at us.

Nothing did, however. Mary closed the door, then led the way down the small dark hall to the kitchen-diner at the rear of the house. Kids' toys were strewn all over the floor, but other than that, the room was clean and tidy. She motioned us toward the table, then sat down opposite us.

"What is your involvement with Radcliffe?" she asked bluntly.

I studied her for a moment. She obviously had no love for Radcliffe, even though RJ was—given both her reaction and what she'd said previously—his son.

"As I said, he has information we need," I said. "Unfortunately, he is somewhat reluctant to part with said information, and he did a runner the last time we went to talk to him."

Mary snorted. "Yeah, he does that. Big on threats, not much personal follow-through."

"So, what is your connection to him, if you're not married?" Jackson said.

Her gaze met his, her expression sharp. Wary. "We

had a brief, three-week fling that resulted in a pregnancy. I wanted marriage; he did not. We came to an arrangement that suited us both."

I wondered what that arrangement was, since she wasn't exactly living the high life here in Coburg. "Is there any way to contact Radcliffe other than his phone?"

Her gaze flicked back to me. "How did you even get hold of it? He's basically outsourced his brain to the thing and can barely function without it."

I couldn't help but smile at the causticity in her voice. She and Radcliffe might share a child, but if she'd ever loved the man, those feelings had died a long time ago. "As I said, he was in a rather large rush to avoid us and left it behind."

"You must have put the fear of god into him, then, because the phone is usually the first thing he grabs." Her gaze swept from me to Jackson and back again. "And considering the wall of goons he keeps close for security purposes, the pair of you must be more badass than you look."

"He happened to catch Emberly on a low-caffeine day," Jackson commented. "It can be a pretty scary experience, believe me."

Amusement touched Mary's lips, and it briefly softened her sharp features. "That's something we have in common, then." She paused and leaned back in her chair. "I'll give you the addresses of all his rat holes, if you do me the favor of giving him a message."

"Done," I said without hesitation.

"Tell the bastard he'd be wise to not only appear at RJ's concert tonight but to bring the money he owes me. Or I'll be contacting his grandmother." She hesitated, and something close to fear flashed in her eyes. "And you will *not*, in any way, mention RJ's relationship to Radcliffe to anyone—especially not to the sindicati."

The last request wasn't surprising, and it was certainly one I had no hesitation in agreeing to. Hell, I may have made the threat, but I wouldn't have followed through. Endangering a child wasn't something I'd ever risk. "His grandmother must be pretty fierce to use a threat like that against someone like Radcliffe."

"Oh, trust me, he may make himself out as a major player, but she's the *real* power behind the pack's activities."

"Then maybe it isn't Radcliffe who will give us the answers we need, but her."

"It would depend on what your questions relate to. She might be the pack's matriarch, but her grandchildren run their various businesses on a day-to-day basis." She paused. "Do we have a deal?"

"Yes." Jackson reached into his back pocket. "In the meantime, you might want to make use of this."

He dropped the wallet onto the table. Mary laughed as she picked it up. "Good grief, he *was* in a hurry to escape, wasn't he?"

She flipped the wallet open and spotted the cash and credit cards. The grin that touched her lips was decidedly anticipatory. "Isn't it lucky for me that I happen to know his PIN and he rarely changes it."

"You might want to make use of the cards fairly quickly," Jackson said, "because if he hasn't already realized his wallet is missing, he will when we confront him."

"Oh, rest assured, that won't be a problem." She rose, tucked the wallet into her pocket, then walked across to the kitchen counter and grabbed a pen and piece of paper. After a few minutes, she walked back and handed me the list. There were six addresses in total; the café we'd raided was second on the list.

"They run from his most secure bolt-hole to his least," she commented. "Just don't tell the bastard you got the list from me. I don't want any flak to fall back on RJ."

"No problem." I tucked the note into my pocket. "Enjoy the spending spree."

"Oh, I most certainly *will*."

She quickly escorted us out, obviously eager to begin wreaking havoc on Radcliffe's credit profile.

"That," I said, once we were both back in the car, "was decidedly wicked. Brilliant, but nevertheless wicked."

"I do have my moments—and it's not like Radcliffe can't afford it. The bastard lives the high life, and yet he can't be bothered paying for a similar level of comfort for his son? I hate people who put their own needs ahead of their offspring."

For all we knew, living in Coburg was Mary's choice, and Radcliffe was supporting his son fully in every other way, but my eyebrows still rose at the vehemence in Jackson's voice. "Personal experience?"

"No. I just can't understand someone bringing kids into this world and not giving them the best start possible." He grimaced. "If and when I ever have a child, you can bet your ass he'll be fully supported *and* loved."

He'd make a damn good dad, too, I thought with a smile. "Are your parents still alive?"

"Yes. Mum lives near Wilson's Promontory National Park, and Dad's a ranger in the high country." He started the car and pulled out into the traffic. "Even though Fae don't do marriage and love, children are considered a rare and precious gift, and both parents remain fully involved in the life of their offspring."

"Even though the fathers aren't involved in the everyday nitty-gritty stuff?"

"Even though."

I leaned forward and typed the address of the first place on the list into the GPS. "Have you got any brothers or sisters?"

He shook his head. "Dad hasn't said anything, and he would have if I'd gained a half sibling. And Mum's got about twenty years or so before her fertile period rolls around again."

"It seems unfair that females get to be fertile only every fifty years or so, whereas males are good to go whenever needed." I shifted slightly to stare at him. "And that being the case, how come there're not lots of little half-breed Jacksons running around the place?"

"Because we only come into 'season' when there's a fertile female in the near vicinity."

"Which is probably just as well for the female half of the population in general," I commented, with a grin. "It'd be hard to hide the existence of your community if there were a ton of half-breeds about communing with trees, doing weird things to weather, or melding the earth into fantastical forms with a mere wave of their hands."

"Earth Fae cannot shape the earth with a mere

wave," he said, his tone severe but amusement flirting with his lips. "It takes a bit more effort than *that*."

"That sort of thing always does." I paused as the GPS gave some directions. "Do you know much about the Dandenong area?"

He grimaced. "Only that it's a mix of industrial and residential, and that it used to have a reputation for being very rough."

Which was about as much as I knew. "If we want to catch Radcliffe unawares this time, we'll need to be more security conscious."

Jackson grunted in agreement. "At least he won't recognize the car."

There was that. "We should have brought Rory along. Or, at the very least, purchased new phones so we could Google the area. There'd be less chance of being seen if we knew what to expect."

"Purchasing phones means creating a trail—paper or electronic—for people to follow. We'll just have to settle for being sneaky." He glanced at me, the amusement touching his lips creasing the corners of his bright eyes. "I'm presuming you *did* learn the art of sneaky sometime in the years before the arrival of the smartphone."

"Given we phoenixes have been hiding our existence from the human population for eons, you presume right." I paused. "Just how old are you?"

"I'm a veritable youngster compared to you and Rory."

"Which does not answer the question."

"When you tell me your precise age, I'll tell you

mine." He raised an eyebrow as he glanced at me, but his expression was decidedly mischievous. "I don't have any children yet, if that's any help."

"It isn't, because I have no idea how long it takes a Fae to reach maturity."

"Longer than both humans and werewolves."

Weres tended to live twice as long as the average human and, as a result, tended to take twice as long to mature sexually. Which maybe meant Jackson wasn't that much older than the thirty or so years he looked.

Of course, since Fae rarely showed their true age and many, in fact, could live for as long as a millennium, that wasn't saying much—especially given the ovulation cycle of Fae females.

It took us about forty-five minutes to get from Collingwood to Dandenong. Jackson slowed the car as we entered Cleeland Street; Radcliffe's building was a grimy two-story place dominated by a dry cleaner on the ground floor. There was a pharmacy on one side and a parking lot on the other. All the windows had roller security screens, as did the entrances, of which there were two—one for the dry cleaner and an unmarked one leading into a stairwell.

"I'm betting Radcliffe doesn't use either of those entrances. They're too visible." I scanned the building as we cruised past it and spotted two security cameras—one at either end of the building on the parking lot side. The building wasn't particularly deep, however, and there were several more businesses at the back of it. They were divided from Radcliffe's place by a small road that went behind both the dry cleaner and the pharmacy. "Care to bet there's a fire escape at the back of the building?"

"No takers on that one. But I doubt he'd use it as his main escape route. Too visible and obvious."

I frowned. "But his office is on the second floor of an old building, and I doubt they saw the need to insert escape routes when they built the place."

"No, but it wouldn't be hard to retrofit some sort of chute, especially if it was rat-sized rather than human."

He turned left into the multistory parking lot of the supermarket just up the road from Radcliffe's and parked in the middle of the three floors. It afforded us a good view over both Radcliffe's building and the road behind it without the danger of being noticed.

An assortment of Dumpsters—some of which were spewing boxes and other assorted paper rubbish out onto the asphalt—lined the service road. None of the buildings had a fire escape, however, which meant Jackson's chute theory was even more likely.

"Since this place is supposedly the most secure of all of them, how are we going to get in there?"

"We don't. We sit here and wait for the rat to come out."

"That's presuming he's even in there."

"The natural instinct of a rat when he feels threatened is to hide somewhere secure. Given we busted his second-most-secure premises, he's bound to run here."

"Have I ever mentioned that I hate stakeouts?" I pulled the hood of my sweater over my hair. Though we'd spotted only two cameras, that didn't mean there wasn't a third trained on this parking lot. "Especially since they're more inconvenient for females than you males."

He grinned. "Maybe you need to head on over to the supermarket and grab a bottle—"

I snorted. "A bottle isn't exactly what I'd call convenient. We can't direct the flow like you males, remember."

His grin widened, but all he said was, "And while you're there, you can grab some munchies and drinks. I seriously doubt he'll come out before dusk."

I grabbed my wallet, then headed into the supermarket to buy supplies—and was cheered to no end by the discovery that the supermarket was part of a complex that also had toilets. Which was just as well, as it turned out to be an interminably long day.

But as the last vestiges of sunset slithered from the sky, the rat finally came out of his hole.

It was time, finally, for some action.

CHAPTER 12

The two husky-looking men who came out of the stairwell door were wearing well-pressed dark suits and shoes that gleamed sharply in the quickly fading light. One positioned himself in front of the door while the other walked into the parking lot. Recognition stirred and, after a moment, I placed him—he was one of the two goons who'd been with Radcliffe at the casino.

I resealed the iced tea I'd been drinking and watched the second guard climb into the driver's seat of a rather standard white Holden sedan. It wasn't quite the type of vehicle I'd have expected Radcliffe to swan about in, but anything fancier would have stood out in an area such as this.

"We can't do anything here," I said as the guard drove the vehicle closer to the building's exit. "There are too many people out and about."

"Agreed. We'll just have to follow them and hope an interception opportunity presents itself."

The man stationed at the door spoke briefly into his lapel, then opened the stairwell door. Three seconds later Radcliffe scampered into the waiting vehicle. It was so smoothly done that if we'd blinked, we'd have missed him.

"What if we don't get the opportunity?"

"Then we'll just have to reassess the situation once we get to their destination." He started our car, then reached back and grabbed a somewhat grubby-looking cap from the backseat. "Tuck your hair up in this—it'll be less obvious you're trying to conceal your hair than if you use the sweater's hood."

"It's night—they're not going to see past the glare of our headlights."

"They're rats, remember, and have very good night sight. Let's not take any chances."

I accepted the cap somewhat gingerly and inspected it for bugs before shoving it on my head. As I tucked up my hair, the white car pulled out of the lot and turned left. Jackson cruised down to street level and ended up several cars behind it.

Unfortunately, not being spotted was about as far as our luck went, because they drove straight onto the busy Monash Freeway and headed for the city.

"Based on the goons' attire, I'd guess he's either meeting someone at a high-class restaurant or going to the casino." I studied the starlike twinkle of Melbourne's lights until I found Crown's oval tower. Was that where Radcliffe had first met Rosen? Not that it really mattered now, given Rosen was dead. "Either way, he's surely realized by now that his wallet and phone are missing."

"Oh, I have no doubt he'd know, given what Mary said about outsourcing his life to his phone, but it won't matter if he's going to the casino. Highfliers usually have a line of credit." He glanced at me. "If he *is* headed there, the parking lot might just provide our opportunity."

"Not with the number of security cameras in the place. We can't afford to have the police as well as everyone else looking for us, and we need this car to remain under the radar."

"We'll park outside."

"And the security cams?"

"Once he parks, we'll burn out all cameras in the area. With any sort of luck, security will take its sweet time coming down to check what's happened."

Radcliffe's destination did indeed turn out to be the casino. As he entered the street that led into the underground lot, Jackson parked illegally on a side street, and we both raced for the stairs. We checked each level carefully, then quickly raced down to the next, until we finally caught up with them. As the vehicle cruised through the near-empty level and moved closer to the elevator entrance, I scanned the roofline for security cameras. Once I'd spotted them all, I sent thread-thin lines of fire snaking along the roofline and promptly burned out the wiring in each one.

"Our best bet is to isolate him from the guards," Jackson said. "Ready to display your party trick?"

I nodded and clenched my hands to hide the flames still flicking across my fingertips. The white car parked close to the door and the goons climbed out; one scanned the area immediate area, then moved toward the casino's entrance while the other moved around the car and opened Radcliffe's door.

Jackson pushed the door all the way open. I slung

fire, then raced forward. My flames shot across the parking lot, far faster than I was, and looped around the first guard, trapping him in a high wall of thick heat. As his curses began to fill the air, the second guard reacted, thrusting Radcliffe back inside the car, then swinging around, his weapon already in his hand. His first shot went wild, pinging off the edge of a nearby concrete pillar and spraying me with dust. He didn't get the chance to shoot again; a ball of flame flashed past my ear and hit the weapon, turning it white-hot in an instant. The guard swore and released it, but rather than clattering against the concrete, it simply oozed away, the bright silver liquid trickling slowly under the car.

"Don't move, and don't even consider reaching for any more weapons," Jackson ordered, his voice loud enough to carry above the crackle of the flames surrounding the first guard. "You'll both fry if you do."

The second guard slowly withdrew his hands from the back of his jacket and held them up. I slowed and glanced at Jackson. He looked a little paler than he had moments ago, meaning the effort of creating flame fierce enough to melt steel *had* drained his strength.

But his gaze was determined when it met mine. "I'm fine. Let's just get our answers." He stopped at the tail end of the car and motioned to the second guard. "Step well away from that door."

Once the guard had obeyed, I leaned forward and peered into the car. Radcliffe glared back at me.

"What the fuck *are* you?" His narrow features were ugly with hate. If he was at all fearful, he was hiding it well. "And how dare you—"

"What we are you don't need to know," I cut in, not

wanting to hear any more of his bluster than absolutely necessary. "And you can be sure that we'll dare a whole lot more if you don't answer our questions."

He snorted. "This place is monitored twenty-four/seven. Security will be on its way even as we speak."

"Then you'd better hurry up and answer said questions, hadn't you? Otherwise they'll just find little piles of soot."

"You won't cinder me." His voice was contemptuous. "Not here. Not when you risk outing whatever it is you are to whatever security is watching."

"True," I agreed, my tone philosophical. "So maybe I'll just ring the sindicati and give them the name and location of your son."

"I have no idea—"

I raised a hand. Fire leapt from my fingers to the vinyl headrests and shimmied toward Radcliffe. He shrank back in his seat, his lips pressed together and sweat beginning to bead his forehead.

"We have your phone," I said. "Unfortunately for you, we also happen to possess an app that breaks numeric codes relatively easily. After that, it was just a matter of basic detective work to track you down."

His gaze narrowed. "Which doesn't explain your belief I have a son."

"Ah, well, listing a contact as simply MJ stirred our curiosity. We did a number search, then sat outside the given address to see who was living there. And if he's not your son, then I'd like to know how you managed to clone a mini version of yourself."

He didn't say anything. He just continued to glower at me.

My smile held a decidedly nasty edge. "Now, tell me why you ordered Rosen killed."

"I didn't," he growled. "He was too valuable an asset."

Given his use of "was," he obviously knew of the hit even if he hadn't order it. "Then who did?"

"The sindicati."

"Which faction? Morretti's or De Luca's?"

"Morretti's no longer a player in *that* particular field." Satisfaction practically oozed from his pores. "And I can't say I'm overly put out by that fact."

"You don't seem overly put out by losing a valuable asset, either," I noted. "Which faction paid you to walk away from your so-called valuable asset?"

He simply smiled and didn't answer. I flicked a finger of flame toward his face, and he thrust back with a slight yelp.

"De Luca's," he immediately said. "Morretti's lot suspected, as I do, that Wilson kept his files securely backed up. They wanted Rosen alive, and your search active, so they could grab it."

"Do they also know that Wilson probably isn't dead?"

His confusion was brief but nevertheless seemed real. "That's not possible. He was torn apart by red cloaks."

So either Morretti's faction didn't have the scientist—which in itself meant they weren't working with the red cloaks, as no one but Luke could control the actions of those within the hive—or they simply wanted to use the research to hasten Wilson's efforts. Either way, it was obvious Radcliffe wasn't being kept informed.

"Why would De Luca want Rosen dead, then?"

Radcliffe shrugged. "He just said that Rosen knew where the notes were, and he wanted to ensure no one else found them before he did."

Meaning he'd tortured the information out of Rosen before he'd killed him? Or, I thought, my stomach sinking as I remembered the cuts on Rosen's face and arms, did it mean that he'd been infected and would also become part of the red-cloak hive mind?

I very much suspected it was the latter, and that meant I'd better warn Sam. PIT probably put security on corpses as a matter of course these days, but just in case . . .

Heat stirred my skin, a caress that was oddly masculine in feel and one that held an indirect whisk of the mother's power.

"Two security guards just appeared," Jackson said. "I've created a wall of flame to stop them seeing anything, but hurry."

Satisfaction oozed across Radcliffe's face. "I told you—"

My flames hit him full in the face. They didn't burn, but he didn't immediately realize that, and his scream was high and fear filled. It was a sound that cut off abruptly as I slapped a hand across his lips; my flames instantly withdrew to my fingers, flicking and dancing brightly in the shadowed confines of the car.

"The only thing I want coming out of your mouth is answers—understood?"

He nodded. I pulled my hand away. His skin was red with heat, even though the flames hadn't been sharp enough to actually burn.

"Who's taken over Morretti's position?"

He swallowed heavily. "Frank Parella."

"And is he the actual leader of that faction, or merely a general?"

"A general. I don't know who the leader is. No one does. And only the generals have contact with whoever is in charge."

Which confirmed what had been in Amanda's notes. "Does that also make De Luca a general?"

He licked his lips. I couldn't tell if it was due to nerves or simply that his lips were still tingling with heat. "The generals are the public face of the two factions. I don't believe anyone else beyond them knows who or what controlled the sindicati before the split."

"Meaning," I said in an attempt to confirm what else had been in those notes, "the sindicati might be led by a committee rather than just one man?"

He shrugged. "As I said, no one knows. It would explain the current fractional split, however."

It certainly would. But who'd interviewed me in that darkened room? Was it De Luca, Morretti, or one of the leaders of the opposing factions? I really had no idea, but if the sense of power that had been evident in both his voice and his presence was any indication, it was someone used to ultimate control.

"How do I get in contact with Parella and De Luca?"

"You don't." He licked his lips again. "And if you're wise, you won't."

"Yeah, but here's the thing—one of them keeps coming after me. That needs to stop. So if I can't get in contact with them, can you?"

"No—"

I singed his whiskers. Sweat began to trickle down the side of his face. "For fuck's sake, the only time I've talked with De Luca was when *he* contacted *me* about Rosen. He wanted to know who had him, and he paid me handsomely to find out."

"So you do have his number?"

"No, it was a burn phone. I checked."

I guess that wasn't surprising, given Radcliffe's inclination to sell information. "And Parella?"

"His number I have." It was said sullenly. The bully boy wasn't so bullish at the moment.

"Was it your goons who snatched Rosen from his office buildings?"

"Yes. Initially they were only supposed to rough him up a little, just to put some urgency into the situation."

"But that changed when De Luca contacted you?"

"Yes. He offered me a large sum of money to snatch Rosen, then look the other way, and I accepted it. Who wouldn't?"

"How large are we talking about? Ten, twenty, thirty grand?"

Radcliffe snorted. "I wouldn't walk from such a valuable source of information for anything less than six figures."

"And it was definitely De Luca on the phone, not Morretti?"

Radcliffe frowned. "Yes, I've already said that."

"So why would Hunt say it was Morretti who contacted him rather than De Luca?"

Radcliffe snorted. "Theodore Hunt is a lying piece of scum."

"But one you're more than willing to use."

"Because he's good at what he does." Radcliffe paused. "At least he was until you got involved in things. I'm betting he gets a hard-on just thinking about killing you."

Hunt's sexual habits *weren't* something I wanted to contemplate—especially if they involved me. "If he tries *anything*, he'll regret it. And right now, I need you to contact Parella for me."

"I don't think—"

"That's right, you don't. You just do," I cut in. "Now!"

To say he looked unhappy would be a major understatement. "Matt, I need your phone."

There was a rustle of movement; then the guard handed the phone to Jackson, who handed it to me. "Hurry," was all he said.

There was an edge of strain in his voice, a slight tremor that spoke of limits being reached. While I could feel the incessant pull of the flames on my strength, Jackson was fading far faster.

I handed Radcliffe the phone, and he quickly dialed a number—one I tucked away in the memory banks for later.

"Parella," he said after a moment. "It's Radcliffe. I have a message for you."

He paused. Parella replied, but his voice was little more than an incomprehensible murmur. Even so, I doubted it belonged to the vampire in the darkened room. The speech rhythms weren't as smooth around the edges.

Radcliffe glanced at me. "It's from the fire witch. She

wants a meet." He paused, then said, "It's not like I had a fucking choice. It was either ring you or be crisped."

I reached forward and plucked the phone from his grasp. "I have to agree with him on the no-choice point. You and I need to talk."

"I can hardly see why." There was an odd, almost aristocratic edge in Parella's gravelly voice that spoke of a cultured upbringing somewhere in his past. "And you certainly have nothing we need."

"If you're so sure of that, then fine, don't meet us. We need to talk to De Luca at some stage, anyway."

He didn't immediately answer, and there was nothing in the way of background noise. Wherever he was, it was deathly silent.

"Fine," he said eventually. "But we do it at a location of my choosing."

"Em," Jackson said, "we need to go."

"When and where?" I said quickly.

"Highpoint Shopping Centre, Hoyts underground parking lot, three a.m."

"Tonight or tomorrow night?"

"Tomorrow."

Meaning he needed time to set his trap. Which was fine, because it gave us the chance to do the same.

"Em," Jackson warned again.

"Agreed." I hung up and handed the phone to Radcliffe. "If I were you, I'd make myself scarce for a little while. The new boss didn't sound too pleased about your actions."

He didn't say anything, but his scowl got darker. I smiled and added sweetly, "Oh, and if you're looking for your wallet, I do believe we accidently dropped it into MJ's mailbox. If you're lucky, she won't find it until tomorrow. If you're not . . ." I shrugged. "Oh, and she said you'd better appear tonight with the money you owe her, or she's going to your grandmother."

He swore vehemently. I left him to it and climbed out. The flames around the door were flickering and fading, which was an indication of how close to the edge Jackson was on the strength front.

"Drop it," I said, and raised a secondary barrier behind his as it faded. A soft ache began behind my eyes, but I ignored it and glanced at the nearest guard. "Very carefully give me the rest of your weapons. Then get into the car."

He handed me a gun and a knife. I checked the gun to ensure the safety was on, tucked it into the waist of my jeans, and handed Jackson the knife. Once the guard was in the car, I slammed the door shut and sealed it—in fact, sealed all of them—by using my flame to weld it to the main body of the car. Radcliffe might be able to smash a window and climb out, but I doubted the goon would. He was too large.

"Go," I said to Jackson.

He took a somewhat shuddery breath, then turned and ran for the stairs. I followed at a slower pace, wanting to be sure he was close to the street-level exit before I reached the stairwell. As the door closed behind me, I claimed fire form and surged upward. It was only once I regained flesh form that I released all the flames. The stretched line of energy feeding them snapped back painfully, making me wince as I exited.

"You okay?" Jackson immediately asked. He was

leaning against a power pull just to the left of the foot-path, and he didn't look great. His skin was ashen, and his face was gaunt.

"Better than you, from the look of things."

He grimaced and pushed away from the pole. Despite his appearance, he strode forward quickly.

"It would appear Rory was right—my body isn't designed to feed the flames of a phoenix. Not for long, anyway."

The stairwell door behind us opened, and I quickly looked around, flames sparking across my fingers. It was a woman leaving the parking lot, not Radcliffe's other goon or one of the security guards.

"You need to eat and rest, and the sooner the better."

"Let's just concentrate on getting the hell away from here first." He tossed me the keys. "You drive."

We made it to the car without anyone coming after us, and within a matter of minutes we were driving through the city, heading for our bolt-hole. I stopped at a local fish-and-chips shop, buying not only several pieces of battered fish for us all but also burgers, the biggest tray of hot chips that they had, and several bottles of Coke. The delicious aroma had my mouth watering as we carried it all into our tiny apartment.

"Good timing," Rory said as he clattered down the stairs. "I was just about to head out—" The words cut off as his gaze fell on Jackson. "What the fuck happened? You look like *shit*."

Jackson pulled out a chair and sat down heavily. "Well, the good news is that we found Radcliffe. The bad news is that creating a wall of flame really does suck the life out of me."

"So I was right."

"Yes." Jackson rubbed a hand across his eyes. "I guess I'll just have to be satisfied controlling fire rather than creating it."

"It might be the wiser choice," Rory commented, walking into the kitchen. "At least until we know whether the draining is a permanent feature or if it's just a sign that your body needs to acclimatize to feeding fire."

"Neither you nor I are immune from the effects of creating flame." I dumped the parcels of food and Coke on the table. "And we're fire spirits, not flesh."

"Yeah, but Jackson may not exactly be flesh anymore after the merging, either." Rory brought plates and glasses over to the table, then helped me tear open the various packages. "Until we understand the full range of consequences, baby steps are required."

"After today, I totally agree." Jackson poured himself a large glass of Coke, gulped it down, and then added, "Even so, it was totally worth it."

Rory raised an eyebrow. "So Radcliffe actually gave you something useful?"

"Yeah. We have a meeting set up with Morretti's replacement in just over twenty-four hours."

"It that a wise move?" Rory helped himself to some of the food. "It'll undoubtedly be a trap, and there're only three of us."

"What choice have we got?" I filled a plate with fish, chips, and a burger and handed it to Jackson. He gave me a tired-looking smile. "We need to stop the sindicati coming after us, and the only way we're going to do that is to confront the bastards."

"Except that we don't know which faction was be-hind the kidnappings. It may not be Morretti's lot."

"Maybe not, but a point still needs to be made." I grabbed a burger, added a layer of hot chips, then bit into it. It tasted as delicious as it smelled. "The main problem will be the location. It's the underground parking area near Hoyts in Highpoint."

Rory grimaced. "That's not good, especially given vampires are very adept at hiding in shadows."

"Almost as adept as we are at banishing them."

"Radcliffe called you a fire witch," Jackson pointed out. "I doubt it was a slip of the tongue."

I frowned at him. "I'm not seeing your point."

"Weren't fire witches another name for female phoe-nixes?"

"A *very* long time ago." My stomach nevertheless fell. "But Parella and the sindicati *can't* know what I am."

"If the red cloaks do have a spy in PIT's ranks, then the vampire faction working with them will undoubt-edly know, given PIT does," Jackson commented. "And even if they don't, both sides have witnessed your abil-ity to create and control fire. I have no doubt they'll be scrambling to find ways to counteract it as we speak."

"The only way to counteract a phoenix's fire is via magic," Rory said. "And witches powerful enough to create that sort of spell are few and far between."

"Which does not rule it out as a possibility," Jackson said.

"No, it doesn't." I demolished the rest of my burger, then, as my stomach grumbled a reminder it needed far more than just a burger to refuel, grabbed some more chips and a couple of pieces of flake. "But what's the alternative? Going in armed is pretty pointless against—"

"Unless," Jackson cut in, "said weapons are water pistols."

Rory blinked. "Water pistols?"

"Loaded with holy water," Jackson said. "I happen to have several of them ready to rock and roll."

"Great idea," Rory said, "but a water pistol will last only so long, and reloading them won't exactly be easy."

"Yes, but we can carry a few extra vials of the stuff to throw."

"And if we miss, we're in trouble. Holy water may work against vamps, but blowing their fucking brains out is far more effective at *stopping* them."

"True." Jackson leaned forward and refilled his plate. "Maybe we need more soldiers."

"The only people I know are the folks at the fire station and the kids I teach kung fu to," Rory said. "I wouldn't want to bring either of them into a fight like this."

"Even though Mike would undoubtedly revel in the opportunity to kick vampire butt," I murmured.

Rory flashed me a grin. "He would, but he's still just a kid beneath all that hate and fierceness."

"Mike being the street kid you mentioned a few weeks back?" Jackson said. "The one you asked to uncover whether there's a black market cure for the N41A drug Sam gave us?"

That was the drug he'd used to enforce his order to stay away from Morretti and stop investigating Baltimore's murder. While it might not have dissipated from our systems, we still needed to find an antidote in case it was used on us again.

Rory nodded. "There isn't, at least not through normal channels. He's going deeper."

"I hope you told him to be careful," I said.

He gave me the look. I merely grinned and kept demolishing my food.

"There is another option help-wise," Jackson said, his tone contemplative. "I could contact a couple of guys I know—"

"You have *male* friends?" I cut in, in a shocked sort of voice. "Who'd have thought *that* possible?"

"They are far rarer than female friends, let me assure you." His tone was dry. "However, I know at least one of them is within driving distance to Melbourne. And they both like a good fight."

"I'm not sure five of us, even if armed to the hilt, are going to be enough," Rory said. "Not if the meet tomorrow takes a bad turn."

"Ah, but there's the rub," Jackson said. "They're Fae. Earth Fae, to be precise."

Meaning the concrete the vampires thought would protect them would actually become a weapon in the hands of an earth Fae, as they could control not only the earth itself but anything that came out of it. I grinned. "Excellent."

Jackson nodded. "Be warned, though—they *are* Fae, and they can no more let a pretty woman pass them by without at least flirting with her than I can."

I raised an eyebrow. "And this is a problem because?"

"Because *I* haven't finished flirting with you yet."

"And here I was thinking Fae didn't get territorial," Rory commented.

"Oh, we don't. I'd just prefer it if Em wasted all her energy on me."

"Yeah, definitely not territorial at all," I murmured.

He grinned and pushed wearily to his feet. "I'll give them a call; then I'm going to hit the sack."

"Sleep tight," I said.

He nodded and clomped up the stairs. I returned my gaze to Rory. "Any luck finding information on the Aswang?"

"Yes and no. I managed to track down an old Filipino medicine man, but he refused to talk to me. He said he needed to see the lady of fire—the one who dreams."

I blinked. "He knew what you—we—are?"

"From the minute I walked into his shop. He told me off for arriving late, in fact." Rory smiled and shook his head. "It was a weird encounter, let me tell you. But you'll soon have the chance to experience it for yourself."

I frowned, not liking the sound of *that*. "Meaning what?"

"Meaning he'll be here in"—he glanced at his watch—"a few minutes."

"Damn it, Rory, why didn't you make the appointment for the morning? I'm dead tired—"

"*I* didn't make the appointment," he cut in. "The old guy did. And, trust me, he would *not* take no for an answer."

"You still shouldn't have given him this address. We've gone underground, remember?" I grabbed the bottle of Coke and topped off my glass. I had a sudden feeling I was going to need the caffeine hit.

"I *didn't* tell him." His expression was bland, but amusement lurked at the corners of his eyes.

Before I could comment, someone knocked on the door. Rory rose, checked the peephole, and then opened the door. The man who stood outside was small in both height and build, and his back was so badly bowed that he wasn't far off being a hunchback. His skin was nutbrown and leatherlike, and his face, when he looked up, was heavily creviced.

But it was his eyes that caught my attention.

They were white—all white. There was color in neither his iris nor his pupil, but they shone with so much power and knowledge it sent a shiver down my spine. Eyes like that had always been an indicator of a true shaman, but they were a rare find in this day and age.

He walked across to the table with a surety that belied his age and posture, and gave me a nod of greeting. "Lady of Fire and Dreams, it is a great honor to meet you." His voice was soft and held only the slightest hint of an accent.

"I'm sure it would have been even more of a pleasure had it not been so damn late." I smiled to take the sting out of my words. "My name is Emberly, and you've already met Rory."

He nodded. "I am Babaylan, but you may call me Lan."

I had the feeling we'd just been bestowed a great honor. "So, tell me, Lan, why would you call me a dreamer? That's not a gift phoenixes have."

"But it is nevertheless one you *do* possess. Do not test

my patience by suggesting otherwise." His tone was sharp, but true shamans were like that. They knew things—saw things—ordinary people never could or would, and they did not suffer fools lightly. "And I'm afraid circumstances do not allow us the gift of a later time. The dreams await, my lady."

"Meaning the Aswang is about to ramp up its attacks?" And that I'd dream about it tonight?

"Yes, but *that* creature is the least of your problems. May I sit?" He motioned to the chair Rory had vacated.

"Sorry, yes. Would you like a drink? Perhaps a coffee?"

"No, thank you." He sat and sighed. "My old bones do not fare so well in the chill of night."

Which made his willingness to come out in it all the more worrying. I glanced at Rory as he claimed the seat next to me, and then said, "Why is the Aswang the least of our problems?"

"Because the omens have been growing worse over this past year, and the darkness is finally rising."

"What darkness are we talking about specifically?" Rory asked. "Vampires? Or creatures like the Aswang?"

The old man's gaze didn't shift from my face, and it made me feel like a kid who'd asked the wrong question—even though I hadn't actually asked it. "You've both been in this world for a very long time. You must be aware that centuries rich in cultural, medical, and political gains are always followed by a period of darkness. *That* is what this city now faces."

Rory and I shared an uncertain glance. "What, like the Dark Ages?" he said.

Lan shook his head. "That term really applies only

to a cultural and economic deterioration. What now approaches is more metaphysical."

I frowned. "Meaning we're about to get flooded by preternatural phenomena?"

"Flooded? No. Not immediately."

"I guess *that's* a relief," I muttered.

Rory asked, "What type of phenomena are we talking about? Creatures or events?"

"Both. And it has already begun. The darkness that grows in Brooklyn, and the Aswang you hunt, are but the first of many who will be drawn to this place." He paused, his expression grave. "There are few dreamers left in this world who have the ability to hunt such things."

"I'm not—"

"A huntress," he finished for me. "But you may yet be forced to become one."

No damn way, I wanted to say, but I held the words in check. I might not have had much to do with shamans over the years, but I did know they were notoriously hard to argue with. "Let's just concentrate on the Aswang for now. How do we stop the damn thing?"

He reached into his pocket and withdrew several charms. "These will stop it from shifting shape."

I somewhat dubiously picked up one of the charms. It was about the size of a five-cent piece, but made of silver rather than alloy, if its weight was anything to go by. There were inscriptions on both sides, though I didn't recognize the language. "What are we supposed to do with them?"

"Throw them into the creature as it shifts between shapes. It will, as I said, pin it to one form."

Hopefully that form would be either human or the

small cat. I really didn't fancy fighting the monstrous black dog, even in spirit form. It might have fled when I'd confronted it in the alley, but who knew how it would react the next time?

I passed the charms over to Rory and then said, "What is the best way of killing it?"

"If it is pinned to a flesh form, either by your flames or by decapitation," Lan said. "They are weaker in the day than at night and impossible to kill in smoke form."

Meaning the damn charms had better work. "How are we supposed to find it? Is there any way to track it during the day?"

"No. They hunt well outside their own territory, so it might not even be based in the city. Your dreams provide the only hope." He smiled and half raised a hand, as if in apology. "I wish I could help you more with this matter."

Rory reached across and squeezed my hand, obviously sensing my frustration. "At least we now have a means of restraining it to one form. That's more than we had five minutes ago."

True. I took a deep breath and released it slowly. "Why is the Aswang moving from dining on the dead to the living?"

"Because the dead provide an easy feed, but as it grows stronger, it becomes more brazen and moves to sweeter, fresher flesh."

"But it's not eating flesh—it's sucking out organs."

"Because it considers them delicacies. And the younger the flesh, the sweeter the taste."

An odd sense of foreboding flooded me. "Meaning it will eventually go after children?"

"I'm afraid so, yes."

Then I had no choice—I *had* to stop it before that happened. I could—and did—sometimes ignore the dreams, but never those that involved children. Perhaps that was why the dreams didn't start until the Aswang's third kill—the prophetic part of me had known it was moving onto not only the living, but young ones at that.

The old man glanced at his watch, then pushed to his feet. "I must go. The time for dreaming approaches." He hesitated, his expression concerned. "Be wary, both of you. Even fire can be doused by darkness."

"Death is something we've faced many times before," I said softly. "It's not something we fear."

"Ah, but death comes in many forms, my lady, and some of them you should definitely fear." And with that warning hanging in the air, he nodded at Rory and left.

"You were right," I said as Rory rose to lock the door. "That was definitely a different experience."

"Yep. Nothing like a bit of doom and gloom to brighten the evening." His gaze swept me as he moved back to the table, and his expression became concerned. "You feel a little low in energy."

I grimaced. "Yeah, but we can't risk a full recharge here, and we certainly can't go home to do it."

"No." He reached across the table and clasped my hand, his flesh becoming flame where our fingers entwined. "But a little foreplay never hurt anyone, and it will at least boost your reserves a little."

"And drain yours in the process." Even so, I drew in his heat and energy, felt it surge through my body, refreshing and renewing the inner fires. It would have been easy—far too easy—to fully refuel at his expense, but that was neither fair nor wise.

After a few minutes, I sighed and pulled my fingers from his. "Thanks."

He smiled, but little warmth touched his eyes. "We're going to have to risk going home in the next day or so—especially if tomorrow night goes down as badly as I think it will."

"I know." I grabbed my drink and gulped down the last part of it. "But right now, sleep will have to suffice."

Rory shook his head. "I don't know how either of you can sleep immediately after a meal like that."

"Cast-iron stomachs." I got up, walked around the table, and dropped a kiss on his cheek. "Don't stay up too late plotting various attack strategies for tomorrow night. We need you alert rather than sleepy."

"I won't. Sleep soundly."

"*That* is doubtful, given what Lan said."

"Shamans aren't always right, Em. I wouldn't read too much into his doom-and-gloom predictions right now."

"It's not the warnings of darkness I'm worried about. It's the possibility of the Aswang's next victim being a kid." I waved good night and headed up the stairs to bed. Sleep found me all too quickly.

And, as predicted, so did the dream.

This time, I found myself at the intersection of two streets. To the left and right there was a mix of large old houses and commercial properties, but the street directly in front was filled with trees and century-old homes. I glanced up at the signs illuminated by the streetlight above them—I was standing at the junction of Edlington Street and Auburn Road. I wasn't familiar with either of them.

For several minutes I didn't move. I couldn't see the creature, and the air was free from the scent of evil. A lone dog barked somewhere in the distance, but otherwise the night was still. Peaceful.

Then the click of nails against concrete began to echo, the sound so harsh and close at first that I had to quell the urge to spin around and look for the thing. It wouldn't have done any good, because the magic this creature employed ensured that the closer it sounded, the farther away it actually was.

I waited, hands clenched against the heat that burned through me. As the clicking of its nails grew ever softer, its scent began to stain the night. I shuddered and kept my breathing shallow, not wanting to draw in its evil even in a dream.

As the clicking faded almost completely away, I glanced left. The creature walked toward me, its form that of a slightly larger-than-normal black cat. Its nose was in the air, tasting the night, and, after a moment, a grotesque smile touched its feline lips, revealing sharp yellow teeth—*not* feline teeth, but canine.

It strolled onto Edlington Street and crossed in front of me. Waves of evil and hunger hit, and my stomach rose as my breath caught in my throat. This thing was getting stronger with every kill.

I couldn't let it kill tonight. I just couldn't.

Looking neither right nor left, it padded down the sidewalk, seeming to know exactly where it was headed. I followed, looking for street numbers and anything else that might lend some clue as to what sub-urb we were in. But the night was dark and the large trees blocked out much of the light.

The creature paused in front of a six-foot-high wooden fence covered in ivy. A large number 7 had been screwed into the middle of the wooden gate, and several large gum trees dominated the small front yard beyond it. The house itself was neat and painted cheer-fully in yellow and green. As the Aswang leapt the fence, it began to shift—change—until it was once again little more than ash. In that form, it slithered up to the front door and slipped inside.

I followed. The creature resumed cat form in the hall and padded past the first two doors. Someone was snoring inside the first, and the second was a bath-room. The third door was its target.

Inside was a child.

A baby.

And she was *alive*.

Horror froze me, even as fires erupted. But I couldn't burn this thing, couldn't help, not in this dream and not if I didn't find where the hell this house was.

As if sensing my desperation, the dream spun and swept me into the kitchen. There on the counter were several envelopes—*Hawthorn East*. We were in Haw-thorn East.

The dream shattered and I thrust up in bed, my heart going a mile a minute and my fear so fierce, I could taste it. Rory knelt beside the bed, his grip almost squashing my fingers as he swallowed the flames that threatened to set the place alight. In the bunk opposite,

Jackson slept on, his body obviously even more drained of strength than he'd been admitting.

"The creature isn't just going after a child—it's going after a *baby*." I shut down my fires and jumped out of bed. "I have to stop it."

"Fuck," Rory said, and immediately began dressing. "When and where?"

I gave him the address as I pulled on jeans and my sweater. "Do you know the area?"

"I think Auburn Road runs off Barkers Road."

"Which is the continuation of Victoria Street, isn't it?" When he nodded, I added, "You have to contact Sam."

"You can't—"

"I fucking *can*." I took a deep breath to calm my anger and gripped Rory's arm briefly. "I'm sorry. It's just that the baby's not dead and—" I hesitated, flames and tears surging in equal amounts.

Understanding flashed through his expression. "Grab the charms and go. There's a public phone box down the street, so I'll ring Sam, then follow."

"Thanks." I kissed his cheek, then raced down the stairs to grab the charms before running outside.

The moon was lower in the sky, but everything was still. Hushed. It was almost as if the night, aware of the terrible thing about to happen, were holding its breath in denial.

I raced into the street but didn't bother getting into the car. It wouldn't be fast enough. The only way I was going to get across to East Hawthorn in time was in spirit form.

It was a risk, a *huge* risk, but I didn't care. Not when the life of a baby was at stake.

I became flame and surged into the sky, streaking through the darkness so fast, anyone watching on the streets below would have thought I was nothing more than a small comet with an odd trajectory.

Thankfully, Victoria Street wasn't far away from Johnston Street. Once I'd found it, I followed it along, dipping lower only once it crossed the Yarra River and became Barkers Road. Parked cars lined either side of the wide road, but once again the street was empty of life and no trams ran along the tracks that ran down the center of the street.

I flamed down the long hill and past the lush sports grounds of Xavier College, until I came to the Auburn Road intersection. There were several more intersections and another long hill before I reached Edlington Street. As I raced onto it, I sent a prayer to all the gods, asking them to give me a break and allow me to stop the creature before it got anywhere near that house or the baby.

But as I shifted to human form, I was confronted by the sharp wail of a child and a woman screaming.

The gods weren't listening.

The creature was already here.

CHAPTER 13

I crashed shoulder first through the gate, then raced up to the front door. The screaming inside was high-pitched and desperate and accompanied by the snarls of a creature that was neither cat nor dog but something in between. With all that noise, no one was going to hear me knocking, even if I had time to waste.

I smashed one of the door's glass panels, then became flame and swept into the hall. As I regained flesh form, a man came staggering out of the baby's bedroom, blood spurting from a large gash down his left arm. I swore, then grabbed a scarf from the nearby hat stand and ran toward him.

"Wrap this tightly around the wound and keep your arm up," I said, and shoved the pretty scarf at him.

He blinked at me, his expression owlish, shocked. "Who the fuck are you?"

"Cop," I said. "Now get back—"

"My fucking wife and child—"

"I'm well aware of just who and what are in that room," I cut in brusquely. "Just do as I goddamn say and let me save them."

I didn't wait for his answer; I just spun and went into the room. The woman I'd heard screaming was hunkered down in the far corner behind the cot, shielding the baby with her body. The creature was standing in the middle of the room, its form pulsating, growing, from that of a large cat to the more-familiar form of the black dog. But it was more ash than flesh, and that meant this might be my one and only chance to use the charms. I dug them out of my pocket and threw them at the creature.

The charms disappeared into its ashy mass, but for an instant, nothing happened. The creature showed no awareness of my presence and simply continued to grow, until it loomed over the pair in the corner. The woman whimpered but otherwise didn't move. The creature raised a wickedly barbed paw, but at that precise moment, a crimson light flared deep in the middle of the creature's ashy heart. It was faint at first but grew fast, until it became a tide that swept through the black mass, staining the sooty particles and clinging to the bits that were already flesh. It stopped the creature from changing, but the form it pinned the creature to was big and strong, and a warped mix of cat and dog. Maybe throwing those coins *hadn't* been such a great idea.

It screamed, a guttural sound filled with anger and frustration, then spun and lashed out with the barbed paw. I jumped back with a yelp but wasn't quite fast enough. The claws sliced through my sweater and down into flesh, parting it as easily as hot knives through butter. As blood began to ooze down my stomach, I spun a lasso of fire around the creature and forced it backward—not only away from the woman and the baby but out through the window and into the night.

It fought my grip every step of the way, pulling at my fiery rope, twisting and tearing at its own flesh in an effort to free itself. I gritted my teeth and held on as I scrambled over to the woman and knelt beside her.

"Are you okay? Is your baby okay?"

She didn't answer. She just shrank away from my touch and screamed again. I swore and hit her. It wasn't nice, but I didn't have time for niceties. Her screaming stopped; she stared at me with wide, frightened eyes.

"Is your baby okay?" I repeated. There was blood on her nightdress, but I wasn't sure if it was the baby's or hers. There wasn't a lot of it, which was at least something.

She nodded.

Relief rushed through me. "Good. More police are on the way, but you need to call an ambulance for your husband."

She licked her lips. "And that . . . thing?"

"I'll take care of it."

But even as I rose, my lasso shattered, and the force of its destruction was enough to send me staggering back. I gripped the side of the cot to steady myself, then took a deep, somewhat quivery breath before pushing away from the cot and diving out the shattered window. I hit the grass hard and rolled to my feet, ready to fight, but the creature was nowhere in sight.

I swore and ran through the still-swinging gate, quickly looking left, then right—and spotted the very end of the creature's black tail as it disappeared around the corner onto Auburn Road.

I swore and bolted after it, changing form as I ran. I swept upward in an effort to avoid being seen by both those who might be peering out their windows to see what was going on and those who were driving along Auburn Road.

The creature galloped along the sidewalk, keeping to the shadows as much as possible, its grotesque form rippling and moving, as if it were trying to shift shape as it ran. Despite its ungainly gait, it was superfast, and I had to dredge up a lot more speed to even catch it.

Up ahead, lights speared the darkness as a car turned onto the road. The creature was briefly illuminated, its red eyes glowing with unearthly fire. I'm not sure whether the driver noticed, but the car's tires squealed as the driver suddenly accelerated.

As the car swept past, I spun another lasso and lashed the creature tight. Then, with a heave that shuddered through my entire being, I lifted it up into the air, surging even higher as I battled to get the creature out of the street *and* out of sight.

Once again it fought my hold, tearing at both my fiery leash and its own flesh. Pain ripped through my being, and my flames began to pulsate, a sure sign I was pushing the limits of my strength. I hissed and battled to hold on, to keep moving. I needed to find somewhere to dispose of this thing, and fast.

As I neared Barkers Road, I remembered the football ovals at Xavier College. It was probably as remote as I was going to get in an area this built up. I swept around the intersection, following the brightly lit road, the creature trailing behind me on an ever-thinning leash of fire. Its fur was beginning to smolder, but it was hate and anger that lashed the night rather than pain.

My leash and energy snapped just as I neared the middle of the four ovals, and it sent us both tumbling down. I hit the ground hard and slid forward, my form rippling from fire to bird to flesh, then back again as I came to a halt in a cloud of dust and cindered grass. But I'd barely had time to gather my thoughts when a snarl of utter fury filled my ears and the air screamed a warning of impact. I twisted around, saw the creature in midair, and called for every ounce of heat I had left.

At the very last minute, the creature must have realized the stupidity of its actions, and it desperately tried to twist away. But it was too close and going far too fast, and it was quickly enveloped in my flames.

It didn't scream. It didn't get the chance. The flames of a phoenix might not be as hot as the mother's lava heart, but the creature was nevertheless soot in little more than a nanosecond.

I scrambled out of the path of the gently falling black rain, then regained human form. Dizziness swept me, and for several minutes it was all I could do to gulp in air and remain upright.

Sirens bit through the night, their blue and red lights washing across the edges of the oval below as they raced by. I watched them swing onto Auburn Street, then slowly pushed upright. Only to have my knees go out from underneath me and send me tumbling backward again.

But I never hit the ground. Arms caught me a hairsbreadth away and hauled me upright again. Rory. I closed my eyes against the relief that threatened to spill in tears down my cheeks.

"Damn it, Em, you're dangerously low on energy. We need to merge—*now*."

Tell me something I don't know. But the words didn't make it past my throat, because the world spun around me and lights began to dance in front of my eyes. His grip tightened as he wrapped his arms around my body and held me close. He smelled of ash and fire and heat, and all I wanted to do was lose myself in his strength.

"We can't," I somehow bit out. "Not here."

"We're in the middle of four goddamn ovals. We're as safe here as we're ever going to be," he growled. "Now flame!"

I obeyed. This time, our joining was no sensual dance, no seduction. We didn't have the luxury of time, and I simply didn't have the strength. I was close to flaming out, and that was a dangerous place to be for a phoenix.

But as our flames combined and his essence flowed across every corner of my soul, strength began to filter through me. It wasn't coming from him, but rather from the connection itself. This merging might be a necessity as much as an affirmation of being, but it was nevertheless filled with power. It was *that* power that renewed me, refreshed me. And it led us, as ever, into a storm of ecstasy.

I came back into flesh still locked in Rory's arms but feeling a whole lot stronger than I had only moments ago. He brushed a kiss across the top of my head, then stepped back, his grip still fierce on my arms as he studied me critically. After a minute, he relaxed and released me. "How bad are the wounds on your stomach?"

"I actually don't know." I lifted my sweater and checked them out. The slashes were long but, thankfully, not particularly deep. The fires of our merging had at least cauterized the wounds and stopped any chance of infection, but they never really healed them. As a result, they were still damn sore. "I wish we had the healing powers of werewolves. It'd be handy at times like this."

"Especially given your recent penchant for going after less-than-savory types."

"Actually," I said, amusement teasing my lips, "the only unsavory thing I've willingly chased *this* lifetime is the creature who's now ash littering the grass."

"What about the sindicati?"

"I'm not chasing them. I'm meeting them." He rolled his eyes at the distinction, and I grinned. "Did you ring Sam?"

"Yeah. He and Adam arrived at the house several minutes ago." He half smiled. "I have to say, it was a pretty impressive sight, you in fire form dragging that thing behind you on a flaming leash."

"Hitting the dirt from that height *wasn't* so impressive, I can tell you."

"I imagine not." He glanced past me, studying the soot that littered the grass behind us. "Good job on incinerating it, though."

"I was lucky." And so were the parents of that baby. It could have very easily gone the other way—a thought that sent a chill running through me. I rubbed my arms and turned around. "Should we return to the house or just go back to the apartment?"

"I'd imagine that if we didn't return, Sam would put out an all-points to find us. Not what we need under the circumstances."

No, it definitely wasn't, especially if Rochelle—or even Sam—was inadvertently feeding the gray cloak information. "Then let's go get it over with."

I trudged through the ovals and followed the extraordinarily high fence—one that was obviously meant to stop both footballs and cricket balls from being smashed into the street—until we found an exit.

By the time we arrived back at the house, there was a mix of cop cars, unmarked PIT vehicles, and several ambulances crowded into the small street.

A cop stopped us at the front gate, but before he could say anything, Sam appeared at the door. It was almost as if he knew I was near, and I couldn't help wondering if that awareness was a result of the virus and becoming a pseudo vampire, or the resurgence of the odd second sense we'd once shared about each other's nearness.

I had to hope it wasn't the latter. He was obviously intent on getting his life back together—as much as was possible given the virus, anyway—and he didn't need a lingering connection to me to mess up the works.

"Jack, it's okay. Let them in." His gaze skimmed me but came to an abrupt halt at the bloody slashes that decorated the middle of my sweater. "Do you need medical help?"

I smiled at the cop as he stepped back to let us through, then shook my head. "It's stopped bleeding."

He didn't move out of the doorway, forcing us both to halt on the veranda. "And the creature?"

"Little more than ashes staining a football field."

"No chance of resurrection?"

"None at all."

He grunted and stepped to one side. "The parents want to thank you. They're down the end of the hall, in the kitchen. After that, we'll need a statement."

"Can't I just say the thing is no longer a problem and leave it at that?"

I brushed past him, my body far too aware of his scent and strength. A regular cop guarded the entrance to the baby's room, and I could see several more down the hall, along with the ambulance officers.

"No, you can't," he said. "But I'll be taking the statement, so it shouldn't be a problem."

Except that it *was*, given the possible leak. I really didn't need the gray cloak learning too much about my capabilities—although I guess, considering what I'd done in Brooklyn, *that* cat was well and truly out of the bag.

Our footsteps echoed softly against the hall's wooden flooring, and the tearstained face of the mother peered past one of the paramedics.

"Oh, thank god," she said, the relief in her expression echoing through her voice. She was still holding her little girl, and I couldn't say I blamed her. I'd have been doing the same after such a close call. "I wasn't sure I'd get the chance to thank you."

"I'm just glad I happened to be in the area and was able to help." As the paramedic moved to one side, I squatted down in front of her and touched the little girl's fingers. She appeared totally unharmed, which meant the blood I'd seen must have come from the woman. As the baby gurgled and clutched at my finger, I added, "Are you okay?"

She nodded. "It's just a minor cut, nothing more. But my husband and I owe you a great debt."

"No, you don't." I rose again and glanced at the husband. "As I said, you're just lucky I was in the area."

"And that thing?" he asked, a slight edge to both his voice and the way he was standing.

"Won't be troubling anyone again."

He nodded, and I could almost see the tension slither from him. I glanced around and met Sam's gaze.

"This way," he said, and headed for the back door.

We followed. Once we were standing in the middle of the small yard, out of immediate earshot of everyone inside, he pulled out his phone and hit the RECORD button.

"Okay, for the purposes of this record, state your name, address, and whether you consent to this statement being recorded."

"I thought PIT didn't operate by the same rules as regular cops?"

"In this case, we have to because the cops got here first. Name, address, and consent, please."

I did so, then, once Sam had identified himself, the time and the location, gave him the bare-bones tales of what had happened.

"And exact location of this thing's ashes?"

"I can't be exact, but it's basically in the middle of the area that divides all four ovals."

He nodded. "Have you anything else to say?"

"Nope." I hesitated. "Will the cops have access to these tapes?"

"No. We just need to appear to be following the rules in this sort of situation." He glanced at Rory and repeated the process, though there wasn't much he could add. Once he'd finished, Sam stopped recording, then saved the file and shoved the phone back into his pocket.

"Is that it?" I asked.

He nodded. "If we need anything else, we'll contact you."

He had to find us first, but I didn't say anything, just wished him good night and followed Rory across the yard.

But just as I was about to enter the house, Sam said, "Em?"

I hesitated and looked around. "What?"

"I've ordered Luke's body to be exhumed. I don't believe he can possibly be the man in charge of the red cloaks, but I need to be sure."

"I really hope he isn't, Sam."

"So do I." His voice was bleak. "I'll let you know either way."

"Thanks." And with that, I left.

Jackson's friends arrived at sunset. Neither was classic Fae in appearance—or, at least, classic as defined by literature and movies. The earth was a solid element, and that very much described the two men. They were both five foot nine and had the same stocky build, with rich brown skin and hair. The only way to really tell them apart was by their eyes—Adán's were the color of chocolate, and Dmitri's more the color of burned earth.

Despite Jackson's warning, neither man flirted out-rageously with me. They were too caught up in the ex-citement and logistics of the upcoming meeting; Fae really *did* live for danger, it seemed.

The five of us discussed every possible scenario we could think of, and we came up with plans and coping mechanisms for each one. Whether it would be enough was anyone's guess, and very much depended on just what, exactly, the sindicati had planned for tonight.

In the end, it was decided that Adán, Jackson, and I would confront Parella and his crew, while Rory and Dmitri would break into the Highpoint complex and make their way down to the Hoyts level. It was the only way they'd be able to get close enough to react if this went down wrong and yet remain beyond the vampires' immediate sensory range. We were presum-ing, of course, that both men would also be able to nul-lify the center's security cameras and avoid on-ground security personnel.

We also went with more traditional means of protection—proper guns rather than water pistols and holy water. It was extremely doubtful that Parella would let us get anywhere near him armed, so it was pointless to waste a precious resource like holy water. Dmitri also offered several blessed knives for us to use, although when I asked why an earth Fae would even possess such weapons, he just grinned and declined to answer.

By the time the meeting rolled around, I was a bun-dle of nerves. We arrived at Highpoint at two forty-five and cruised down the road that led into lower-level parking. There was no gate on the entrance, but Jackson stopped the car regardless, keeping the headlights on and the engine running. The security lights that dotted the various buildings at regular intervals provided brief spots of brightness, but the parking area was a wasteland of darkness. But I guess that was no real surprise, given we were here to meet vampires.

"I can't see or sense anything." Jackson glanced at me. "You?"

I shook my head. "But that's hardly surprising, considering a phoenix's senses aren't exactly wolf sharp."

"But they are *very* prettily packaged," Adán commented, his voice gravelly and pleasant.

Jackson's grin flashed. "Already used that line, my friend."

"Which does *not* make it any less true." Adán leaned forward, and his scent spun around me, fresh and earthy. "Someone's watching us from the shadows."

I glanced around in surprise. "How can you tell that? It's pitch-black, and Fae don't have infrared."

He smiled. "Earth Fae don't need it when the earth is more than willing to whisper its secrets. There're another five deeper within."

"Only six?" My gaze went to Jackson's. "That's not what I was expecting."

"No. And it makes me nervous."

"Maybe they're playing it straight," Adán said. "They have nothing to lose by doing so."

"We're talking about the vampire mafia here," I said. "I very much think they'd play *every* situation to their own advantage."

"I daresay we'll soon find out," Adán said, "as our watcher is about to reveal himself."

Even as he spoke, a thin man with dark hair and pockmarked skin stepped into the pale light that washed the parking entrance. He studied us for a moment, then motioned to the pedestrian-access gate to the left of the main gate. Obviously, they didn't want us driving any farther.

"And so the fun begins." Anticipation rolled through Jackson's voice. He pulled on the parking brake and stopped the engine. "Adán, you want to warn Rory and Dmitri that we're about to head in?"

As Adán spoke into the small two-way we'd purchased for the night, Jackson and I climbed out of the car. The night was cool and crisp, and the promise of rain filled the light breeze that teased the ends of my hair away from my neck. I flexed my fingers, and sparks flew, bright fireflies caught by the wind and flung away.

Once Adán was out of the car, Jackson locked it, then led the way in. The vampire stepped back and once again disappeared into the shadows. But while he was invisible to the eye, I knew precisely where he was. Vampires might naturally run cooler than the rest of humanity, but they weren't beings of ice and, in most circumstances, I could sense the heat in them, whether they were shadowed or not. Of course, given the tension and my heightened state of awareness right now, I'd probably sense the heat of a gnat half a mile away if it so much as twitched the wrong way.

"Straight ahead," the shadowed vampire said. His voice cracked as he spoke, and it made me wonder just how old he'd been when he'd turned. Not very, I suspected. "Walk slow. Don't try any of your tricks."

"I might ask that you do the same," Jackson commented, "or this could get really messy."

"Yes, it could," the kid said. If he was at all concerned by the prospect, he didn't sound it. But then, he was one of six here, and that suggested Parella had a whole lot of trust in his capabilities.

We walked through the cavernous parking lot, Jackson and I side by side and Adán at our back. The vampire shadowed our movements but kept a good six feet between us.

When we'd walked about a third of the way through the first part of the lot, he said, "Stop and divest yourselves of weapons."

Though we'd expected this to happen, it didn't mean we had to be happy about it. Or comply too easily.

"The only way we're going to leave our weapons here is if you lot do the same." I glanced ahead, at the usually brightly lit Hoyts cinema entrance. They might be nothing more than shadows, but the remaining vampires were near there, watching.

"We are not armed," the kid said. "There's no need for us to be."

It wasn't so much the statement that ramped up the tension already twisting through me but the confident manner in which it was said.

"Yeah, well, you're vampires," Jackson said. "You'll have to forgive our hesitation about dropping our sole means of self-defense."

"They are hardly your sole means," the kid came back. "We have all seen what the fire witch is capable of."

What *I* was capable of, not what *we* were capable of. It very much suggested they weren't aware that Jackson was a fire Fae—and that one point could make the difference between surviving this meeting and not. I flexed my fingers, this time controlling the sparks. "Then why fear guns when fire is far more dangerous?"

"Do you wish this meeting or not?" he said. "Because the only way it will proceed is if you drop all your guns."

That he'd avoided answering my question could mean only one thing—they didn't fear my fire because they believed they could counter it. And *that* was the one situation for which we'd had no answer. If there *was* a containment spell here somewhere, then what I could and couldn't do would very much depend on the strength and scope of the magic itself.

But if they truly believed I was some form of witch rather than a phoenix, then there was at least hope. They could restrict my own fire, and they might even be able to restrict my access to the mother—especially if whoever produced this spell was old enough to realize that some fire witches could draw on the heat of the earth itself. But if they didn't know I was actually a phoenix, then a spell would not inhibit a change to my true form. But it was a change I could make only if there was absolutely no other choice, because I had no desire to out myself to anyone, much less the likes of Parella and his crew.

I glanced at Jackson, and he nodded. We pulled out our guns and tossed them on the concrete.

"I trust that is it?" the kid said.

"Yes, so can we please get this show on the road?"

My voice held an edge I hoped they took for annoyance rather than fear. "We're here for your boss's benefit as much as our own."

"That," the kid said, "remains to be seen. This way."

He stepped away from the shadows and led us deeper into the underground complex. I glanced at the glassed-off Hoyts entrance as we passed it, looking for some hint that Rory and Dmitri were in there. I couldn't sense them, and maybe that was just as well, because if I could, the vampires no doubt would, too.

As we moved into the deeper darkness beyond the Hoyts entrance, an unnatural energy began to stir around me. It was little more than a whisper that caressed my skin in gentle waves, but it had the hairs at the back of my neck standing on end. I paused instinctively, and the two men instantly stopped.

"You okay?" Jackson asked.

"Yeah."

I forced my feet forward and brushed my fingers across both his hand and Adán's, silently letting them know that the magic we'd feared was here. Jackson swore under his breath. Adán merely flashed me a smile and murmured, "And the challenge has been set."

Fae really *were* crazy people.

The magic grew stronger the deeper into the parking complex we moved, until it felt like a blanket settling around. My breathing quickened and my skin crawled, although the magic's touch was neither clean nor foul—a fact that suggested its creator sat somewhere in the middle in terms of good and evil. And whoever she was—although it could have easily been a male, because the term "witch" applied to both genders even if literature generally thought otherwise—she was well practiced in her art. The spell not only felt strong but tight.

Whether it would be enough to fully restrict me remained to be seen.

The kid eventually stopped. Although they didn't immediately reveal themselves, four of the five other vampires stood six feet away—three in front, one slightly to the rear. The fifth now stood about ten feet behind us. The kid became shadow again and joined the vampire at the rear.

"What is it you wish of us?"

It wasn't Parella who spoke. The voice wasn't gravelly enough.

"We came here to speak to Parella," I said. "Not his second, or third, or whatever the hell you are. If he's not here, then we're leaving."

There was a pause; then a familiar voice said, "I'm here. Now say what you came here to say."

"We haven't got Wilson's research," I said bluntly. "And we currently have no idea where his backup files are, because the only person who might know has now been killed."

"And who might that person be?"

"Denny Rosen."

That produced a reaction, even if it was one I couldn't actually see, just sense. But the mere fact they were surprised meant they weren't up to date on the current state of affairs when it came to the virus and the research. But why? I would have thought knowing everything that was going on—and what moves the other players in the search were making—would be vital if they wanted to grab the research for themselves.

"How did he die?" Parella asked.

"He was murdered." I paused. "And, depending on who you believe, by either yourself or De Luca."

"Why would we want him killed? Surely Radcliffe has mentioned we were paying him to track your movements and grab the files."

Radcliffe hadn't actually mentioned the tracking bit, but maybe our paranoia over the car's being bugged hadn't been that far off the mark.

"For that same reason, I cannot imagine De Luca wanting Rosen killed," Parella continued. "He's after the research every bit as much as we are."

"Actually, I believe he already has it."

The shadows abruptly parted, and a man stepped forward. He was tall, well built, and very tanned, especially for a vampire. His steel gray hair was cropped short, and his face was dominated by a Roman nose and a chin dimple you could lose a finger in. His eyes were the same color as his hair but totally devoid of life. It was almost as if there were nothing going on beyond them—and that could only mean Parella was a very *old* vampire. *That* depth of emotional control came only with time—centuries and centuries of it. Of course, if they remained alive long enough, then time also leached any vestiges of humanity from them. And that, in turn, made them *very* dangerous, because a vampire devoid of emotion also had no remorse, no guilt, and nothing in the way of a conscience. Parella might not be at that stage yet, but, looking at his eyes, I couldn't help but think he wasn't that far away from it, either.

"And how would you know something like that?" His voice was lower than before, and thick with menace.

Though neither Jackson nor Adán moved, I felt their sudden readiness for action. We might have lost our guns, but we still had the blessed silver knives and, among the three of us, we could certainly take out at least a couple of them before they realized what was happening. And even if the magic did restrict my abilities, Adán could still give them hell in this concrete cavern.

I crossed my arms and met Parella's gaze evenly—and hoped like hell he wasn't catching the rapid pounding of my heart or the quivering of my insides.

"I very much suspect we know a whole lot more about De Luca and his exploits than you do at the moment."

"That," Parella said, "is highly unlikely."

I smiled. "And are you willing to bet your life on that?"

He raised an eyebrow, the movement oddly elegant. "Are you?"

"I wouldn't be here if I wasn't." I shrugged. "But I want something in exchange for our information about De Luca."

"And what might that be? The ability to walk out of here rather than crawl, perhaps?"

I snorted, even though the cold amusement in his voice had goose bumps skittering across my skin.

"That would undoubtedly be good, but what I actually want is a guarantee you'll stop your people coming after us."

"My people haven't been chasing you."

"Perhaps they haven't, but I still want that guarantee."

He considered me for a moment. "And the research notes?"

"The research notes—which may or may not exist, by the way—are not part of this agreement."

"Then we have no agreement, and you have wasted my time. And *that* is very vexing."

And we didn't want him vexed if the sudden rush of anticipation coming from the other vampires was anything to go by.

"De Luca has access to both Baltimore and Wilson," I said quickly. "And he's working with someone who poses more of a threat to you and your organization than me or PIT or anyone else for that matter."

Parella studied me for a moment, his expression contemplative. "Go on."

"Do we have an agreement?"

He hesitated, then made a "whatever" motion with his hand. "We will allow you to walk out of here, and we will also not come after you—not until the notes are found, anyway."

All bets were off if we *did* find them, obviously. But until we did, it at least offered us some maneuvering room. I glanced at Jackson and he nodded.

"Then we have an agreement." I held out a hand. "I do hope you realize it would not be wise to break it."

His smile was as cold as his eyes as he clasped my hand briefly. "And I do hope you realize that the information had better be worth it."

"Oh, I think you'll find it illuminating." I released his hand and flexed my fingers to rid them of the cool, almost dead feel of his flesh. "What do you know about Brooklyn and the red cloaks?"

"Possibly as much as anyone does," Parella replied. "They are insane, and they now control much of that area. Like most sensible people, we abandoned Brooklyn once we realized what was happening."

"Except that they're not all insane. The red cloaks work along the lines of a hive, and there's a queen bee controlling them all. He—the aforementioned queen bee—and a few others are not as affected by the virus as those with the scythe burned into their cheek." I smiled grimly. "Unfortunately for you *and* us, that queen bee is working with De Luca."

"Impossible," Parella growled. "This virus poses as much of a threat to vampires as it does to humanity. He and his ilk would not risk it."

I didn't bother arguing the point. He could find out the hard way if he wished. "The problem for us doesn't end there. Both scientists are alive and in their hands."

"Again, impossible. I know for certain Baltimore was killed—"

"Because your people tortured and killed him? And took his research?" Jackson cut in.

Parella didn't even spare him a glance. "Yes. And unless he ingested vampire blood—and I would have known had he done that—there is no way he could have survived."

"He didn't drink vampire blood, but he *was* somehow infected by the virus," I said. "He recently walked out of the morgue and joined the red-cloak crew."

"You know this for certain? How?"

"PIT told me."

"Ah." Parella contemplated me. "And what of Wilson?"

"If you believe the police and witness statements, he was attacked by red cloaks, and his body was dragged into the sewers to conceal it. We believe they dragged him down there so that they could keep an eye on him until the infection took over and he became one of them."

"All of which is possible, but it does not explain your belief that De Luca's faction is working with the red cloaks."

"Did your faction kidnap both Jackson and me, and hold him hostage in return for the research notes Baltimore gave me just before he was murdered?"

"Obviously not, since we already have them."

"Then you weren't aware that I exchanged a rather special laptop containing those notes for Jackson up at Hanging Rock recently?"

"No, I was not." His gaze swept over me, and though his expression gave little away, I very much suspected he was trying to judge whether I was playing him or not. "I gather they will gain no access to the notes on that laptop?"

"You'd gather right."

"Excellent." He paused. "Describe the man you met at the exchange."

I did so. He swore. "*That* is undeniably De Luca."

"Which is why I have no doubt he's working with the red cloaks," I said. "They were in the forest with De Luca and his crew, and attacked us the minute the exchange happened."

"I cannot believe even *he* would sink to that level."

"Believe," a new voice said, "because it is *very* much the truth."

Chapter 14

The cool voice came from our left, and it belonged to the man who'd now been identified as De Luca. But I had no sense of him—no sense that there was anyone with him—and I had no idea why. Maybe the spell had something to do with it, but if that was the case, why could I still sense the five other vampires?

Except, I suddenly realized, there'd been six. One of the vampires who'd stood behind us was no longer there.

Did Parella have a turncoat in his own crew? It was certainly possible, given there was no other way De Luca could have known about this meeting. But even with help on the inside, De Luca wouldn't have come here alone. If he didn't have his vampire buddies with him, then he'd at least have the red cloaks.

But how had he gotten so close without anyone sensing him? I glanced at Adán, eyebrow raised in question, and he pointed downward.

"Sorry. I didn't sense them until it was too late. I was intent on the vampires already here."

"Can you stop any more of them getting into this place?"

"I can reshape and block the sewer entrances, but it'll take time and I'll be vulnerable to attack."

"I have your back," Jackson said.

Adán nodded and closed his eyes. A tremor ran through the concrete under our feet and began to radiate outward in ever-increasing circles. If the vampires noticed, they gave no indication.

"What are you up to, De Luca?" Parella growled. "Surely even you can see—"

"What I can see," De Luca said, "is an opportunity to cleanse the sindicati of your faction's stain and bring the organization into the current century. That it comes with the prospect of great profitability is a bonus."

"If you think the man in charge of the red cloaks is about to share wealth *or* power," I said, "you're seriously deluded."

"About twenty have now entered the area via the sewer grates," Adán murmured. "But they feel . . . wrong. Warped."

"Because they're the red cloaks." Fire burned through me, and I flexed my fingers in an effort to remain calm. Sparks skittered across my fingertips, but they were a pale imitation of their usual strength.

But at least there were sparks—even if I couldn't create a full flame, Jackson would be able to catch and shape the sparks into something far more deadly. But history had already told us they wouldn't be deadly enough to take care of the red cloaks. I just had to hope I could reach the mother's heat.

"Oh, I'm well aware of my counterpart's untrustworthiness," De Luca said, amusement in his tone. "However, our deal currently suits us both—and it has certainly benefited us both."

"I'd be wary of deals with the devil, De Luca," Parella growled. "They have a habit of turning."

"Yes, they do, don't they?" The underlying rancor in De Luca's voice suggested there was a very long history between these two men.

"Why have you brought so many red cloaks here, De Luca?" I said.

Parella glanced at me sharply. "There are red cloaks here? Why can we not—?" He paused, and swore again. "They're coming up through the sewers."

"Yes," De Luca said. His voice was now coming from a different spot, though I'd had no sense of movement. But then, I couldn't sense the red cloaks, either, and I wasn't sure if that was the spell or something else—especially since Parella hadn't sensed them until I mentioned it. "And you have so kindly employed magic to nullify the one person who can actually stop them."

"So that's what this is all about?" I asked. "You're going to snatch me and kill them in the process?"

"Kill them? No, what I have planned for them is far dirtier than that."

The amusement and confidence in De Luca's voice was so strong, I wanted to punch him. But I had no doubt that the minute I so much as moved, or even sparked, the red cloaks we couldn't see would attack. Besides, I doubted De Luca would be an easy target— at the very least, he'd be protected. He, like Parella, didn't seem the type to put his own safety at risk if he didn't have to.

"I will not become a cloak," Parella said. "I will slice my own throat before it ever comes to that."

"That, too, would be an acceptable outcome," De Luca said. "I'd like to say it's been a pleasure knowing you all, but the true pleasure will come when you all are a part of the hive and as mad and mindless as any of the soldiers."

And with that, the red cloaks screamed and charged.

Fire burned instantly to my fingertips, but even as the flames came to life, the magic surged and snuffed them out. But Jackson caught the fading sparks and breathed new life into them. As they grew into flame, Adán threw out a hand, the gesture imperial, demanding. There was a mighty roar as the ground beneath us answered his call; then the concrete split, forming jagged fissures that ran like fat fingers through the concrete, allowing the earth to surge through the gaps. It was a fierce brown tide that quickly solidified, forming a wall that was thick and strong. Adán made a sweeping gesture to the right, and as the tide of earth followed, a circular cage began to form around us. The cloaks screamed again and threw themselves sideways, racing the earth, trying to get around it. Half a dozen managed to scramble over the wall before it reached the ceiling and charged at the vampires. They didn't panic—they simply produced several rather large guns each and began to fire.

So much for their *not* being armed.

Not that I was about to complain right now.

Jackson cast a ball of flame toward the ceiling. As the shadows fell away, the true depth of our situation was revealed.

There had to be at *least* thirty red cloaks here.

"Oh fuck," I muttered. Luke—or whoever else might be leading this mad rabble—really *was* intent on winning this particular battle. He surely had to be throwing most of his resources at us. Unless, of course, he had far more soldiers than anyone had thought possible.

And yet he was nowhere to be seen, and that was unusual, given he'd been at every other major confrontation I'd had with the cloaks. Did that imply he'd been seriously injured when I'd blown that building apart? He wouldn't be dead, because I couldn't imagine the red cloaks leaving De Luca standing untouched if he wasn't under some sort of protection order.

"It's worse than it looks," Adán muttered, sweat beginning to trickle down his brow, "because there're another twenty trapped underground. They may yet find a way in."

Jackson swore. "Is it possible to lock off this entire area? If we can stop any more of them getting in, we might stand a chance."

Three more red cloaks made it around the wall. The vamps calmly shot them. As blood and gore and brain matter splattered across the still-moving earth wall, the younger vampire who'd been left alone went down under the weight of another three cloaks. They tore him apart in an instant. He didn't even have time to scream.

It was a fate that might well be ours if we weren't very careful.

Adán glanced around, his face paler and more drawn than only minutes before. "I can try, but I can't finish the earth wall and lock off the entrances. Pick one, and do it fast."

"Entrances," Jackson replied, even as I said, "What about Rory and Dmitri?"

"They're in the first section of the parking lot." Adán paused and tilted his head slightly to the left, his expression closed, as if he were listening. "The red cloaks are not the only soldiers De Luca brought. Rory and Dmitri are engaging his vampires."

"This just gets better and better," Jackson said, and flung a ball of flame at a red cloak as it screamed toward us. The creature went up in an instant, but that didn't stop it. It took a bullet from Parella's gun to achieve that. "Do it, Adán."

I swore violently and hoped like hell that Rory would be okay, that he and Dmitri would survive even if we didn't. It was a purely selfish thought since I could be reborn and the others here could not, and I thrust it away and swung around. The earth wall came to a shuddering stop, leaving a breach of about twenty feet between the two ends. The red cloaks filled it in an instant.

"Parella, if you want to survive, you might want to get your arse over here," I bit out, "because the only way any of us are going to get out of this is by joining forces."

His hesitation was only brief; then, with a silent glance at his men, the four of them moved over to us— Parella and one vampire on either side of Jackson and me, and the other two behind. Adán stood in the middle of the rough semicircle, his sweat beginning to stain the concrete at his feet as he concentrated on locking off the entrances to this section of the underground lot.

"I don't suppose you can undo the damn spell," I added, frustrated by my continuing inability to reach my flames.

"Not from here, I can't." Parella raised his weapons and fired as he spoke. One red cloak went down. The others just ran over the top of him. "And, unfortunately, we have a limited supply of bullets."

"Then fucking don't fire until absolutely necessary."

"Define 'necessary,'" Parella snapped back. "Because none of us are waiting for the bastards to get within slashing distance before we take them out."

It was a viewpoint I could only agree with. Besides, Parella and his men knew the dangers of running out of bullets just as much as we did.

I reached for the mother. Only it felt like I was reaching through a wall of glue. Whatever the spell was, it really *was* powerful. Sweat broke out across my brow as I kept reaching; gunshots echoed, and the smell of burning flesh fouled the air as Jackson's fire hit the nearest cloaks. They screamed but kept on coming. I wasn't going to reach the mother in time. The red cloaks were too close. More shots rang out, but the sound was lost to the screaming of the cloaks.

So I did the only thing I could do. I thrust my knife at Jackson, then became spirit. As my inner fires answered my call and tore away my flesh form, Parella swore. But, to his credit, he didn't move—even though the heat of my natural form had to be damn unpleasant, given how close he was standing—and he kept on firing. But as one gun clicked over to empty, the nearest red cloaks literally launched at him.

The last of my human body burned away, freeing

me. Flicking out two ribbons of fire, I caught the red cloaks in midair, stopping them and burning them. As their ash fell like black snow to the concrete, I surged forward, my body incandescent as I flung my arms wide. Three red cloaks smacked into me; they tore at me, bit me, even as their screaming stopped, their flesh cindered, and their bones became little more than soot staining the ground.

The rest of the cloaks simply slipped around me. I spun so fast, my fires trailed like a comet behind me, bright and fierce against the fading light of Jackson's flaming light that still hovered above us, providing light.

I flung ribbons of flame left and right and flared them high, creating a wall of fierce fire. But I wasn't fast enough. Two red cloaks got through, and one of Parella's men went down. The other two spun and fired, taking out the cloaks. The vampire was bloody and torn but alive. But not for long, because Parella turned and fired. As the vampire's brains bled out across the concrete, Parella growled, "We need to end this. I only have a few bullets left."

I swore, though no one here would have heard anything remotely resembling speech. If he had only a few bullets, then it was likely the other two were in a similar situation. And while Jackson might be armed with fire, it was fading fast and wasn't really stopping them anyway; Adán was still attempting to lock the area off. There were simply far too many red cloaks here for me to cope with alone.

We weren't going to survive. Not if I didn't pull something special out of the box.

I threw as much strength as I could into my wall of

flame and once again reached for the earth mother. The glue was still there, but this time, desperation won the day. I burned through the barrier, and the ground underneath us began to tremble and shake as she responded. Then her energy exploded through me, a wild force that—as had happened up at Hanging Rock—would not be contained or in any way directed. She erupted outward, a wave of flame and heat so fierce that the air beyond my barrier briefly became unbreathable. Fingers of fire that burned with the color of all creation wrapped almost lovingly around the throats of the remaining red cloaks and cindered them in an instant.

When there was nothing—not even ash, her force retreated, leaving me back in flesh form, on my knees, and shaking with weakness.

But we were alive, and the red cloaks were not.

And that was more than I'd thought possible only minutes ago.

"Fuck," Jackson said. "That was *close*."

"Yeah, it was." I pushed to my feet and met Parella's gaze. "Can you sense De Luca?"

He hesitated, then shook his head. "He's not in this area."

I glanced over my shoulder. "Adán?"

The earth Fae took a shuddery breath and wiped the sweat-dampened hair out of his eyes. "As the vampire said, he is not in this area."

"Is he in the other area, with Rory and Dmitri?" Jackson asked.

"Meaning you did not come alone," Parella commented. "*That* is a breach of our trust."

"So say the vampires who swore they didn't need weapons but who subsequently produced something of a small armament," I snapped. "Kindly remember we survived, no thanks to those guns *or* the damn spell."

"I have no idea if De Luca is among those who still battle our companions," Adán said. "But there is movement in the locked-off area to our left, and it is vampiric in feel, but not fouled."

Meaning it was De Luca and his people rather than the red cloaks. It had to be. Highpoint's security people would be well aware by now that hell had broken loose under their feet, but even if they had vampires in their employ, I doubted they'd come down here themselves. But the cops would have been called, and that meant we were now on a countdown. I certainly didn't want to tangle with the law right now, and I doubted Parella and his crew did, either.

"If it *is* De Luca," Jackson growled, "we can't let the bastard escape."

"De Luca is our prob—," Parella began.

But I cut him off with a quick "Like *fuck* he is."

I didn't wait for his reaction. Neither did Jackson. The two of us bolted forward as one, but the vampires were after us in an instant. Only Adán remained behind— and I very much suspected he simply didn't have the energy to follow.

None of us got far. Fifty feet from the wall of earth was another wall, this one made of concrete and stone. It blocked the entrance into this section of the lot from the rest of the parking area on the Warrs Road side of the complex. Jackson swore and swung around, but before he could say anything, Adán said, "Working on it."

The wall began to shiver and quake. Bits of stone broke away and fell around us, a less-than-gentle rain that quickly became something more dangerous. We jumped out of its reach, and, a heartbeat later, the wall came down, spewing rocks and concrete chunks around our feet as dust plumed into the air.

I didn't wait for it to settle. Neither did anyone else. We scrambled over the still-moving pile of rubble and raced into the next section.

"De Luca is ahead but not alone," Parella growled. "There are at least a dozen others with him."

"You boys don't do anything by halves when you plan a trap, do you?" The words came out as little more than a wheeze of air, and it wasn't due to just a shortness of breath. I was pushing my limits physically, but I wasn't about to be left behind. Not when the bastard was so damn close. "Can you at least destroy the spell and give us a fighting chance against them?"

I wasn't even sure I had enough strength left to make flame, but I certainly couldn't call to the mother in my current state of weakness. She'd claim me, of that I had no doubt.

"Fredrick," Parella snapped; then, as the vampires peeled off as one, he added, "De Luca is mine to deal with. Understood?"

"I don't care who places the final blow, just as long as the bastard dies."

"Then that is something else we agree on."

We raced up the ramp to the next level, heading toward Warrs Road. Six vampires blocked our path. Jackson thrust the knife back into my hand; then, with a yell that was all anticipation and fury, he raised his own and charged. Flames still flickered across his fingertips, which lent the silver blade a bloody glow. Parella and the remaining vampires were silent but no less angry or determined as they surged past Jackson.

And they all left me in their dust.

But that was okay. I didn't need to get involved in this fight. What I needed—what I wanted—was De Luca.

The clash of flesh against flesh was fierce and ugly. As the vampires fell on one another, Jackson slashed left and right, and his flames flared higher, burning flesh even as he sliced and diced. I skirted around the lot of them and ran on.

One of De Luca's men sensed me at the last moment and lunged for me. I yelped and dove away, but I was far too slow. We went down in a tumble of arms and legs, and came to a halt abruptly against the edge of a concrete pillar. Air hissed from my lungs and I swear something broke inside, but I ignored the pain that ripped down my side and thrust a hand into the vampire's face, clawing at his eyes. He swore and jerked away even as he threw a punch—not at my face, but at the side that was burning.

It hurt, god how it *hurt*. Just for a moment, all I could see were stars dancing merrily in a field of gathering black.

But at that precise minute, my flames surged. Fredrick had broken the spell.

And while I was fast approaching the end of the line, when it came to strength, I *wasn't* there yet. I slapped a hand against the vampire's chest and pushed, as hard as I could. Flames erupted from my fingertips, the force of them enough to both set him alight and throw him off me.

I scrambled to my feet. Just for an instant, the world spun. I took a deep, shuddery breath, then forced myself on.

Another blockade of vampires soon appeared, although this time there were only three of them. Even so, that was probably two too many in my current state. I swore and slithered to a stop, fire dancing across my fingertips. It lit the shadows and highlighted the anticipation in their eyes. If they were afraid, they certainly weren't showing it.

They attacked en masse. I yelped and threw up a wall of flame between them and me, but it was weak and nowhere near high enough. They simply leapt over the top of it and charged on.

I ran backward, not daring to take my eyes off them, the silver knife in my hand, raised and ready. It wouldn't be enough. I knew that; they knew that.

Awareness surged through me; Rory was close. Even as relief washed through me, threatening to buckle my knees, the concrete under my feet began to shift and crack. Out of the small fissures that formed as a result, earth, stone, and concrete erupted, forming a wall that swept around the vampires in less than a nanosecond and locked them inside.

"Go," Dmitri growled. "I will take care of this filth."

A hand grabbed mine and pulled me forward. "Flame," Rory growled, even as his fingers became fire.

This time I didn't argue; I simply sucked down the strength he was offering, refueling my energy even as I drained his—but only to the point where our levels evened out. Neither of us could afford to be close to the point of exhaustion since we had no idea what might await if and when we caught up with De Luca.

"What happened to the vampires you and Dmitri were battling?" I asked as we continued to race forward. Our footsteps echoed through the dark silence, a warning we still were on the hunt to anyone up ahead.

"They retreated not long after Adán raised the walls to shut off your area. We gave chase but came back the minute I realized just how close to the edge raising the mother had brought you." His eyes glittered in the shadows as he glanced at me. "I don't think I've ever been so scared in my life."

"That makes two of us."

I squeezed his fingers, then released him. We ran on. But as we neared the Warrs Road exit, three more vampires stepped from the shadows on either side, raised their guns, and fired.

We both became flame.

The bullets tore into our spirit forms and melted in an instant. The vampires' eyes went wide, but before they could move, before they could react in *any* way, we hit them and swept on. Not even dust remained in our wake.

The headlights of a car speared the night as a big black vehicle spun around in the open parking area beyond the exit and accelerated away. Rory hit it with a ball of flame so powerful that the rear end of the vehicle rose high in the air and the car teetered on two front wheels for several seconds. Then it tipped over, with odd grace. It landed on its roof and slid forward for several yards before halting against the concrete wall of the building.

A vampire scrambled out of the passenger's side of the car and raised a gun. A brave man, but he was ash in an instant.

There were two others inside the car, one at the front—presumably the driver—and one behind. That *had* to be De Luca.

I flung a ribbon of fire at the door, wrenched it free from the car, and then dragged De Luca out. I wrapped him in fire but didn't actually burn him; I just burned the weapons from his grasp. As the metal dripped onto the concrete, I became flesh once more and walked toward him.

"It doesn't matter if you kill me," he said, his voice cool and amazingly calm. "Another man will just take my place."

"Oh, I'm not going to kill you." Ignoring Rory's surprised glance, I stopped in front of De Luca and crossed my arms. It was an action that hurt like blazes; I really *had* broken something inside—possibly a rib. Or two. I swallowed bile and said, "I just want answers."

"Answers will not help you," he said. "Answers will not save you from either the wrath of my faction or the rage of the red cloaks."

"Maybe they won't, but I'd still like them."

"Then ask away."

Alarm slithered through me. He might be a very old, very powerful vampire, but we'd ensnared him *and* wiped out all his soldiers . . . all except for the ones who'd fled Rory and Dmitri, that was.

I spun around and glanced up, catching a glint of metal as a weapon was raised.

"Rory—," I warned, even as I became flame once again.

Several bullets ripped through me. Others pinged off the car and zipped into the darkness. I twisted around and saw blood plume from Rory's arm a heartbeat before he attained full fire form.

"They're mine," he growled, and surged upward. The bullets kept raining around me, through me, and then abruptly stopped as heat boiled through the darkness and screams shattered the silence. They were screams that cut off as abruptly as they'd started.

I regained flesh and shook De Luca violently. "No more. If any of your men are still alive, tell them to run."

"None remain." He was still far too calm and self-assured for my liking. Did he really care so little about his life? Or did he believe, perhaps, that the red cloaks would come to his rescue?

If so, why? He had to be aware that we'd cindered the lot of them. Why else would he have fled?

"Good," I said. "Now tell me the name of the man who controls the red cloaks."

His smile was thin, amused. "I'm surprised you have not already guessed."

"Maybe I have. Maybe I just want confirmation."

He raised an eyebrow. "Then you can have your confirmation. It is indeed Luke Turner."

Well, *fuck*. Even though I'd suspected all along that my guess would be right, part of me had been hoping for a miracle. Hoping that even if fate couldn't give me a break, it would at least give Sam one.

I should have known better.

Sam was not going to take the news well at all—not that I intended to say anything to him. He'd have confirmation enough when PIT exhumed his brother's grave.

"And what do you really get out of the deal with Luke? It has to be more than full control over the sindicati and mere monetary gain."

"If you do not think power and monetary gain are enough, then you have no understanding of those within the sindicati."

"But this virus provides just as much threat to vampires as humans. You cannot believe that Luke will leave the sindicati standing untouched. Especially since he now has control of the two men who have any chance of quickly finding a cure."

"Ah, but there is the rub," De Luca said. "He may have control of the scientists, but to proceed where they left off, they must have their research. And that is something *I* control."

"Except that you don't. Parella's faction stole Baltimore's files, not you."

His smile held little amusement. "They may have stolen them, but I now control them."

So Parella *did* have a mole in his organization.

"If you *do* control all the information, I'm surprised you're still alive to boast about it." I hesitated, studying him through narrowed eyes. But there was no stain in him, no hint of the darkness I'd often sensed in Sam. "You're not even infected."

"No, because the few vampires he's turned simply became insane. They do not fall under hive control and cannot be read by either the hive mind or by Luke."

"He learned this the hard way?"

"Oh yes. And since the notes are inaccessible to everyone but me, he is forced to abide by our deal."

"Until the moment you dole out the last of the notes and your usefulness comes to an end," I said.

"Perhaps. And perhaps I have other cards up my sleeve." His gaze went past me, and I suddenly realized Parella was moving up behind me. Once again, De Luca's too-confident smile flashed. "So, you see, it would appear that neither you, nor Parella, nor anyone else can kill me. Not without risking a quick end to this virus."

"That's where you would be wrong," Parella growled.

And with little other warning, he blew De Luca's brains apart.

CHAPTER 15

I swung around, fist clenched. "Why the fuck did you do *that*?"

Parella raised an eyebrow, obviously surprised at my reaction. "I warned you at the very start of all this that De Luca was mine to kill."

"Yes, but didn't you hear him? He has the research notes—the very ones *you* claim to have."

"And if that *were* true, he could never be made to tell us their location. If you think otherwise, you are indeed a fool." His gaze swept over me. "And, up until this point, that has not proven to be the case."

"But even so, your actions—"

"My actions," he cut in, "have evened out the playing field. The cloaks may have the scientists, but without the use of their notes, they are back to square one. That gives us the chance to either find the notes or to at least develop a vaccination, if not a cure."

"It gives PIT and the government the same sort of chance," Rory said as he regained flesh form behind Parella.

Parella didn't even glance around. "That it does. But

De Luca was sindicati, even if a general on the opposition side. I believe that gives *us* a far greater understanding of both his habits and mind than either PIT or you."

It probably did. The sound of sirens began to bite through the air. We had to get out of here, and soon. "What happens now?"

"Now, *we* depart and leave you to walk away alive, as promised. Till we meet again, lady of flame."

He bowed slightly, then disappeared into the shadows. The heat of his presence slipped away into the night and quickly faded.

I blew out a relieved breath and walked over to Rory. "We'd better gather the troops and get the hell out of here before those cops—and undoubtedly PIT— arrive."

"The troops are already gathered," a familiar voice intoned.

We turned. Jackson appeared at the parking lot's exit, limping a little and looking the worse for wear. His clothes were torn and bloody, and one eye was swollen and almost completely closed, but he was grinning like a loon. So were Dmitri and Adán, even though Adán was leaning heavily against Dmitri for support.

"Fae really are weird people," Rory said, amusement in his tone. "And I think the first place we should all be headed is the hospital to be patched up."

"The hospital won't help us," Dmitri said. "We need communing time with our element."

"Take the car I rented, then." Rory reached into his pocket and tossed the keys over. Dmitri caught them. "I'll catch a lift with these two."

"My thanks," Dmitri said. "I'll return it in a day or so."

"No hurry."

As the two men shuffled off, Jackson stopped in front of us and said, "Now that we've pulled off the biggest fucking miracle in living history, let's get the hell away from here."

I laughed. It hurt like hell, but I didn't care.

We really *had* pulled off a miracle. And sure, this whole mess was far from over. We might have killed off a good portion of the red cloaks, but Luke could easily make many more. And he had the scientists, so both he and De Luca's faction—if their deal actually *survived* De Luca's death—were still in the driver's seat when it came to finding a cure.

But Baltimore's notes were out there somewhere. So were Wilson's, if Rosen was to be believed. There was a chance they could be found if we could piece together enough about both Wilson's and De Luca's lives. And if we couldn't, then surely PIT could.

The chance of it actually happening might be slim, but that was better than no chance at all.

But best of all, we'd lived to fight another day.

And once we'd all recovered, that was exactly what I intended to do.

I was over being hunted. It was time to become the hunter.

Don't miss the next Souls of Fire novel
from Keri Arthur,

FLAMEOUT

Available from Piatkus in June 2016

The throaty roar of machinery shattered the peace of the old cemetery. Deep in the old trees and on the other side of the road that channeled drivers up to the mausoleums, light shone. It was fierce and bright against the thick cover of night, but it oddly cast the man who stood at the very edge of its circle into shadow.

I paused on the side of the road and took a deep breath. It did little to calm either my nerves or the churning in my stomach. I had no right to be here. No right at *all*. And I certainly knew that shadow wouldn't be, in *any* way, happy to see me.

But I couldn't stay away. I had to see with my own eyes the lack of a body in the grave the excavator was digging up. While it might have been only a few days ago that I'd physically confronted the man who was *supposed* to be buried there, some insane part of me couldn't help but hope that it *hadn't* been Luke, that it had instead been some sort of doppelgänger. Not for my sake, but for the sake of the shadow ahead.

After another useless deep breath, I crossed the road and walked as silently as possible through the old eucalypts that dominated this section of the cemetery. Although, given the man ahead was infected by a virus that had basically turned him into something of a pseudo vampire, I'm not sure why I bothered. He'd sense my presence long before I actually got there.

Whether he'd acknowledge it was another matter entirely.

The excavator's engine suddenly cut out and the ensuing silence was eerie. It was almost as if the night were holding its breath, waiting to see the outcome of the grave's being opened.

As I neared the site, the shadow turned. Despite the darkness, his blue eyes had an almost unnatural gleam and, as ever, I felt the impact of them like a punch to the gut. But if he was in any way surprised to see me, it didn't show.

But then, Sam Turner probably knew me better than almost any human alive, given our rather intense—if all together too brief—relationship five years ago.

"Evening, Emberly." His voice gave as little away as his expression, yet it ran over my senses as sweetly as a kiss. "I was wondering when you'd turn up."

"There was always a chance the sindicati were lying when they said the leader of the cloaks was your brother." I shrugged. "I needed to be sure."

He raised an eyebrow. "Why would you disbelieve them when you confronted Luke face-to-face?"

"I know. I just—" I paused and shrugged again.

"You just keep hoping that you're wrong, that it's someone who looks like my brother in charge of the red cloaks rather than Luke himself." A bitter smile momentarily twisted his lips. "I know the feeling."

The red cloaks was the nickname given to those infected by the Crimson Death virus—or the red plague, as it was more commonly known—and it was a virus Sam had running through his veins. Those infected generally fell into two categories: the ones who were crazy and kept under control only by the will of the red cloak hive "queen," and the ones who kept all mental faculties even though they were still bound to the hive and its leader. No one really understood why the virus affected some more than it did others, although the powers that be suspected it very much depended on whom you were infected by. Of course, there *was* a third category, involving people such as Sam and Rozelle—Sam's lover and another member of the Paranormal Investigations Team. They may be infected, but they had no attachment to the hive and did not fall under the will of its leader. How long that would last, no one could say.

All anyone really knew for sure was that the virus had the potential to become a plague even worse than the Black Death. It wouldn't just *kill* millions; it would change them, thereby making them an even greater threat to those who remained uninfected.

Unfortunately, the two scientists who'd been leading the charge for a vaccine were now infected themselves, and under the control of the hive.

As situations went, it was pretty damn dire.

And it wasn't helped by the fact that the sindicati—the vampire equivalent of the mafia—were also after both the scientists *and* the missing research notes. Vampires could be infected as easily as humans, but I suspected their interest in a cure was more monetarily based than in the interest of self-preservation. The government had already gone to great lengths to keep the outbreak secret, so it was a obvious they'd pay millions—or more—to get either a vaccine or cure.

The man who'd been operating the small excavator climbed out of the cabin and walked to the edge of the grave, where a second cemetery worker already stood.

He looked down into the hole for a second, then glanced at Sam and said, "Do you want me to start the opening procedure now, sir?"

Sam nodded, the movement sharp. Abrupt. Tension rolled off him in waves, and held within it hints of fear and resignation. He might not want the leader of the cloaks to be Luke, but he, like me, had all but come to accept the fact that this time, the sindicati had been telling the truth.

Not that Anthony De Luca—the factional leader who'd given me the information—had had any reason to lie. He'd thought he was safe simply because he had sole control over Mark Baltimore's research notes and that *that* would protect him from both his red cloak partners and from his opposition in the sindicati. He'd been wrong—at least when it came to the latter.

With De Luca now dead, the notes he'd so carefully guarded were out there somewhere in the wider world to be found, and apparently so were the backups of Professor Wilson's notes. Of course, the two sindicati factions and PIT weren't the only ones currently scrambling to find those notes. The red cloaks undoubtedly were, too. They might control the two scientists, but their job would be made far easier if they didn't have to start from scratch.

The cemetery worker climbed into a harness and was lowered into the open grave. There was a soft thud as he landed on the coffin's lid. It wasn't a wooden sound; it was metallic.

I glanced at Sam in surprise. "You buried him in a metal coffin?"

"It's lead lined rather than mere metal, and the choice was out of my hands." His voice was grim. "The government didn't want to risk toxins leaching into the soil—not when we have no real understanding of the virus."

I frowned. "But isn't the virus transferred via a bite or scratch? Besides, it can take twenty years or more for a normal coffin to decompose, so it's doubtful whatever is left of the body by then would actually infect the soil."

"Maybe. Maybe not." He shrugged. "I can understand their not wanting to take the risk since there *are* toxins out there that remain viable basically forever."

"Yeah, but this is a virus, not a toxin."

"A virus that transforms cells in a way no one yet understands. In *any* case like this, it's better to be safe than sorry."

"So why not cremate him?"

"Luke didn't believe in it. I gave him that, if nothing else."

If the authorities were so worried about contamination, I had to wonder why they didn't insist. But then, maybe they'd also feared this thing could mutate and become airborne.

As the worker aboveground tossed what looked like a bolt cutter down to his partner, Sam made a low sound deep in his throat and strode into the circle of the nearby floodlight. It gave his short black hair an almost bluish shine and somehow emphasized the leanness of his athletic frame. There wasn't a scrap of fat on him these days; it had all been eaten away by the virus he was still fighting. But while all that was left was muscle and bone, he was still a very good-looking man.

Of course, given that the heart of a phoenix is fated to fall only once each lifetime, and Sam was my allotted love *this* time around, I'd be attracted to him no matter what.

I trailed after him. The metal coffin gleamed in the shadows of the grave pit, its surface untarnished by time or earth. There was no indication of damage or attack from either within or without; it could have been buried yesterday instead of more than a year ago.

The worker inside the grave seemed to be struggling to get the casket open, even with the use of bolt cutters. The padlock was *huge*. The government really *had* been serious about not letting any contaminants out.

So how the hell had Luke escaped?

"Is that the same padlock he was buried with?" I asked.

Sam shrugged. "It looks like the same type, but I guess we'll know for sure when the damn thing is opened."

I could have gotten it open in half a second. Even if the lock was made of tungsten metal, it would have melted quickly enough under the full force of the flames that were mine to call. But that would have meant revealing myself as something other than human to the two cemetery workers, and I wasn't about to risk that. Vampires and werewolves might be out and proud, but the rest of us remained well and truly closeted—and with damn good reason. While humanity had, on the whole, accepted the presence of vamps and weres in the world with surprising calm, there were still many who figured their very existence was a crime against nature, and one that needed to be dealt with. Nightly hunting parties were a growing problem, even if it was one the vamps and weres had so far ignored.

If they ever *did* decide to react to the situation, heaven help humanity.

The lock finally snapped. The coffin was unlatched, and then the bolt cutter was exchanged for a rope. Once the rope was tied securely to the lid of the coffin, the worker was hauled out.

"We've been ordered to stand well clear of the grave when the coffin is opened." He tossed the rope to Sam. "Give us five minutes before you do so."

Sam nodded. His grip on the rope was so tight his knuckles were white, but his expression remained as neutral as ever. He hadn't always been this calm, this controlled. And while it would have been easy to blame the virus, I doubted that was the true source. Any man who'd killed his brother, and who felt a personal obligation to hunt down as many of the cloaks as he could, would have both witnessed *and* caused much bloodshed. In that sort of situation, you had two choices—control your emotions or go crazy. The former was always a better option than the latter. I knew that from experience.

The two men climbed into the excavator. A heartbeat later, the machine had turned and begun to trundle away, its bright headlights piercing the shadows.

Once it was out of sight, Sam moved around the grave, then glanced at me. "You ready?"

I nodded and took my hands out of my pockets. Sparks danced across my fingertips, tiny fireflies that spun into the night and quickly disappeared. Just because I knew Luke wouldn't be in that coffin didn't mean someone—or some*thing*—else wouldn't be. Luke had never been stupid; he'd known he couldn't possibly keep his resurrection a secret forever and that eventually his grave would be checked. He'd have something planned; of that I had no doubt.

Sam took a deep breath and released it slowly. His tension echoed through me.

With a quick but powerful motion, he yanked the rope. With little sound, the lid opened.

The coffin was empty.

Nothing waited within. Not a body, not a trap. The sparks died as my tension slipped away.

"Well, the sindicati weren't lying. Neither were your eyes." Sam's voice still held little in the way of inflection, yet I could feel the rise of anger in him. It wasn't in any way aimed at me, but it was fierce, dark, and thick with the desire to hunt, to kill. Goose bumps fled down my spine and it was all I could do to stay where I was and *not* run from the sheer force of it. "Luke is alive."

"Not only alive, but in charge of the red cloaks." The words were out before I could stop them, and I silently cursed. I really didn't need to poke the proverbial bear any further, if only because the darkness within him—the darkness that was the virus—had risen along with his anger, and *that* was very, very dangerous. He might not want to harm me, but who knew what would happen if that darkness ever gained full control?

"Yes." His gaze rose to mine. In the blue of his eyes, grief shone. Grief and disbelief. Despite the evidence, despite his words, despite my telling him what I'd seen, he still didn't want to believe that his brother was capable of so much chaos.

"What will you do now?" The desire to comfort him was so strong that I actually took a step toward him. But while the Sam of old might have welcomed such an action, this one certainly wouldn't. Not from me, at any rate.

"I'll do exactly what I've been doing." The grief disappeared from his expression, but the anger remained. "And this time, when I find him, I'll make sure he stays dead."

"Good luck with that," an all too familiar voice said. "Because you certainly haven't had much success so far with your quest to erase us."

I jumped and swung around, flames instinctively burning across my fingers as I scanned the night. Luke's voice had come from the trees to the left of the floodlight, but there was absolutely no sense of him. As far as I could tell, there was no one and nothing nearby in that section of the cemetery.

"Come out and face us, Luke." Sam's voice was low and very, *very* controlled. "Or are you still that same little coward hiding behind excuses and the strength of others?"

"My, my, we have gotten bitter since the infection, haven't we?" There was an almost jovial note in Luke's cool tone. "But then, I guess hunting a killer that is little more than a ghost will do that to anyone."

"You're no ghost," I snapped. I desperately wanted to unleash my flames, but it would be a pointless action until I actually had a target. "You're not even immortal. And you certainly bleed as profusely as anyone else when shot."

"You're right." His voice was still amused, but the edge of ice was stronger. "I do owe you one for that shoulder wound, you know. And bringing that building down on top of me was *very* impolite of you."

I snorted. "Next time we meet, I'll make sure the damn building *actually* kills you."

"Oh, I have no doubt that the next time we meet *will* be the last time—but for you rather than for me."

"Says the man who's currently hiding behind shadows and trees," Sam said. "Come out and face us if you're so damn confident."

"I would love to, but, unfortunately, the aforementioned building collapse has seriously curtailed my movements in the short term."

Which suggested he wasn't actually near. I frowned and glanced over at Sam. He half shrugged and motioned for me to keep on speaking.

"I can assure you, Luke, that *wasn't* my intention."

Sam stepped out of the floodlit area and merged with the deeper darkness of night. It was a vampire trick, one the virus had gifted him. I wasn't sure whether all those infected with the virus got the ability, as few of the madder red cloaks—the ones who had the scythelike brand burned into their cheeks—seemed to use it. Luke *did* have the ability, but even if he was using it, I should have sensed him—unless, of course, he was using some form of magic to distort my senses.

But if he *was* close, why hadn't he said anything about Sam's leaving the gravesite? Was that exactly what he wanted—me and Sam separated—or was there something else going on?

"Oh, you made your intentions clear enough." The last shred of amusement had left Luke's tone. All that remained was ice and fury. "Now, let me make mine clear—"

"We're all *very* aware of your intentions," I cut in. The quickest way to annoy Luke had always been to interrupt when he was speaking—and when he was angry, he tended to react without thought. Right now, with Sam off in the trees trying to find him, keeping his attention *and* annoyance on me would hopefully mean he wasn't paying attention to everything else that was going on around him. "But history is littered with would-be dictators like you, and each and every one of them was doomed to failure from the beginning. Just as you are."

"They weren't in possession of a virus capable of infecting the world and making it theirs," he spat back.

"The world would be yours only until a cure or a vaccine is found." I crossed my arms and wondered why the hell Sam was taking so long. Surely, given the clarity of Luke's voice, he couldn't be *that* far away.

"By the time that happens—if it ever happens—my army will be vast," Luke growled, "and not even your flames will be strong enough to stop my rampage."

"I wouldn't be so sure of that, Luke. You've had only a very small taste of what I'm actually capable of."

"Ah, but now that I have, I can work on ways to counter it."

A chill ran through me. The flames of a phoenix certainly *could* be curtailed, and one of those methods had been employed by the sindicati only a few nights before. The last thing I needed was a psycho like Luke getting his hands on *that* sort of magic.

"You might want to talk to Parella about how well that worked out for him," I snapped back, glad my voice was absent of the fear churning in my gut.

"Oh, if I ever get near *that* piece of vampire scum, talking is the last thing I'll be doing with him."

Meaning Parella had better watch his back, because I needed him alive. I had no love for vampires *or* the sindicati, but Parella and I had something of a truce going—he'd agreed to keep his men off my tail until I found Wilson's backup notes. It gave us breathing space—not much, granted, but at least it meant there was one group fewer we had to worry about. If he got himself killed, there was no guarantee his replacement would keep that agreement.

My gaze swept the tree-filled darkness beyond the floodlight. I still had no sense of Luke, though I was aware enough of Sam's position. His presence reminded me of a winter storm—filled with ice and the promise of fury. So why was it taking so long to uncover where Luke was—or wasn't?

"Look," I said, my tone holding a hint of the frustration that swirled through me. "It's been nice catching up with you again, but is there *any* point to this whole conversation? Have you decided to hand yourself in or what?"

He laughed. It was a high, unpleasant sound. He might not be one of the crazy ones, but he sure as hell wasn't far off it, either.

"There is a point to *everything* I do," he replied. "And you had better remember that."

I snorted. "Yeah, okay. If you say so."

He made a low sound that was an odd mix of a growl and a curse. "Perhaps a small demonstration—"

"Oh, don't feel obliged," I said. "Because we both know it will seriously hamper your domination plans if you lose any more of your soldiers right now."

"Oh, I have no intention of losing soldiers." His tone once again held an edge of smugness, and the flames flickering across my fingertips flared brighter as he added, "After all, we both know that if you're incapable of making fire, you're of very little threat."

And with that, an unnatural force began to unfold around me. It was a wash of energy that stung my skin and had the hairs at the back of my neck standing on end.

Because it wasn't just energy—it was magic. The type of magic that could restrict a phoenix's fire.

And not only would it curtail my ability to create fire, but it would also hamper my access to the earth mother—and the mother was the only force capable of utter and instant annihilation of the cloaks . . . or anyone else I decided to direct her against, for that matter. She was the heat of the earth, the energy that gave life to the world around us, a power that was dangerous and deadly to even those of us who could call her into being. But the risk was often worth it, especially in a case like this. My own flames, while they burned the cloaks, took longer—and that was never a good thing when fighting against greater numbers.

And I had no doubt that, despite his words, Luke would throw more than a few red cloaks at us. He'd always favored having the odds on his side.

I reached for my fire form, but even as I changed from flesh to spirit, the magic tore at my skin, trying to restrain me, to stop me.

It failed.

I surged up, away from the ground and the net seeking to encase me. Threads of energy briefly chased me, then snapped away. I paused and turned, but didn't relax. The magic was still active, even if it couldn't get me right then. What I needed to do was find the source of the damn spell and deactivate the stupid thing.

My gaze swept the ground but I didn't immediately see anything odd or out of place. I moved out of the floodlit area, my flames casting an orange glow across the ground.

That's when I saw them: four stones, each gleaming a soft grayish silver in the darkness. Spell stones—stones that provided both a base for the magic to latch onto and a means to restrict and control the size of the spell. The color of the stones themselves suggested the creator of this spell walked a dark path with his magic. White witches drew on the energy of the world around them in conjunction with the strength that came from within, and few would use stones this color. Those who used black magic—or blood magic, as it was more commonly known these days—often didn't need them.

A twig snapped in the trees behind me. I spun, my flames surging in response. But it wasn't Luke or the cloaks, as I'd half feared. It was Sam.

"Luke isn't here," he said, his voice vibrating with fury. "He was using a fucking speaker."

He threw some wiring on the ground, then stopped abruptly as he spotted me. "Emberly? What the *fuck* is going on?"

It was pointless answering, given only another phoenix could have actually understood me when I was in my fire form. Instead, I spun and surged toward the nearest stone. I had no idea how the spell was constructed, but I knew it could usually be undone if one of the stones was dislodged.

But even as I moved, figures erupted from the trees behind me. They were twisted, ugly beings with scars that resembled death's scythe burned into their cheeks.

Red cloaks. The *mad* kind.

They didn't run at me. They ran at Sam.

"You always were an untrustworthy bastard, brother dearest," Sam muttered. With that, he pulled out a gun and began firing. Blood and brain matter sprayed across the nearby tree trunks, but it didn't stop the tide. There were far too many of them for one man with one gun.

I cursed and reached for the force of the world, for the mother herself. She answered immediately, her energy wild, powerful, and difficult to contain. Not that I wanted to do that right then. I flung my hands wide and aimed her force at the cloaks. She surged through me and leapt almost joyously into the night, separating into multiple streams of flame that burned with all the colors of creation. Each finger hit one of the red cloaks and wrapped almost lovingly around it. Her flames pulsed, briefly darkening, as if in distaste.

Then she burned.

In an instant, the cloaks were little more than ashes fluttering gently to the ground.

When they were all gone, I released my hold on the mother. Her flames shimmered brightly for several seconds, then dissipated, the energy of them returning to the air and the earth itself.

Weakness washed through me. There was always a cost to calling such power into being, and this weakness was just the start of it. If I ever held on to her for too long, she would drain me until there was nothing left—no heat, no flame, and no life. She would take me into her bosom, into the earth itself, and there would be no escape. No rebirth.

Not something I ever wanted. I might be tired of the curse that bound phoenixes to endless lifetimes of having their hearts broken, but I wasn't yet tired of life itself.

I spun, dropped to the ground, and, even as the magic surged toward me, sent a lance of fire at the nearest gray stone. Its surface began to glow as my flames hit it, but it wasn't immediately moved out of alignment. I cursed and pushed harder; the color of my flames changed from orange to white, but it seemed to make no difference. Then, just as the magic began to twine around the fiery edges of my spirit form, the stone exploded. Sharp splinters speared through the night and a shock wave of energy sent me tumbling. I hit the ground and skidded along the dirt for several yards, ending up in flesh form and hard up against the trunk of an old pine.

I winced as I rolled onto my back. "That fucking *hurt*."

"Hitting a tree that hard generally does." Sam squatted beside me. "You okay?"

I opened one eye and glared up at him. "Do I look okay?"

The smile that briefly teased his lips was a pale imitation of the one that sometimes haunted my dreams, but I was nevertheless happy to see it. It meant that, despite the shadows in his eyes, despite the darkness I could almost taste, he was in control.

"You look pale, tired, grubby, and your lovely red hair rather resembles a bird's nest." His smile grew a fraction, briefly touching the corners of his bright eyes. "But other than all that, yeah, you do."

I snorted and pushed upright. His hand hovered near my spine, not touching me, but close enough that I could feel the chill radiating from his skin—another gift of the damn virus.

"If Luke wasn't actually here, how did he know we were? Was there a camera attached to the speaker?"

"No, but there was a microphone." He rose and offered me a hand. "There must have been some form of alarm in the casket that let him know when we opened it."

I gripped his fingers and allowed him to pull me upright. "But how did he know we were going to be here tonight?"

Sam released me and stepped back. I couldn't help noticing that the hand that had held mine was now clenched, as if to retain the lingering heat of my touch. Or maybe that was just wishful thinking by the stupid, deep-down part of me that refused to give up hope.

"He couldn't have. I checked both the perimeter and the cemetery itself before I gave the go-ahead to exhume the body. There was no one and nothing here."

"Then how did those red cloaks get here so fast?" I tucked my shirt back into my jeans. Thankfully, the magic that allowed us to shift from one form to another also took anything that was touching our skin—clothes, watches, et cetera—with it. Unlike werewolves, we didn't end up half undressed after shifting shape.

He shrugged. "The virus endows many vampirelike qualities, including speed."

"Not even Superman could have gotten here on foot from Brooklyn so fast," I said. "There were barely ten minutes between our opening the casket and their attacking."

"Maybe he had a small squad of them on standby. There are plenty of drain outlets nearby, and that seems to be their chosen method of moving about."

That was certainly possible, but part of me doubted it. He had to have known Sam, at least, would be here. And he would have guessed that curiosity would also drive me here, if only to support Sam.

"You don't believe that any more than I do." I paused, then added softly, "He knew we were coming, Sam."

"It wasn't Rozelle."

"Are you sure?"

"Yes, because I didn't tell her. Only my boss knew what was going on tonight."

"Your boss and the security team that monitors your every move."

He hesitated, then nodded. "They wouldn't have given her the information, though."

"Are you sure of that?"

"Yes." His voice was flat. "It wasn't her, Em."

I let it go. It was pointless arguing, because he was

never going to believe that the woman he was sleeping with would betray him in that way.

Which was odd, given his belief that I *had*.

Of course, my betrayal had come out of necessity, not choice—something he'd refused to hear back then. He knew the truth now, when it was all far too late.

"Then, there's the magic—"

"Magic?" he cut in. "Where?"

I waved a hand to the black patch of soil that had once held the silvery spell stone. "And it was a strong spell, too, but it's one that can't be set up too far in advance."

His gaze swept me, and it was a cold, judgmental thing. "Since when did you become an expert on magic?"

"I'm not, but I've been around a very—"

He clapped a hand over my mouth, the movement so fast I squeaked in surprise. He released me almost immediately and motioned me to remain silent as his gaze swept the night and his expression grew dark.

"Fuck," he said, his voice a low growl. "That's all we need."

"What?" I kept my reply low and studied the trees around us. I couldn't see anything out of place, nor could I sense anything or anyone approaching. But the senses of a vampire—or even a pseudo vampire—were far sharper than that of a phoenix. I might be able to sense the heat in others, but if they had none, or if it was concealed in some way, it left me as blind as any human.

Which meant, if there *was* a threat out there, it could really have only one source.

His next words confirmed my fears.

"Vampires," he said. "Six of them. And they're coming straight at us."